Beneath a Frosty Moon

BY RITA BRADSHAW

Alone Beneath the Heaven
Reach for Tomorrow
Ragamuffin Angel
The Stony Path
The Urchin's Song
Candles in the Storm
The Most Precious Thing
Always I'll Remember
The Rainbow Years
Skylarks at Sunset
Above the Harvest Moon
Eve and Her Sisters
Gilding the Lily
Born to Trouble
Forever Yours
Break of Dawn
Dancing in the Moonlight
Beyond the Veil of Tears
The Colours of Love
Snowflakes in the Wind
A Winter Love Song
Beneath a Frosty Moon

RITA BRADSHAW

Beneath a Frosty Moon

MACMILLAN

First published 2018 by Macmillan
an imprint of Pan Macmillan
20 New Wharf Road, London N1 9RR
Associated companies throughout the world
www.panmacmillan.com

ISBN 978-1-5098-2923-1

1 3 5 7 9 8 6 4 2

A CIP catalogue record for this book is available from the British Library.

Typeset by Palimpsest Book Production Limited, Falkirk, Stirlingshire
Printed and bound by CPI Group (UK) Ltd, Croydon, CR0 4YY

For Jane, my lovely bestie. Over forty years of friendship filled with joy and sometimes sorrow, fun and laughter and occasional tears, walks with the dogs when we'd put the world to rights and marvel at the beauty in God's creation, and overall a spiritual oneness that is infinitely precious.
Love you, bestie. Always will.

Author's Note

Whenever I've thought about the question of evacuation during the Second World War, the iconic picture of small children with little cardboard suitcases and labels round their necks standing at a train station comes to mind. A sweet, heart-tugging picture on the face of it, but that was how the government of the time wanted the subject presented. Those snapshots of time were far from being the whole story, of course. With over three million British children being targeted in private and government-sponsored schemes aimed at sending them away to the safety of the English countryside, to Canada and the United States of America, South Africa, New Zealand and even as far as Australia, there was untold heartache and misery for parents and children alike.

Today, with the emphasis on child protection and an increased awareness of paedophilia and other dangers, it seems incredible that thousands upon thousands of vulnerable little people of all ages would be billeted with anyone who was willing to foster them, and even those who weren't so willing. The major towns and cities of England were seen as places of potential intensive bombing by the enemy, and parents were encouraged – forcefully – to put their own feelings aside and to do 'what was right'. In a vast number of cases neither the evacuees nor their parents knew where the destination was, and parents would have to wait until notices were hung outside schools to find out where their little ones were. It could be a week or more before they received word of specific foster parents and their addresses.

During the period known as the 'Phoney War', between the declaration of war in September 1939 and Dunkirk in June 1940, many of the evacuees returned home, only for a number to then have to face evacuation for a second time once the threat of invasion became real. There were no niceties of trying to match the evacuees with families of similar cultural backgrounds, no consideration of emotional impact on children and parents alike, no taking into account the consequences of returning home eventually after months or years away when the strangers the evacuees had been placed with had become their new families.

The scars which the war left on many evacuees were not visible but they were there, and the more I delved into facts and figures, the more I thanked God that I hadn't been called upon to decide whether to send my little ones away or flout public opinion and government demands and keep them with me. The government of the day looked at the problem as one of administrative planning, but the real

Acknowledgements

Thank you to all those evacuees who shared their stories. You are amazing.

Research that was particularly helpful for this book:
When the Children Came Home by Julie Summers
I'll Take That One by Martin L. Parsons
Millions Like Us by Virginia Nicholson
War in the Countryside by Sadie Ward
Wartime Women by Dorothy Sheridan
The Man Who Broke into Auschwitz by Denis Avey with Rob Broomby
Yesterday's Farm by Valerie Porter

Contents

Preface

'What if he tries to come in here when we're asleep? We wouldn't hear him.'

'Yes, we would. That's why we've moved the chest of drawers in front of the door, isn't it? We'd know if he tried to sneak in.'

'I'm scared.'

'Well, don't let him see it, all right? That's what he wants, for people to be frightened of him.'

'Aren't you scared?'

There was an infinitesimal pause. Then, as though to make up for it, the second voice was fierce in the darkness: 'No, I'm not. He's just a bully, and you know what Da always used to say about bullies. At heart they're lily-livered cowards and you have to stand up to them.'

'Da was talking about Linda Fox and her gang at school when he said that.'

'It doesn't matter who it is. The principle is the same. Bullies like people to be scared of them and that's that. You have to pretend you're not, however you might be feeling inside. It's the only way. Bullies threaten and carry on but you have to stand up to them. You stood up to Linda and her pals when Da told you and you didn't have any more trouble, did you?'

There was a longer pause. Then the first voice came small and trembling: 'I wish I was like you. You're not scared of anything or anybody.'

'I don't know about that, but I do know that we have to stick together and look after the little ones an' all and everything will be all right. You trust me, don't you?'

'Aye, you know I do.'

'Well then, go to sleep now. Tomorrow's another day and everything always seems worse at night. We're together, that's the main—'

The voice was cut off as footsteps sounded on the floorboards of the landing outside. They lay not daring to breathe for what seemed like minutes but in reality was only seconds. Then the floorboards creaked as the footsteps walked away.

'There, you see? What did I tell you? You've got nothing to worry about.' But the reassuring whisper shook a little . . .

PART ONE

Evacuation

1940

Chapter One

'But why, Mum? It's [illegible] and we want [illegible]'

Nancy Stubbs stared [illegible] her thirteen-year-old [illegible] the reaction from [illegible] and [illegible]

The year before when [illegible] war had [illegible] people to [illegible] the Nazis. The Luftwaffe was going to rain death and destruction from the [illegible] would come under [illegible] would be [illegible] had believed [illegible] brothers and sisters had [illegible] to the safety of the countryside.

But what had [illegible]

Chapter One

'But *why*, Mam? It'll be the same as before, I know it will, and we want to stay here with you. Don't send us away again.'

Nancy Stubbs stared down into the indignant face of her thirteen-year-old daughter. She had been expecting this reaction from Cora when she told the child about the evacuation, and in truth she couldn't blame her. She sighed heavily.

The year before when everyone's worst fears had come true and war had been declared, the government had scared people to death with their dire prediction about the Nazis. The Luftwaffe were going to rain death and destruction from the skies; every town and city in Britain would come under attack, and industrial places like Sunderland would be a special target. She, like so many other parents, had believed every word. So Cora and her brother and sisters had been duly dispatched to the safety of the countryside.

And what had happened? Nowt. No bombing. No

German planes. No bodies for the thousands upon thousands of cardboard coffins the government had made such a song and dance about requisitioning. Everyone had been left wondering what all the fuss had been about. She'd fetched the bairns home in time for Christmas and normal life had been resumed, or as normal as life could be with Gregory over the water in France.

Telling herself she had to be patient with Cora, Nancy said quietly, 'It's not the same as before, lass, and you're big enough to understand that. The war's begun proper now, what with Dunkirk and everything.'

'But it was horrible the last time, Mam. Right from the minute we got off the train and people walked about picking the children they wanted like we were in a cattle market. They wouldn't let us stay together and I didn't know where Horace and Anna and Susan had gone—'

'I know, Cora, I know.'

'And Horace lost his suitcase because I couldn't look after him and he didn't get it back for days. *Please*, Mam, let us stay here with you.'

'Don't you think I want to do that, lass? I missed you even more than you missed me.'

Cora's truculent expression told her mother what she thought of that.

'I did, really. But I knew it was for your own good.'

'But it wasn't, was it? Nothing happened here. We could have stayed.'

'That was then and this is now, and like I said, it's not the same.' Hitler had shown all too clearly what he was capable of when he'd sent the German air force to bomb Guernica to support Franco two years ago, Nancy thought, a chill flickering down her spine. The terrible outcome for the undefended town had shocked everyone and she'd never forget a word of what she'd read. The reporter had written that the whole town had been systematically pounded to bits and reduced to just charred bodies, flames, smoke and debris. It'd been a calculated act of terror by Hitler, and it hadn't even been his war, not like this one. What that madman would do now didn't bear thinking about. Her thoughts making her voice sharper, Nancy said, 'Don't argue, Cora. You're going and that's that. I'm not having you and the others put in harm's way when I can do something about it.'

'I'd rather be in harm's way than living with Mr and Mrs Riley. They wouldn't let us stay in the house except to eat meals and sleep, even if it was pouring with rain. Weekends they'd turn me an' Maria out after breakfast and we'd have to walk the streets. I'm not going back there.'

'You won't have to. It'll be somewhere different.'

'Where?'

'I don't know, Cora, but that's enough now. I mean it.'

When her mother spoke in that certain tone Cora knew she meant business. For a moment the temptation to scream and shout and stamp her feet like a bairn in a tantrum was strong, but as the eldest of five siblings she was expected to be sensible and grown-up, besides which she had promised her da she'd help her mam while he was away fighting.

The thought of her father melted the hard ball of resentment in her chest. She knew her mam was worried to death about him and so was she. He hadn't been one of the vast number of men who had been rescued from Dunkirk, and they had no idea if he had been killed or taken prisoner by the Germans. She felt sick just thinking about it.

She put a tentative hand on her mother's arm. 'Sorry, Mam,' she said quietly, her voice subdued. 'I – I just want us to stay together as a family in our own home.'

'So do I, lass. So do I. But I have to think about what's best for you and the others first and foremost and that's not staying here. Now go and pack your things and then you can help me get the other suitcases ready. You've got to be at the school for eight tomorrow and you can't be late.'

She didn't want to start packing. It made this too real. Cora bit down on her bottom lip as she glanced towards the kitchen window. Beyond their yard her brother and three sisters were playing in the back lane, oblivious of what was afoot. The four of them had had instructions to stay in the lane and not venture into the streets as they sometimes did, especially her brother who was always disappearing given half a chance. But a few days ago there had been a nasty accident involving one of Cora's class-mates, Godfrey Taylor, a lad who lived in the next street. He'd been playing with some pals when he'd fallen under a tram and had had both legs chopped off above his knees. They had been told at school by a grim-faced teacher that he was in hospital and fighting for his life, and that if he recovered he would be in hospital for a long, long time. Cora had sat next to Godfrey in class and she had always liked him. He was the class clown and made her laugh; sometimes they had sat talking together at playtime, and he'd taken to walking home with her and carrying her bag. Now he would never walk again, not on his own legs. It was horrible, just horrible.

Dragging her mind away from Godfrey she returned it to the matter in hand. Her mother had kept her back when the others had gone out to play, ostensibly to help with the ironing. She had thought that was strange on a Sunday because her mam normally kept Sundays free of jobs, but she hadn't argued. She didn't mind helping her mam, in fact she liked it. Sometimes she and her mam would have a right good crack when they were working together and the others were out playing or what-have-you. She loved those times.

She sighed heavily. It was the first of July tomorrow and the evening was hot and muggy, the air sticky with a sultry heat devoid of the normal north-east breeze. Some of the neighbours' privies in the back yards had begun to stink to high heaven and she had complained about the smell earlier, grumbling about the fact that some of the women in their street were less than particular, unlike her mam. Now she felt she would never find fault with their neighbours in Lumley Street any more if only her mam would change her mind about sending them away again. But she wouldn't. Cora glanced at her mother's set face.

Mind, compared to poor Godfrey she supposed being evacuated again was nothing. He'd been a tall, well-built lad who'd loved playing football, and now . . . She had thought Godfrey was the reason her mam had taken them all to the lovely beach at Roker the day before, to take their minds off what had happened. Her mam had known she liked Godfrey. They'd had an ice cream each and a donkey ride and had used up all their bacon ration on butties when they'd got home. But all along their mam had known they were going to be evacuated.

Swallowing the lump in her throat, Cora turned to her mother. 'Will you at least come and see us off?'

Nancy sighed. They hadn't been told exactly what time the children would leave the school for the train station, but the headmaster had stated in his letter that the powers-that-be thought it would be less distressing for all concerned if parents were not present. She could see why but it made it look as though they didn't care about their bairns, and she knew Cora had been angry with her the year before when she wouldn't wave them off.

'Look, lass, I told you last time why I didn't come and it's no different now,' she said with as much patience as she could muster. 'The school doesn't hold with it.'

Cora scowled. 'Blow the school. Anyway, some mothers did come before.' She didn't add that the previous year, when word had spread that the bus taking the children to the train station was about to leave, a group of women had run down the street trying to catch up with it. Children had become hysterical, the grown-ups' distress adding to their own. A couple of women had fallen over and others had stood with their aprons to their faces to hide their anguish. It had been pandemonium.

'I'm not coming, Cora,' Nancy said firmly. 'I don't think it would be good for your sisters if I came. I know you'll look after the others for me till you're all back home again. You're a good girl, pet.'

It was scant comfort.

Within the hour, five gas masks and five small cardboard suitcases had been placed out of sight in the front room and the door closed, and the luggage labels each of the children were required to wear round their necks had been duly written. Cora had been warned not to mention their imminent departure to the others when they came in.

'Time enough in the morning,' Nancy said firmly as the two of them walked through to the kitchen. 'Not a word till then, mind. I don't want your sisters carrying on and upsetting themselves.'

She didn't include her son in this statement; Horace, at nine years old, was a tough, independent little boy blessed with a cheerful personality and resilient nature. He'd landed on his feet the year before with the family he had been placed with and had got on with them like a house on fire. She had no worries about Horace, Nancy thought fondly. Cora had some of this toughness too, in spite of looking as though a breath of wind could blow her away with her slender figure and mass of curly red hair that refused to be tamed by brush and comb.

Cora's sisters were a different kettle of fish. Maria, who was ten, Anna, who was seven, and little Susan, the baby of the family at six years old, were shy and timid and easily reduced to tears. The three of them even looked the same, Nancy reflected. With their mousy brown hair and pale blue eyes they took after their da, whereas she liked to think Cora and Horace got their spirit, as well as their colouring, from her side.

'What if we get separated again, Mam?' Cora stared at her mother. It was all very well her mam saying she should look after the others but her mam hadn't been there before. It had been horrible, her worst nightmare come true. Horace had been taken off to one place and Anna and Susan to another despite her loud protests, and probably because she had been so vocal and tried to prevent it happening, even going so far as to hold on to Susan as the woman who'd taken the younger two had tried to haul her sisters away, she and Maria had been left with others who hadn't been selected. Maria had been crying and hanging on to her and one of the billeting officers had lost his temper with them and told them they'd never be homed if they carried on being so disruptive and naughty. The frightening ordeal had ended with the billeting officer, who had been sharp and terse, marching them and a few other unwanted children round the streets at ten or eleven o'clock at night, knocking on doors and demanding that unwilling householders 'do their bit' and take the tired, grubby and tearful small people into their homes. The experience would for ever be engraved on her memory.

'Just because you couldn't stay together before it doesn't mean you won't be able to this time.' Nancy plonked the big black kettle on the hob; if ever she'd needed a strong cup of tea it was now. Not only was she losing her bairns to the war for the second time, but unbeknown to them she was starting work as a shipping clerk at the docks the next day. What her Gregory would say if he knew she'd got herself a job outside the home she didn't know, but things had changed in the last months since the war. Women were being brought in to do all kinds of work which hitherto had been a man's domain; with the menfolk away fighting, needs must. And a position in an office was a step up from the munitions factory or working on the buses or on a production line sewing uniforms. She'd tell him that.

Thoughts of Gregory brought the ever-present anxiety about him to the forefront of her mind, and when she turned round and saw her daughter's woebegone face, worry expressed itself in anger and irritation. 'For goodness' sake take that look off your face, girl. The others take their lead from you and it won't help matters if you look like a wet weekend when they come in. I expect you to be a help, not a hindrance. Now go and call them and act normal. That's not too much to ask, is it?'

As Cora flounced out of the back door, banging it behind her, Nancy wanted to slap her, but in the next moment her annoyance had been washed away by a flood of guilt and despair. She shouldn't have shouted at the bairn like that, it wasn't fair, but somehow she and her eldest daughter always seemed to rub each other up the wrong way. Probably because they were so alike. Both strong-willed and fiery. She grimaced to herself. And like Cora, she'd always been top of the class at school, and even now, if she ever had a minute to herself – which wasn't often – she liked nothing more than sitting down with a good book from the library.

While she mashed the tea she asked herself, as she did more and more of late, why she had let herself be talked into marrying so young. She'd been fifteen when she'd met Gregory and less than two years later, on her seventeenth birthday, she had walked down the aisle. Part of it had been the thrill of being loved so much; Gregory was six years older than her and for this tall, kind-natured man to be head over heels about her had been flattering to the girl she'd been then, especially because she had never known love at home. Her father had been killed in an accident down Wearmouth pit when she was just a toddler, and her four older brothers had always been the apple of her mother's eye. Even on her deathbed her mother hadn't been able to say 'I love you' to her, the way she had to the lads.

Nancy's lips tightened as her mind touched on Gregory again. She'd fallen pregnant within a week or two of her wedding night and from that point on the pattern had been set. It had only been then, when the trap had closed, that she'd realized she wanted more. More than being a housewife and a mother. She'd told Father Grant this once at confession not long after Maria's birth when she'd found out she was expecting again. The priest had told her such thoughts were wicked and from the devil and she must resist them. It had been following the arrival of Susan, just eleven months after Anna, that she'd made a stand against more bairns though. She would accommodate Gregory's needs, she'd told him, but only if he ignored the Church's teaching on the matter and made sure she couldn't fall for a baby again. And his desire for her had been stronger than that of being a 'good' Catholic.

The children bursting pell-mell through the back door cut short her musing, and it was her son who caught Nancy's eye. His cut lip and bloodied nose told their own story, and as she glanced from him to Cora, her daughter said flatly, 'He's been fighting with Archie Chapman.'

'Archie said we're gonna be invaded by the Nazis and we'll all have to speak German.' Horace was fairly quivering with rage. 'He said now the French have given up, we're next, and Hitler's gonna live in Buckingham Palace and we'll all have to eat German sausages and do the Nazi salute, and I said he was a traitor.'

'So Archie punched him,' piped up Susan.

'Aye, and I hit him back. Bawled his head off, he did, like a lassie.'

Nancy shut her eyes for a moment. Wonderful, this was all she needed. Ten to one she'd have Beryl Chapman coming round screaming blue murder. Archie was an only child and the apple of his mother's eye, Beryl having had him late in life when she and her husband had given up on a family. Everyone had been thrilled for Beryl at first, but as the baby had grown into a screaming, petulant toddler and then a thoroughly unpleasant little lad, enthusiasm had waned.

Nancy drew in a long breath, then let it out slowly as she said, 'Wash your hands and face, the lot of you, and then up them stairs. It's already well past your bedtime.'

Horace stared at his mother in surprise. He'd expected at the very least a clip round the ear for fighting. Never one to look a gift horse in the mouth, he was the first into the scullery to wash his face and hands with the hard blue-veined soap that never lathered, leaving the bowl of cold water in the deep white sink a pale brown by the time he'd finished.

Cora was the last one to leave the kitchen, and she stood for a moment staring at her mother who was now sitting at the kitchen table with a pile of mending in front of her. Nancy returned her stare while her lips moved one over the other as if she was sucking something from them.

'Will you –' Cora paused, then tried again through the emotion that was blocking her throat. 'Will you write more often this time? Not just every couple of weeks?'

'Aye, lass. Aye, I will.' The year before the two of them had had a barney once Cora and the others were home because Cora had accused her of not caring about them, citing the fact that she had written four letters to her mother's one each time as proof. 'Like I said before, I thought it best only to write if there was a bit of news or something.'

'I don't care about news. I just –' Cora gulped hard – 'I just like to hear from you.'

'All right, hinny.' And then as Cora's face crumpled, Nancy said quickly, 'Come on, lass, don't cry. The others'll cotton on something's amiss. And it'll be different this time. You won't be with the Rileys for a start so that'll be better, won't it? Aye, course it will. You might even grow to like being in the country with the birds and animals and things.'

Cora didn't even bother replying to this absurdity. Instead she said, 'The Rileys were told by the billeting officer that they had to censor our letters and destroy them if we said we weren't happy. I had to smuggle out any to you where I spoke the truth. I think it's disgusting that they can treat people that way, don't you?'

It was a loaded question, and Nancy was well aware of prevaricating when she said, 'I suppose they were thinking it would be less upsetting for everyone concerned.'

'Huh!'

The exclamation had been loud and as the door banged behind her eldest offspring and Nancy was left alone, she sat for a moment staring into space. Then she stretched out her arms on the table, rested her head on them and let the silent sobbing shake her body.

Chapter Two

The headmaster of Rowan School had been in the building since six o'clock that morning, and he had run his hands through his coarse grey hair so many times it was now sticking straight up on his head like the bristles on a brush.

This second wave of evacuation was perhaps even more of a headache than the first the year before, he thought wearily. Then the hundreds of thousands of women, children and disabled were bussed, trained, paddle-steamed or driven out of Britain's towns and cities to the countryside over a period of four days, and on the whole, and certainly as far as the children from his school were concerned, the procedure had run relatively smoothly. In a purely statistical sense, he supposed Operation Pied Piper had been a success and certainly Whitehall had been pleased with itself, if the euphoria in the newspapers was to be believed. 'Exodus of the Bible dwarfed: three million people on the move', 'A Great National Undertaking', 'Triumph of Planning'; he'd read them all. He shook his head. The chorus of self-congratulation had been all very well, but the government hadn't taken into account the far-reaching emotional consequences on both children and parents, not to mention the foster parents and billeting officers on the other side of the coin.

Clarence Wood stood up from behind his desk that was littered with piles of paper, all to do with the legalities of evacuation, and sighed loudly. Paper, paper, paper – he was drowning in it. Reports, timetables, surveys, maps, but the whole question of billeting his children was done on a numerical basis by those on high yet again; nothing had been learned from the first time. Profiling little ones and trying to match background and characters was apparently not even considered by those responsible for the evacuation, in spite of the heartache and distress caused last year.

Walking to the window of his office, he pulled up the paper blind and stood staring out into the as-yet empty playground. When town met country and country met town the shock had been intense on both sides. From last September right until the present day a propaganda war about each other had raged. From the country had come a cry of horror that the mothers and children from the towns and cities were verminous, lousy, unsuitably dressed for the country and ill-mannered. From the town-dwellers had come stories about outside earthen lavatories, girls being used as unpaid maids, boys being kept back from school to work on farms, and children being forced to eat food to which they were unaccustomed and that had often been killed and plucked in front of them. Both sides had been pleased to see the back of each other when it had become clear that the predicted bombing wasn't happening. And now it was going to start all over again.

He glanced at his wristwatch. Seven-thirty. Within a short while the playground would begin to fill with those of his pupils whose parents deemed it right and proper to evacuate them for a second time. In the letter he had sent to each family he'd made it clear that if any parents did not wish to avail themselves of this opportunity, their children would not be expected at school until after lunch. This edict was with the benefit of hindsight. The year before it had added to the strain and awkwardness for his teachers attempting to keep control when those pupils staying put had been somewhat vocal to the ones leaving, saying their parents loved them too much to send them away and that country folk still lived in the dark ages. Such comments had been less than helpful, to put it mildly.

He turned from the window and sighed again. He certainly wasn't against the government-sponsored schemes to send little ones out of harm's way to the countryside or coastal towns, or even to Canada, the USA, South Africa, New Zealand or Australia in some cases; the threat of invasion was all too real now France had fallen. And of course evacuation was voluntary, but enormous pressure had been, and was being, put on families to do the right thing by their children and allow them to go to the safety of the countryside and beyond, and he wasn't sure if he agreed with all the propaganda involved. Government ministers making radio appeals imploring 'responsible' parents to get their children away from danger; the 1939 leaflet that had been sent to every home in the country claiming that 'the main way to avert the enemy's intention of creating panic and social dislocation is by removing children from endangered areas'; the poster campaign aimed particularly at women which featured a mother sitting beside a tree in the countryside with a town in the distant background, and frolicking before her two happy, robust little boys, but behind her, in ghostly outline, Hitler in uniform whispering, 'Take them back, take them back.' The woman had been anxious and confused, and the caption along the bottom in blood red read, 'Don't do it, Mother. LEAVE THE CHILDREN WHERE THEY ARE.' No, he hadn't liked that or the implication that women would be regarded as traitors if they ignored official advice and brought their children home.

Shaking his head, he said aloud, 'Poor people,' and he wasn't sure if he felt sorrier for the children or their parents. He had never imagined before the war that he would be glad he and his wife had not been blessed with a family, but since September last year he'd thanked God for it. Their next-door neighbours had three sons and over the last couple of decades as he'd watched the lads grow up he'd had moments of bitter envy. But no longer; all three had been killed at Dunkirk and it had turned their poor mother's brain. Even his Mary, the most dependable and level-headed of women, had announced that she no longer intended to listen to the news on the radio or read the papers, and he could understand why. The distress in Europe was horrific but worse still was the prospect of a German invasion, and fear of the unknown could dominate you if you weren't careful. When the unthinkable had happened and France had surrendered, it had knocked everyone for six.

But we'll win, he told himself in the next breath. We have to. Britons couldn't live beneath a brutal power; they'd rather die fighting than succumb to the life of a slave. His Mary had said that last night over dinner and he agreed with her.

A knock on his door brought him out of his reverie and in the next instant it opened and one of the teachers popped his head in to say, 'The first few children have arrived, headmaster.'

'Right you are.' He nodded briskly. No more navel-gazing, Clarence, he told himself as he left the room. You've a job to do so get on with it. In times like this it was the only way, after all.

Cora had had a wretched start to the day and it wasn't getting any better. As she had expected, her sisters had wept and wailed when they'd realized what was afoot and Susan had made herself sick before they'd even left the house. And now on the train the two youngest were still snivelling although Maria had pulled herself together.

Horace, on the other hand, was full of beans, which was only just less irritating than Anna and Susan's tears.

She had no idea where they were bound for. All one of the teachers had said when she'd asked was that it would be the country, which was a fat lot of help. This same teacher was sitting opposite, deep in conversation with an elderly matron wearing a badge stating 'Rowan School Evacuation Assistant'. They were supposed to be whispering but Cora had no trouble hearing every word.

'I couldn't believe my eyes when I got that leaflet from the Ministry of Information,' the older woman was saying in a tone of deep disgust. 'I mean, what a load of old codswallop. If the Germans arrive by parachute like it said, it'd be no good trying to hide our food and bicycles and maps, or anything else. And "See that the enemy gets no petrol." I ask you. And that picture showing a smiling mother in a housecoat secreting her biscuit tin at the back of the coal cellar made me laugh out loud, it did straight. Do them daft so-an'-sos in Whitehall really believe that a sweetly smiling little lady politely informing the Nazis that she can't give 'em a biscuit will stop them beggars from doing their worst? My Eric's nailed the pamphlet up in our kitchen; he says it's better than a bottle of beer for cheering him up.'

The teacher's voice was lower than her companion's but Cora could still eavesdrop as she pretended to look out of the train window. In a tone that suggested disapproval of said Eric, she whispered, 'I copied out the speech Churchill made to the nation on the eighteenth of

June and put that on *my* kitchen wall where I can see it every morning when I have my breakfast. Now that is worth having up. "The whole fury and might of the enemy must very soon be turned on us. Hitler knows that he will have to break us in this island or lose the war. If we can stand up to him, all Europe may be free and the life of the world may move forward into broad, sunlit uplands. Let us therefore brace ourselves to our duties, and so bear ourselves that if the British Empire and its Commonwealth last for a thousand years, men will still say, 'This was their finest hour.'" I like that bit about broad, sunlit uplands. I can see it in my mind's eye.'

The other woman clearly hadn't appreciated the covert criticism of her husband because her voice was distinctly frosty when she said, 'Aye, well, be that as it may, it'll be our English sense of humour that keeps us going rather than speeches by them as never gets their hands dirty. I've nothing against Churchill, and even my Eric says he's the man for the job and it was high time Chamberlain went in May, but Churchill's no friend of the working class, war or no war.' She sniffed a very pointed sniff. 'When the bombing starts and the Germans invade, it'll be the ordinary man and woman fighting the beggars in the streets and on the beaches.'

'Shh.' The teacher had noticed Cora's interest. Turning from her companion, she looked at Cora as she said brightly, 'We'll soon be there, and don't you worry, you'll be nice and safe in the country.'

And what about her mam? Cora thought sickly. And

her aunts and uncles who all lived in the town, and her grandma and granda, her da's parents, in Monkwearmouth? They lived right by the docks; they'd be first in line when the Germans landed.

For a moment she seriously considered jumping off the train at the next station and making her way back home, but then reason kicked in. Her mam would only send her off again, besides which she had to look after Maria and the others.

Her thoughts drew her eyes to Horace who was sitting further down the carriage with a couple of his pals and Wilfred, their next-door neighbour. Wilfred was the same age as her and they had always been friends; she knew he was keeping an eye on Horace today to help her. He was like that. Last year when they'd been evacuated and she and Maria had been with the Rileys, it had been Wilfred who had persuaded his host family to let her and Maria come in out of the cold sometimes, and he'd surreptitiously stowed food away for her too because he knew they were hungry all the time. She'd hated the Rileys; at least they weren't going back there, to the cold, cheerless house and Mrs Riley who had a permanent drip on the end of her thin pinched nose.

Wilfred's eyes had been waiting for her and now he smiled, raising his thumb and mouthing, 'It'll be all right.'

She smiled back but it was an effort. Wilfred didn't understand that she was more worried about her mam and the others at home than about being evacuated again, but then how could he? She knew full well what Wilfred's mam and da were like. Evil, her mam had called them once when she hadn't been aware that she was listening. She knew Wilfred's older brothers had scarpered the minute that they'd left school and were earning enough to take lodgings, and everyone in their road knew why. You only had to look at the boys and see the bruises and marks their da regularly left on their thin, scrawny bodies. Her mam had said she didn't know what was worse – Wilfred's da knocking the living daylights out of the bairns at the drop of a hat, or their mam starving them. And her mam said the Huttons' house was filthy; certainly their privy stank to high heaven if you were in the back lane.

Anna and Susan had drifted off to sleep at last, lulled by the chugging of the train and exhausted with all their crying, and now Cora looked out of the window once more although she wasn't really seeing the trees and fields they were passing. She was still thinking of Wilfred and what he'd said the last time they were evacuated. It had been on the day when she'd received the letter from her mam saying she was going to come and collect them and bring them home for Christmas, and, beside herself with happiness, she had gone straight round to Wilfred's to tell him. He had stared at her in a strange way before saying slowly, 'I thought it was too good to last.'

'What?' she'd answered, not understanding. 'What's too good to last?'

'Being here.'

'But don't you want to go back and for everything to be normal again?'

'No.' It had been flat, stiff.

'Well, you don't have to go back anyway, not if you don't want to. You can stay here.' She had made to put her hand on top of his but he had pulled away jerkily, looking as though he was going to cry. 'Wilfred—'

'It's all right.' She could see the effort he had made to smile. 'I shall come back with you. I – I wouldn't want to be here without you.'

The conversation had made her feel uncomfortable although she wasn't sure why, but once they were home again the old pattern had re-established itself and the feeling had melted away. Wilfred was often at their place, more than his own, and her mam fed him along with them – she always had. He was the only one of her friends her mam allowed in the house and she treated him differently from everyone else, as though he was one of the family. And he was, he *was* one of the family, Cora told herself. Even though he was the same age as her he was like an older brother and she'd always been able to tell him anything.

The teacher and her companion had started their whispering again but now it was about the payments made to host families. The teacher considered that the ten shillings and sixpence per week for the first child, and eight shillings and sixpence for each subsequent child, wasn't nearly enough to cover board and lodging, but Cora thought it sounded like a small fortune. She soon lost interest as the two went on about the cost of clothes and shoes and medical expenses, and with Maria wedged at the side of her and also now asleep, her own eyes began to close despite her anxiety about the prospect ahead.

They had changed trains twice, and it was four o'clock in the afternoon when they arrived at their final destination which turned out to be a small market town deep in Northumberland. Hot and tired, the children were formed into a crocodile and marched out of the train station and along a lane to a field, clutching their suitcases and gas masks and wearing their now bedraggled luggage labels.

Cora and Wilfred kept the younger four children close to them, and although Cora was hoping the selection process wouldn't be a repeat of the cattle-market of the year before, her worst fears were soon justified. The prospective foster mothers were waiting for them, and although Cora heard one of the adults say the hosts shouldn't be allowed on the field at all, they soon invaded the space. They walked about, picking out what they considered the most presentable or suitable specimens before harassing the billeting officers for the registration slips which were essential if they were to get the necessary cash for food and lodging from the government.

As this was farming territory, it soon became clear to the children that boys of eight or nine and upwards were the most popular choice. Therefore it was something of a surprise when two women approached them, one looking at Cora and saying, 'You four sisters then? Want to stay together, do you?' at the same time as the other lady said to Wilfred and Horace, 'I can take you two.' And when Cora nodded, the woman pursed her lips before adding, 'I dare say I can stretch to four.'

Cora and Wilfred stared at each other, the same thought in their minds. It was the best they were going to get and much more than Cora had hoped for.

'Cora?' Wilfred's voice was low.

She answered the unspoken question by nodding as she said, 'Look after Horace, won't you,' and to her brother, 'You behave and do as Wilfred tells you, all right?'

The woman who was taking Wilfred and Horace said kindly, 'Don't worry, lass, you'll all meet up at school every day and Stone Farm is the next one to ours so you won't be a million miles away from your brothers.'

Cora didn't bother to correct the lady's assumption that both Wilfred and Horace were her brothers; she just nodded and smiled. At least she and Maria and Anna and Susan could stay together which was better than last time, and Horace was with Wilfred.

She looked again at her benefactor. The other woman was small and fat with rosy cheeks, the way she had always pictured farmer's wives to be, but the one who was taking them was tall and thin with sparse brown hair pulled tightly into a bun at the back of her head and sharp features. Swallowing hard, Cora said quietly, 'Th–thank you.' The other foster mothers were selecting one child or at the most two; they were lucky this lady was prepared to take them all.

'That's our horse an' cart over there.' The woman pointed to a big brown animal standing patiently in the lane some distance away. 'An' I'm Mrs Burns.'

The four girls stared at the horse. They had seen others in fields out of the train window but at home the only ones they came across were the rag-and-bone man's animal and the coalman's, both of which would bite given half a chance. Mrs Burns's horse appeared twice as big.

'You go an' wait while I sort things out with the billeting officer an' I'll be across shortly,' Mrs Burns went on. 'There's some bales of hay in the back of the cart for you to sit on.'

Cora nodded. For better or worse they had a new home and whatever was ahead of them they could face it together. Anna and Susan were huddled in to her and Maria was standing slightly behind her, and now she said briskly, 'Come on, the lot of you, pick up your suitcases. We're going for a ride.'

Wilfred stood, his arm round Horace's shoulders, and watched as the horse and cart holding Cora and her sisters trundled off. This had turned out better than he'd expected. Cora's farm was close to theirs and he was with Horace. He smiled down at the younger boy as he said, 'All right?' and Horace grinned back at him.

Their lady came bustling across from where she had been talking to the billeting officer.

'Come on then, lads,' she said brightly. 'I daresay you'll be wanting your tea?'

'The farm where the girls are going,' Wilfred said as he and Horace walked with the woman towards a similar horse and cart to the one Cora had disappeared in. 'Have they got other evacuees there already?'

'Two little lassies, I think, lad.'

Better and better. Wilfred flexed the tense muscles in his neck. He'd been wound up like a spring all day wondering who Cora would be billeted with and whether there would be any lads around. Last year he had made sure Cora and Maria came to where he was staying when the Rileys threw them out in the daytime and that had been fine. Of course, Godfrey Taylor had had his eye on her then but his host family had been more like the Rileys and there had been no chance of the girls going there for a meal.

Godfrey Taylor. Wilfred's lip curled. He'd given him fair warning to stay away from Cora but Godfrey had just laughed at him. Well, he wasn't laughing now and his days of muscling in when they were walking home from school and hanging around her all the time were over. One little push was all it had taken.

He climbed into the back of the cart with Horace and they settled themselves on a straw bale, chatting with the farmer's wife who had introduced herself as Mrs Croft. She was a motherly sort but could talk the hind leg off a donkey, and he let her and Horace natter on as he gradually relaxed more and more.

Aye, he thought, raising his face to the sky, he'd been surprised how easy it had been to send Godfrey into the path of the tram but then he'd been following him for weeks off and on, making sure he was never seen and waiting for an opportunity like the one that had presented itself that day. A swift push from behind on a crowded pavement and then he had melted away. No one had noticed him, not with Godfrey screaming and the blood and mayhem. A 'little runt' Godfrey had called him, the last time he had warned him to keep away from Cora. Well, one of the advantages of being a little runt was that no one noticed him – he could be practically invisible when he wanted to be.

Wilfred smiled to himself. Who was the runt now with half his legs gone? No one was going to take his place in Cora's affections, he'd make sure of that. She was his. End of story.

Chapter Three

The summer evening was glorious. The still air was heavy with the perfume of the hundreds of dog-rose bushes lining the country lane, and the blue sky above the trundling cart echoed to the cries of swallows as they circled, dipping and rising on the wing, hawking for flies and small insects. The area was much more countrified than the small town near Bishop Auckland where Cora and the others had been billeted the previous year, but also further away from her mother and home, and for this reason Cora was blind to the natural beauty as they bumped along.

They had travelled for a few minutes in silence before the farmer's wife spoke from her plank seat at the front of the cart. She didn't turn as she said, 'You're lucky I took the four of you – no one else would have done. You know that, don't you? I did you a good turn, especially in view of the two youngsters not being good for much. You two older lassies will have to work twice as hard to make up for your sisters once you're home from school and at weekends. There's always too much to do on a farm and not enough hours in the day, and since our farmhand went off to war and his wife and family moved to stay with her parents, I've had my work cut out and so has Farmer Burns. Rob used to do the work of two men.'

Cora turned her head and stared at the back of Mrs Burns's tight, upright body. Without thinking, she said, 'Why didn't you choose boys to help then?'

There was a moment's pause and immediately Cora knew she'd said the wrong thing, even before the farmer's wife said sharply, 'You an' your sisters would have been in a fix if I had, miss.'

'Oh, I know,' Cora said hastily. 'I didn't mean—'

'Like I said, I did you a good turn and I expect some gratitude.'

'I'm sorry, Mrs Burns, and I *am* grateful, we all are, and we'll work hard, I promise.'

'I should think so an' all.' There was another pause and then the farmer's wife went on, 'We've already got two lassies from last year, and my husband don't hold with lads and lassies in the same house, all right? Not respectable, see?'

'Yes, yes, Mrs Burns.'

'With the government making us plough up pasture-land for food crops and then the frost and heavy snow all through January and February meaning we lost the winter wheat, it's been a trial all round, I can tell you. The cows and pigs and chickens still need to be fed, don't they?'

'Yes, Mrs Burns.'

'Potatoes and carrots and leeks don't jump out of the ground by themselves, and the wheat won't harvest itself come August either. Ploughing, weeding and hoeing, dung-spreading and hedges to trim and ditches to clear out, it still all has to be done, war or no war. Milking the cows and making cheese and butter, that's not going to be done by one of these ministry types who sits on his backside all day, is it?'

'No, Mrs Burns.'

'No, that's right. So there'll be no larking about and you'll do whatever you're asked to do whether you like it or not. That's if you want to stay together. The littl'uns can feed the hens and collect the eggs an' such and clean the coops – there'll be stuff for them but not heavy work – but you two older ones look fit and strong enough to muck in. Enid and Maud'll show you what's what.'

Cora and Maria looked at each other and Maria was biting her lip to stop herself crying. Suddenly the Rileys didn't seem so bad after all.

It was another half-an-hour before the horse turned off the dusty lane and passed through two big open wooden gates onto a farm track. They had journeyed through several hamlets, the last one, some minutes ago, being the largest and boasting a cluster of stone cottages, a small church, several shops and some other buildings. Mrs Burns hadn't spoken for a while but as they'd trundled through she had pointed to a brick-and-timber building saying briefly, 'The school.'

As they approached the farm in the distance, the fields either side of the track were full of grazing cows, and then they reached the farmyard, which had a large stone barn forming one side of a courtyard of other farm buildings under mossy mellow-tiled roofs. On the far side of the yard an archway through the buildings led Cora's eyes up a long, straight path to the heavy front door of a three-storeyed farmhouse which was much larger than she had expected. They scrambled quickly out of the cart, clutching their suitcases and gas masks; Mrs Burns was already walking towards the archway. As they followed her, passing an octagonal stone structure in the centre of the yard, its walls perhaps three feet high with big, age-bleached oak uprights supporting the tiled roof, Cora realized where the terrible smell was coming from. The structure was used for storing dung from the cow houses surrounding the cobbled yard. This, combined with the run of corrugated-iron pigsties with their own small yards which had been built on the outside of the farmyard, with one of its walls forming the back of the sties, made the stench overpowering to their uninitiated noses, and little Susan was heaving by the time they'd left the yard.

'I don't want to stay here.' Susan clutched hold of Cora's sleeve, her bottom lip quivering. 'I don't like it.'

Neither did Cora but she couldn't very well say so. Her voice low but fierce, she whispered, 'If you want to be with the rest of us you have to stay here and you don't want to be somewhere on your own, do you? It's a farm – you'll soon get used to the smells and it won't smell so bad inside. If you start carrying on, Mrs Burns will send you back to the billeting officer and you could end up anywhere. You heard what she said – no one else would take the four of us. They didn't last time, did they?' And at Susan's small forlorn shake of the head, she added, 'Come on, you'll feel better when you've had your tea.'

Mrs Burns didn't enter the house by the front entrance but followed the path round to the side of the building, and as the children filed through the door which she'd opened they found themselves standing in an enormous, stone-flagged kitchen. The biggest iron range Cora had ever seen took up a large part of the far wall with built-in cupboards either side of it, and a huge number of pewter pots and copper pans filled shelf after shelf. Two deep white sinks stood under two windows and these had a long wooden table between them, but the main table was in the centre of the room. A great wooden chair with fancy arms was positioned at the head of it, and down its two sides were eight-foot-long wooden benches.

Cora stared about her in awe. This one room was far larger than the whole of their downstairs at home and held everything, and more, that she could imagine a kitchen would need.

'This is the kitchen,' said Mrs Burns, as though it wasn't perfectly obvious, 'and through there –' she pointed to an open doorway – 'are the back rooms. The scullery and larder first, then the wash house with the copper and sinks, and beyond that the salting house and the dairy. The copper has to be filled using buckets of water from the pump – all the water for the house comes from our well. That'll be one of your jobs. Enid and Maud have been doing it but I daresay you can do it every other day between you. Wash day is a Saturday and we need plenty of boiling water then. There's a door out of the dairy into the rear yard, so you don't have to bring pails of milk through my kitchen. Understand?'

They all nodded dazedly, trying to take it in.

'None of you venture into the parlour or dining room or Farmer Burns's office at the front of the house without permission. I used to have a girl from the village who came to do the cleaning once a week but she's hightailed it off to a munitions factory somewhere, so Enid and Maud take it in turns. You two older ones can do that an' all so it'll be once a month for each of you. There's four bedrooms all told but the top floor's not used. Your bedrooms are in the attics and aren't reached by the main staircase.' So saying, she opened a door into a long narrow corridor. 'That's the door into the main house,' she said, pointing to the end of the whitewashed passageway, 'and there's the staircase to the attics.'

They looked at the steep narrow winding staircase in front of them. It looked unwelcoming and forbidding.

'Enid and Maud have one room and you'll have the other one, all right? There's a bed big enough for you two older ones and the littl'uns can have the smaller one. Take your things up and put 'em away and no dilly-dallying.'

In spite of the whitewashed walls the corridor was dark once Mrs Burns shut the kitchen door behind her after ushering them into the passageway, practically shoving Susan out when she was a little slow. They stood for a moment, and then Cora said, 'Come on, follow me. Maria, you come last in case Anna or Susan slip on these steep stairs. Here, give me your suitcase, Susan, and Maria, you take Anna's.'

They climbed the worm-holed wooden treads carefully, up and up until they came to a kind of tiny landing, a narrow slot of a window casting a meagre dusty ray of sunlight over the bare floorboards. There were two doors in front of them but when Cora opened the first one she saw the little room held one bed with rumpled covers and some clothes in a heap on the floor. Shutting it quickly, she said, 'That must be Enid and Maud's.'

The second room was larger, its slanted ceiling joists coming right down to the top of the small window which was only a couple of feet from the floorboards. One bed was slightly wider than the other but both were really only singles, and apart from a dilapidated small chest of drawers that looked as though it had been cobbled together from different types of wood and a row of pegs on one wall, the room was devoid of furniture.

Cora walked over to the bigger bed and plumped down. The flock mattress didn't give an inch. Nevertheless, the sheets and blankets were clean and although the eiderdown was old and patched in several places it looked thick and warm. As did the one on Anna and Susan's bed.

Forcing a bright note into her voice, she said, 'Well,

isn't this nice, our own room where we can be together. Mam'll be pleased when I tell her we haven't been split up and that Horace is with Wilfred.'

'It's hot and stuffy in here.' Maria wrinkled her nose. 'And fusty.'

'It's summer, what do you expect?' Cora had already noticed the window didn't open. 'And in the winter you'll be glad it's snug and warm.'

'I don't like Mrs Burns. She nearly pushed me over.' Susan had begun to snivel. 'I want Mam.'

So did she, oh, so did she. 'Mam sent us here to be safe and we can't go back till the war's over so we've got to make the best of it.' Cora's voice sounded flat now.

'She's going to work us every minute we're not at school, Mrs Burns, isn't she?' Maria said quietly. 'She's got it all worked out. That's why she took the four of us, not out of the kindness of her heart.'

There was no denial from Cora, only a downward movement of her head.

'And she probably wanted only girls 'cause she thinks she can bully us better than boys.'

'You don't know that, Maria, and don't put ideas in the little ones' heads. Listen, the three of you. We're here and here we remain unless Mam sends for us, and she's not going to do that until any bombing is over. If any of you play up you won't go home to Mam but to someone else, and you'll be on your own. We can look after each other here – *I'll* look after you, all right? And you heard what the lady said who took Horace and Wilfred, their farm is next to this one and we'll see them at school every day. Things could be a lot worse, believe me. And there's always plenty to eat on a farm, don't forget that. Everything's going to be fine, you'll see.'

Three faces that were as alike as peas in a pod stared at her, and the weight of the responsibility she'd been feeling all day became heavier. But it *would* be fine, it had to be, Cora told herself. Whatever was in store, she had to make this work so they could remain together. Failure simply wasn't an option.

An hour later Cora was reminding herself of this. The four of them were sitting at the kitchen table with the farmer and his wife, and Enid and Maud. It appeared that Enid was a year younger than herself and Maud was nine years old, but the two looked very different. Enid was small, plump and stocky, and Maud was as slight and ethereal as a will-o'-the-wisp. The two sisters had arrived at the farm the year before after being evacuated from Newcastle, but apart from this Cora had been able to get little out of the pair. It had been difficult enough to have a conversation in the short time which had elapsed between Enid and Maud arriving back from school and Farmer Burns entering the kitchen, but once the farmer had taken his place at the head of the table the two sisters hadn't said a word.

Cora glanced at Farmer Burns under her eyelashes, continuing to devour the plateful of food in front of her as she did so. True to her prediction, it appeared Mrs

Burns wasn't going to be a stingy cook. Several big crusty cottage loaves and a round pat of golden butter, along with thick slices of ham, a great slab of creamy cheese and a large bowl of hard-boiled eggs, adorned the table, and Mrs Burns had encouraged them to help themselves to as much as they wanted.

The food was heavenly, and there wasn't so much as a whiff of rationing. If it hadn't been for the farmer himself, Cora would have been congratulating herself that they had landed on their feet this time, in spite of the smells outside and their bedroom and the work they were clearly expected to do.

Farmer Burns was a big man, in height as well as breadth, and he smelt of the farmyard and stale sweat. His bulk was emphasized by the way his head and neck flowed into his shoulders and he was extremely hairy, like a gorilla. His arms and hands were covered in thick black hair and his open shirt collar sprouted a growth that suggested his chest was the same, unlike his head that was practically bald. But it was his eyes that had caused Cora's gaze to fall away from his when he had walked into the kitchen. Small and bullet-shaped under beetling brows, they had caused a shiver to slither down her spine. She had seen a photograph of a great white shark once, in a geography lesson at school, and the creature's black cold stare had chilled her blood. Farmer Burns's eyes were like that.

He must have noticed her covert gaze because he suddenly spoke to her. 'So, what's your story then?'

'Story?'

'Aye. Any more of you in the family? Brothers? Sisters? And what of your mam an' da?'

'We've got a brother, Horace, he's at the next farm.'

'Older than you?'

'No, younger.'

'An' your da? Fighting, is he?'

'In France, yes.'

'An' your mam, liable to want to visit, is she? We don't encourage that, too disruptive. You can tell her that when you write. Told their mam the same.' He nodded at Enid and Maud who were eating with downcast eyes. 'Enough to do here without pandering to visitors, all right?'

Cora made no comment to this. She certainly wasn't going to tell her mother not to come and see them; not that she expected her to do that anyway. Their mam had made it quite clear the last time that she considered it would upset the little ones too much. But something deep inside warned her not to explain this to the farmer although she couldn't say why. Instead she said, 'My mam will do what she wants to do, she's like that.'

'Is she? Is she now?'

'Feisty, my da calls her.'

This clearly didn't sit well with Farmer Burns. He stared at her for some moments more and she stared back, determined not to be intimidated even if she was all butterflies inside.

'Strikes me someone needs to know their place,' he said after the silence became excruciating, and Cora didn't know if he was referring to their mother or to her. Either way she didn't like it and as her chin lifted and her lips tightened, her body language spoke for itself.

It was Mrs Burns who spoke hastily into the tense atmosphere. 'Finish what's on your plates and I'll fetch the apple crumble an' cream, and then you, Enid, can show Cora and Maria how to milk the cows, and Maud, you take the two little ones to the chicken coop and collect any eggs before getting them in for the night. The fox was about early last night, I saw it with me own eyes when I left the milking parlour. Bold as brass, that one.'

It was a moment more before Cora did as she was told, and only then because the farmer's gaze had dropped from hers and he'd begun to shovel food into his mouth again. She ate quickly but not through hunger; funnily enough her appetite was quite gone and the butterflies in her stomach were making it churn. There was something wrong here. She couldn't put her finger on it but she was sure there was something very wrong. But if Farmer Burns was like Wilfred's da, if he thought he could knock them about and treat them rough, he'd got a shock coming. She wouldn't put up with that and she'd tell him so. They would work their socks off doing what was required of them and she would see to it that the farmer had no complaints on that score, but she wasn't going to stand for any ill-treatment and it was as well he knew that from the beginning. If he *was* like that, handy with his fists. And he might not be – she might be reading this all wrong but she didn't think so.

She thanked Mrs Burns for the bowl of apple crumble topped with thick cream which the farmer's wife had just placed in front of her, and began to eat with every appearance of enjoyment although in truth she was barely tasting it.

Chapter Four

During the month of July the children became familiar with the way the farm operated and with what was expected of them. And that was a lot.

Stone Farm was a dairy farm, and Mrs Burns demanded that Cora, Maria and Enid rise at five o'clock in the morning to present themselves in the cow yard where Farmer Burns had already brought in the cows for milking. Once they'd pulled thick smocks over their clothes, the three of them, along with Mrs Burns, washed each cow's udders with warm water and disinfectant, and then squirted a little milk from each of the animal's four teats into a small can to check for any signs of mastitis or other problems that would mean keeping that cow's milk separate. Then sitting on their stools, the bucket between their legs, they would begin the milking proper, as Mrs Burns called it.

Mrs Burns had been surprisingly patient in showing Cora and Maria exactly how to sit on the low, three-legged stools, the exact position of their legs and the right way to balance the bucket between them. They watched as she pushed her head well into the flank of the cow she was milking, keeping her left side against the animal's leg and one arm ready to ward off a kick. Not that the herd were difficult on the whole; they were used to being handled twice a day and accustomed to human company, and they were a rather matronly bunch. There were two or three that could prove awkward and deliver a stinging blow with their long muscular tails across the milker's face when the mood took them, but Mrs Burns handled these cows.

On the first morning she explained the correct way to hold the cows' teats, showing how fingers and wrists had to work together to draw the milk, but for three or four days it refused to flow for Cora and Maria and all they had to show for their efforts was the sweat of frustration and fingers that were stiff and aching, along with a dribble of milk that barely covered the bottom of the bucket. But then, on the fifth day, there was suddenly the wonderful sound of milk rhythmically thrumming into the bucket with a frothy head like a glass of beer. They went into the house for breakfast that morning on the crest of a wave, and even the farmer's brooding dark presence at the table couldn't dampen their joy. Admittedly, Mrs Burns milked twice as many cows as the three girls, but as the lady said herself, she'd had plenty of practice.

Cora found that she liked the cows; they were peaceful, placid creatures, and one in particular always screwed her great head round to watch the milker intently with her dark, heavily lashed eyes and liked nothing more than having her nose rubbed every so often. The plough horses were gentle giants too in spite of being the muscle power on the farm. The stables had an airy loft to insulate the animals against extremes of heat and cold as well as storing hay and bedding straw. There were head-high hay racks in the stalls and low feeding troughs, along with a tack room where harness equipment was hung on stout pegs and a wooden corn bin for the horses' fodder. Farmer Burns saw to his precious plough horses and it was clear he valued them more than the other animals, probably more than Mrs Burns too if it came to it. Certainly the farmer and his wife had a strange relationship in Cora's opinion; only speaking to each other when they had to and in a way that was devoid of even a hint of affection.

Much to Susan's dismay, she and Anna took over Maud's job of feeding the pigs their whey and other waste products, as well as looking after the chickens and collecting any eggs each day. Susan cried and sulked at first – the smell of the pigs made her feel sick and the chickens frightened her when they flapped and squawked – but Mrs Burns was adamant that she needed more help in the dairy, and thus Maud joined the three older girls. Susan, realizing she had met her match in the farmer's wife, accepted defeat.

It was a tough life on the farm and the daily routine was grim, especially at weekends when there was no school. The house had no running water or electricity and as the oldest evacuee it fell to Cora to empty the chamber pots onto the fields every morning, which was a filthy task. In the day the household used the outside privy at the end of the rear yard, and this was nothing but a narrow brick hut with a rickety door and a wooden structure holding a plank of wood with a hole in the middle of it. The stench was overpowering and there were always big fat bluebottles buzzing around inside. Farmer Burns only cleared it out once every two or three weeks and the ashes from the range that were dumped down the hole daily did little to disguise the smell. Cora and the others visited the privy before they went to bed and then tried to last until morning, but the farmer and his wife had no such compunction. They made full use of the chamber pots under the beds.

The first morning that Mrs Burns led her along the corridor and into the main house, Cora stood amazed in the wide tiled hall that had a great grandfather clock ticking away in one corner and framed pictures on the walls. She followed the farmer's wife up the wide staircase and on to a landing, whereupon Mrs Burns opened the first door, saying, 'This is Farmer Burns's room. Before you bring the pots down I expect you to make the bed.'

The room was full of heavy dark furniture and the bed was a big one, but it was the stench coming from the pot under the bed that took Cora's attention. It was the same in the next room which was a smaller version of the previous one and was where, apparently, Mrs Burns slept. Again the smell knocked you backwards when the door opened, but Mrs Burns appeared impervious to Cora's distaste beyond saying, 'On a fine day open the window before you leave.'

Compared to this task, which she undertook every morning just before she left for school, milking the cows was a pleasure. Certainly they smelt a lot sweeter. And in the first week or two at the farm, many was the time Cora thought she was going to bring up her breakfast of home-cured bacon and eggs, toast and porridge, which she'd devoured so eagerly after the milking, as she carried the stinking chamber pots to the fields. It was Farmer Burns's pot that turned her stomach the most, not that it smelt any worse than Mrs Burns's. It was the fact that it *was* his, that he had parked his massive backside on it and sat there squeezing out the contents of his bowels, knowing that she would have to empty the pot, that made her feel somehow unclean. And she knew the moment she had begun to feel that way. It had been the first Saturday at the farm when they had been there five days.

She and Maria, along with Enid and Maud, had spent most of the morning after milking washing the household's dirty linen and clothes, carrying pail after pail of water from the pump to the boiler. That had been the easy part. Then had come the pummelling and scrubbing in the wash tub with blue-veined slabs of home-made soap that wouldn't lather, the rinsing, the mangling, then carrying basket after basket outside to hang on the three lines in one of the fields close to the house where the laundry could blow in the wind and the sun.

After a hasty midday meal of bread and cheese washed down with mugs of milk, the four of them trooped off to scour Mrs Burns's dairy from top to bottom with hot salted water and disinfectant. Mrs Burns made all her own cream, cheese and butter and sold a good amount, along with milk, to the surrounding hamlets, something – she told the girls with some pride – that was becoming rarer since the Great War. It was all hard work but especially the butter-making. The churning seemed to be endless and every time she did it Cora felt as though her arms were dropping off by the time the precious yellow flecks began to appear in the milk. But there was no denying that Mrs Burns's butter was better than anything she had tasted before. The farmer's wife said the finished rolls were so rich and golden because the cows ate the buttercups at this time of the year, and the whey benefited from the flowers and sweet herbs in the fields. Certainly every time Farmer Burns drove off in the cart with his deliveries, he returned having sold everything to the last drop of milk.

On that particular Saturday, Cora and Maria had tackled the mountain of ironing once the scrubbing of the dairy was finished, leaving Enid to clean the farmhouse and Maud and the little ones doing the umpteen jobs Mrs Burns had lined up for them. At dinnertime they were too tired to speak, eating the delicious pot roast Mrs Burns had left simmering most of the day in silence, and then the older ones had gone to the milking and the little ones to collect the last of the eggs from the chickens and bed them down for the night.

When they had all gathered once more in the kitchen, preparatory to going to bed, Cora had seen the tin bath set in front of the range. Mrs Burns had left them finishing the last of the milking, and now Cora watched as the farmer's wife tipped the boiling contents of the big black kettle into the few inches of cold water in the bottom of the bath. She glanced questioningly at Enid and Maud but both had sat down at the table without a word and had their eyes downcast. It was their usual stance, Cora had found. Indeed, she and her sisters had found it difficult to get more than the odd monosyllable out of the two girls since they had arrived at the farm. It wasn't that they were unfriendly exactly, more as though they were terrified of something, but when she had said this to Maria her sister had shrugged.

'Just the way they are, perhaps, like Alma Potts. She never had two words to say to anyone, did she?'

Cora had said no more on the matter but she didn't think Enid and Maud were like Alma Potts who had lived in their street in Sunderland. Alma had been a little simple with a vacant look in her eyes and a constantly snotty nose.

They always had a mug of milk and a slice of bread and butter for their supper before they went to bed but tonight it wasn't ready on the table. And Farmer Burns was sitting in his chair with his pipe in his mouth rather than being outside as he normally was at this time of night.

'Right, Enid and Maud, you first,' Mrs Burns said

briskly after bending and feeling the temperature of the water in the bath. And to Cora's amazement, which rapidly turned to horror, the two sisters stood up and silently divested themselves of every item of clothing until they were as naked as the day they were born. Still without a word they climbed into the bath and sat facing each other, taking the old coarse flannels that Mrs Burns handed them and beginning to rub themselves.

Cora watched dumbstruck, aware that Maria had moved along the bench and was pressing into her side, and Anna and Susan's eyes were as wide as saucers.

The fact that the four of them were so flabbergasted clearly prompted Mrs Burns to say something, because in the false bright voice she had used before, she said, 'Saturday night is bath night at the farm, girls,' but she didn't look at them as she spoke. Instead she bent and dipped a tin jug into the bath water and then emptied it over Enid's head before doing the same to Maud, passing them a tablet of soap which the sisters then rubbed into their hair before Mrs Burns repeated the procedure with the jug, rinsing the soap off.

Cora was aware of Farmer Burns puffing harder on his pipe as the moments ticked by, and as she glanced at his face she was unnerved by what she saw there. She didn't understand it, but she knew it was bad, dirty. She tried to swallow but her throat was too dry and her stomach was turning over and over.

'Cleaned all over and between your legs?' Mrs Burns said briskly, and as the girls nodded with their heads bent and their eyes downcast, she handed them a small threadbare towel each. 'Out you get and dry yourselves.' And as though they had been programmed, the two sisters stood up and stepped out of the water to stand shivering on the stone slabs, clutching the meagre pieces of towelling.

Mrs Burns looked at Anna and Susan. 'You next.'

'No.' Cora jumped up to face the farmer's wife, and as she did so Anna and Susan slid off the bench opposite her and Maria and sidled round the table to stand behind her. Young as they were they knew that what they had witnessed was wrong. 'They're not doing that, none of us are.'

'I beg your pardon, madam?' Mrs Burns straightened, her thin body rod-like.

'We're not washing in front of –' she had been about to say Farmer Burns, but changed it to – 'everybody. We haven't been brought up that way and our mam wouldn't like it.'

'Your mother isn't here.'

'That makes no difference. It's . . . it's not seemly.'

'You dare to question the way we do things here? You'll do as you're told, m'girl.'

'Not in this.'

'You're defying me? Refusing to obey?'

It was strange, Cora thought, but in spite of the farmer's wife's stance and her words, she felt that Mrs Burns wasn't as angry as she was trying to make out.

Whether Farmer Burns recognized this she didn't know, but he suddenly shot to his feet, stretching himself so he appeared to stand a good foot taller and his face red with suppressed rage. 'You're trouble, girl. I knew it the minute you walked in. Take after your mother, I'll be bound. Well, we can do without your sort so think on.'

Cora didn't ask herself at this moment what she would do if the farmer and his wife turned them out and they were split up again, because deep down inside she knew there was something very bad here and if she weakened now it would affect not just her but Maria and the little ones. Farmer Burns had liked looking at Enid and Maud in the bath and she had seen his big body move slightly forwards in his chair when the sisters had been handed their flannels by Mrs Burns and told to wash themselves. So *this was the reason there were no boys at the farm*. It was nothing to do with decency as Mrs Burns had suggested; just the opposite, in fact.

Her mind grappling with knowledge she didn't quite understand and couldn't grasp, she stared at the man in front of her. She was as slender as a reed and the farmer was three times the width of her and more than twice as heavy, but as she continued to glare at him it was he who turned from her, muttering vile profanities as he stomped out of the kitchen, banging the door behind him as he stepped outside.

For a moment silence reigned. Enid and Maud were still standing with their pitifully inadequate towels held in front of them, Mrs Burns appeared frozen, and Cora felt light-headed with the relief that the immediate danger had passed. It was the familiar sound of Susan snivelling behind her that brought Cora back to herself. 'Stop it.' She turned, her voice unusually sharp. 'There's nothing to cry about. Go and get ready for bed, the lot of you.' And when no one moved, she said again, more sharply still, 'Go on, all of you.'

As Maria ushered the others out of the kitchen after Enid and Maud had picked up their clothes, Cora found she was shaking inside, the enormity of what had occurred fully dawning on her. But she couldn't dwell on that, not right now. Instead she forced herself to continue to stand upright although her knees felt weak with shock.

'There will be no more baths like this, not for anyone,' she said to Mrs Burns, 'or I'll tell someone. Mr Travis. He'd listen. He'd believe me. He'd think it's not right.'

Mr Travis was the headteacher at the village school and taught the seniors, of which Cora was one; two other teachers – Mrs Fallow and Mrs Dennis – each being in charge of the juniors and infants. She had no idea if Mr Travis would believe something was wrong if she told him what had happened. Children, adults too, bathed in baths in front of the fire all the time – they had done the same at home – but this was different. Farmer Burns made it different.

Rachel Burns said nothing for a moment. She was aware that if she had spoken the truth to this indignant slip of a girl in front of her, Cora would have been surprised. Oh, yes, very surprised. But of course she wouldn't do that. All she had left in life was her standing within the community, and if Bernard was exposed for what he was, it would reflect on her. She had been fifteen years old when she had married Bernard Burns, although being thin and flat-chested she'd looked younger. And at first she had mistaken his lust for love. It wasn't until the tenth year of marriage, when she had caught him handling one of the young children of their farmhand, that she had understood why his passion for her had waned. She no longer looked like a child.

He had been more careful after that, going further afield for his pleasures, but she had known what he was about when he came home after dark on market days or disappeared for the evening on 'farm business'. He disgusted her – in fact she loathed the very ground he walked on – but she had been nothing more than a little village brat from the poorest family hereabouts when he had picked her out and courted her, and the life of a fairly well-to-do farmer's wife was infinitely preferable than returning to her roots. And so, without a word being said, she had moved out of the master bedroom and their life had continued fairly passively until the war had brought the evacuees into their home. Bernard had chosen Enid and Maud and when he had arrived home with them in the back of the cart she had known instantly what he was about, but had made no comment. And she had departed to pick up the next batch with his instructions ringing in her ears. No boys on the grounds of propriety. But again she'd made no demur.

Now, her voice flat, she said to Cora, 'Farmer Burns has important friends in the community, child. Mr Travis is one, along with the local magistrate and others in authority.'

Mrs Burns was saying she wouldn't be believed. Cora stared at the farmer's wife. In spite of herself, her voice shook a little when she said, 'I don't care. I'll shout it in the village square, I'll go into the shops and everywhere until someone takes notice. I will, I mean it.'

'I believe you would.'

'I won't have my sisters treated like that.'

Mrs Burns nodded slowly. Saturday night bath time had always turned her stomach from when Bernard had insisted upon it shortly after Enid and Maud had arrived, and not just for the children's sake. Every Saturday she had felt as though he was rubbing her nose in his filth. 'I daresay the six of you could have your bath in the wash house. The bath's always kept in there anyway. It'll save me bringing it into the kitchen and it'll be more convenient all round. I don't know why I didn't think of that before.'

They surveyed each other for a moment more, what had been left unsaid vibrating in the air between them before Cora turned and followed the others. As she walked up the narrow stairs to the attic rooms her head was whirling. *She knew. Mrs Burns knew that her husband liked to look at Enid and Maud naked.*

They were all waiting for her in the larger bedroom. Anna and Susan had changed into their nightdresses and were snuggled down in their bed, half asleep, but the three older girls were sitting bolt upright on the other one, faces chalk-white. For once, it was Enid who spoke first. 'What happened? What did she say?'

'She's agreed we can have a bath in the wash house from now on, and we'll make sure the door's shut, all right?'

'He – he won't like that.'

'I don't care what he likes.'

'He'll be mad.'

Again Cora said, 'I don't care.'

Enid's plump body slumped and Maud put her arm round her sister. Looking at Cora, she said, 'He'll take it out on Enid, he always does.'

Cora and Maria glanced at each other and then Cora crouched down in front of Enid who was staring at the floor. 'What does Maud mean? How does he take things out on you?'

'He doesn't.' There was a note of fear in Enid's voice, shriller than before, and she glanced at the bedroom door as though the farmer was going to come bursting in at any moment.

'He does.' Maud wouldn't be shushed by her sister. 'He makes her do things.'

'Shut up, Maud.' Enid jumped to her feet, yanking her sister with her and practically dragging her out of the room.

Cora stared after them and as the door was slammed shut, Maria said, 'They're scared stiff of Farmer Burns, Cora. Maud's just told me their da's in prison and when their mam came to visit them last year he chased her off the farm and wouldn't let her talk to them.'

'He can't do that.'

'Well, he did, and she's not been back since or written to them.'

'Or if she has, they haven't got the letters,' said Cora meaningfully.

That had been nearly a month ago, and when she had told Wilfred about it the following Monday at school he had been highly indignant, but on her behalf, not Enid's. 'If he tries to bully you like he does them, you tell me,' he'd said angrily, for all the world as though he was a full-grown man rather than a thirteen-year-old lad.

Cora had smiled and said she would, although she had known she wouldn't. What good would it do? She was the one living at Stone Farm, not Wilfred. She had to fight her own battles for herself and her sisters. But at least she didn't have the added burden of worrying about Horace. Not only was her brother under Wilfred's protection, but Appletree Farm was altogether different from Stone Farm from what Horace and Wilfred had told her. Horace had landed on his feet yet again. Wilfred described the farmer and his wife, who'd had three sons, as salt of the earth, and he and Horace were treated as members of the family. They were expected to do their bit round the farm when they weren't at school, but they didn't mind that. Neither did Cora. It would keep her brother out of mischief.

The youngest son, Jed Croft, was a year older than

herself and Wilfred. Cora saw him at school in the company of a couple of friends every day but had never really spoken to him. Being the oldest pupils, Jed and his cronies were the undisputed hierarchy at the small village school – apart from twin girls from a nearby hamlet who had shades of Alma Potts about them – and to Cora they seemed very much aware of their exalted position.

She didn't know if she liked Jed or not. He and his friends kept themselves somewhat aloof from the rest of the fifty or so children. But there was no doubt he stood out from the crowd, being a good head taller than his pals and handsome to boot, with thick black hair and vivid blue eyes. But handsome is as handsome does, as her mam used to say in a disparaging fashion. Cora had never really understood what that meant but nevertheless it seemed to fit Jed Croft. Everyone appeared to hero-worship him, even her brother and Wilfred, and for some reason Cora found that grated on her. Not that she had time to muse about Jed once she was home from school, Mrs Burns made sure of that. Every minute until they climbed the stairs for bed was accounted for. School hours were more in the nature of a rest most days.

The school itself was very different from the one in Sunderland, being a small village building that until the commencement of war had only housed fewer than thirty children. There was a tiny dirt yard outside, divided by a fence into Boys and Girls, with one rudimentary lavatory each. The school had no water supply and every morning several of the boys fetched buckets of water from a horse trough outside the church. The juniors and infants shared one small room with their two female teachers, and Mr Travis taught the seniors in the other. Cookery lessons were conducted at the vicarage due to the kindness of the vicar's wife who took batches of children from the Seniors and Juniors several times a week, and physical exercise and nature study involved working in the vicarage garden and outhouses where the children were expected to do everything from weeding and growing vegetables and flowers, to digging and bagging potatoes and other produce in due course. 'You scratch my back and I'll scratch yours,' Wilfred said drily to Cora when they were first told of the arrangements. There seemed quite a bit of this. 'Agricultural Studies' turned out to be a team of children from the Seniors class working on any local farms who requested the unpaid help three hours a day twice a week, and science lessons involved practical animal husbandry and crop production with the children being part of the management of resources.

Farmer Burns never availed himself of the free labour though, and there were no visitors in any capacity to Stone Farm, but it was through the school that Cora first got to see Appletree Farm at the beginning of August. The Seniors, who consisted of Jed and his two friends, the twins, and several other children besides Cora, Maria, Wilfred and Enid, were told that Farmer Croft had consented to furthering their education by allowing them to assist with the haymaking which occurred well before harvest. They would merely be required to rake the cut grass, they were told, but it was an important stage in the process which ensured that all parts of the precious crop were dried out to the right degree to avoid pockets of mould, mustiness or moisture.

Cora didn't know what she had expected to see as they had arrived at Appletree Farm. Probably something along the lines of Stone Farm. The day was soft and warm, the sky blue with long streaks of white clouds, and the morning air promised a rising heat to come, but it was the sight of the farmhouse that gripped her as she sat squashed in the back of the horse and cart that Farmer Croft was driving. The house was two-storeyed, with soft red-brick walls spread with vines and climbing roses and the chimneys muffled in ivy. Arched lattices overgrown with honeysuckle framed the windows and front door, and in the small fenced rectangle of front garden grew a profusion of flowers – roses, hollyhocks, pinks, lavender. She stared, spellbound. It was everything she had ever imagined a farmhouse to be and was as different from Stone Farm as chalk from cheese. It spoke of peace and warmth and comfort; it was a home. She wanted to cry.

The fourteen children who comprised the Seniors worked all morning in the fields, the skylarks swooping and calling overhead and the air scented with the perfumes of summer. The farm had a burn running through the bottom of one of the fields over gleaming pebbles and smooth rocks, the water crystal clear and pure, and mid-morning the group took a break there when Jed's mother brought them a huge basket of teacakes hot from the range oven and dripping with butter. Cora took off her shoes and socks and dabbled her feet in the icy water as she ate, Maria on one side of her and Enid on the other, and as had happened several times before when she was in close proximity to Enid she noticed the smell that clung to the other girl now and again. It was an unpleasant odour, not least because there was something about it that was faintly reminiscent of Farmer Burns, but perhaps she was imagining this. And sometimes, for days on end, there was no smell at all.

She glanced at Enid but the other girl was stolidly eating her third teacake, her eyes on the babbling water, not looking to left or right. Cora didn't attempt to make conversation knowing it was a fruitless exercise, and when in the next moment someone plumped down behind the three of them she looked round, expecting it to be Wilfred. Instead Jed's cornflower-blue eyes laughed at her. 'Well?' He grinned, raking back a lock of black hair that always fell over one eye. 'What do you think of my mam's teacakes then?'

It was the first time he had spoken directly to her and for a moment she was too taken aback to reply; the full force of the beautiful blue eyes was unnerving. And then she collected herself. 'They're lovely. It's kind of her.'

'Aye, well she's like that, my mam.'

He seemed different here, on his farm, Cora thought. Nicer. Much nicer. For the first time she could see why Wilfred and Horace liked him. And as though the thought had brought him over, Wilfred sat down beside Jed, his eyes on her face as he said, 'Didn't have times like this in our school back home, did we, lass? Old Woody wouldn't have allowed it.'

It wasn't so much what he said as the way he said it that made Cora feel odd. Wilfred's voice was jolly and he was smiling, but she didn't think he was smiling inside.

'Bit of a stickler for the rules, was he?' Jed said, but to her, not Wilfred.

Cora shrugged. 'Mr Wood's all right.'

'Bit handy with the cane.' Wilfred stretched his legs out so that Jed was forced to move back a little. 'Remember when he caught Oscar Todd and Larry smoking some tippers Larry had scrounged off his brother? They couldn't sit down for a week.'

'Tippers?' said Jed, again to her.

'Fag ends,' said Wilfred shortly. 'By, Jed, don't you know anything?' He dug the other boy in the side as though he was just joking but Cora had caught a definite edge to his voice. Before anyone could speak, he continued, 'You lot don't know you're born here with Travis, I can tell you. Me an' Cora didn't have it so easy back in Sunderland, did we, lass? It's as different there as chalk to cheese. But we stuck together. We've always stuck together, haven't we, Cora.'

Cora saw Jed's eyebrows give the slightest movement upwards. Embarrassed, she reached for her socks and shoes and busied herself pulling them on without replying. She felt flustered and annoyed with Wilfred and all at odds. Maria and Enid followed her lead and as the three of them stood up Cora didn't look at the two boys.

The rest of the morning passed by without incident but as Cora worked at fluffing out the hay with the other girls, she found she was aware of Jed Croft in a way she hadn't been before. Her senses heightened, she knew exactly where he was at any given time, and when she heard him laugh or call something to his friends, her heart would thud faster.

They had been packed into Farmer Croft's cart like sardines in a can on the way to the farm earlier, and on the ride back she made sure she was in the middle of the cluster of girls at the front of the cart with her back to the boys. But even without glancing his way, she could see Jed's deep blue eyes and black hair, and the way he'd looked at her when he had first sat down earlier. He was there on the screen of her mind.

He liked her. Jed Croft liked her in *that* way, and Wilfred had taken umbrage at it. Which meant . . . This thought was unwelcome but had to be faced. Which meant that Wilfred might like her in that way too. She'd suspected this in some recess of her mind for a while, she realized unhappily. She just hadn't wanted to admit it to herself because if she did then everything would change, one way or another, and she didn't want it to. Wilfred was her friend. No, he was more than that. He was like a brother and she loved him, she loved him very much, but only as a brother. She could never like him in the way a lass liked a lad when she walked out with him, whereas Jed . . .

Upset and confused, angry with herself and Wilfred and even Jed Croft, Cora sat with her back rigid in the cart as it bumped along, her head whirling. She hated it here, she told herself fiercely. She hated Stone Farm and the way everyone was frightened of Farmer Burns, even Mrs Burns, truth be told, and yes, herself too. Her stomach knotted. He wasn't violent, not like Wilfred's da, but he terrified her and she knew there was something bad happening at the farm, something she couldn't put her finger on but that was real, nevertheless. The hard work, the smells, the stifling little attic room, the lavatory arrangements, *everything else* wouldn't be so bad without Farmer Burns. Even the constant ache of missing her mam. And now there was Wilfred too. Her world was rocking like this cart, not only from side to side but backwards and forwards. From today things would never be the same as they had been.

By the time the horse and cart deposited the children outside the school, Cora's stomach was aching and she felt nauseous. She grew worse as the afternoon progressed, but once back at the farm she somehow got through the jobs Mrs Burns had lined up for them and then the milking after dinner. She was thankful to climb into bed, curling herself into a little ball beside Maria as she tried to ease the pain in her stomach. The others had been asleep for an hour or more when she became aware of a stickiness between her legs and carefully climbed out of bed.

In the deep summer twilight that pervaded the attic

room, she realized what had occurred. Before she had left home, her mam had warned her this would happen one day, and had packed her some little pads and a sanitary belt to insert in her knickers when it did. It was all part of growing up, her mam had said, and she would explain it fully to her when it became necessary. But once it began it would happen every month, it was the same for every girl. That had been the end of the conversation.

Cora rummaged in her suitcase for the pads. None of them used the rickety chest of drawers; it was full of silverfish and spiders so they kept their things in their suitcases under the beds. Once she was sorted, she climbed into bed once more.

Her mam had said this was part of growing into a woman, but right at this moment she didn't want that. She wanted to stay the same, she wanted Wilfred to be the Wilfred she'd always known, she wanted to be at home with her mam and da safe, she wanted . . . She wanted the moon. She bit down on her lip and cried until there were no more tears left, drifting off to sleep only when she was too exhausted to think any more.

Chapter Five

Nancy Stubbs stood staring out of her kitchen window at the snowstorm outside, her mind only half on the weather which added to the prospect of a bleak Christmas for a besieged Britain. This time last year, a week before 25 December, she had already fetched the bairns home and there had been no real food shortages to speak of. Now everything was different, in more ways than one.

She turned restlessly, the familiar feeling of guilt mixed with excitement strong. She always felt like this before Ken came. More than once she had told herself that as soon as she opened the door to him she would say it was over, but she never had. She only had to look at him and she melted, that was the trouble. And the thought of an existence without him was intolerable. It had taken meeting Ken to show her that she had never been in love with Gregory.

She plumped down at the kitchen table, her head in her hands, as she relived the first time she'd laid eyes on Ken Preston on a sunny Friday morning in August. She had just left work to take an early lunch when seemingly out of nowhere a single German aircraft had dropped its bombs along the riverside, one falling twenty yards in front of her. She had been blown off her feet, narrowly missing being run over by a steam traction engine which had just delivered steel plates, and ending up under a mound of debris comprising the remains of the plasterer's shed roof and a hydraulic crane arm that had been broken off. Ken had helped dig her out, shaken and cut and bruised but with no serious injuries, and then offered to see her home when her boss had insisted she take the rest of the day off.

Five people had lost their lives that day and umpteen others had sustained life-changing injuries. Had it been that, her narrow escape, that had made her fall into Ken's arms the next week when he had called, ostensibly to ask how she was? Certainly since that day in the yard when she had come round to find herself buried alive, only to emerge minutes later almost unhurt, she had felt a new sort of inward aliveness and happiness she couldn't have explained to anyone. It was as though the incident had awakened violent passions and she hardly recognized herself any more, passions that were emotional and physical. It was heady, and more of an aphrodisiac than any man-made substance. One Ken had taken full advantage of. But no, that wasn't fair. She couldn't blame him.

She stood up and walked over to one of the built-in cupboards either side of the range, opening it and extracting a half-full bottle of whisky. Ken worked at the docks and had a sideline in black-market goods; he was always bringing her something or other. It had been four pairs of silk stockings the other day, whisky the week before that along with half a dozen eggs and a side of bacon, and tinned peaches and chocolate another time. At first she had been uncomfortable about accepting the illicitly obtained goods, not least because it felt as though Ken was paying to sleep with her, but he had been miffed and she hadn't wanted to upset him so she'd swallowed her objections. She was finding he was forceful, in bed and out of it, but that was part of his attraction. Gregory had worshipped the ground she walked on and there had been times when his adoration was suffocating. Ken was a different kettle of fish.

She set the bottle of whisky on the kitchen table and fetched two glasses, glancing at the clock on the mantel-piece over the range as she did so. He was late again. He was often late; she never really knew where she was with him. In the first weeks after they'd got together she'd worried herself silly that he'd been caught in an air raid but there had been no bombs dropped on Sunderland since October, thank God. And although the town had been bombed on a number of occasions it hadn't suffered the same kind of wholesale destruction and loss of life as London or Coventry. She pitied the poor folks caught up in that. What good were the extra Christmas rations of four ounces of sugar and two ounces of tea if your home and everything you held dear was gone?

Her eyes moved involuntarily to the tea caddy that

was full to the brim thanks to Ken, and again a feeling of guilt assailed her. Even the King and Queen were making sacrifices if the newspapers were to be believed, and certainly they'd put their money where their mouth was by staying at Buckingham Palace in spite of being bombed a few weeks ago, but truth be told she was better off than she'd ever been. Ken ate his evening meal with her most nights and he always made sure there was plenty on the table. There was a stuffed roast breast of lamb cooking in the oven tonight that would have fed the lot of them before the war and she'd still have saved some for Gregory's packing up, but it'd all go once Ken sat down.

Gregory . . . She poured herself a good shot of whisky and drank it straight down at the thought of her husband, wincing as the neat alcohol burned her throat. Shortly after Cora and the other bairns had been evacuated she'd received word that he was alive and unhurt after Dunkirk and had escaped being taken captive by the Germans. The day after the telegram had arrived he'd turned up on the doorstep, full of how the French Resistance had got him and a number of his comrades out of France under the noses of the Germans, but within two days he was back with his regiment. Since then she'd had one letter from him in which he had written that he was likely being sent to North Africa. That had been a week before she had met Ken, and she'd heard nothing from Gregory since.

Was she wicked, carrying on with another man while Gregory put his life on the line for King and country? She didn't need to think about the answer and it caused her to pour another glass of whisky. The thought had come more than once that if Gregory were to die then everything would be so much simpler, and in spite of her shame and disgust at herself she couldn't get it out of her mind. She had felt so bad that she had blurted it out in confession one day and she could tell how scandalized Father Grant had been. She hadn't been back to church since, and when the priest had called at the house to see her some weeks ago she had hidden upstairs until she was sure he had gone.

The back door opened and Ken Preston walked into the kitchen as though he owned it. Tall and good-looking, with dark brown hair, a fresh complexion and heavily lashed eyes a few tones darker than his hair, he had always been used to running his life exactly as he pleased and saw no reason why a war should interfere with things. Since leaving school he had worked at the docks, and had very quickly become involved in the network of pilfering that went on, graduating to a spot of smuggling and other crimes as the years had gone on. He liked to think he'd got some standing in the criminal underworld that operated in Sunderland, and when there had been a danger that he'd be conscripted he'd used one of his contacts to put him in touch with a doctor who'd been more than happy to sign a certificate saying he'd got dodgy eyesight and flat feet – for a fee, of course. But it had been worth every penny.

He slung a bag containing a box of coffee and some

chocolate on the table, smiling as he said, 'For after we've eaten.'

Aye, he thought as he looked at the woman in front of him, it'd been worth every penny to buy himself out of trouble. Let the other daft beggars go away to fight if they wanted to; he'd prefer to keep their women warm for them. That was his bit towards the war effort.

His smile broadening at his silent joke, he nodded at the bottle of whisky. 'I see you've started without me. Getting in the mood for later? That's m'girl, hot and steamy, eh?'

Nancy stared back unsmiling. She hated it when he spoke like that; it made her feel cheap. Her voice cool, she said, 'You're late.'

'I'm here, aren't I?'

'Aye, you're here.'

His face straight now, he narrowed his eyes. 'I've told you before, if a spot of business comes up then I have to see to it when it suits. The blokes I deal with expect it.'

'And it doesn't matter what I expect?'

He shrugged. 'Take it or leave it, Nancy. If I'd wanted a nagging wife, I'd have married one.'

She felt the colour sweeping over her face. This was where she should tell him to clear out and not come back, but even through the bewildering feelings of rage and hurt the words wouldn't come. She would die if he walked out; she couldn't survive without him now. Gregory had been a sedate, circumspect lover – mostly the whole thing had been over in less than five minutes and she had never experienced any pleasure from the act apart from a mild satisfaction that he was content and happy – but from the first time with Ken she'd felt as though she was reborn, a different woman. He had taken her right here in the kitchen that day in the summer, and done things to her that had had her crying out with an abandonment that had shocked her. Afterwards, when he had gone, she had felt horrified and ashamed by what she had allowed because Gregory wouldn't have dreamed of ravishing her with so little respect or regard, but when Ken had returned the following evening she had let him spend all night in her bed.

Ken had been scrutinizing Nancy through lowered lids and he had a good idea of the turmoil inside her. It amused him. He knew he had awoken her sexually, in spite of her being a married woman with bairns, and for his part he had been surprised at the liberties he could subject her to in the throes of their mutual passion.

His point having been made, he now leaned towards her and took her hands. 'Don't be mad, sweetheart,' he coaxed softly. 'I only wanted to get you some chocolates after all. They're your favourites.'

Nancy gulped in her throat but she didn't resist him. 'There's times . . .'

'What?'

'There's times when you don't seem to care whether we're together or not.'

'Now that's not true, darling.' He pulled her against

him, kissing her hard. 'I adore you, you know that. Aren't I always saying how much I want you?'

As the kiss deepened she briefly found the strength to jerk away muttering, 'The dinner . . .'

'Damn the dinner.'

He pulled her in to him again, beginning to undress her as he whispered sweet nothings against her hot skin. She was his and she'd remain his until he tired of her or until her husband came home, whichever occurred soonest. It was really no odds either way.

It was the day before New Year's Eve, but as Nancy and Ken sat listening to the wireless over cups of coffee heavily laced with whisky from a new bottle Ken had acquired, celebrations for the next night were the last thing on their minds. For once even Ken was subdued. The city of London was an inferno. The Germans had chosen the previous night, a Sunday, to set fire to the capital.

'*The raid had clearly been planned with typical German thoroughness*,' the newsreader announced sombrely. '*It was timed to coincide with the tidal low point in the Thames, and the water mains were severed at the outset by high-explosive parachute mines. At least ten thousand fire bombs fell on the city with the fires raging out of control, the belaboured firemen unable to use the mains supply or pump water from the Thames. When the water came on again, pumped from more distant mains, the exhaust pipes of the fire engines became red hot through the continued high-pressure pumping by twenty thousand firemen, but as ever the people of London rallied to the emergency. Soldiers and civilians alike did what they could to help, but it was an act of God that saved the city from total alienation. Just when the Luftwaffe seemed to be winning, the raid was called off due to the weather unexpectedly deteriorating over low-lying German airfields.'*

'Act of God!' Ken reached for the whisky, slurping a good measure into his now almost empty cup. 'Where's God when little bairns are blown apart and whole streets demolished, eh? It's survival of the strongest in this world and to my mind that means Hitler's going to win this war hands down.'

'Shush,' said Nancy, still listening to the newsreader who had gone on to say, '*In a dramatic incident, one of many no doubt on such a terrible night, an unknown soldier lost his life. As yet no one knows his name. He was just an old soldier – no stripes, just many ribbons – but he and a fireman were playing a hose on a sixty-foot wall engulfed in flames when it crashed down, burying them both beneath a ton of bricks. There have been many other reports of extreme bravery in the face of overwhelming odds during the raid, and the city is pulling together today as only the British do.*'

Ken made a sound in his throat, bringing Nancy's eyes to him. 'What?'

'Extreme bravery my backside – extreme foolishness more like.'

She stared at him. 'He was trying to help. Everyone was trying to help.'

'You look after yourself if you've got any sense, lass, and leave the heroics to them who've a mind for it.'

'You don't mean that.'

'The hell I don't.'

'But you helped rescue me, when the bombs fell along the riverside.'

'That's different. The plane had gone, hadn't it? It wasn't like in the middle of a raid.'

Nancy didn't know what to say. His face had taken on the slightly amused expression he adopted at times, but there had been something in his voice that told her he was deadly serious. More to change the subject than anything, she said, 'You don't really think Hitler's going to win, do you?'

'I think him and his Nazis have got a good chance, aye.' He drained his cup. 'They're strong and we're weak. Look how Chamberlain handled things. Hitler must have been laughing his head off. He had Chamberlain under his thumb from day one and he knew it.'

'But Winston Churchill's in charge now.'

'Might be too late. Hitler is ruthless and determined and he knows what he wants and isn't afraid to go for it whatever the cost.'

'You sound—' She stopped abruptly.

'What?'

'You sound like you admire him.'

He shook his head impatiently. 'It's not a question of

that. And of course I don't hold with what he's doing to the Jews and the rest of it. But he's strong and he's powerful, and first and foremost he looks out for number one. If you're going to get anywhere in this world that's what you have to be like, Nancy. Weakness isn't a virtue. My father was a weak man, he let everyone push him around. It made me sick.'

Her eyes opened a little wider. He never talked about his past. All she knew was that he was an only child, that his mother had died when he was born and that his father had passed away just after Ken left school.

'You didn't get on with your da?'

'No.'

She looked at him closely for a moment. 'Because you felt he was weak,' she clarified.

'He *was* weak. After my mam died he let himself be talked into marriage by the woman who looked after me during the day when he was at work. She took in bairns like that, being a widow with no man to support her and four kids of her own. She had him up the altar within twelve months.'

'You didn't like her.' His tone had made that plain.

'She was a lazy fat lump. She stank, the house stank and us bairns brought ourselves up amid the filth and chaos but did my da ever say a word? She doled out his beer and baccy money and spent all day sitting on her backside guzzling stout with a couple of her cronies who were at our house more than they were at their own, but not once did he raise his voice, let alone his fist, to her. I was out of there the minute I was earning. Rented a room with a mate of mine to start with. It was small and cramped but it was clean and bug free which was all I asked.'

So that was why he had never married. A feeling of tenderness swept over her as a number of traits in his personality suddenly made sense. She reached out and touched his cheek. 'I'm sorry.'

'Don't be.' He pulled her to her feet, taking her into his arms. 'It was damn good training for life. I wouldn't be where I am now if it wasn't for dear Jinny, may she rot in hell.'

'She's dead?'

'Fell down the stairs when she'd got a load on a few years after my da died.' His tone was suddenly impatient. He was tired of the conversation; after all, he hadn't come here to converse. 'Come on,' he said, smiling the smile he knew worked wonders with the ladies. 'Let's go upstairs.'

PART TWO

Conflict Within and Without

1941

Chapter Six

She could hardly believe they had been living at the farm for over a year.

Cora stood up straight to ease her aching back. The warm air, scented with the smell of freshly cut wheat, was bearable now that the heat of the day was past. It was gone ten o'clock at night but they were still harvesting; the clocks had been put forward two hours during the summer months to extend the hours of daylight and facilitate a longer working day. It was dirty work, sweat and dust combining into a mixture not unlike mud, but in spite of that Cora enjoyed being out in the open air. Once they returned to the farm she knew the little attic room would be stifling.

Cora and the other girls had spent all day and the ones before it setting up the sheaves in stooks in the fields, ready to be taken to the rick yard to await the arrival of the travelling threshing machine. This had a crew of two men and four land girls, but the year before Farmer Burns had made it clear he expected them to help where they could. She remembered it had been pure bedlam from start to finish, but especially when the bottom two or three layers of sheaves were moved and the rats and mice left the ricks. She knew Farmer Burns hadn't wanted the crew at the farm, she'd heard him talking to Mrs Burns about it, but due to the war and the output he was expected to achieve he had no choice in the matter. They had been forbidden to talk to the men and land girls, ostensibly because it would interrupt the flow of work, but that was ridiculous.

She nodded at the thought as she stood gazing over the field. He just didn't like anyone setting foot on his farm. Unconsciously her eyes went to Enid who was working some yards away, her big straw hat pulled well down over her face even though the sun had long since lost its power. Enid had never been talkative, but in the last few weeks since they had broken up from school for the summer holidays she'd barely said a word to anyone. And it was all to do with Farmer Burns, she knew it was. She had lost count of the number of times she had tried to talk to Enid about him since they'd been at the farm. Just last week, when she had seen Enid emerging from behind one of the barns, her face smeared with tears, only for Farmer Burns to follow her a moment or two later doing up the belt of his trousers, she had attempted to get to the bottom of things. But the other girl wouldn't be drawn; instead she'd put on what Cora described to herself as Enid's gormless face. But Enid wasn't gormless, far from it. She was good at her lessons; bright, Mr Travis called her.

She had spoken to Jed about it and he'd said it was possible Farmer Burns was interfering with Enid. She had a vague idea of what this meant, but as her mother had never explained the facts of life to her, any information had been picked up here and there from other children. But one thing was certain – if the farmer *was* making Enid do bad things that should only be done between married folk, Enid wasn't about to say so. She'd said as much to Jed and he had shrugged his shoulders. 'Then I don't see what you can do.'

She didn't either. Cora sighed. But it left her feeling all at odds, nevertheless. What with Farmer Burns, the fact that her friendship with Jed had caused something of a rift between herself and Wilfred, and the worry about her mam, she didn't know if she was coming or going half the time. Her mam had written nearly every week when they had first been evacuated to the farm, but now she was lucky if she had a letter every couple of months. With the Germans bombing Sunderland fairly regularly now she couldn't help imagining all sorts of things when she was in bed at night. The trouble was, when a letter *did* eventually arrive it was never reassuring. Not that her mam was full of woe or anything, just the opposite. She was always bright and cheerful, too bright and cheerful. And detached. Yes, that was the thing that worried her the most, Cora thought. She was detached. As though she didn't care about them any more.

And then she admonished herself sharply. *Enough*, she was being stupid. Of course her mam cared about them.

She started work again in the falling twilight, swallows swooping in the sky above her in their quest for flies, and a large flock of lapwings gleaning amongst the sheaves in the distance, in search of grain. Hard though life was at Stone Farm, she had come to realize in the last twelve months that she preferred the country to the town, which had surprised her. In the town, the seasons came and went with just the inconveniences of the weather being noted – cold and wind and deep snow in winter; rain and damp in the spring; heat and smells from the privies and docks and industry in the summer, and gales and storms in the autumn. Here, each time of the year possessed its own individual treasures, whether it be the first springtime primroses dotting the verges of the lanes on the way home from school; corn fields shimmering in a summer's haze with scarlet poppies changing their radiance with every twist and turn of their silky heads; the smell of wild hops hanging thickly from autumn bine; or the woods and meadows thick with snow in a rolling frozen landscape that intensified the barest colour and shade.

Yes, she loved the country and Jed was the same. Only the other day he had confided in her that he dreaded the war not being over by the time he was old enough to fight. His two older brothers had chosen to join up as soon as war had been declared. He wasn't afraid to fight the Germans, he had said in the next breath as though she had voiced it, but it was the fact that he would be away from the farm and everything he loved that would be the hardest to bear. He had looked at her intently as he'd spoken and their eyes had held for a long moment, causing Cora to shiver inside. He had left school for good at the beginning of the summer holidays but they had arranged to meet every Sunday afternoon whereupon they walked and talked in the fields and down by the river. They were still just friends – he hadn't asked her to be his lass or anything or tried to kiss her – but she knew she was in love with him. She just wasn't sure how he felt. And then there was Wilfred.

Cora's eyes narrowed. The friendlier she'd grown with Jed, the more awkward Wilfred had become, which apparently caused tension at Appletree Farm. Jed had tried to stay pally with Wilfred, but Horace had told her on the quiet that Wilfred wasn't having any of it and picked quarrels whenever he could. Horace had taken Wilfred to task after the older boy had 'accidentally' let the bull out into a field where Jed was working, causing Jed to vault a five-bar gate in the nick of time. Wilfred hadn't admitted anything to Horace, but he had finished the conversation muttering that he wasn't about to touch the forelock to anyone, be they the farmer's son or no, which was ridiculous because Jed never looked down on anybody. It was all horrible.

She gave a mental shrug. Her da had always said that worrying about things you couldn't change was wasted effort and he was right. And Wilfred wouldn't have meant to actually physically hurt Jed, he wasn't like that, but perhaps scare him a little? Not that that was acceptable.

But the only way that Wilfred would be himself again, the old Wilfred she'd grown up with, was if she stopped her Sunday walks with Jed and told the farmer's son their friendship was over. She would rather die than do that.

A sudden longing to see her father, to hear his voice and look into his face, swept over her so powerfully it brought tears pricking at the backs of her eyes. She'd been euphoric when she'd read her mam's letter telling her he had survived Dunkirk, but she had found herself wishing he could have been injured – not badly, just enough so he could have stayed with her mam and not had to go away again, and not just for his sake. For her mam too. There was something wrong with her mam, she knew there was.

The others were downing tools and Cora followed suit, but as she walked back towards the farmhouse with Maria's arm in hers and her sister nattering away ten to the dozen, she was only half listening. Nothing in life was straightforward these days and it was all down to the war turning everything on its head; how she hated Hitler and his Nazis.

It was the last week of a blazing hot August and the threshing machine and its crew had arrived at the farm. It was a different group to the year before, but still consisted of two burly farm workers and four land girls. By now, much of the initial hostility to land girls had been overcome as the women from all walks of life had proved themselves by their physical as well as their mental ability to be tough and resilient. Indeed, some land girls delighted in rivalling men at their jobs by taking on the hardest work, often under atrocious conditions, despite being born and bred in towns and cities. The compulsory working week of fifty hours in the summer and forty-eight in winter with little chance of time off was taken in their stride, and woe betide any male who talked down to them.

One such girl was Phoebe, a ravishing blonde from a well-to-do family if her upper-class accent was anything to go by, who despite her tall, slim figure and small hands and feet was as tough as old boots. She had told Cora the story of how, when she had first been trained and sent to a farm in the middle of nowhere, the farmer had instructed her to stand in a shallow, smelly dyke and then put her arm down a nearby rat hole to find out which way the hole ran. The farmer, standing safely on top of the bank, had then started pumping Cymag gas into another exit hole, causing a huge rat to run out of Phoebe's, shocking her into falling on her back in the fetid stinking mud. 'And do you know,' Phoebe had drawled, 'the wretch actually laughed. Believe me, sweetie, the worst rats in the world are the two-legged ones. I've actually got a lot of respect for the rodent kind, for their tenacity and will to live, but men . . .'

It was this same land girl who now came and sat by Cora on a straw bale during their lunch break. Cora had chosen the spot to be by herself and go over in her mind the latest development in the feud Wilfred seemed determined to have with Jed. According to Horace, who had turned up at Stone Farm the night before specifically to have a word with her about the matter, Wilfred had – again 'accidentally' – sprayed artificial fertilizer in Jed's face the day before. Fortunately, after washing out his eyes in water, Jed seemed to be suffering no ill effects apart from redness and itching, and Wilfred insisted it was unintentional.

She'd been so deep in thought that she hadn't noticed Phoebe until the other girl said, 'Your friend, the quiet one. Got a beau, has she?'

'What?' Cora stared into the beautiful face.

Phoebe motioned with her head towards Enid who was sitting stolidly eating the bread and cheese Mrs Burns had brought them all, Maud by her side. 'Her, the oldest one. Seeing a boy, is she?'

'Enid?' The idea was ridiculous. 'No, no, of course not.'

'There's no "of course" about it. Lots of girls have a beau about her age. I know I did.'

'At thirteen?'

'Oh, yes.' Phoebe smiled. 'Algernon Braithwaite, his father was an earl or something. He was home from school in the summer hols and we met every afternoon in the walled garden until Daddy's gardener got wind of it. Anyway, that's by the by. Are you sure she hasn't got a pimply-faced boy calling on her? I mean, she's out from under her parents' eye, isn't she, and while the cat's away, the mice will play, and all that.'

'I'm absolutely sure.'

'No shadow of a doubt?'

Cora shook her head.

'Oh, dear. I thought you might say that.'

Cora was nonplussed and it showed. Phoebe smiled, kindly. 'You're such an innocent, aren't you. I don't think I was ever like you.'

'Phoebe—'

'No, no, it's all right, I'll deal with this. Of course, I could just go on my merry way and forget all about it but if he—' She stopped abruptly. 'There's the rest of you to consider. Oh, why are some men so foul? If it is that, of course. I might be putting two and two together and making ten. She could have a tumour or something.'

Cora was completely at sea, but later that night she saw Phoebe take Mrs Burns aside as the crew were preparing to leave, and casting her scruples aside she hid in a doorway to eavesdrop unashamedly. She was still some distance away, but she heard Phoebe's high, clear voice say something about being an abnormal shape for a girl of her size and age. She couldn't catch Mrs Burns's reply, but then Cora heard every word as Phoebe said sharply, 'I do not accept that, Mrs Burns, and I insist you take the girl to a doctor immediately. Do you hear me? I have never known puppy fat to consist of a round mound in the stomach. There's something there for good or ill and it needs to be investigated. I won't let the matter drop, believe me.'

Cora's eyes opened wide as the penny dropped. Phoebe suspected Enid was in the family way, and if she was then Farmer Burns . . . She felt physically nauseous. Jed had been right. Farmer Burns had indeed interfered with Enid which had resulted in a baby. A *baby*. Thinking about it, for the last two or three months Enid had made sure she washed alone, but then so did she, so she hadn't thought anything of it.

She watched as Mrs Burns turned on her heel and walked swiftly away, her face white and grim. Phoebe joined the other land girls, saying something that made all their faces stare after the farmer's wife.

Her heart thudding hard in her chest, Cora wondered what to do. Should she tell Enid what had been said? It didn't seem right not to warn her. Perhaps it was all a mistake? Enid had always been rotund, after all. Oh, Enid, Enid. And Maud too. If Enid was expecting a baby and Farmer Burns was the father, what was going to happen?

In the event, the decision of whether or not to tell Enid was taken out of her hands. When she entered the farmhouse it was to find that Mrs Burns had taken Enid into the main house without any explanation to anyone, and Enid didn't return to sleep in the attic room with Maud. A tearful Maud came into Cora's room and while the younger two slept, Cora and Maria sat up with her till gone midnight waiting for Enid. When it became apparent Enid wasn't coming back that night, they made room for Maud in their bed and tried to get some sleep. Cora said nothing of what she had overheard.

In the morning, they trooped downstairs to milk the

cows and found Mrs Burns waiting for them in the kitchen. 'Enid is unwell,' she said without any preamble, 'and I'm taking her to see the doctor in Rochester. You all know what you have to do so get on with it as normal, and you, Cora, see to the food and drink for the threshing crew midday if I'm not back.'

They nodded silently. Something about the farmer's wife's rigid posture and tight voice forbade questions.

Mrs Burns and Enid were gone by the time Cora, Maria and Maud finished the milking. Farmer Burns was seeing to the cows his wife usually dealt with and was still in the barn when the girls left, and the milking was done in silence. Shortly after the breakfast of cold ham, hard-boiled eggs and crusty bread which Mrs Burns had left for them, the threshing team arrived at the farm. Cora saw Phoebe walk purposefully towards Farmer Burns as soon as she climbed down from the vehicle. She said something which the farmer answered with a shrug, leaving Phoebe staring after him, hands on hips. As soon as the land girl reached Cora, she said, 'Mrs Burns has taken Enid to the doctor then?'

Cora nodded. After a moment's hesitation, she whispered, 'You think she's going to have a baby, don't you?'

Phoebe made a small movement with her head which could have been taken as affirmation but did not speak.

'I think Mrs Burns does too. After you'd spoken to her yesterday she took Enid into the main house and we haven't seen her since.'

Phoebe sighed. 'Look, Cora, if this goes the way I

think it will the police will be involved. Enid's only thirteen, after all. They'll probably ask you some questions, all of you, and you must tell them anything you know. Are you sure Enid didn't have a boyfriend?'

Cora drew in a deep breath. 'I'm sure, but—'

'What?'

'Ever since we got here Enid's been frightened of Farmer Burns. Enid and Maud were here a year before us and Maud once said—'

'What? What did Maud say?'

'That Farmer Burns made Enid do things.'

'What things?'

'I don't know. Enid denied it and I think she told Maud not to say anything else.'

'Have you ever seen anything? Think hard. Anything at all.'

Cora told Phoebe about the time she had seen Enid coming out from behind the barn. 'She was crying. She often cries but you can't get a word out of her.'

'The dirty swine.' There was no doubt as to the conclusion Phoebe had come to. They stared at each other and then the land girl took Cora's arm. 'Come on, we'd better get to work. It'll all come out in the wash now, don't worry.'

Cora was to think of Phoebe's words often in the ensuing weeks. Enid didn't come back to the farm but the only explanation they received from Mrs Burns when she returned was that Enid was unwell and had been sent somewhere to be looked after. The police visited the following day and spent some time with Farmer Burns and his wife in the farmhouse. The threshing team had finished their stint at Stone Farm the day before and Cora would have given the world to be able to talk to Phoebe, but it wasn't to be.

A few days after Enid had been taken away, the police came back to the farm and Mrs Burns called Cora and the others into the kitchen. Maud had been in tears on and off since her sister had gone and was clearly terrified, but refused to say anything to Cora beyond that Enid had told her to keep her mouth shut no matter what. When Cora had asked what she had to keep quiet about the girl wouldn't reply and had become hysterical when Cora had asked if it was anything to do with the farmer.

Mrs Burns stared at each one of them in turn but her eyes rested longer on Maud who was white and trembling. 'Farmer Burns's friends, Inspector Shaw and Sergeant Irvin, want to talk to you,' she said at last, a slight emphasis on the word 'friends'. 'As you know, Enid has gone and she won't be coming back.'

This prompted fresh sobs from Maud which the farmer's wife ignored. She cleared her throat, her face grim and her eyes unblinking. 'Enid has got herself into trouble. Do you know what that means?' she said flatly.

Anna and Susan stared wide-eyed at Mrs Burns, clearly at a loss. Whether Maria and Maud realized what the farmer's wife meant Cora didn't know, but something inside her was saying, *You say it, you spell it out*, because the more she had reflected on the situation the more sure she had become that Mrs Burns had known exactly what was going on with poor Enid and hadn't lifted a finger to help the girl.

'She is going to have a baby.' Mrs Burns stared at Maud. 'And the police need to ask you some questions.'

Cora's chin went up a notch. 'Where's Enid now?'

Her voice had been abrupt and for a moment it appeared as though Mrs Burns had taken umbrage. Then she swallowed and with obvious effort spoke calmly. 'Enid has been taken to a home where she will stay until she has the baby. She is refusing to name the – the father.' Again her eyes rested on Maud for a moment. 'But obviously it is a boy from round here so the police need to know if she has confided in you.'

Cora stared at Mrs Burns. She didn't think she had hated anyone as much as she hated the farmer's wife at this moment. Not even Hitler. He was evil and killing people right, left and centre, but this was a different sort of badness and it was directly in front of her. 'It might not be a boy,' she said harshly.

There was a second's pause, and then Mrs Burns's back straightened and her voice took on a steely quality. 'The police aren't interested in "might"s, girl, but facts. Do you understand me? Folk can get into a lot of unpleasantness with "might"s, unpleasantness that could cause them to be taken away and put somewhere else, away from everyone they know. Your mother asked you to look after your sisters, didn't she? So think on. Facts, girl.'

Cora knew she was glaring at the farmer's wife; she couldn't help herself. She turned to Maud who had tears streaming down her cheeks. 'Enid spoke to you, told you things, I know she did,' she said urgently. 'She's your sister, Maud, and they're going to say she's bad if you don't speak up about what you know. And Enid isn't bad, we all know that.'

Rachel Burns took a step towards Cora before checking herself. She would have liked nothing more than to shake the girl until her teeth rattled, but now was not the time to lose her temper. Gossip spread like wildfire, and if Bernard was tainted with it all the folk who had been jealous of a nobody like her becoming the wife of a well-to-do farmer would make sure the mud stuck till their dying day. Oh, she knew how people were, and the old school friends and her cousins and family who still lived hereabouts would be the worst. They might smile and nod and show deference now to her position in the community, but once the knives were out it'd be a different story. She didn't doubt that nothing could be proven even if Enid named Bernard; he would deny it and his friends and associates would back him rather than a bit of a girl whose father was in prison. They knew which side their bread was buttered and the stuff that Bernard slipped them every month wasn't to be sneezed at in this time of rationing. No, Bernard would get away with it all right, but the common folk, the people she saw now and again, would make her life miserable.

Her voice icy cold, she now directed her gaze to Maud. 'No one is saying Enid is bad,' she said stiffly, 'merely that she was taken advantage of by some lad still wet behind the ears or even a passing vagrant. There was a tramp sleeping under the bridge down by the river for some weeks; he was at the kitchen door a few times asking for bread and cheese. Do you remember?'

Maud gulped and tried to speak but choked on her tears.

'Do you remember?'

'Don't shout at her.' Cora's brown eyes were fiery as though they were reflecting the red of her hair, and her hands were clenched into fists at her side. 'Don't you bully her.'

'Don't talk to me like that, madam.'

Rachel Burns glanced at Cora but what she read in the girl's face deterred her from continuing down that line. Instead, her voice took on a conciliatory note as she looked at Maud again. 'Don't get all het up, lass. No more crying, now then. I was just saying that when the police ask you questions there's always that tramp to remember, along with any lads Enid knew at school. Girls like to flirt and carry on a little, it's natural, nothing wrong in that, but lads take it too far sometimes. Force the issue. Anyway –' her voice became brisk – 'sit yourselves down, the lot of you, and I'll get the mid-morning snack while we wait for the police to call you in. It'll be one at a time and I doubt they'll want to see Anna and Susan, just you older three. But think on about what I've said, all of it.'

Maud sat down at the table with her eyes on the oiled tablecloth. Maria glanced helplessly at Cora, tears welling. She was clearly shocked and scared, and Cora placed her hand on her sister's. She would have liked to reassure Maria that all would be well and the truth would out, but suddenly she didn't believe that. It seemed to her that Farmer Burns could do whatever he liked. Enid was clearly so afraid of him that she would not name him as the father of her child, and however little or however much she had told Maud, Maud was going to say nothing.

Cora bit hard on her lower lip. Her mother had sent them away. She didn't care about them any more or she would have come to see them and make sure they were all right, or at least have written every week. She had forgotten about them, and so had everyone else in Sunderland. They were on their own and the only person she could rely on was herself. Maria and the two little ones and even Maud had no one to protect them but her, and she couldn't afford to be sent away somewhere else as a punishment for speaking out her suspicions about Farmer Burns. Mrs Burns wasn't going to help them. No one was. Maud and Enid's mother couldn't even read and write, Maud had told them that, and worked long hours in a shirt factory just to pay the rent. She would be no match for Farmer Burns and his powerful friends.

Mrs Burns placed a glass of milk and a wedge of stottie

cake still warm from the oven in front of each of them. Anna and Susan tucked in immediately, and after a moment Cora and the others followed suit. Cora's stomach was churning and she was sure Maria and Maud's were too, but what could she do?

A thought occurred to her and she looked the farmer's wife straight in the face. 'Maud's going to sleep in our room from now on.' It was a declaration, not a request. 'And when we clean the farmhouse we'll be doing it in twos with the other one staying with Anna and Susan.' There had been the odd occasion when she'd thought back that Enid had returned tearful and upset from her Saturday stint. Cora pictured Farmer Burns's room and the big bed and the smell and she shuddered.

Rachel Burns recognized a trade-off when she heard it. Her eyelids blinked. If she agreed to this it would be tantamount to admitting she knew of her husband's guilt, but she was in no position to argue. And in truth part of her had no wish to. If Cora could keep herself and the others out of Bernard's reach, it would bode well for the future. He could take himself off elsewhere for his depraved practices, rather than fouling his own doorstep. She could feel the colour hot on her cheeks but aimed to retain some semblance of dignity as she said, 'As long as the work gets done it's no odds to me how you arrange it amongst yourselves.'

As she spoke the kitchen door opened and Farmer Burns stood there, his bullet eyes moving over them. 'You.' He pointed at Maud. 'Follow me.'

Maud cast an agonized glance at Cora before standing up and doing as she was told.

When the door closed, Cora drew in a deep breath. 'Is he staying in the room while the police ask their questions?' When the farmer's wife didn't immediately reply, she said again, 'Is he? Is he going to be there?'

'I believe so.'

'I shall say I don't want him in the room.'

She watched Mrs Burns sigh and shake her head slightly. 'While you live here with us we're standing in for your parents.'

'I don't care. I don't want him listening.'

'What you want is neither here nor there, I'm afraid. The police will expect him to stay and if you cause a fuss it will rebound on you and your sisters, he'll make sure of that.'

Cora was near to tears but she knew she must not show it. And now there rose in her an anger that enabled her to blink them away and straighten her back, but her fury wasn't directed towards Mrs Burns, nor the police, not even Farmer Burns. It was her mother she was angry with, and in that moment she told herself she would never write to her again. Her mam didn't care about them – well, that was fine. She didn't care about her either. Her mam had abandoned them here, left them at the mercy of strangers she'd never met, and forgotten all about them. She was as bad as Wilfred's mother; worse, because her mam had pretended to love them. She hated her. Cora's full mouth pulled tight. She'd never forgive her for this.

It was a few minutes before Maud came back and she was ashen white. Farmer Burns beckoned to Cora. 'Come on.' Once in the corridor leading to the main house, he walked in front of her, the smell of him causing her nostrils to flare with distaste. He opened the door into the hall and stood aside for her to pass him, his voice threatening as he murmured, 'Watch your Ps and Qs, girl. None of your lip,' before again walking ahead of her and flinging open the door into the parlour where the two police officers were sitting.

Cora noticed three half-full glasses and a bottle of whisky on the low table in front of the two men who were sitting on a sofa, and as Farmer Burns sat down in a chair at the side of them, he took one of the glasses and drained it.

Cora stood in front of the three men. No one suggested she sit down and she stared at the two policemen, determined not to show how frightened she felt. After a moment or two, one of the policemen said, 'I'm Inspector Shaw and this is my colleague, Sergeant Irvin. I understand your name is Cora Stubbs, is that right? You're an evacuee from Sunderland?'

She nodded.

'And you're here with your three sisters?'

Again she inclined her head.

'You're most fortunate.' The inspector smiled. 'There's not many folk who would have taken four sisters so that you could all stay together. You're the eldest, I understand? And you're fourteen years of age?'

'Yes.' Fortunate? she thought. Did he really have no idea?

'Do you understand why we need to ask you a few questions today, Cora? Questions that you need to answer truthfully.'

'It's because Enid is expecting a baby.'

'Quite. Unfortunate business, most unfortunate. Now, Enid's sister mentioned a man, a vagrant, who hung around these parts for a while some time ago in the spring. Do you remember such a person coming to the farm asking for food? I understand he requested that he be allowed to sleep in one of the barns, a request Farmer Burns wisely refused. Do you know if Enid talked to this man? Did you see them together?'

'No.' She looked at the farmer for a moment. 'Definitely not.'

'Did Enid ever mention him? Or a boy perhaps? One of the lads from hereabouts?'

'Enid would never have had anything to do with a vagrant and she didn't have a lad.'

'Are you sure about that, Cora? Think carefully before you answer. Are you absolutely sure Enid wasn't meeting a lad on the quiet?' It was the sergeant who had spoken.

'I'm sure. Enid wasn't – wasn't like that.'

'Hm.' The inspector had kept his eyes trained on her and now he finished his whisky; Farmer Burns immediately refilling the glass. 'And you were close, were you? Best friends?'

'We were friends, yes, but Enid was—'

'What?'

'Shy, quiet.'

'Not shy enough, it seems,' said the inspector in an aside to his sergeant who gave a smirk in reply.

Cora glared at the policemen. They were making Enid out to be bad, that this was somehow partly her fault. 'Enid's a nice girl,' she said hotly. 'She would never have done anything like this if she hadn't been forced.'

Ignoring her, the inspector turned to Farmer Burns. 'And the father's in prison, you say?' he murmured. 'And the mother is illiterate? Dear, dear. We open up our homes to all and sundry and this is the result. The war's got a lot to answer for, if you ask me.'

Cora felt sick. They had made up their minds; whatever she said they would believe Farmer Burns over her. Involuntarily her gaze went to his face. His expression was deadpan but something in the depths of his eyes caused her stomach to jolt. He was enjoying this, she thought with horror. Taking some weird satisfaction in proving how influential and untouchable he was. Showing her how he was fooling the police. He knew she knew about him and Enid.

'Enid talked to Maud, I know she did,' she said desperately.

'How do you know? Did you hear them? Has the

sister told you what happened?' The inspector's voice was sharper.

Cora shook her head. 'I think Enid told Maud not to say anything, but I know Enid's been unhappy and upset since we came to the farm.'

The inspector turned to Farmer Burns again. 'That tallies with what you and Mrs Burns have told me about the girl not really settling. With her state of mind and her background it's highly possible she was reverting to type, if you get my meaning. In my job we see the seedier side of life and –' he lowered his voice but Cora could still hear him as he whispered – 'they start young in the slums.'

Without looking at her again, the inspector said, 'Thank you, Cora. You can go now,' as he wrote something in his notebook. 'Send your sister along, would you.'

She stood quite still for a moment, a sense of utter helplessness making her feel very small as though she was shrinking, reducing to nothing. It was a frightening feeling, something alien to her bold spirit and therefore all the more terrifying.

She didn't glance Farmer Burns's way but she knew his eyes were on her and it was this that stopped her from crumpling. Her back straight and her chin high, she swung round and left the room, and again it was his footsteps behind her that enabled her to march along the passageway and into the kitchen where Mrs Burns and the others were still seated at the kitchen table. 'They want you,' she said to Maria, amazed that her voice sounded almost normal, and as her sister walked past her she reached out and squeezed Maria's arm. 'Chin up,' she said softly.

Farmer Burns remained standing in the doorway for a full ten seconds, staring at her after Maria had left, and then without a word he turned and walked back along the passageway. Mrs Burns glanced at her. 'You and Maud'd better wait in the house for now in case there's further questions, but you needn't be idle. Get yourselves into the scullery and start on them pots and pans in the sink. I'll call if you're wanted.'

She had placed two baskets containing cheese and butter and cream on the table as Cora had walked in, and now she spoke to Anna and Susan. 'Go and collect the eggs from the hen house. Farmer Burns has promised them both a few bits before they leave.' She looked full at Cora then; the unspoken message clear before she turned away.

Cora stared back, sickened. So justice for Enid was to be sacrificed for a couple of baskets of food? She watched as the farmer's wife wrapped some thick rashers of bacon in greaseproof paper and added them to the baskets. Without looking up, Mrs Burns said, 'What are you two still doing in here? The pots won't clean themselves.'

Maud was silently crying as they walked into the scullery, and once Mrs Burns was out of earshot, she whispered, 'I couldn't say about Enid, Cora. I couldn't. Enid made me promise on our mam's life. And he said he'd kill her if she told, me an' all, and he would, Cora. He drowned one of the farm cats in the water barrel to show Enid what he'd do to us if she let on. He made her watch and she was sick after and he laughed.'

Cora put a hand to her mouth, her eyes wide.

'He made her do things to him at first when we came here – he'd come up to our room at night and take her in the room you have now. Enid made me pretend to be asleep so he didn't start on me. But then he'd make her do things in the day an' all if he got her alone, and one day she came back from feeding the calves and there was blood on her legs and she was crying. She said he'd put his – you know what –' she paused – 'inside her and she could hardly walk. It – it was awful.'

Maud wiped her face with her sleeve. 'After that she wouldn't talk about it but he carried on. I know that. I'm – I'm scared, Cora.'

Cora rubbed her lips, her head spinning. It was useless to try and persuade Maud to talk to the police and even if she did would it accomplish anything? She thought of how the inspector and sergeant had been and knew the answer. But he mustn't be allowed to hurt Maria or Maud or the little ones. Very quietly, she said, 'Listen, Maud. From now on none of us must be on our own here, all right? You or Maria or me must always be with Anna and Susan, and the other two must be together. No matter what he says or what Mrs Burns says, we must do that. She's agreed you can come into our room and that'll start tonight.'

Maud nodded, her face a picture of misery.

'It'll be all right if we stick together. If he knows we're not going to give him a chance to do anything, he'll give up. And Mrs Burns knows now, I'm sure she does.' Cora picked up one of the small kitchen knives out of the sink and ran the blade carefully along her finger. Slipping it into the pocket of the thick linen smock they wore over their clothes at the farm, she offered another one to Maud. 'If he tries anything, use this,' she said grimly. 'It'd be enough to keep him off you.'

Maud backed away, eyes wide. 'I couldn't.'

'Well, I could.'

They stared at each other for a moment and then began the task of scrubbing the pots and pans from the meal the night before. After a few minutes, Maud whispered, 'What will happen to Enid now?'

'I don't know.' Cora thought of the small plump girl with the eyes of a wounded doe, and her stomach contracted. But one thing she did know was that she wouldn't let Farmer Burns hurt another one of them, no matter what she had to do to keep them safe.

Chapter Seven

Jed stared at Cora. Her face was drained of colour like a piece of bleached calico. There was no doubt she'd meant every word she'd just said; the little knife she'd shown him was proof of it. He didn't like to say a small thing like that would be no defence against the big burly farmer; if it gave her some peace of mind so be it. When she'd spoken of her suspicions before, even though he'd suggested that Farmer Burns might be trying it on with the girl, he'd never seriously thought . . . 'And Enid's been sent away?' A baby, at her age. Her life was ruined.

Cora nodded sadly. 'Mrs Burns told us it's a special place where girls like Enid can be looked after and have their babies, and then the babies are usually adopted by married couples.'

'Enid should have told someone,' he said at last. 'And why on earth didn't Maud speak up when she had the chance?'

'I've told you why.'

Cora's voice had verged on sharp. Placatingly, he said,

'I know, I know, I'm sorry, I didn't mean . . . I wasn't criticizing. I didn't mean it like that. I'm just worried about you.'

Cora glanced at him. He hadn't said, 'about you all', but 'you', meaning her. She shrugged, but her voice was soft when she said, 'I'll be all right. I've told the others we stick together and must always be on our guard – safety in numbers and all that.'

It was the Sunday afternoon after the police had come in the week to question the girls. After instructing Maria and Maud to stay together and take care of Anna and Susan, Cora had gone to meet Jed as arranged the week before. The two of them were sitting in their favourite spot on a grassy bank overlooking the fields. The next day was the first of September. Cora was due to return to school but Jed would be working on the family farm. She'd miss seeing him at school, she knew that, but there were still Sunday afternoons to look forward to. That was if Jed wanted to continue their rendezvous. It was hard to fathom him out sometimes.

As though he'd read her mind, Jed said, 'First of September tomorrow, autumn's nearly upon us.'

Cora nodded. Already along the lanes and wayside the elms and sycamores were faintly touched with yellow, and the fruits of blackberry, sloe and elder were ripe in the hedgerows. She and the others had collected great basketfuls of blackberries the day before for Mrs Burns to make into jam and wine. There had been none of the usual chatter though, each of them, even Anna and Susan, aware of the absence of one of their number.

'Cora, I want to ask you something.' Jed turned to face her, his blue eyes reflecting the sky above them and his jet-black hair shining like silk. His shirt collar was undone and his shoulders, broad and muscled for a youth of his age, strained against the material.

He was so handsome, Cora thought, as her heart began to thud erratically. She would die if he said he didn't want to see her again.

'I should probably wait until you're fifteen, I know that, until you've left school and so on, but I can't. I want to ask—'

'What?' she asked breathlessly.

'I want to ask you if you will be my lass. Mine. So if any other lad asks you, you can tell them you're spoken for.' He had said it in a rush and with a dart of surprise she realized he was nervous. 'I – I know we're young and all that but I love you, Cora. I'll never feel about anyone else the way I feel about you, I know that. And you like the country, don't you? I mean, you wouldn't mind living here when – when the war's over?'

Cora smiled. Now it had happened she wondered how she could ever have worried it wouldn't. 'I'd like to be your lass,' she said shyly. 'Course I would.'

Jed leaned forward. The kiss was sweet and inexperienced, but they were both trembling when it ended. 'There,' he whispered, 'it's signed and sealed.' He took her hand, turning it over and kissing the palm. 'I love you,' he said again. 'For ever.'

'Me too.' She touched his face, her eyes shining.

They stared at each other and then began to laugh as he pulled her to her feet, twirling her round as he shouted to the sky, 'We love each other, do you hear? Cora and Jed love each other for ever.'

Wilfred ground his teeth. He was hidden in the hedgerow, a spot he'd found early on when he had begun following Jed on a Sunday. He was always careful to keep hidden and although it was torture seeing them together he couldn't stop. During the night hours when he lay awake in the room he shared with Horace, he'd tell himself he'd fix Jed the way he'd fixed Godfrey Taylor but it hadn't proved as simple as that. He had been banking on the fact that now Jed had left school it would mean he'd have Cora to himself during school hours and they could get back on their old footing. They were meant to be together, him and Cora. She was his world, she always had been.

He ran his hand across his face, telling himself he had to remain strong. She was so beautiful, so lovely, and of course other lads would want her, but there was a cord binding him and her together that was unbreakable.

He heard them laugh again and the fear swamped him despite his attempt to keep it at bay. She didn't really love Jed, he knew she didn't, she couldn't. She was his and she had always been his. He had known from a young lad that they would be together. Get married, have a family.

That was how it should be. That was *right*. He couldn't let anything or anyone get in the way of that. It was for Cora's sake after all; no one could possibly love her the way he did and she just had to understand that. Somehow he had to make her see.

In spite of himself the tears came, bitter and hot, giving no relief but making his head ache.

How could she let scum like Jed Croft touch her, contaminate her? But it wasn't her fault, he told himself in the next breath. She was perfect, but she was also so innocent, so naive. Jed's fancy looks and the fact that he was kingpin in their age group would turn any lass's head, especially one as trusting as Cora. But Jed wouldn't have her.

His hands were bunched into fists and now he shut his eyes, slowly relaxing taut muscles and gaining control of himself. This was his strength and he had recognized it some time ago after he had dealt with Godfrey. It was all about believing that you could make things happen, things that other people wouldn't have the guts for. He might look puny on the outside but his mind was super-strong and that was what mattered. He would dispose of Jed somehow and Cora would turn to him again, he knew she would. She loved him. Perhaps not in the way she felt about Jed, but that was girlish infatuation. It wasn't real.

He lifted his head, taking a deep breath of the clean air as he opened his eyes. Jed was brawn but he had the brains; he would win. More and more of late he had realized how gullible people were, people like the Crofts, for instance. He had determined some time ago to get Jed's parents on side and it had been easy. He said and did what they expected and wanted him to do and say, and he knew Mrs Croft especially had a soft spot for him.

He could hear Jed and Cora talking but couldn't make out what they were saying. Now and again she would laugh, a little giggle that made him want to bash Jed's face in. He imagined himself lying in wait somewhere, a big rock in his hands, and then how it would feel to bring it crashing down on the back of Jed's skull. He could almost feel the impact; his fingers were tingling and he was sure he could smell the metallic tang of blood on the breeze. But it couldn't be like that; he had to be cannier from now on where Jed was concerned. He'd been going about things all wrong by showing he considered Jed an enemy and alienating Cora.

He nodded at the thought, frowning. And he'd be careful what he said and did in front of Horace too. He had always thought that the youngster saw him as an older brother, but after the incident with the bull, Horace had been different, the little turncoat. But no matter. He knew he could win Horace round if he put his mind to it.

The drone of aircraft high above in the blue sky drowned out Cora and Jed's voices and brought his eyes peering upwards. Fighters flying home from yet another sortie over German-occupied territory in Europe, perhaps. He wondered how many of their company hadn't made it. It was all very well for Churchill to declare that the V-sign was the symbol of the unconquerable will of the occupied countries and a portent of the fate awaiting the Nazis, but people were dying in their tens of thousands, weren't they? The BBC had urged listeners in Europe to go out at night when it was dark and chalk the V-sign on doors, walls, pavements, anything, in order to rattle the Germans. Fools.

He shook his head at the thought of chalk marks compared to German panzers and machine guns. Hitler must be laughing his head off. Didn't people realize that might triumphed over right in the real world? He and his brothers had learned that early on. There was nothing like having the living daylights beaten out of you day in, day out, to teach you how to survive. What didn't kill you made you stronger – that was what one of his brothers had told him after a particularly vicious hammering by his da.

He came out of his thoughts to realize that the planes had gone and Cora and Jed were leaving too by the sound of it. He watched from his hiding place as the two of them walked off in the direction of Stone Farm, hand in hand. After the first time of being evacuated, he had prayed and prayed they'd be sent away again once he was back home. He didn't mind where he ended up, he'd told God, as long as Cora was with him. It could be the worst place, the worst hovel, because anywhere was better than where he was. Now a saying of his old teacher in Sunderland came back to him as Jed and Cora disappeared from view down the country lane.

She had been a strict old spinster, had Miss Lindsay, but nice enough at the bottom of her. Any time a bairn had started a sentence with 'I wish', she had stopped them, saying, 'Be careful what you wish for because it just might come true.' Well, he had wished, hadn't he, and it had come true. They had left Sunderland again and Cora was here too, but he'd got a darn sight more than he had asked for. Miss Lindsay had been right. But this wasn't the end of the story, not by a long chalk.

He normally followed Cora and Jed back to Stone Farm to watch their leave-taking, but this afternoon it was beyond him. He came out of the hedgerow and looked down the lane, his shoulders hunched. A mist had lingered in the fields that morning, rolling across the newly ploughed earth that broke the harvest stubble and bringing a chill to the air. And he had been glad. It had meant the summer was drawing to a close and school would begin again. He would have Cora to himself now that Jed had left and he could sit with her at lunchtimes and walk home with her when their lessons were done. He had told himself she would soon lose interest in Jed and it wasn't as if they had actually kissed or anything, but now . . .

He stood for a moment more and then straightened, his mouth a thin line and his eyes narrowed. Now he would have to change tack a little. He would start being civil, even friendly, to Jed. Not immediately – he'd go about it bit by bit, a thawing if you like so Jed wasn't suspicious, and he'd hold his tongue about Jed when he was with Cora. If she mentioned him, he'd be nonchalant, interested but not too interested. He could do that, he was clever enough to fool them all. And he'd watch for an opportunity to take care of Jed for good. It could be a while and he would need to use all his wits, but he could bide his time if he had to. It made sense.

He began to walk towards Appletree Farm, slowly at first and then faster, with more purpose. This latest was a hiccup in his plans for the future, but that's all it was. That was all he would allow it to be.

Cora returned to the farm in time for milking. The three hours after Sunday lunch that Mrs Burns allowed them to have to themselves was on the understanding that it was work as usual at six o'clock. Cora had insisted Anna and Susan were kept with them; she didn't think Farmer Burns would attack the little ones but she couldn't be sure so she was playing safe. He was a devil, and how could you fathom what a devil might do? Jed had agreed. As they had parted at their trysting place, he'd said urgently, 'Be careful every minute you're there, won't you, all of you. And if he tries anything, get your sisters, Maud too, and come to our farm.'

She knew he meant well and her voice had been soft when she'd said, 'I don't think your parents would appreciate the five of us turning up on the doorstep and I couldn't drag them into this anyway. The police are on Farmer Burns's side – your parents would get into trouble if they kept us and they might not believe me anyway.'

'Of course they'd believe you.' She had sworn him to secrecy, and now he added, 'I wish you'd let me tell them what's gone on.'

'Tell what? That Enid's going to have a baby but she won't name the father? And Maud told the police she thinks it might have been a tramp who was around in the spring? Maud's so scared she'd still say that to anyone else but me. But I will be careful, I promise.'

They hadn't kissed again after that first time, but he had taken her hand and pressed it to his heart, the look on his face saying more than any words could have expressed.

Cora thought of this as she joined the others. Mrs Burns and Maria and Maud were already at their milking stools, and Anna and Susan were standing some distance away in front of the big trough used for cleaning the churns and buckets, scrubbing at some cans and pails. They flashed her quick smiles as she sat down, Mrs Burns glancing up briefly to say, 'You're late.'

'No, it's just six o'clock.'

Muttering something about 'gallivanting', the farmer's wife continued milking her cow, one of the few short-tempered ones who took pleasure in using her tail like a whip. Cora hoped Primrose was in a bad mood this evening.

Once the milking was over the five of them went to the hen house and settled the birds down for the night. Cora wasn't sure how much Anna and Susan had understood about the happenings at the farm and Enid's departure, but they had accepted her stipulation that at least one of the older girls be with them at all times without argument.

Once back in the kitchen they finished the supper of bread and jam washed down with milk that Mrs Burns had ready for them, and climbed the stairs to their attic room before Farmer Burns came in from the fields. Maud now slept in the slightly larger bed with Anna and Susan, and Cora and Maria shared the other one. It was a squash for them all but no one complained, and since the evening after Enid had been taken away in the morning, Cora and Maria dragged the chest of drawers in front of the door before they got ready for bed.

The room was stiflingly hot but with the chest of drawers in place at least Cora felt she could sleep with some degree of safety. There was no doubt that since the inspector and sergeant had questioned them all and left, Farmer Burns was feeling invincible. Far from being deflated as Cora had half-expected, she and the others had found him watching them at various times, the expression on his face curdling her stomach. If he had noticed the new arrangements that Cora had insisted upon he had made no comment to the girls, but the night before, when the others had drifted off to sleep and she was still awake, Cora was sure she had heard footsteps on the landing and the door of the room Enid and Maud had occupied being opened. She'd lain as stiff as a board for what had seemed like hours but had heard nothing more, and eventually had fallen into a doze that had remained fitful till morning.

*

It was an hour later and Cora still hadn't fallen asleep, her ears straining for any sound outside the room. The old farmhouse was full of creaks and groans as it settled down for the night, and every faint noise brought her ears straining. She wasn't aware that Maria was awake too – her sister had kept as still as she had – until Maria's voice came very soft as she whispered, 'I'm scared.'

Cora didn't pretend she didn't know what about. Turning on her side to face Maria, she murmured, 'Well, don't let him see it, all right? That's what he wants, for people to be frightened of him.'

'Aren't you scared?'

'No, I'm not. He's just a bully, and you know what Da always used to say about bullies. At heart they're lily-livered cowards and you have to stand up to them.'

Their conversation continued – Maria pouring out her fears and Cora trying to reassure her – until they heard heavy footsteps on the landing outside the room. They lay still, frozen in terror, and then Cora heard him walk away, the floorboards creaking, and down the narrow staircase, and she prayed with all her might he would lose his footing and fall and break his neck.

Even as she comforted Maria, telling her sister he wouldn't come back and that she was safe, Cora wondered how long it would be before the confrontation came. And it would come. What she'd read in Farmer Burns's face was proof of that. So she had to do something, something that would convince him there were no easy pickings here. It was different from when he'd started on poor Enid; there were five of them now and they'd fight him tooth and nail.

Long after Maria had gone to sleep, snuggled tightly into her arms despite the heat, Cora lay wide awake, thinking and planning. Attack was the best form of defence. She'd read that somewhere. It might even have been Churchill who said it. Things would be easier on a day-to-day basis from tomorrow when they were back at school, but there were still the evenings and weekends to contend with. The last few days she'd felt as though they were being stalked by a predator. That was the only way she could describe it to herself, and she knew Maria and Maud felt the same. Farmer Burns *wanted* them to be frightened of him, he enjoyed it, and so, however she felt inside, she had to square up to him. The thought brought her heart pounding in her throat so hard she put a hand on her chest. It was the only way.

Bernard Burns walked into the stables, humming to himself. Seth and Polly, the two great plough horses, were in their roomy stalls munching on the mash he'd prepared, a mixture of chaff, beans, oats and different types of clover, with a generous amount of molasses added to it. He always made the mash himself and wouldn't have trusted anyone else to do it, using the hand-turned chaff cutter that had been his father and grandfather's before him.

He was proud of the stables. His ancestors had known all about animals requiring good ventilation and the stables were warm and airy in the winter and cool and airy in the summer, as well as being high – sixteen feet to the eaves – which gave plenty of room for the dust to get above the horses. The stables had their own yard which could give the animals more freedom, and Seth and Polly shared their home with Sadie, Farmer Burns's smaller horse used for driving and riding, unlike the big workhorses of the fields.

He walked across the stone-slabbed floor into the tack room, only to come to a sudden halt. His eyes narrowing, he said, 'What're you doin' in here?'

Cora faced him without flinching although inside everything in her shrank away from the man she considered monstrous and repellent. Since Enid's situation had come to light there was barely an hour in the day when she didn't think of her and what she must have gone through, berating herself that she hadn't forced Enid to tell her the truth or cornered Maud and questioned her or . . . oh, a hundred scenarios.

Her back straight and her head high, she said coolly, 'I wanted to talk to you.'

'Oh, aye?' The bullet eyes narrowed still more, becoming black slits. 'And what could you have to say that's worth listening to?'

Bernard Burns had never had any real feeling of love for anyone. The nearest he came to genuine emotion was the firm attachment and regard he felt for his horses. His father had been of the same ilk, and Bernard knew that his father had treated his mother badly but he didn't think any the less of the man who'd sired him because of this. His mother had been a weak character in his view, easily cowed and given to tears, and she had irritated him at best. He couldn't remember how old he'd been, no more than five or six because he hadn't been long started school, when his father brought his mistress and her three brats to live on the farm in one of the farm workers' cottages.

The youngest of Vera's girls had been a babe in arms and the eldest three, and over the next decade until his father died of a heart attack whilst forking farmyard manure out of the dung cart into furrows before sowing the new crop, Bernard had watched him take all three of them at one time or another in the hay barn whilst he'd hidden in the loft. Even before his father was buried, his mother had turned Vera and the girls out of their cottage, but she hadn't lived long to glory in her victory. Within six months the fever had taken her and he had inherited everything. Become master of his own small empire.

And it was as the master of all he surveyed that he now looked at the slender young girl in front of him, the girl who'd been a thorn in his flesh since the day she had come to the farm. She was beautiful with her mass of red hair and great eyes but it wasn't her beauty or unconscious grace that made him want her; it was the itch of longing to tame her that kept him awake some nights. In the child brothel he'd frequented before Enid had arrived, and then with Enid herself, he'd let his depravity have free rein, subjecting the children to any and every perversion he could think up, and now as he looked at Cora he was imagining her beneath him, screaming and squirming and helpless. He had never had anyone defy him as this girl had; even Rachel, when she'd still appeared young enough to excite him, had submitted to his more unnatural demands with nothing more than pleas and tears.

He watched her as she drew in breath and then his eyes widened when she said, 'We, my sisters and Maud and I, want you to know that if you ever try to lay a finger on any of us we'll make sure everyone knows what kind of man you are, and even your so-called friends in high places won't be able to save you. We'll make sure of that.'

Cora looked at him as his head moved forward and his shoulders rose. His whole attitude spoke of incredulity. For a moment he stared at her in amazement and then his face became convulsed and he took a step towards her, rage causing him to spit as he cried, 'You dare to threaten me? *Me*?' He swore viciously. 'I'll teach you a lesson you'll never forget, m'girl.'

It wasn't Maria and Maud coming out of one of the stalls where they had been crouching down out of sight and standing either side of Cora that halted him so much as the knife she brought out of her pocket. Her eyes as fiery as her hair, she said with soft intent, 'I'll use this, I mean it. You touch me or any of us and I'll use this on you and so will they. You might think you've got away with what you did to Enid, but no more. We won't be handled, any of us.'

Bernard looked at the bit of a girl as he had termed

her in his mind before this day. His mouth opened and shut but without any sound coming from it; he couldn't believe his ears. That she meant every word he was in no doubt. All his life, like his father before him, he had used his standing as a well-to-do farmer as a springboard for getting what he wanted. He had cultivated colleagues of influence in the community and in the police, always making sure they were well looked after even before the war had begun and rationing had reared its head. Early on his father had told him that everyone had their price and he'd found this to be true and made good use of it. Bribery, if sugar-coated as gifts of friendship, was a powerful tool.

Still speaking softly, Cora said, 'I've got Maud to write down every single thing that Enid told her about you and put it in a sealed envelope and given it to someone for safe keeping. Should anything happen in the future to any of us, we'll make sure the police have it. Not the inspector and sergeant who came to the farm but proper policemen.'

He wanted nothing more than to wring her neck, to watch the life seep out of her. Swallowing hard, he said, 'And you think anyone would believe it? You think anyone in their right mind would believe you over me?'

'Aye, I do. There's already talk about you –' this was a lie but spoken with such conviction he didn't doubt it – 'and folk always think there's no smoke without fire.'

His voice was a growl as he said, 'Get out of my stables, the lot of you.'

'We're going.'

Cora was looking at him as though he was something putrid, and again the desire to wipe the expression off her face was so strong he could taste it, but not so strong that he dared act on it because he believed she would do what she'd threatened. He could hardly take it in and it was sticking in his craw but she had the upper hand, her, a bit of nowt from the streets of Sunderland.

The three girls walked past him and out of the stables but he didn't move for a full minute. Behind his still facade his mind was racing, rage and humiliation uppermost. He uttered a deep, thick, unintelligible sound as he glanced around the tack room where he prided himself on keeping everything in immaculate order, almost stumbling across to a leather-topped stool where he sat down heavily.

It wasn't to be borne. Talking to him as though he was the scum of the earth, it wasn't to be borne. He drew in a snarling breath. But this wasn't the end of it, not for that little madam. There were more ways to kill a cat than drowning it and he wouldn't rest till she was crawling at his feet begging for mercy.

His fingers gripped his knees, the heavy cloth of his trousers bunching, and he squeezed and squeezed as though it was Cora's neck he was wringing.

He sat for some minutes more, and by the time he stood up his mind was clearer. He'd let the dust settle for a while, allow this talk about him that she'd mentioned to die down. This with Enid had been unfortunate but with the girl out of the way, people would find something else to gossip about eventually. It was an inconvenience, and for the present he'd have to go further afield to have his needs taken care of, but that couldn't be helped.

He flexed his shoulders, glancing across the room to where Cora had stood a short while ago. His chance would come. He nodded to himself. And when it did he would take great pleasure in breaking her spirit along with her body. With her out of the way – he didn't qualify what he meant by 'out of the way' at this juncture – the others wouldn't stand up to him, he had the measure of them. Maud could retrieve this damn letter and he'd stand over her while he forced her to eat it, every damn word, and he hoped she choked on it.

One of the plough horses snorted, drawing him out of the tack room and over to their stalls. He spent some minutes stroking Seth's great head that had lowered at his approach, the huge horse nuzzling at him as he caressed the velvety nose. After giving Seth and Polly a carrot each, he left the stables, walking out into the balmy September evening and sniffing the smells of the farm as though they were the finest perfume.

'Why did you tell him I'd written everything down?' Maud's voice was shaking as the three of them walked away from the stables towards the hen house where they were to join Anna and Susan.

'I don't know, it suddenly came to me, but perhaps you should, Maud.' Cora turned to face Enid's sister.

'I couldn't, Enid wouldn't like it, and besides, who could we give it to?'

'We'll think of someone.'

'No, I mean it, I won't do that.'

It was said with such finality that Cora accepted defeat. 'All right, but it's important that Farmer Burns believes that you've done so. You do see that? If he thinks that there is something written down it's a sort of protection for you and the rest of us too.'

'I agree.' Maria added her two penn'orth.

'And you mustn't let him see that you're so scared of him, Maud.' Maud had been trembling from head to foot in the stables. Cora's voice was gentle but firm. 'We've got to be a united front, like in the war.'

'But I *am* scared.'

'I know. We all are. But he mustn't see it.'

Maud nodded doubtfully.

Cora sighed, aware that she wasn't making any headway with Enid's sister. As the field where the hens were came into sight, she said, 'Look, try and imagine that Farmer Burns is Percy, the rooster. Percy throws his weight about and hollers and turns nasty, doesn't he, but when he's shut up in his box he quietens down because he knows he can't do anything. That's what we've done today in standing together against Farmer Burns, Maud. And saying about you writing everything down is part of that, part of shutting Farmer Burns in his box.'

Maud stared at her and then, as Percy caught sight of them and did one of his little war dances, prancing about and squawking, she began to giggle. Maria joined her, and as Maud gasped, 'Farmer Burns, Percy's Farmer Burns,' they both went into a paroxysm of helpless laughter as they held on to each other, their mirth an outlet for their previous terror.

Cora grinned. It was the first time she had seen Maud smile since Enid's abrupt departure, but in truth she couldn't enter fully into the moment. Nor could she laugh at Farmer Burns. Every day and night that they stayed at Stone Farm they were in danger, that was the truth of it, but she had done all she could for the present. She couldn't do anything for Enid now, it was too late, but she would look after Maud the best she was able. Enid had endured what she'd endured to keep Farmer Burns from molesting her sister and she wouldn't let her sacrifice be in vain. Not while she had breath in her body.

Chapter Eight

'Oh, those poor lads. Those poor, poor lads. To be attacked like that with no warning. They must have thought hell had opened up and dragged them in.' Nancy stared at Ken as they sat at the kitchen table listening to the wireless. The day before, three hundred and sixty Japanese warplanes had made a massive surprise attack on the US Pacific Fleet in its home base at Pearl Harbor in Hawaii. At the same time Japanese planes had also attacked American bases in the Philippines and on the Guam and Wake islands in the middle of the Pacific. In two hours the Japanese had sunk or seriously damaged five battleships, fourteen smaller ships and two hundred aircraft, killing over two and a half thousand people.

'*Imperial headquarters in Tokyo have announced that Japan is at war with the United States of America and Britain,*' the newsreader intoned, '*and this comes after assurances less than two weeks ago from Premier Hideki Tojo that there was nothing to fear from Japan. In a further escalation of hostilities, Britain has today declared war on Finland, Romania and Hungary after the failure of the three Axis satellites to respond to ultimata demanding they stop military operations in support of the German armies. It would indeed seem that now every nation in the world needs to decide where their loyalties lie and whose side they are on in this war that Adolf Hitler has forced upon us.*'

Nancy had her hand at her throat, plucking at the skin there as she said, 'The world's gone mad, Ken. Who would have thought even a few years ago we'd be in this mess? It's wicked, the murder and mayhem. What's going to be left at the end of it?'

Ken shook his head in silent commiseration but continued eating the pot pie that Nancy had dished up before the news had begun. The pie was stuffed full of the steak and kidney he had acquired from a contact the day before in exchange for other black-market commodities. In truth, and he wouldn't have voiced this to Nancy because he was fully aware of how she would have responded, he was making a packet due to the war. Certain imports were like gold dust and British produce was becoming scarcer by the day. It could be a bit of a juggling act at times at the docks, keeping the bosses in the criminal underworld happy whilst raking off a nice profit for himself on the side, but he managed all right. He swallowed a big chunk of meat and belched appreciatively. Aye, he was no one's fool.

'I've had a letter.'

He looked at Nancy; her voice had been flat suddenly. 'Oh, aye? Gonna tell me who from?' He wasn't in the mood to play games. It had been the first of December eight days ago and right on cue the weather had changed and turned foul. Freezing cold, with winds that cut to the bone, had been followed by what every dock worker dreaded – thick snow. It made every day doubly long or it felt like it. Grindingly hard work and wet clothes that were often frozen to his skin wasn't his idea of the good life but he'd get there, he was determined on that. The plans he had for the future and the money he salted away were worth the risks that he took. War or no war, he was going to come out on top.

Nancy had barely touched the food on her plate. Quietly, she said, 'It's from Gregory. He's been injured and they're shipping him home once he's fit enough in a little while.'

'Oh, aye?' Ken raised his eyebrows. She didn't seem too pleased about it but then she wouldn't, would she. It hadn't been a marriage made in heaven, not on her side. 'How bad is he?'

'I don't know, he didn't go into details. He – he wouldn't want to worry me. It was just a line or two, nothing more.'

Ken nodded. He knew Gregory was no letter writer. In the last eighteen months or so since he'd got together with Nancy he'd formed a pretty good picture of the man he was making a cuckold of.

'He – he's had a raw deal from me, hasn't he.'

Ken shrugged. 'What he doesn't know doesn't hurt him.'

'But he will. Know, I mean. When he comes home.'

Ken's eyes narrowed. 'Only if you tell him and why would you want to do that?'

Because I love you. Because I want us to stay together. Because you're the most important thing in the world to me. Nancy swallowed hard. 'It's not as simple as that. The neighbours aren't daft, Ken. They've seen you coming and going and will have put two and two together. There's more than one of them who'd take great delight in informing Gregory about us, believe me.'

She was spoiling his dinner. 'So you just deny it and keep denying it,' he said coolly. 'No big deal.'

It wasn't the answer she wanted.

She stared at him with wounded eyes and he found it difficult to stop his irritation from showing. He didn't need this on top of everything else. He was having a bit of trouble with one of the blokes he dealt with – a gangster, he supposed Dan Vickers was, and a nasty blighter – who he suspected had cottoned on to the fact that he'd short-changed him once or twice. It'd got to the point where the last few days he'd been looking over his shoulder and feeling uneasy. Of course he could be wrong – it might just be his guilty conscience that was making him imagine things – but Vickers hadn't been himself the last time he'd spoken to him and he'd been on edge ever since.

'Eat your dinner,' he said shortly. 'We'll discuss it later.'

She could see she'd annoyed him. Nancy's stomach was turning over. She'd been hoping that when she told him about Gregory he'd declare his love for her – not the way he did in the throes of passion but in the cold light of day – and say that she must leave her husband for him. That he'd move out of his lodgings and see about getting a house for them, somewhere where the bairns could live too once the war was over.

And if he said he didn't want her bairns living with them? Yes, she'd asked herself that too because deep down she knew he wasn't a family man. And she'd come back with thinking that the bairns would be all right with Gregory. He was a good da, he'd look after them and Cora was already of an age where she could keep house if need be. Things would rub along just fine without her.

She couldn't lose Ken. She felt sick at the thought. Whatever happened, whatever she had to do, she couldn't lose him. She hadn't told him she'd had Gregory's letter for a week or two and had been plucking up the courage to mention it, fearing he might react exactly as he had. He had never talked about the future in all the time they'd been together, and when she had tried to bring up the subject he'd always deflected the issue.

She forced down a mouthful of food, feeling as though it would choke her. What was she going to do? What *could* she do? One thing was for sure, she couldn't go back to being a dutiful wife to Gregory. She *wouldn't*. Things had changed since the war had begun; the stigma of divorce was lifting. The Abdication crisis had nudged public opinion about such things closer to leniency, and now the winds of war had further blown away the idea that a divorce meant guilt and disgrace. She knew at least two or three other women in her position who had started off by not meaning any harm, just desiring a little change from the monotony of their lives while their husband was away fighting. True, such conduct was still disapproved of by many, but self-righteous condemnation seemed unnecessarily cruel in a world of bombs and shortages.

Nancy gave up trying to eat and poured herself another cup of tea before pushing her plate to one side.

'Don't you want that?' Ken reached for her plate after she shook her head, tipping the contents onto his own before continuing to shovel food into his mouth. It wasn't until he had finished his meal that he said, 'It'll be all right, lass. Things have a way of working out if you let them.'

Nancy's tone had a sharp edge to it now as she said, 'By that do I take it you mean you want to do nothing?'

'Don't start, Nancy.'

'I'm not "starting". I just want to know where I stand, that's all. I love you. I thought you loved me. Don't – don't you want us to be together? Properly, I mean.'

It was the last thing he had in mind. Regretting that he hadn't ended the affair some time ago but not wanting a scene, Ken took a long deep breath. 'Of course I love you but I've never pretended the whole hearth and home thing is for me, now have I? Bairns and everything that goes with them isn't something I could take on, lass. I thought you understood that.'

'I do, oh, I do.' She could hear the eagerness in her

voice and hated herself for it. 'And I wouldn't ask you to do that. It would be just the two of us, I promise.'

What the hell had he let himself in for? In the past there had been the odd tear or two from the women involved when he'd finished with them, but his sweet-talking had enabled him to go on his merry way with no hard feelings. Something told him it wasn't going to be like that with Nancy. For a while now he'd felt somewhat stifled, but the sex had been the best he'd ever had and it had kept him coming back for more. Just the thought of some of the things they did made him as hard as a rock.

Moving his chair back slightly, he held out his arms. 'Come here.' Once she was sitting on his lap, he traced the full contours of her mouth with his finger before kissing her hard. He could afford to let her down lightly, cool things slowly, bit by bit. He didn't want Nancy causing trouble for him and she could. Oh, aye, she could. She knew a sight too much about some of his more questionable deals for him to risk her shooting her mouth off to the dock police. Working as she did as a shipping clerk, she came into daily contact with quite a few folk he wouldn't want to run foul of. A woman scorned and all that.

'You know how I feel about you,' he murmured in her ear before kissing her again and feeling her melt against him. 'I've told you often enough, haven't I? All I mean is that with the war and everything life's uncertain enough as it is. Looking into the future does no one any good, but we can enjoy the time we have together here and now and that's what counts. I adore you and we're good together, perfect in fact.'

His hands were moving all over her now and he felt her begin to tremble and smiled to himself. Moving her so she was sitting astride him on his lap, he set about making love to her, knowing it would deflect more awkward questions, at least for tonight.

For a moment the back door opening barely registered on Nancy. For an endless moment she gazed at Gregory in the doorway, snow dusting his uniform, one arm in a sling and the other holding his kitbag, a patch covering his right eye and an angry red scar distorting the cheek beneath it. Then all hell broke loose.

It was ten o'clock. Ken had long since gone, nursing his bloody nose and minus two teeth. It hadn't been a fight as such. After Gregory had hit Ken, Ken had grabbed frantically for his coat and cap and been away on his toes as Nancy had held on to Gregory with all her strength, begging him to stop as he had tried to throw her off and go after the other man.

She continued to cling on to his good arm for some moments after the kitchen door had slammed behind Ken, and then as Gregory went limp and sat down suddenly she took a step backwards, feeling sick and faint herself. For the life of her she couldn't speak; not until his voice came rasping and shaking as he said, 'Who is he?' did she manage to pull herself together enough to form words through the whirling in her head.

'He's a friend from – from work.'

'He's a damn sight more than a friend.' He turned his head to look at her. 'How long has it been going on?'

'Gregory, please—'

'How long?'

'Months.'

'Do you love him?'

'Don't do this, let me get you a drink—'

'I said, do you love him?'

He looked ghastly, grey and ill and so thin his face was almost skeletal, and it was this that made her unable to speak the truth. Instead she whispered, 'Your eye? Is – is it serious?'

He didn't answer, staring at her until she had to turn away. Walking to the cupboard she took out a bottle of whisky and poured a good measure into two glasses, offering him one. When he didn't take it, she put it down on the table in front of him and then drank hers straight down. The neat alcohol burned its way into her stomach and helped the trembling deep inside.

'Since when have you taken to drinking whisky?' he said grimly.

Again she didn't answer this, saying instead, 'Drink it, it'll help.'

'It'll take more than whisky to do that.' Nevertheless he swallowed the contents of the glass in two gulps.

'Greg, I'm so so—'

'Don't say you're sorry, Nancy.'

The tone was one he had never used to her before and

for a moment a sense of loss pierced her through. She had always known he adored her, worshipped her even, but that was gone for ever. She had fallen off her pedestal good and proper.

Her voice low, she said, 'Well, I am whether you believe it or not. I – I didn't want to hurt you. I've never wanted to do that. It just happened.'

He swore as he stood up, pushing back the chair with the backs of his knees. 'Don't give me that. Things like this don't just happen – it's a series of steps involving choices. You're a grown woman, not a bit of a lass who doesn't know her own mind.'

She stared at him. He was right. Of course he was right.

'I'm going to ask you again and I want the truth. Do you love him?'

She felt she was drowning in shame and guilt. He looked so ill, a broken man, and he didn't deserve this. He had thought he was coming home to a wife who loved him, to normality, to his family. But, bad as she felt, it wasn't enough for her to lie for him. She couldn't live without Ken; she would sacrifice anything or anyone to be with him, and nothing else mattered. She had known this day would come eventually, she just hadn't expected it to be so hard.

'Yes.' It was a whisper.

'And him?'

'He loves me. We – want to be together.'

When she had imagined telling Gregory about Ken she

had pictured a hundred different scenarios. Knowing how much he loved her, she had expected rage and fury, that he would be incensed and perhaps even violent before pleading with her, begging her not to leave him, promising her the earth if she would stay. Much as he loved the children, she'd known his feeling for her was a thing apart, all consuming, that she was as necessary to him as the air he breathed. Hadn't he told her so every night in the depths of their bed and not just in the act of physical love? Many nights he would just hold her close, whispering endearments in the darkness, words he would never have expressed in the day. But that was the way with lots of tough working men like Gregory, northern men who weren't given to fancy words and such. That was what made Ken so special, so thrilling, so intoxicating.

Now, as she waited for Gregory's wrath to fall on her head, she was aware of a slight feeling of bewilderment mixed in with all the raging emotions. His face was stony cold and likewise his voice when he said, 'Then there's nothing more to be said. I suggest you go to him.'

In all her imaginings she had never expected this. As her mouth fell slightly open in shock, she stammered, 'What, now?'

He closed his eyes for a split second, his voice losing the iron control for a moment and shaking as he said, 'Aye, now.'

'But Gregory, you're ill—'

As her hand reached out to him his voice was a bark: 'Don't touch me, Nancy. I won't be responsible for my actions if you touch me. Just get out and go to him if that's what you want. Pack what you need and clear off.'

'You don't mean that.'

'The hell I don't. You think I'd want you after what I've seen? You've made your decision. It was made the first time you opened your legs for him.'

The crudery was so unlike him that again she recoiled in shock. She had thought she knew him inside out but this was a stranger. She stared stupidly at him as he walked across to where she had placed the bottle of whisky, picking it up and bringing it back to the table where he sat down and poured himself a glass, filling it to the brim.

Utterly at a loss, she whispered, 'We'll need to talk at some point, about the bairns and everything.'

She waited another moment and then walked into the hall and climbed the stairs to the bedroom. There she stood looking around her in a daze. After a full minute she went to the big mahogany wardrobe and pulled an old battered suitcase off the top of it. Placing it on the bed she opened it and again stood staring blankly before beginning to pack some of her clothes and bits and pieces. A couple of nights before, Ken had lain with her in this bed and after they had made love he'd had her in a fit of the giggles as he'd told her about a funny incident down at the docks. No one could make her laugh the way Ken could.

She shook herself. Now she felt as though she would never laugh again.

After she had snapped the suitcase shut, she stood

hugging herself round the middle for a few moments. Her heart was pounding against her ribs and she felt sick with the swiftness of how her life had changed in the last few minutes, but there was an element of relief there too which added to her guilt about Gregory. She had known this had to happen one day, hadn't she, if Gregory came back from the war? And now he had. It settled things. Even to herself she couldn't admit that what had happened downstairs had forced Ken's hand regarding her. Ken wanted them to be together, she told herself for the umpteenth time since meeting him. He just found it hard to say so.

As though flinging something off, she grabbed the suitcase. She couldn't be glad the war had occurred, not with all the horror and suffering, but it had created a chance for her that would never have happened otherwise. Her life had been mapped out into old age, a life of routine and respectability – housewife, mother, grandmother, a life lived in the stifling cage that was her marriage. Now nothing would be the same as it had been before, not just for her but for everyone. The war had changed things and not before time. No, not before time.

The thought carried her down the stairs and into the hall where she put on her hat and coat. She stood hesitating. No one ever used the front door. Practically the only time it was opened was if the priest or the doctor called, but she couldn't face walking into the kitchen again. Gregory had told her to go and so she was going, she told herself with a touch of defiance. Then she recalled the look on his face when he had first entered the kitchen, the smile that had lit his countenance only to change into a spasm of what she could only describe to herself as horror, and the defiance melted and she wanted to weep. For a moment, just a split second, she wavered. Then her back straightened. If she went into the kitchen, if she went to Gregory to try and comfort him, it would only delay the inevitable. It was less cruel to go now.

She didn't let herself think any more. Opening the front door she stepped over the drift of snow that had been banked against it and which collapsed in a soft pile on the old cork mat. Ken had a room in a lodging house in East Cross Street close to the docks and it was a fair walk in weather like this. She'd better get on with it.

Lifting up her head, she breathed deeply of the icy air starry with snowflakes, gripped the suitcase more firmly, and began to walk.

Gregory heard the front door shut but he didn't move from his seat at the kitchen table. After a few moments he refilled his empty glass for the third time and drank deeply, aware that he was well on the way to being pie-eyed. Pie-eyed. He smiled grimly. The blast that had mangled his right arm, breaking bones and stripping skin and flesh, had also taken his eye and disfigured his face, but he had fared better than his closest friends. He was alive.

He got up and walked into Nancy's front room – he always thought of it in those terms, it was practically a holy of holies and woe betide anyone who entered it without permission. He found it strange, in view of what he had come home to, that everything looked exactly the same. The stiff three-piece suite in dark jade green, the small table with the aspidistra set in the centre of the window and the staid wooden clock ticking the time away on the mantelpiece, all as it had been when he had gone off to war. His life had exploded into a thousand pieces and yet this room continued to be a mausoleum to Nancy's idea of respectability.

Respectability . . . The word mocked him as he parted the lace curtains to peer out, but he could see nothing but the driving snow. She'd gone. To him. To her fancy man. All the time he'd been wallowing in blood and guts, she'd been having it away with some bloke. When his hand came out and swiped the aspidistra to the floor it was without conscious thought, the crash of the fancy pot and the earth and leaves and jagged pieces barely registering. He was back in Tobruk, in the disastrous offensive in which half of the British tanks fighting Rommel were destroyed in a single day.

He staggered back into the kitchen but it was no good, the genie was out of the bottle. He was in hell. They were all in hell, and facing a major strategist who was the hero of the German army. The Desert War, where the battleground was large, featureless wastes of rock and sand, had its own character and its own rules, and made unique demands on the men who fought it. Rommel had understood that so why hadn't the British generals, damn them? They'd been overstretched and unprepared for the speed and ferocity of Rommel's highly trained and mobile fighting force that had been perfectly suited to war in the desert. And the German panzers and huge 88-millimetre anti-tank guns; it'd been lambs to the slaughter. Frank Robson, his pal from schooldays, had been blown to smithereens in front of him along with countless others, their blood soaking into the sand and body parts cascading down like grotesque lumps of raw meat.

He sank down on a chair, running his hand across his face which was pouring with sweat.

Joe McGuigan, Adam Harley, Tim Mallard – all gone. And the noise, the deafening noise. It numbed the brain and turned you into a mindless automaton.

Reaching for the bottle he didn't bother to pour the liquid into a glass, glugging it down as though it was water, wanting only to deaden the images in his mind. He didn't understand why every single one of the men he had trained with and become close friends with should have died and he should have been spared, even more so now he had come home to no wife, no bairns, nothing. Adam's wife had twin boys, two years old, but now they'd never know their da; and Tim Mallard had been the baby in their group, just eighteen years old. When he'd first come round in the field hospital it had been Tim he'd remembered; one moment he'd been there in front of him and the next his head had gone, his body in the sand pumping blood. He'd screamed and yelled about Tim apparently – one of the nurses had told him – begging them to find his head so he could be whole again. They'd stuck needles in him then, soft voices telling him it would be all right and he must sleep and get well. Well . . . He shook his befuddled head. What signified well? The fact that he could walk and talk and act normal? Because that was all it was, acting.

The bottle was empty and he slumped in the chair, too exhausted and too drunk to move. *Nancy had left him.* He ground his teeth. She had been the only reason for him to keep trying, to keep living. Oh, he loved the bairns, of course he did, but Nancy . . . From the first moment he had set eyes on her he had loved her – it had been as swift and final as that. And when she had agreed to marry him he had known he loved her more than she loved him, but that hadn't mattered. There was always one person in a marriage who loved their partner more, that's what he'd told himself, and more often than not it was the man. A woman was taken up with homemaking, bairns – that was natural.

The whisky had done its job – he could feel himself sinking into oblivion and he didn't fight it. He was finished, he knew he was finished now. It just remained for him to decide how the end would come, that was all.

By the time Nancy reached the house in East Cross Street she was wet and cold and the suitcase seemed to weigh a ton. The pavements were lethal and twice she had nearly gone full length on patches of ice hidden under the fresh layer of snow that was falling. There were few folk about, the snow was keeping all but the hardiest indoors, and she had felt very small and very alone as she had plodded along in the dark night.

She had been to the house where Ken rented a room

twice in the time they had been seeing each other. It was a two-up, two-down terrace and he occupied the front room, two of his pals from the docks having a room each upstairs. Ken had told her the landlord owned quite a bit of property in the East End, some of it used for legitimate purposes and some not. She'd raised her eyebrows enquiringly and he'd grinned: 'Brothels, gambling dens, that sort of thing.'

Her shock must have showed and Ken had laughed out loud. 'Skelton's all right, lass. He started from nowt, just a snotty-nosed urchin with his backside hanging out, and he's made it big by being canny. He's a good bloke as long as you don't cross him. Believe me, his rent collector never has any trouble.'

The conversation had troubled her, more because of Ken's admiration of the man than what he had disclosed about Skelton. Eventually, though, she'd brushed it aside. Ken dabbled on the wrong side of the law but that was all, she'd told herself. He wasn't a proper criminal, not like Skelton.

She had to knock twice before the door opened, and then it wasn't Ken standing in the hallway but Edwin, one of the men from upstairs. He stared at her in surprise, his gaze going to the suitcase, and Nancy said quickly, 'I need to see Ken.'

'He's not here, lass, but come in, come in.' He reached out and took the case from her, the simple act of kindness bringing the tears she had been fighting closer to the surface. 'Come in and get warm and I'll make a pot of tea.'

She followed him into the kitchen and sat down at the table. It had surprised her in the early days with Ken that he hadn't got his own place and was content to continue to rent a room, but the more she'd got to know him the more she had realized that he didn't like the thought of permanence in any realm. It had bothered her, it still continued to bother her, but that was Ken and she accepted him as he was. And since he'd been with her they'd established a pattern; most evenings she cooked him dinner and he often stayed the night so they had breakfast together, although they always took care to arrive at the docks separately. Not that that had fooled anyone. Her boss, a nice family man with umpteen grandchildren, had taken her aside not long after she had taken up with Ken and warned her that he was not someone she should get too friendly with. But it had been too late by then. She had already been head over heels in love.

She looked at Edwin who was busying himself putting the kettle on the range. 'Do you know where Ken's gone?'

'He came in not so long ago and then went straight out again. Someone had left a note for him earlier, a spot of business down at the docks, I think.'

Edwin hadn't met her eyes as he had spoken and she knew Ken had told him about Gregory turning up. Mind you, with the state of his face she didn't suppose he could have done much else, to be fair, and her arriving unannounced with a suitcase was a giveaway. 'Did he say how long he'd be?' She was feeling a bit funny now, truth be told, odd, sick, light-headed.

Edwin must have guessed – probably she looked bad – because the next moment he fetched out a bottle of brandy, pouring her a glass and one for himself as he said, 'We'll have a snorter before the tea, eh, lass? Get that down you. It'll make you feel better.'

She didn't argue and the alcohol did help. Edwin made a pot of tea and poured two cups, adding a liberal dollop of the brandy to both before he passed her one. Sitting down opposite her he said nothing for a little while, clearly at something of a loss. Distressed females weren't Edwin's forte.

She liked Edwin. He was rough and ready and built like a brick outhouse but his heart was in the right place, and it was this that enabled Nancy to say, 'I suppose Ken told you about Gregory?'

Edwin nodded uncomfortably.

'You must think I'm an awful woman.'

'Don't be daft, lass. Course I don't. It's this blasted war, it's thrown everything up in the air. Anyway, it's nowt to do with me or anyone else.'

'Ken doesn't know yet but I've left Gregory.'

Again Edwin nodded, but now something in his face sharpened her tone when she said, 'What? What is it?'

'Nowt, nowt.'

'Edwin, say what's on your mind.'

'It's just . . .' His head made a quick little movement. 'Have you talked it over with Ken before, about you leaving your husband, I mean?'

Had she? *She'd* talked about it for sure but Ken had

usually changed the subject or come out with some platitude or other. 'Of course,' she said quickly, but they both knew she had hesitated a mite too long.

'The thing is, lass, Ken's a good bloke, none better, but some fellas never have it in 'em to settle down.'

'I wouldn't expect him to settle down, not in that way, a family way. I've had my bairns and I wouldn't want any more.'

'Well, like I said, it's nowt to do with me.'

She had just opened her mouth to reply when the air-raid sirens sounded. The last raid had been in the first week of November when there had been quite a few bombs falling in the region of South Dock. One had fallen on the docks railway line, hurling a steam train twenty yards down the track where it had ended up overturned and at right angles to the rails. Others had fallen on the foreshore and in the streets close to the docks with considerable damage to property and loss of life. The Luftwaffe had targeted the harbour and industrial installations, and although some bombs had failed to detonate, enough had exploded to cause terrible fires, death and horrific injuries. It was this that was on Nancy's mind now as she said, 'Ken! He's at the docks you say?' as she jumped to her feet. 'I must find him.'

'Hold your horses, you can't go looking for him, Nancy. Ten to one you wouldn't find him and even if you did he wouldn't thank you for turning up when he's about a spot of business, you know that as well as I do. He's a big boy, he can look after himself. Now come on, come into the shelter and wait. He'll come back, never fear. Only the good die young.'

It was Edwin's attempt at a joke and one Nancy didn't appreciate. Nevertheless, she allowed him to lead her out of the kitchen and into the back yard where the three men had dug out an Anderson shelter at the beginning of the war. Maurice, the other member of the house, joined them seconds later, grumbling at being woken up and smelling strongly of beer. In minutes he was asleep on the top bunk of the rickety structure the men had built inside the shelter.

Three quarters of an hour or so later Nancy and Edwin could hear bombs exploding in the distance. 'Seaburn,' said Edwin. 'They're getting it tonight, poor blighters.'

Nancy sat in the pitch darkness, listening to the anti-aircraft fire and praying Ken was somewhere safe as Maurice snored on. Perhaps God was going to punish her for her sin on the very day she had left Gregory, she thought wildly. They hadn't had a raid for four weeks and for it to happen tonight was no coincidence. Hail, Mary, full of grace. Hail, Mary, full of grace . . . The words kept repeating themselves over and over in her head through the noise outside. Sorry as she felt for the folk Seaburn way, she prayed the Luftwaffe would stay on the north side of the river. Unbidden, a memory from the past flashed into her mind. She had been heavily pregnant with Cora who'd been born at the end of May, and in the middle of the month an unseasonably hot spell had hit the north-east. One Sunday Gregory had taken her to Seaburn for a treat, and he had hired one of the bulky canvas tents that were stored on the promenade and rented out to sun-seekers for the day. It had been a wonderful day, special, she had thought about it for months afterwards. Gregory had danced attendance on her, fetching them ice creams and lemonade, and then dishes of whelks and mussels from one of the old fishwives who plied their trade on the beach. They had laughed and dreamed, talking about the baby and whether it was a boy or girl, what it would look like, whether it would have her red hair. And it had. Cora had.

A shaft of emotional pain that was so real it physically hurt shot through her chest. Cora would hate her now. She had always been something of a daddy's girl and Gregory had adored her from the moment she was born, saying she was a miniature of her mother. Cora wouldn't forgive her for hurting him.

She squeezed her eyes tightly shut in the blackness, telling herself it was too late for any regrets. And she didn't regret leaving Gregory because she couldn't have done anything else, not loving Ken as she did. She would write to Cora and explain; she owed her and the rest of the bairns that. Anna and Susan wouldn't understand, of course, and no doubt Cora would colour their view of their mother given time. Her lips tightened. She would get no mercy from Cora, she knew that. And perhaps she didn't deserve any.

The all-clear sounded at twenty to one in the morning.

Maurice was snoring so soundly that Edwin decided to leave him in the shelter when he and Nancy went indoors, whereupon he insisted on making another pot of tea despite Nancy urging him to go to bed while she sat up for Ken. 'You need your sleep,' she said, 'and I'll be all right sitting here.'

'Don't you worry about me, lass,' Edwin smiled, bringing out a tin of biscuits that was no doubt one of Ken's acquisitions that had 'fallen off the back of a lorry'. 'Never needed much sleep. Me mam, God bless her soul, always used to say that's why I was as thick as two short planks – never rested me brain.'

Nancy smiled. He was a nice man, Edwin. A gentle giant.

It was three o'clock when they heard the front door open and close. Edwin stood up. 'Wait here, lass. I'll tell him what's what, all right?'

Nancy waited. She heard the murmur of voices and then Ken's '*What*?' followed by Edwin's deeper voice saying something she couldn't quite make out except that it ended with '. . . brought it on yourself.'

The sick feeling was back, worse now, because she was having to face what Edwin's concern and sympathy had been hinting at all night. The door to the kitchen was slightly ajar; now it was thrust open and Ken walked in. It wasn't so much the visible result of Gregory's handiwork that caused Nancy's heart to lurch, although Ken's face was undoubtedly something of a mess, but his furious expression. 'What the hell are you doing here?'

She made herself talk calmly. 'What do you think? After what Gregory walked in on?'

'He's thrown you out?'

Had he? Not really. She supposed it had been her decision when she had told him she loved Ken and they wanted to be together. Something warned her to prevaricate. 'What would you have done?' she said quietly. 'Coming home from the war and finding that.'

'Aye, aye.' He understood that line of reasoning. 'Well, it couldn't have come at a worse time, that's the thing.'

She felt a cold shiver although the kitchen was warm. 'What do you mean?'

'I'm in a spot of bother. I need to get away for a while.'

'What sort of bother?'

'Ending up in the Wear with me throat cut sort of bother.'

Shocked but still suspecting it was an excuse, she said, 'What do you mean? What's happened?'

His face was grim and he poured himself a good measure of brandy from the bottle Edwin had left next to the range, swallowing it before he answered. 'There's a bloke I know, Vickers is his name, and I got it on good authority tonight that he's marked me card.'

'But why? What have you done?'

'That doesn't matter,' he said irritably, pouring another brandy and wincing as the neat alcohol met his bruised mouth. 'The fact is, I need to make meself scarce, disappear.

I've a couple of pals in Newcastle who'll put me up for a while till I decide what to do. I've got a bit salted away –' more than a bit, but he wasn't going to tell Nancy that – 'so I'll be all right and mebbe it's time to start again somewhere new. I'm sorry, Nancy, but there it is.'

She stared at him. 'I'll come with you.'

'Don't be daft.'

'It's not daft. There's nothing for me here and we can be together. You said you wanted to start again somewhere new, well, so do I. I mean it, Ken. I've burned my boats here.'

'I never asked you to do that, Nancy.'

'Well, it's done anyway.'

'You don't understand. I need to go today, straight away.'

'That's all right. I can write to Gregory and tell him, that's only fair, and to – to the bairns.'

'It'll be no life for you, not with me.'

'It will, it will.' Aware that she was pleading but unable to stop herself, tears pricking her eyes, she said, 'I can't go back to him, Ken. I can't. And – and I love you, and you love me. We – we could see how it goes, couldn't we?'

After a few moments, during which he returned her stare, Ken said flatly, 'Very well. Have it your own way.'

It wasn't how she had wanted it, how she had imagined their being together would start. What did it portend? And then she caught at the thought, refusing to dwell on it. It would be all right. *They* would be all right.

She would make sure of it. She would make him need her like she needed him; it would only be a matter of time. And so great was his power over her that what she was giving up – her home, her bairns, her friends and her respectability – was as nothing compared to the gain of him.

Chapter Nine

Cora sat on the edge of the bed staring at the single sheet of paper in her hand. She had recognized her mother's handwriting on the envelope that Mrs Burns had handed to her on their return from school that day, and after telling Maria and Maud to stay with the little ones, she had gone upstairs to read it without the others being present. She knew something was wrong. There had been no Christmas presents, not even a card from her mam, let alone a visit, and it was now the third week of January. Their old headmaster, Mr Wood, had promised all the evacuees that he would see to it that they were notified of any news from home, from which Cora and the older children had assumed – correctly – he meant bad news, and as there had been nothing from him or anyone in authority she knew her mother hadn't been bombed out or worse. So that meant she just hadn't bothered about them, even at Christmas. She had been upset and angry and it had further hardened her heart towards the woman who had given birth to her.

But this, this was worse, a hundred times worse, than her mam merely forgetting about them. She glanced again at the sheet of paper but without really seeing it, every word burned on her brain.

Dear Cora,

This is a difficult letter for me to write but first of all I want you to know I love you, all of you, and I wish things could be different. There's good news in that your da is home and he won't be going back to fight. The other thing is that I have gone to live in Newcastle with a friend of mine called Ken who I met through work. I'm sorry, lass. From the depths of my heart I'm sorry and I hope one day you will forgive me. I know you won't understand now but perhaps when you're older you might see that as good a man as your da is, he wasn't the one for me and I found that out too late. Please don't think too badly of me, lass. If it wasn't for this war probably things would have gone on as they were but it's changed everything and there is no going back. I love you all.

Mam xxx

Her mam had run off with another man, the way Mrs Fraser, their neighbour several doors down in Sunderland, had done three years ago just before the war had started. It had been the talk of the street and even though Mr Fraser was a drunkard and had been known to knock her about as regular as clockwork, it had been Mrs Fraser who'd been universally condemned and Mr Fraser had acquired the halo of sainthood. But her da wasn't like Mr Fraser, Cora told herself bitterly. Her da had worshipped her mam, she'd heard her grandma say so on more than one occasion, and anyway you'd have to be blind not to see it. And her mam had said her da was home from the war. Did that mean he was all by himself in their house? It must do. And he would only be back if he had been injured. Oh, Da, Da.

She jumped up and paced about the room for a few moments before sitting down again, her stomach churning. Her mam had left them all. It seemed impossible but it was true. It was as though a great chasm had opened up and everything that had been normal and good and right had been swallowed up. She wanted to cry but she knew she couldn't; the others were waiting for her. Besides, her eyes were dry and burning and the crying was all inside, in a great aching lump below her ribs.

How could she tell Maria and Horace their mam was gone? Anna and Susan wouldn't really understand, besides which they rarely mentioned their old life these days, but Horace, and Maria especially, would know what this meant to them as a family. She would have to press home the fact that her da was back from the war, but she didn't know how he was or anything, and her mam going would crush him, she knew that. She wished her mam had died, she wished she had been killed by a bomb. That would have been better than this. For her da, for her, for them all. She hated her mam. Oh, she did, she hated her.

I love you, that's what her mam had written, and I wish things could be different. The liar. If she had wanted things to be different she wouldn't have done what she'd done. And to blame the war. Cora's lip curled as an icy rage filled her. Her mam was to blame for hurting her da, her mam and her mam alone. She was filthy, wicked.

She had to go downstairs and talk to Maria. She wouldn't tell Anna and Susan yet, not until she'd had a chance to discuss everything with Horace and Wilfred. Strangely, Jed didn't enter her mind at this point; it was Wilfred she needed and who she knew would understand. He had always loved her mam, so he would know how devastating this was. Since the summer they had got back on their old footing and she had been so thankful for it; until things had righted themselves she hadn't realized how much she had missed him. He might not be related to her by blood but he was her brother in every way that counted, and she knew now she had been mistaken that he thought about her in *that* way. He was the old Wilfred again, family.

Folding the letter into a small square, she tucked it in the pocket of her dress. She wouldn't tell Mrs Burns about her mam running off but she would write to her da straight away and post it without the farmer's wife knowing. He was her main concern now. She had washed her hands of her mother.

She came downstairs to find the others in the scullery melting the small scraps of soap saved by the household into a soap jelly by pouring a little boiling water over them and adding a teaspoonful of borax to every pint of the solution. Now that rationing was biting and countless personal and household items had become virtually unobtainable, it made the large weekly wash even more of a trial for the girls. They also added borax to the laundry to loosen the grease and dirt and soften the water so that less of the soap jelly was required to make a good lather, but the mixture was nothing like the old soap powders that were now unavailable. Mrs Burns had taken them into the nearest market town the week before Christmas because they had all been wearing shoes that were too small for them for months and which had eventually fallen apart, but had flatly refused to use any coupons on clothes except for underwear. Instead she'd obtained some plain material and some tweed from a farmer's market and set Cora, Maria and Maud to sewing new dresses for themselves. Maud's clothes were too threadbare and patched to pass down to Anna and Susan, but Mrs Burns told the older girls to alter the frocks that they had brought with them to the farm for their sisters.

Mrs Burns was full of bright ideas for saving a penny or two, Cora thought grimly, shaking her head warningly at Maria as her sister raised her eyebrows as she joined them. She would show Maria the letter as soon as they had a minute together without the others around. Oh, yes, the farmer's wife had them reducing the amount of furniture and floor polish needed by sprinkling the cleaning cloths they used with paraffin so the polish didn't soak into the material. They had to stick a knife into warm candle-ends that Mrs Burns saved, rubbing it over the soles of their shoes to make the leather waterproof. Coal dust mixed with damp tea-leaves kept the range going at night. There were a hundred and one other little cost-saving devices Mrs Burns insisted on, most of them being smelly or dirty or both. Not that the farmer's wife cared.

Mrs Burns's motto of 'save and mend' was a constant refrain and one Cora was heartily sick of, and yet she noticed that the farmer's wife had bought herself a brand new hat and coat on the shopping trip without batting an eyelid. By the same principle, Mrs Burns insisted they save all spent matches and put them into old matchboxes for lighting candles or the fire in the main house, whereas she always availed herself of unused ones. And at the beginning of the winter when the farmer's wife had had to fork out for replacement gum boots for her because she had outgrown her old ones, you'd have thought she was paying for the crown jewels. Maria would use them next winter when her feet had grown anyway, so it wasn't as if they were being discarded. Mean as muck, that's what Mrs Burns was.

Cora sighed heavily. What was she doing, wittering on to herself about Mrs Burns when her mam had run off with someone and left her da all alone? She bit hard on her bottom lip. She'd put up with Mrs Burns for ever if only her mam and da were still together.

It wasn't until much later when they were in bed and the others were asleep that she was able to show Maria the letter. Maria read it by the dim light of the flickering candle, crying silent tears by the time she came to the end. 'Cora, you don't think she'll change her mind?'

Maria stared at her, and Cora found it impossible to endure the look in her eyes. Taking the letter from her sister she pretended to read it again as she said, 'No, I don't. Anyway, Da wouldn't want her back after this. Everyone – everyone will know.'

'Are you going to write back to the address on the letter?'

'No, I'm not.' It was a harsh whisper. 'I'll write to Da but not her. I never want to see her again, not ever.'

'Oh, Cora.'

'Well, do you? After what she's done?' Maria's silence was her answer, and after a moment Cora said, 'Well, I don't. I hate her. She's ruined everything. The war is bad enough but this . . . It's Da that matters now. You can write to her if you want but I'm not.'

'Are you going to tell Mrs Burns?'

'It's none of her business. She doesn't care about us, you know that.'

'She feeds us well.'

That was Maria all over, seeing the good in someone even if she had to search for it, Cora thought irritably, and then she softened. Maria was nice. It was her who wasn't. Gently, she said, 'Yes, I know she does, but that's partly because she wants us to be strong and well to work for her. Anyway, if we tell her she'll tell him –' they both knew she was talking about Farmer Burns – 'and he'll think with mam gone it makes us more helpless. And we won't tell Susan and Anna either – there's no need. Horace is different, and Wilfred needs to know, but I shall tell them not to say a word to anyone.'

In a small voice, Maria said, 'And Jed?'

'Of course I shall tell Jed.'

Maria nodded. Beginning to cry again, she whispered, 'I hate this war.'

'It's not the war that's made Mam do this. Nothing made her and no one. She made the decision, Maria.'

'Well, I hate the war anyway.'

They talked for an hour or more, and long after Maria had fallen asleep, Cora lay wide awake in the darkness. The little room was freezing, there had been ice on the inside of the window for weeks, but snuggled next to Maria she wasn't cold. It was her thoughts that kept her from sleeping. She didn't want to cry any more when she thought of her mother; her hate had burned that weakness away, and she hugged it to her. It was strengthening, sustaining. Her da was the one she felt bereft for. She lay quietly, formulating the letter she would write to him in her mind, and eventually drifted off into a troubled, restless sleep full of disturbing dreams she couldn't remember in the morning.

Wilfred stared at Cora, his thin face reflecting his shock. If she had told him her mam had walked through the town naked he would have believed it more easily than that Mrs Stubbs had played Cora's da for a sucker. It just showed you never really knew anyone else. He would have bet his life on Mrs Stubbs being a good'un.

Horace, standing at the side of him, looked bewildered and then angry. 'I don't believe you, our Cora. You've got it wrong. You and Mam were always at odds with each other.'

Cora's response to this was to thrust her mother's letter into his hand. He read it in silence, the angry red draining from his face and his mouth tightening. Wilfred put his arm round Horace's shoulders but he shook it off, throwing the letter on the ground and running off to join a group of his pals who were playing football with a rusty tin can.

'He's upset,' said Wilfred quietly. 'He didn't mean that about you and your mam.'

'It's true and he meant it.' Cora looked at Wilfred. 'I know you've always thought a lot of my mam but there's another side to her as this shows all too clearly. No one could have been a better husband than my da, Wilfred. You know that.'

He nodded. Cora's da had loved her mam like . . . well, like he himself loved Cora.

'I'm not going to tell Susan and Anna yet. Time enough when they're a bit older. Nor Mrs Burns or him.' Like Maria, Wilfred knew who Cora was talking about. 'He'd just love that, to think our mam's run off with a fancy man.'

'Oh, Cora.' Her bitterness was tangible and pity welled up in him.

'It'll be just us four and Jed who know. All right?'

'Have you told Jed yet?'

'Not yet.'

Wilfred felt a surge of pleasure that she had told him first, which evaporated when she continued, 'Can you tell him I want to see him tonight when you get home? I'll meet him near the old barn when everyone's gone to bed. Say eleven o'clock?'

'You shouldn't be out late at night.' Apart from his jealousy he was worried about the farmer waylaying her. It was a constant gnawing anxiety after she had confided in him about Enid and the way Farmer Burns was, regularly causing him sleepless nights and when he did fall asleep, nightmares in which terrible things happened and he was left writhing and in agony because he was unable to protect her.

Cora waved his objections away with an irritable gesture. 'Will you tell him?'

'Of course, if that's what you want, although I don't see why you can't wait till Sunday. Nothing's going to change.'

Today was Thursday and the thought of waiting till Sunday afternoon to see Jed was unbearable. Since the summer when they had declared their feelings for each other the time between Sundays seemed like mini eternities as it was, but the work the girls were expected to do once they were back from school in the evenings meant it was virtually impossible to meet in the week. They rarely fell into bed before ten o'clock as it was. Besides which,

Cora was terrified Farmer Burns might find out about Jed. The girls always went for their Sunday-afternoon walk in a group from the farm, Cora breaking away from the others to meet Jed once they were sure they were alone and Farmer Burns wasn't around. They would then meet later and arrive home together.

Cora's fingers went involuntarily to the dainty silver locket hidden under her dress. Jed had given it to her for Christmas and she had been thrilled. 'Just tell him, Wilfred.'

Wilfred knew about the locket and he had to call on all the self-control he had learned to exercise in the last months not to betray himself as he said, 'I'll tell him. Don't fret.'

'Thank you.'

The bell to call them in after lunch sounded in the next moment. They had been talking over the fence that separated the boys from the girls in the small yard, and as they walked into the building through separate doors and then joined up again to enter the seniors' classroom, Cora gave Wilfred a small smile and he smiled back. 'Don't worry, lass,' he said softly. 'It'll be all right.'

The words were meaningless in the circumstances but his concern and comfort were balm to her sore heart, and as she had done many times in the past, she thought, What would I do without Wilfred? She knew he cared about her and her sisters and Horace as though they were his own family, more so because he had told her he had never been close to his own siblings. And for her part she loved him every bit as much as Horace, more, she thought ruefully, as her brother gave her a filthy look when he passed her as though the situation at home was her fault.

'Her mam's run off with another bloke?' Jed's face was a study in surprise. 'How does she know? Who told her?'

'Her mam wrote to her,' said Wilfred flatly. He had just told Jed that Cora wanted to see him and why, and now he added, 'And she wants it kept quiet. She hasn't even told the two youngest, just Maria and Horace and me and you.'

Jed, shaking his head as though coming out of a trance, rubbed his hands that were blue with cold up and down the rough material of his work trousers. He had been breaking the thick ice on the water troughs in the yard when Wilfred and Horace had come back from school, and although Horace had gone straight into the farmhouse, Wilfred had come across to Jed to impart the news. 'How's she taken it?'

Jed was showing no annoyance that Cora had told him first, Wilfred noted, feeling peeved. He had felt it was a small triumph over his enemy but Jed's reaction was dispelling his satisfaction. 'As you'd expect. Her mam told her that her da's home from the war an' all so she's imagining all sorts about him.'

'Poor blighter, coming back to that.'

'Aye.'

Jed straightened, throwing back his shoulders as he stretched his spine. He had grown a good five or six inches the year before and now at six foot four towered over Wilfred, which was another nail in his coffin as far as Wilfred was concerned. He had thought it impossible for his hate of Jed to find a deeper level, but when he spied on them on a Sunday afternoon the height and breadth of his rival against the slim perfection of Cora forced him to admit they made a breathtaking couple and he loathed Jed still more because of it. He himself hadn't grown an inch in the last couple of years and Cora was now taller than him, and in spite of the good food that he stuffed himself with at the farm he was as thin as a rake.

'I'm glad she had you to talk to at school earlier, she must have been in a state.'

Again Wilfred said, 'Aye,' whilst thinking derisively how easy Jed was to fool. He had no idea how much he hated him and wished him dead, or of his real feelings for Cora. Mind, he'd worked hard to make sure of this, constantly curbing his natural responses around the older boy and acting the part of a pal. He'd gone about it bit by bit after that day in the summer, knowing a sudden change in his manner might make Jed suspicious, and Jed had been only too eager to let bygones be bygones, the idiot. 'She said to meet her by the old barn at eleven o'clock,' Wilfred said quietly, his love for Cora which was a thing apart from his jealousy making him add, 'But I'd get there early and make sure Farmer Burns isn't around.'

'Aye, I'll do that, lad.' Jed clapped him on the shoulder.

'Go and get a hot drink – you look frozen.' The thick snow of November and December had melted the week after Christmas when a thaw had set in, but a severe drop of temperature at the beginning of the New Year had brought heavy frosts, and the sub-zero conditions showed no signs of abating. For the last three weeks any winter sun had been so weak and fleeting as to make no inroads on the barren sparkling ground, the only colour in the white sky a few fleeting wisps of silver and feeble glimmers of yellow which stained the expanse as the shadows of twilight approached. It made life even harder at the farm, but at least the thick glutinous mud that had been inches thick at the end of December had become rock-hard ridges that made walking slightly easier as long as you took care not to turn your ankle.

As Wilfred walked off towards the farmhouse, Jed stood looking after him for a few moments. He was a funny one, was Wilfred, but he was glad he seemed to have come to terms with him and Cora walking out. And he was friendly enough now – they were more or less back to the way they'd been when Wilfred and Horace had first arrived at the farm before his friendship with Cora had upset Wilfred. And yet . . . Jed narrowed his eyes as Wilfred disappeared from view. He didn't know if he altogether trusted him. There were times, just now and again, when he sensed something else was going on behind the pally front Wilfred adopted.

He shrugged the thought away, his mind fully concentrating on Cora and what she must be feeling like as he continued with his work. His poor lass, his poor, poor lass.

At half-past ten Jed was already standing in deep shadows with his eyes on the kitchen door from which Cora would exit. The night was frozen and still and the moon was high, casting its light over the frosty ground that, along with rooftops and trees and fields, glittered and sparkled as though strewn with diamond dust. An owl's muffled hoot sounded in the far distance a few times and the occasional lowing of the cattle in the cowshed, but otherwise the night was silent.

At five to eleven the kitchen door opened and Cora came out, walking quickly across the white glinting yard towards the old barn in the distance that was used for storing feed for the animals along with the fodder barrows and other equipment. He moved out of the shadows when she would have walked right past him, causing her to squeak in alarm before she realized it was him.

'Sorry, lass.' He took her hand and together they hurried away from the farmhouse, continuing past the barns and outbuildings until they reached the small beech wood some five hundred yards from any buildings. The interior of the wood was a dark and silent place for much of the year, cowled in shadows and screened from sunlight by dense columns of foliage. In winter, however, the trees were laid bare, allowing the bitter north-easterly winds to drive snow into the very heart of the wood, and tonight the trees stood clothed in their thick mantle of frost, the ground beneath their feet crisp and white and the moon casting eerie silhouettes and outlines here and there.

Once they were in the heart of the wood he took her into his arms, kissing her long and hard beneath the frozen branches overhead. Cora hung on to him, kissing him back. She had been so worried something would prevent him from coming or that she would be discovered trying to leave the house. It was Jed who drew away, moving her to look down into her face as he murmured, 'I'm so sorry, lass. I'm so, so sorry.'

She hadn't wanted to cry since she had read her mother's letter but now the tears were overwhelming. He held her for long minutes, not saying anything beyond soft comforting sounds and muttered endearments, and when she finally composed herself he handed her his handkerchief to wipe her eyes.

'I – I didn't mean to cry all over you.' She gave a little hiccup as she spoke.

'Don't be daft, that's what I'm here for.' He smoothed a tendril of flaming red hair from her damp cheek as he said again, 'I'm so sorry.'

She sniffed, giving a shaky smile. 'I know it could have waited till Sunday but I just wanted to see you.'

'I should hope so.'

'I just can't believe she's done such a thing, Jed. Not my mam. It'll kill my da, I know it will.' She shook her head despairingly. 'Just to leave him, to leave us all as though we don't count for anything.'

'No, don't think like that.'

'I can't help it. The war's turned everything upside down and now this. She couldn't have loved us like I thought she did. It's all been a lie, everything I thought was real.'

'Look, lass, you're in shock, all right? And I know it's hard but if there hadn't been a war we would never have met and that's got to count for something, hasn't it? And I tell you something else, Cora. I will never leave you, you can count on that. If we live to be a hundred I'll be at your side. I might be toothless and bald by then, but I'll be there.'

She gave another shaky smile as he'd hoped she would.

'I mean it, lass. I love you beyond words and if I could change what your mam's done I would. But I can and do promise you that we're different to your mam and da. What we've got happens once in a lifetime – you know that, don't you? I'd die before I left you and I know you feel the same.'

They kissed again, their white breath mingling, and as they did so she felt her world – which had been rocked to its foundations – beginning to stabilize again.

In spite of the bitter cold they spent another hour talking and kissing and cuddling beneath the white skeletons of the trees, feeling as though they were the only two people alive in an enchanted landscape where the normal laws of nature were suspended. And it helped. She'd needed this time with Jed, Cora told herself, as they walked back towards the farmhouse hand in hand. She didn't fool herself that it had solved anything but it had somehow set her back on course; that was the only way she could describe it to herself.

As they reached the spot where Jed had been waiting for her earlier, Cora lifted her eyes to the black sky and frosty moon. 'It's beautiful,' she whispered softly. 'The sky, the moon, the trees and fields, it's all beautiful. It's only men and women who spoil the world and make it ugly.'

'But our world will be beautiful, lass, and filled with love, you'll see.' He kissed the tip of her nose. 'I promise.'

'I know.' And she did. Nothing could come between them and that was the only thing that mattered, the thing she had to hang on to. Whatever happened in the future, she had Jed.

PART THREE

When Opportunity Comes Knocking

1943

Chapter Ten

'The tide's turning, you know.' Mrs Burns nodded her head at Cora as she spoke. 'You mark my words, the tide's turning and not before time. Them blighters being beaten at Stalingrad has taught old Hitler a lesson. He's not as invincible as he likes to make out.'

'I hope so, oh, I hope so.' All the news the year before had been a catalogue of disaster, but since the war's greatest battle had come to an end the month before at the end of January and the German siege of Stalingrad had collapsed into abject defeat for the enemy, everyone's spirits had lifted a little.

'You think what's happened in the last few weeks. The Red Army's started to drive the Nazis out of the Soviet Union and they won't stop, you know. The Russians can be as ruthless as the Germans when they want to be, history tells you that. And the Yanks are doing their bit all over. Them coming into the war was the beginning of the end for the Nazis, and Japan'll live to regret catching a tiger by the tail. Evil so-an'-sos, them Japanese. Every bit as bad as Hitler's crew if you ask me.'

The two of them were attending to the business of washing out everything that had been in contact with the milk now the morning milking was over. It was still early and the stars were shining outside the huge cowshed, but inside, the cows were chomping on their milking-time breakfast and the storm lanterns provided a soft light. Mrs Burns had sent Maria and Maud and the two little ones back to the farmhouse to set the table for breakfast and check the porridge she'd left simmering on the range, and as Cora glanced at the farmer's wife she marvelled, and not for the first time, at the camaraderie that had grown between herself and Mrs Burns since she had left school the previous summer after turning fifteen in May. As the end of the school term had approached she had been in turmoil at the prospect of being alone at the farm without her sisters and Maud once the summer was over, but then Mrs Burns had taken her aside one day.

'You've turned fifteen now,' the farmer's wife had said quietly, 'and likely you'll be wondering how things'll pan out once you've left school? I could do with you working alongside me, Cora. You're a good worker and the two of us together could get through more than double the work, and I mean the two of us together, all right? Side by side. I'll keep an eye on you.'

Cora had stared at the older woman. For months now Farmer Burns had taken to silently watching her whenever he could. He would stop whatever he was doing and just stare, without saying a word, not bothering to hide what he was thinking. Sometimes his hand would work at the bulge in his crotch if his wife wasn't around, other times he would stand, legs apart and with a small sneer twisting his thick lips. Cora had known he meant it to be intimidating and she braved it out by totally ignoring him, but inside he made her shrink. Much as she hated to admit it, she was every bit as terrified of him as her sisters and Maud. She hadn't realized Mrs Burns had noticed his tactics though.

She could have pretended she didn't know what Mrs Burns meant or merely acknowledged her meaning with a nod, but something made her go a step further and she had said, 'He frightens me, Mrs Burns. I try not to show it but he does.'

Mrs Burns had blinked and then let out a long, slow breath. Her voice had been softer than Cora had ever heard it when she'd said, 'Like I said, lass, you'll be with me all the time. I can't undo what's been done, I know that, but I can and will make sure it doesn't happen again.' She had hesitated for a moment before saying, 'I've been putting off telling you this and it's best you don't tell Maud, but the home wrote some time ago to say Enid had her baby, a little girl, but – but there were complications. Enid – Well, Enid passed away two days later. I'm sorry, lass.' Cora's hand had gone to her mouth but she hadn't been able to reply. After a few moments Mrs Burns didn't commiserate with her but said below her breath, 'A woman's conscience can be a terrible thing, Cora. Especially when it's awakened too late.'

She had walked off then, leaving Cora staring after her, but from the first day after the summer holidays when the others had gone back to school, Mrs Burns had kept her word. Gradually Cora had relaxed and a kind of tentative understanding had grown between them.

And they worked well together, Cora thought now, as the two of them left the barn and walked towards the farmhouse for their breakfast of porridge, toast, and eggs with home-cured bacon. Whether it was in the dairy or in the house or attending to the cows. The herd took up a lot of time now they were indoors for the worst of the winter. The cleaning out every morning with shovel and brush and a wheelbarrow to cart the old manured bedding to the midden was warm work, as was supplying the constant meals Mrs Burns fed 'her girls' as she called them. An individual ration of corn into each cow's manger before milking in the morning, followed by oat straw during the cleaning out, and then later turnips – cut into small pieces through the root-chopper. After Cora and Mrs Burns had their own lunch it was back to the cowshed to feed a few hundredweight of potatoes mixed with a little corn followed by hay to 'the girls', after which the cows settled down to chew the cud and gossip until the evening milking and another meal of turnips and corn, followed by hay to see them through the night. But in spite of the hard work and the smell and the occasional cow like Primrose that could prove awkward, Cora was finding she enjoyed working with the animals more than anything else. She now knew the cows all by name, and the anticipatory joy in their big brown eyes and excited puffing and scrambling when they knew a meal was on its way was reward enough for the hard labour.

She'd said as much to Jed and he was thrilled she was taking to a farming life so well and soaking up all that would be expected of her as a farmer's wife through Mrs Burns's instruction. Jed's parents had been devastated the previous summer when his two brothers had been among the heavy Allied casualties in the assault on Hitler's Fortress Europe in Dieppe. Jed was now the sole heir to take over the farm which had been in his family for generations.

He had finally persuaded her to let him introduce her as his girlfriend to his parents one Sunday afternoon just before Christmas, insisting that it was ridiculous they continue as they were just because she didn't want Farmer Burns finding out about their relationship. She had told Mrs Burns the day before the visit and the farmer's wife had been non-committal but not discouraging, merely nodding and then continuing with the job the pair of them were doing in the dairy. The next afternoon Jed had met her and her sisters and Maud and they had all gone for tea at Appletree Farm. Wilfred and Horace had been there and Jed's mother had made them very welcome, insisting that they must make Sunday afternoon tea a weekly habit.

As Cora and Mrs Burns entered the kitchen they found the farmer already seated and eating, the four girls sitting in a row as they too ate their porridge. It was noticeable that in spite of the length of the kitchen table, all four were squeezed close at the opposite end to the farmer.

Rachel Burns said nothing to her husband as she and Cora sat down after filling their bowls from the huge black pot on the range. She rarely spoke to him if she could help it, neither did she look at him unless necessity demanded it. When she had received the letter from the home a while ago, and told him that Enid had died and the baby had been adopted by a childless couple, he had stared at her unblinking. 'So?' he'd said eventually.

'Is that all you can say?' In spite of what she knew he was, she had expected some reaction. Remorse would have been too much to hope for, but a glimmer of shame or regret or guilt? But there had been nothing; she could have just informed him of the state of the weather. In fact, being a farmer, he would have taken more notice of that. 'She's dead. Enid's dead.'

His eyes had narrowed. 'What do you want me to say? The girl was a little whore. With her background what more could you expect?'

'I don't believe Enid was bad, just the opposite, in fact.'

'I don't give a monkey's cuss what you believe.'

'No, I know that.'

They had glared at each other for some moments before he had stomped away, and as she'd stared after him she'd felt sick and guilt-ridden at her part in causing Enid's demise. She remembered a sermon she'd once heard when she was a young lass in the village, long before Bernard Burns had come across her path. The vicar had been preaching about sin and the fires of hell and a lot of it had gone straight over her head, but he'd finished by saying something that had made sense to her in its simplicity. '"The most effective way for sin to abound is for good men and women to do nothing when they encounter it and look the other way."'

And that's what she'd done, she thought, as Bernard disappeared into one of the barns. Knowingly and intentionally. But she hadn't thought the child would die, never had she imagined that. She had stood with her hands knotted against her thin chest praying for forgiveness to a God she wasn't sure she believed in. That was another thing Bernard had done in the early days of their marriage, crushed the simple, childlike faith she'd once had by the things he had subjected her to.

But that day something had changed in her, Rachel thought now. She'd carry Enid with her to her grave but she wouldn't let him molest little Maud or the other girls; she'd fight him herself to prevent that. But it wasn't Maud he wanted, she knew that. By Cora standing up to him the way she had, she'd made him twice as dangerous where she was concerned.

As though in confirmation of her thoughts, Bernard said, 'Heard some interesting gossip at the market yesterday.'

It was unusual for him to speak at the table; normally he shovelled his food down and demanded more with a grunt or a growl, and it brought her eyes sharply to his face. 'Oh, aye?'

'Aye.' He pushed his empty bowl away, his signal that he was ready for his eggs and bacon, and belched long and loudly.

Rachel got up, aware that though the four younger girls were sitting in terrified immobility, Cora was continuing to eat her porridge. There were many little ways that Cora stood her ground with his bullying tactics, refusing to let him see that she was intimidated, and whilst she inwardly applauded the girl's nerve it made Rachel fear for her still more. She hadn't expected to become fond of any of the evacuees; she had never particularly wanted children herself and since finding out what Bernard was she'd been glad she hadn't fallen for a bairn in those first two or three years of their marriage when they'd still slept together. However, over the last months since Cora had left school she'd found she enjoyed the girl's company very much and her life was richer because of it. If she had had a daughter, she would have wanted her to be exactly like Cora, a lass she could have been proud of.

Rachel dished up Bernard's eggs and bacon and brought the plate to the table along with the stack of toast she'd left keeping warm on the range, but as she placed the plate in front of him and went to turn away he caught hold of her wrist.

'Did you know?' he said, his voice coming from deep down in his broad chest. 'Have you been a party to it?'

'Know what?' She tried to jerk her wrist free but he was having none of it.

'About her playing the whore with Croft's youngest lad.' He gestured with his head at Cora who raised her eyes to stare at him, her face white but expressionless.

'If you mean did I know that Cora and the others go to tea there on a Sunday afternoon, then aye, I did. And I gather Cora and Jed are fond of each other. He's a nice lad, respectful.'

Bernard flung her hand away from him with a snort of disgust. 'Nice lad!' He sent a venomous glare at Cora before looking at Rachel again. 'There's no such thing as a nice lad, not at his age. They're all after one thing and he knew he was all right with her. Laid on your back for him already, have you,' he growled, his gaze swinging back to Cora. 'You dirty little—'

Cora was barely aware that she had hurled her bowl at him until it hit him square in the face, sending him rocking back on his chair with a roar of fury and pain. She was up and facing him as porridge and blood from his bleeding nose ran down his face, Rachel hanging on to his arm as he attempted to shake her off and dive at Cora. Terrified by what she'd been driven to do but full of fury at the injustice of what she was being accused of, she didn't move, not until Rachel screamed at her, 'Get upstairs, all of you, get upstairs,' and then it was only Maria and Maud pushing and pulling at her that freed her locked limbs.

Rachel's strength as she held her husband back verged

on superhuman and was born of the certainty that if she let go of his arm murder would ensue. It wasn't until after the door had banged behind the children and she heard their footsteps on the stairs to the attics and then the door to their room shutting that she dared relinquish her hold, and by then she was panting and sweating. As he felt her grip lessen Bernard pushed his wife so violently that she staggered back and would have fallen but for landing against the wall. Winded and bruised, she stared at his livid face as he swore at her, calling her every name under the sun before sinking back onto his chair, a handkerchief to his face. 'She's broken it, she's broken me damn nose.'

Rachel straightened, her shoulder blades throbbing. 'What did you expect, talking to her like that? She's not like the rest of them, she's got some spirit.'

'I'll "spirit" her all right. An' you, stopping me getting to her, what's the matter with you? You're me wife, dammit.'

'Don't pretend that means anything.'

He cursed again, moving the handkerchief away from his face and staring at the blood before saying, 'Get me a bowl of warm water.'

She did as she was told, moving his plate and placing the bowl in front of him with a flannel in the water and a towel at the side of it. His nose was so swollen she couldn't tell if it was broken or not but she wouldn't be surprised, she thought, and not without some satisfaction. She watched him as he dabbed at his face before drying it with the towel and shoving the bowl away so that the pink water slopped all over the table. She picked it up without a word, using the towel to mop up before she said, 'I'll make another pot of tea. Do you want your breakfast?'

He glared at her and by answer stood to his feet, sending his chair flying with the backs of his knees so it skittered across the flags and then fell over. 'I'll see my day with that one, you see if I don't.'

'You won't lay a finger on her, nor none of the other bairns either, else I'm straight to the police and I don't mean your crooked pals, them that turn a blind eye to anything as long as you keep 'em supplied with this and that. I mean it, Bernard. Anything happens to any of them bairns and I'll see you sent down the line for it.'

He stared at her now as if he was stupefied and in truth she was as amazed as him at her temerity. But she meant it, every word. At first she thought he was going to hit her but he didn't; he stood swaying slightly backwards and forwards as if he was drunk and the silence became filled with their mutual hate.

It was in that moment that Rachel realized she had always been frightened of Bernard Burns; even before they had got married and whilst they had been courting and he had been very circumspect and proper, never trying anything more than a kiss goodnight, she had been scared of him, and after their wedding night . . . But the fear was gone. Quite gone. She could hardly believe it, but she knew if he came at her now she would fight him tooth and claw and with anything that came to hand.

Whether her face betrayed her she didn't know, but instead of his usual foul ranting he wetted his lips, then dug his teeth into the flesh of the lower one, the action seeming to drag his head down and his shoulders with it so he looked like old Silas, the bull, before he charged. Still uncertain of what he was going to do, it was his turn to surprise her when he said, 'I don't want us to fall out over that little slut, now then. Nothing's been the same since she came, you have to admit that. We used to rub along all right together, didn't we? We had a good goin' on, you've never wanted for owt.'

Knowing that the balance of power had shifted somewhat with her threat to go to the police, she was further emboldened to say, 'I agree nothing's been the same since Cora and her sisters came to the farm and it's all to the good in my opinion. As for us "rubbing along" as you put it, we've never done that. Your mind's a cesspit, that's the truth of it, and likely always has been. That little lass has got herself a lad, a nice lad who respects her and is good to her, but you can't understand that, can you, not being the way you are. And I tell you, you do anything to spoil things for her and I'll follow through on what I say. I've kept my mouth shut about you cooking the books and all your dodgy dealings for years, but there's them in high places who wouldn't take too kindly to your cheating and double-dealing, not now it comes under the heading of the black market.'

He was glaring at her again, anger turning his face and neck a turkey red, as red as the blood staining the collar of his shirt. His lips moved and he mouthed words that were soundless before he ground out, 'I should have known better than to take a bit of scum from the village as me wife. Sure as hell you can't make a silk purse out of a sow's ear. But *I* tell *you* now, if I go down you'll be right alongside me so think on that. I'd swear on oath you were party to it all.'

'I don't doubt it would be a case of your word against mine, Bernard, but there's not a court in the country who wouldn't believe an ill-used but faithful wife against a husband who has little bairns for his own pleasure.'

Now his glare was maniacal, and with his teeth grinding and his eyes bloodshot he looked as though he was about to murder her. Somehow she stood her ground and glared back without wavering. It wasn't until he swung round, spitting an oath, and walked out of the kitchen into the driving snow that was falling outside that she allowed herself to slump down on a chair, her legs finally giving out.

She sat quite still for some moments, shaken to the core but strangely full of a pleasure that was almost joy. She was still Bernard's wife, still living in his house; she would still have to see him every day and cook his meals and wash his clothes, but . . . She shook her head as she tried to marshal her racing thoughts and pin down the source of the peace that was filling her. *She was free of him*. In her head, where it counted, she was free of him.

She stood up and began to clear the table and after wiping the oilcloth free of drops of blood, splatters of porridge and the remains of the water from the washing bowl Bernard had used, she reset it for herself and the girls, bringing the big dish of bacon and eggs she'd kept warm on the range to the table, along with a large crusty loaf and a pat of butter.

She didn't call to them, but instead she climbed the stairs and then knocked on the bedroom door, saying, 'Cora? It's Mrs Burns. Come down and finish your breakfast, all of you.'

She heard the sound of the chest of drawers which they'd obviously pushed in front of the door being moved, and then it opened. Cora looked at her, Maud and Maria standing behind her and the two little ones sitting on their bed. 'Come down and finish your breakfast,' she said again, very gently. 'He's gone outside, don't worry. I'll make another pot of tea for us all, shall I? And Cora –' she added, even more softly – 'you keep seeing that lad of yours, all right? He's a nice lad or you wouldn't like him.'

Cora gulped hard. 'We haven't – He wouldn't –'

'I know, I know, lass.' Rachel patted Cora's arm. 'The trouble is, if you've a mind like a sewer it dirties everything.'

Rachel saw Cora's tense face relax, her voice a whisper when she said, 'Thank you, Mrs Burns.'

As Cora's bottom lip began to tremble Rachel turned away, saying briskly over her shoulder, 'Come on then, the lot of you. It's snowing a blizzard out there and if there's ever a day you need a full stomach, it's this one. It's no good thinking about going to school in this, there'll be drifts six foot high in places. You four can stay home and help me an' Cora today, all right?'

As the children followed her downstairs and into the kitchen Rachel busied herself with mashing the tea, but as she did so she was remembering the chest of drawers in front of the door, and it came to her, with something of a shock, that from this night forth she would lock her bedroom door. She wouldn't put anything past her husband and if she was to wake up and find a pillow over her face . . .

Chapter Eleven

The thick snow and bitter cold of January and February gave way to squalls of blustery sleet in March and the arrival of spring was gradual, but despite the cruel weather Cora was much happier than she had been in a long while. Since the confrontation in the kitchen Farmer Burns had taken to ignoring her existence most of the time, which suited her perfectly, but it was the deepening friendship between herself and the farmer's wife which lightened Cora's heart. What she saw as an utter betrayal by her mother had brought such a sense of loss that it would have been impossible to put it into words, but one morning when the others were at school and she and Rachel were alone in the cowshed, she had confided her secret to the older woman.

Rachel had listened quietly, making no comment until Cora had fallen silent, and then she had said gently, 'Let the bitterness go, lass. It'll eat you up if you don't and that won't help your da, will it.'

'I can't help it.' She had written to her father straight

after her mother's letter had arrived and received an answer within days. More by what he hadn't written than by what he had, she had realized that what she was feeling was just a reflection of his suffering. His letter had cut her to the quick and she had been desperately worried about him for weeks, but his subsequent correspondence had gradually become more cheerful. Apparently, Beryl Chapman's husband had been killed in Dieppe and with Archie having been evacuated she, too, was all alone. Beryl had suggested they pool their rations and she cook for the pair of them each night, and she had offered to clean house for him and do his washing and ironing for a small fee to which her father had readily agreed. Knowing that someone was taking care of him, even if it was Archie Chapman's mother, whom her own mam had always described as being as nutty as a fruit cake, had put Cora's mind at rest to some extent. Besides which, she'd asked herself bitterly, who was her mam to pass judgement on anyone? At least Mrs Chapman hadn't abandoned her family and run off with a fancy man.

Towards the end of March the war news regularly became more uplifting with bombing raids by the Allies smashing the heart out of German industry, and Rommel and his troops taking a beating in North Africa. The posters the government produced began to reflect the change in fortune: 'Dig For Victory Still', followed by 'Victory may be in sight, but there's no time to relax yet and there's still plenty of digging to do,' was cheering in its way, even if the budget in April raised the price of drinks and put a hundred per cent tax on luxuries. Not that such things really affected Cora and the others. The farm was its own little world and one of hard, unrelenting work. Girls in the towns and cities might bemoan the fact that their clothes had been reduced to utility designs with ration-book fabrics and hardly anything at all in the shops, but on the whole such sentiments passed Cora by.

One thing that did make a difference to how she felt, along with the rest of Britain's war-weary folk, was Churchill's decision to let the country's church bells be rung regularly once again. With the threat of invasion over, church leaders had been campaigning for the restoration of the bells – for so long the warning of impending invasion – saying it would make a huge difference to the morale of ordinary men and women, and so it proved. Hearing church bells on Sundays and other special days to summon worshippers to church was so quintessentially a part of normal life that it seemed, in spite of continued bombing raids by the enemy, as though Hitler and his Nazis were already beaten; and when, on the day after this news was announced, the newspapers and wireless reported that the RAF had bombed Berlin and three other cities to mark Hitler's fifty-fourth birthday, many a glass was raised to Britain's brave lads.

Now that Cora and Jed's relationship was out in the open and Sunday afternoons weren't secret affairs any more, Jed would often come to their agreed meeting point at the back of the old barn and the two of them would go for a walk together without Maud and Cora's sisters.

Rachel had offered to keep the others under her wing on these occasions, saying it was natural the courting couple wanted some time alone. Cora didn't know what Farmer Burns thought about this; although Jed had never come to the kitchen door or into the house itself, she had no doubt the farmer knew about the arrangement and would be silently seething. However, Jed was now seventeen years old and could easily have passed for a man ten years older, being so tall and well built with shoulders on him like a wrestler. In a fight with the farmer one would be hard pressed to say who would fare worse, besides which, Jed had youth on his side.

April had been a changeable month, showers and even storms one day and then the next lukewarm sunshine. The Sunday before, Cora and Jed had gone for a walk along the river bank; wandering along in dappled shade, their conversation punctured by kisses and laughter. They had come across a grass snake that had recently emerged from hibernation lying basking in the weak sunshine on the path in front of them. The serpent had shot into the moist seclusion of the hedge bank once it had sensed their presence, and whether it was the sight of the snake that had caused Cora to feel unsettled she didn't know, but for the rest of the afternoon she'd felt strangely on edge, as though unseen eyes were watching them. Jed had teased her about it, along with her fear of snakes which she couldn't conquer no matter how she tried. She knew that grass snakes were harmless and that if she touched one it would be warm and smooth rather than slimy and cold because Jed had told her so, the same as he'd also informed her that the forked tongue flicking in and out of its mouth was merely an organ of smell and not, as some supposed, a sting; but nevertheless, the creatures terrified her. She didn't think that her unease was solely due to the encounter though; she'd had the same feeling lots of times in the past when she was with Jed and wouldn't have been surprised at any moment to have Farmer Burns jumping out at them.

They had arrived at Jed's farm for tea just a few minutes before Wilfred had walked in. He had been mending a fence in one of the fields. Since leaving school at the same time as Cora he'd begun to work full-time for Jed's father, but unlike Cora, he got paid for what he did. He had listened to Jed teasing her about the snake and her misgivings without making comment, but Cora had got the idea from the look on his face that he didn't like snakes any more than she did.

Now it was the last Sunday in April, and although the morning had been bright and fresh the sky had begun to cloud over come midday. As Cora left the farmhouse and walked towards the old barn she glanced up at the pearl-grey sky, willing it not to rain. She was a little early to meet Jed and had planned to begin walking along the route he'd take, but just as she reached the barn a few big raindrops stung her face. And then, in a matter of moments, the heavens opened and it was a deluge.

Flinging open the door of the barn she darted inside, glad she hadn't been on the road between the two farms or in the fields because she would have been soaked through within a minute or two. As it was the water was dripping off her curls and running down the back of her neck. She took off her coat and shook it, the sound of the rain pounding on the roof of the barn deafening, and she was just about to put it on again when something, a sixth sense, caused her to turn round.

A feeling of shivery fright like that which a small child might experience on being faced with something dark and ghoulish caused her to freeze. Farmer Burns had been sitting on a bale of hay towards the back of the barn. He must have come there straight after Sunday lunch because he was clearly already drunk, a nearly empty bottle of whisky hanging loosely from one hand, and he had moved to within a few feet of her.

Cora rarely looked at him if she could help it and even then it would be a fleeting glance, but now she was close enough to see the bristles on his chin and his mottled complexion and the hairs protruding from his bulbous red nose. His drunken breath wafted over her as he said softly, 'Well, look what the rain's brought in.'

The smell of him, not so much the whisky but *his* smell, a mixture of dirt and sweat and a thick musty odour that always caused bile to rise in her throat, made her take a step backwards, her nostrils flaring.

'Get away from me.'

'You're in no position to give orders but that's you all over, isn't it, acting like Lady Muck? I knew the first time I set eyes on you that you were trouble. Oh, aye, I did, I did.' He nodded his head, almost falling over as the action caused him to lose his balance for a moment. 'And her in there, you've got her on side, haven't you, smarming round her. I know, I know. Filthy little whore, I know.'

Cora took another step backwards away from him, her eyes flashing to the door of the barn that she'd pulled to behind her. The cloudburst was still thunderous outside but if she could get into the open she would escape him. In the same instant he lunged at her with such force that they were both borne to the ground. Winded and dazed and with the full weight of him on top of her, she struggled ineffectually but she still tried to claw at his face, causing him to swear as her nails caught him on one cheek. He was sitting astride her now and he grabbed a wrist in each hand as he ground out, 'I knew me chance would come one day and it has.' He let go of one wrist long enough to slap her hard round the face, making her ears ring. 'With you out of the way the rest of 'em'll toe the line.'

'No, no, they won't, and there's the letter—'

'Damn the letter. I'll take me chance with that if need be but Maud'll do what she's told. She's like her sister, is Maud. No, I can manage 'em all with you gone.'

Gone?

As though she had spoken out loud, he gabbled, 'The river's running high in the bottom field with all the rain. Who's to say you didn't slip an' fall in, eh? Aye, that's the answer, you slipped an' fell in.'

He was talking to himself as much as to her and even

in her panic and pain it came to her that he was unhinged and that without realizing it she had always sensed this. The weight of him on her stomach and chest was crushing the breath out of her now, and much as she wanted to scream, the sound emerged in a strangled choke. It was enough for him to slap her again so hard that for a moment everything went black.

When she came to herself, it was to the feel of his hands yanking up her dress and trying to pull down her knickers. Terror at what was happening to her and the fact that he'd moved enough for the breath to come back into her lungs enabled her to emit one high piercing scream as she pounded at him with her fists. His hand came tightly across her mouth and nose as he cursed her while fumbling to open his trousers as he held her pinned down.

In the next instant Cora heard a loud whack. The farmer collapsed on top of her, a dead weight, crushing her so that even with her mouth and nose free she couldn't breathe. Through the horror of it all, she was aware of Jed swearing as he yanked the inert body off her, and then he was on his knees gathering her against him, murmuring her name over and over as she began to cry hysterically.

It was some moments before she could gain control and during this time Farmer Burns lay still, the old rusty hoe that Jed had hit him with lying to one side. Jed was frantic, and it was this as much as anything that enabled her to take hold of herself and gasp, 'I'm all right, really I'm all right.' She sat trembling as she took his handkerchief to wipe her eyes. 'He didn't do what he wanted. You got here before he could – you know.'

'Thank God.' Jed pulled her up and then into his arms once more, and they stood holding each other tight. 'He needs locking away, the dirty swine, and after this I'll make sure the police take notice if I have to raise merry hell till they do.'

The farmer still hadn't moved, and now Cora whispered, 'He's not dead, is he? You haven't killed him?'

Jed was shaking with the shock of what could have happened if he hadn't heard her just now, and his voice was fierce when he said, 'I don't care if he is dead, the filthy pervert.'

Neither did Cora, except that Jed could get in serious trouble. The farmer had powerful friends as she knew only too well. What had happened with Enid had proved that. She watched as Jed bent over the sprawled figure, silently praying that the farmer was alive. Her face was throbbing and the back of her head was aching – in fact she hurt all over – but fear for Jed was uppermost. She had been so happy going to meet him; how could a day change so quickly into a living nightmare?

'He's breathing, more's the pity.' Jed stood up. 'And he reeks of drink.'

'It's whisky.' Cora pointed to the bottle which had rolled some distance away. 'I think he's had most of it.'

'He might as well have the rest of it then.' Jed picked up the bottle, his face grim and white and his eyes narrowed.

Cora didn't realize what he was going to do until he unscrewed the top and then stood above the farmer, pouring the whisky over his face. There was no reaction for a moment and then the liquid brought Farmer Burns round and he began to moan and splutter, opening his eyes and then swearing as he struggled to sit up. That he was concussed was evident but Cora didn't care about that; he was alive and that meant Jed was safe.

Jed knelt down again, his eyes like chips of blue ice as he said softly, 'You're not fit to draw breath. You know that, don't you? Things like you should be put down at birth, you sick perverted swine you, but I tell you now you'll regret the day you touched her. I'll see you go down the line for this, you see if I don't.'

They had both thought he was more stunned than he was because in the next moment the farmer lunged at Jed, grabbing him round the throat with a strength born of hate and frustration, and then they were rolling about on the floor. Jed managed to prise the farmer's fingers from his throat and then punch him in the jaw with enough force to render Farmer Burns semi-conscious. As Cora helped him to his feet they looked down at the figure on the floor where he lay cursing and mumbling to himself, his language turning the air blue.

'Right, we're going.' Jed took Cora's hand, his tone brooking no argument. 'We'll go to mine and tell my parents what's happened. Da'll know who best to report it to. He needs putting away, Cora.'

'He said he was going to kill me.' She looked at Jed,

her face bleached of colour. 'He said everyone would think I'd fallen in the river.'

'If anyone's going in the river it'll be him,' said Jed grimly. 'The man's stark staring mad.'

'We must go and tell Mrs Burns before we see your da. It's only right.'

'No.' Jed shook his head. 'Think, Cora. I know you're on fairly good terms with her now but she's his wife when all's said and done. For years she's known what he is and never said a word – gone out of her way to protect him, in fact. Look at what happened with Enid. You can't trust her.'

'She's not like that now.'

'A leopard can't change its spots.' Jed pulled her towards the door of the barn which was ajar. 'Come on, we're going to mine. My mam can take care of you while Da and I sort this.'

They were about to step outside into what was now merely a drizzle of rain when a voice behind them said, 'I'm bleeding. I need help.'

They turned to see Farmer Burns trying to sit up. He was holding his head, his hands bloody. 'I'm bleeding, get someone, damn you.'

'Get someone yourself.' Jed's voice was cold.

'I can't.' It was a whimper. 'I'm bad.'

'Jed–'

'No, Cora.' Jed pulled her outside, taking her arm and walking her away from the barn towards the path that ultimately led to Appletree Farm. 'There's not much wrong with him apart from being three sheets to the wind. He'll have a headache tomorrow but again that'll probably be more the whisky than anything else. I want you at mine where I can be sure you're safe and Da and I can come back for Maria and the others.'

'But we can't just leave him. What if he bleeds to death?'

'Believe me, Cora, he's not going to bleed to death. The devil looks after his own, and if ever there was a devil in human form it's that man.'

Still protesting, she allowed herself to be led away from the farm, but within five minutes she whispered, 'Jed, we have to go back and at least tell Mrs Burns. There was a lot of blood.'

'A little blood goes a long way.'

'Please, Jed. Before we tell your da. What if he bleeds to death before you and your da come back?'

'Cora, for the second time, that's not going to happen,' said Jed, exasperation in his tone, but then, when she stood still staring at him, he said, 'All right, all right, if it's going to put your mind at rest.'

They had just climbed over a stile into a meadow that bordered the land between the two farms, dandelions, shining like miniature suns, reflecting the light and providing a rich supply of nectar for the hundreds of bees buzzing busily about their business. The scene was so peaceful, and such a contrast to what they'd just experienced, that it brought a lump to Cora's throat, tears pricking at the backs of her eyes.

In one way she didn't want to return – she'd be happy never to see the farm again now – but something was telling her they had to go back and at least tell Mrs Burns what had happened so she could see to her husband.

Jed offered her his hand to climb back over the stile and she took it, but he kissed her first, stroking back a tendril of hair from her brow as he murmured, 'It'll be all right, my love. I promise.'

Wilfred had been close enough in his shadowing of Jed to hear the scream faintly and he knew immediately it was Cora. Forgetting all about keeping hidden, he raced for the barn where he knew Jed usually met her, catching a glimpse of his rival as Jed disappeared inside. It was only when he reached the door of the barn which was open a crack and heard voices that caution reasserted itself.

Peering through the gap, he could just about see the farmer spreadeagled on the floor and Jed holding Cora in his arms as he endeavoured to comfort her. His stomach turned over as his heart began to pound fit to burst. It was obvious what had occurred.

The dirty swine, he thought sickly. I'll kill him. He was on the verge of betraying himself and bursting in, when Jed lifted Cora up from the ground and the action made Wilfred think again. If they saw him Jed would demand a reason for his appearance, and once that can of worms was opened who knew where it would end?

His hands bunched into fists at his side, he forced himself to remain where he was and listen. He'd heard

Cora say the farmer hadn't succeeded in raping her before Jed had pulled her to her feet and now she was urging Jed to make sure the man wasn't dead. Within a moment or two the farmer and Jed were scuffling on the floor and he watched as Jed hit him, wishing it was his fist bashing into the farmer's face. And then Cora and Jed were coming towards him and he knew he had to make himself scarce, darting round the back of the barn just in time.

A moment or two later they emerged but it became clear Cora was reluctant to leave, and he heard Jed persuading her to go with him. 'Aye, take her out of this,' Wilfred whispered to himself, for once in agreement with his rival. 'Get her away.' If he'd been Jed he would have made her leave the farm months ago before something like this very thing occurred. When the two of them had disappeared from view, he found himself pushing open the door of the barn. Farmer Burns had pulled himself into a sitting position with his back against a bale of hay and he appeared to be dozing, but as Wilfred approached him he opened his eyes and squinted up at him, clearly unable to see properly.

His voice thick, he muttered, 'Come back, have you?'

'It's not Jed.' Wilfred's voice was cold. 'I'm a friend of Cora's.'

The name sparked life into the farmer, if not his body then his voice, as he hissed, 'Her, the little whore. They're all whores but she's the worst of the lot, damn her. But she's as good as dead, you tell her that from me. Good as dead.' The words were slurred but the naked hatred behind them was crystal clear. The farmer screwed up his eyes when Wilfred didn't answer, mumbling, 'Who did you say you were again?'

'That doesn't matter.' As Wilfred stared down at the farmer he knew what he was going to do, and in the same instant he realized it was no spontaneous thing bred of the moment. The seed had been set a good while ago when he had begun to understand that Cora was frightened of the farmer and that he was a danger to her.

Farmer Burns had slipped back into a drunken stupor and Wilfred knew he'd never have a chance like this again. The hoe was lying on the ground and he bent and picked it up, walking behind the bale of hay. The farmer was now snoring, his head lolling forward and his chin resting on his breastbone, exposing his grimy neck.

Although still small and wiry, Wilfred had toughened up considerably since working full-time for Jed's father. He had developed muscles he'd never known he had and the hardest jobs on the farm no longer daunted him.

He stood a moment more and then brought down the hoe onto his victim with all his strength. Blood spurted from a gaping wound in the farmer's neck and he fell to one side, squirming and moaning. Wilfred stood back a pace, savouring the death throes as a sense of power made his chest expand.

The ever-widening pool of red stained the ground as the farmer's groans grew fainter before stopping altogether. Wilfred waited a full minute, standing in the quiet of the old barn. The rain had stopped and he could hear chirruping in the rafters above. Must be a nest up there, he thought inconsequentially, before stooping over the body and checking for signs of life. There were none. It was over.

He left the barn carefully, checking no one was about, and then began to follow the route he knew Cora and Jed would take to Appletree Farm. The cloudburst had cleared the weather and now patches of blue showed in the sky above, the sun shining and the air fresh and clean. He had gone a short way when he saw two figures in the distance and realized with some surprise it was Jed and Cora retracing their steps. Quickly he left the path and plunged into the thick hedgerow, concealing himself until they had passed by. He had expected they would go straight to Appletree Farm but it looked as though they were returning to Stone Farm. His brow wrinkled. What the hell was Jed doing taking her back there, the idiot? He hadn't got the sense he was born with. He could only surmise they were going to check on Farmer Burns.

Until this moment his only thought in getting rid of the farmer had been to remove the danger from Cora, but as he stood there in the sunshine it dawned on him what the pair of them would assume – that Jed had killed him. He'd heard Cora remonstrating with Jed that they shouldn't leave him.

His mind racing, he attempted to weigh up what this could mean for him and slowly a smile lifted the corners of his mouth. Jed would go down the line for this. If he tried to plead self-defence he'd be laughed out of court. As far as he'd been able to see, Jed hadn't got a mark on him; certainly not anything that warranted practically decapitating a man. And from behind too. No, that wouldn't go down well with the law. Well, well, well. This particular Sunday was turning out better than he could ever have expected. He'd get back to Appletree Farm and await developments.

Cora had come to a petrified stop a foot or so inside the barn, her hand across her mouth to stifle the scream that nearly escaped. There was so much blood, a great dark pool of it. He had said he was bleeding, she told herself frantically as Jed approached the body. They shouldn't have left. She watched as Jed knelt down and she wanted to ask if the farmer was breathing but she couldn't speak; all she could do was to stare stupidly as he checked for signs of life.

Jed turned a chalk-white face to her. 'He's dead.'

She was about to scream. No, no, she mustn't scream. That wouldn't help Jed. He hadn't meant to do it – he had been protecting her – but would the police, especially Farmer Burns's cronies, see it like that? Her mind racing, Cora forced herself to walk forward.

'Are you sure?'

The farmer's dying convulsions had left him lying on his back and now Jed gingerly moved his head before jerking away. 'It's from the back of his neck. Perhaps he cut it when we were fighting, I don't know, or from when

I hit him with the hoe. Maybe the fight opened it up or something.'

'It wasn't your fault, Jed. He was trying to rape and kill me and then he went for you.'

Jed stood up and Cora could see he was shaking. 'I never thought . . . I mean, if I'd have known he was bleeding this badly I'd have got Mrs Burns.'

'I know, I know.'

'Although part of me . . .'

'What?'

'Part of me is glad he can't hurt you any more. He was evil, wicked.'

'Yes, he was.' They stood looking at each other for a few moments and then Cora said, 'It was an accident, we both know that. You were trying to protect me and you never meant to kill him. He reeks of drink – he could easily have fallen on something and cut his neck, couldn't he?'

'Aye, but he didn't.'

'But only we know that.' Cora was looking round the old barn that was full of this, that and the other. There were bits of broken, rusty machinery, old cartwheels, a rotting wooden plough and other cannibalized odds and ends dating back to the farmer's great-grandfather's day. Farmer Burns hadn't believed in getting rid of anything. Next to a wooden tub holding the remains of a root-cutter and other implements stood a cracked granite trough that had once been used for salting pig meat, the top lethal and jagged in one corner. 'We have to move that across here, where all the blood's soaked into the ground.'

'What?'

'The old trough. Look at the top of it, it's as sharp as a scythe. We can –' she gulped hard – 'smear blood all over it and make it look as though he fell on it while he was drunk.'

She watched his face stretch as the penny dropped. Then he shook his head. 'No, I can't involve you like this. I'll go to the police and tell them what happened. Truth's on my side.'

'That won't mean anything, not round here, not with his pals. For a start they won't like it that their supply of black-market goods stops. And anyway, I *am* involved. The only reason it's happened is because of me.'

'Oh, no, let's be clear about that.' Jed took her into his arms. 'The reason it happened was because of him and only because of him.'

Cora drew in a long breath. 'Jed, we have to make it look as though he did this himself. I can't – I can't lose you.'

He held her a moment more before saying, 'All right. I can see it makes sense. He's bought and bribed his way into favour with those who have a bit of power hereabouts and that sticks in my craw but it is what it is.'

It took a good few minutes to drag and pull the trough inch by inch across the ground because it was even heavier than it had looked. It left a deep groove in the dirt floor of the barn and by the time they had seen to that, sprinkling bits of straw and other debris on their handiwork, they were both sweating.

The smell of blood, metallic and sickly sweet, was making Cora feel nauseous, and she turned away as Jed smeared it over the jagged top of the trough and down the side. By the time he had finished no one could have guessed that the trough hadn't been the cause of the farmer's demise. Cora picked up the whisky bottle, handing it to Jed who placed it near the body.

'I'll go and get Mrs Burns.' Cora spoke softly, almost in a whisper, although she wasn't sure why. 'I'll say we came in here out of the rain and found him.'

'No, you can't say that, the rain stopped some time ago.'

'Well, what then?'

'Just leave him and come home with me. Someone will find him and you won't be around.'

'And that someone could be Maria or Maud or the little ones. No, I can't do that, Jed. I'll say . . .' She thought for a moment. 'I'll say you brought me back early 'cause I wasn't feeling well and we came in here to say goodbye before I went in.'

'My hands are covered in blood.' He looked down at them as though he had just realized.

'You tried to help him, see if he was still alive.' And when he shook his head, she said, 'I can't risk one of the others finding him like this, Jed.'

It was a few moments before he nodded. 'Go on then, go and get her but be careful what you say. We hadn't reached mine before you started to feel bad so I brought you straight back, all right? They might question my mam an' da.'

'Who?'

'The police, of course. They'll have to be told straight away. Mrs Burns will need to report it. Even with an accident there'll be lots of questions.' They stared at each other and then Jed gave a shaky laugh. 'Where's one of Hitler's bombs when you want it? If this barn could be flattened that'd be that.'

She couldn't dredge up a smile in return, merely looking at him and saying softly, 'It's true it was an accident, Jed. Whatever happens, that's true, and it's only you and me who know he didn't fall on the trough. I love you.'

'I love you too, lass. For ever and a day. And like I said, at bottom I can't be sorry he's where he can't hurt you no more. It's just I'd rather it have happened a different way.'

She nodded. The tops of her legs were throbbing from where the farmer had manhandled her and she knew she would have a whole host of bruises tomorrow. Her face hurt, everything hurt, and if Jed hadn't come when he had she would have been raped and probably killed because Farmer Burns had had murder in his face. But for it to end like this . . . Jed had to be kept safe, that was all that mattered now.

Chapter Twelve

The next few hours were chilling and Cora would remember the terror she felt for the rest of her life. Mrs Burns came to the barn with her and looked at the body on the floor and then at Jed who was standing as though he was guarding it. Her eyes rested on Jed's hands and Cora, seeing this, said quickly, 'Jed tried to see if there was anything he could do but it was too late. He wanted to check if he was breathing.'

Mrs Burns didn't reply to this; instead she said, 'What have you done to your face? It looks sore.'

'I tripped earlier and banged it.'

The farmer's wife nodded. 'I see.' What she saw, Cora wasn't sure, but then Mrs Burns said, 'I always said his drinking would be the death of him and it's got worse lately. Had you noticed?'

'What? Oh, aye, yes, much worse.'

'He must have tripped and fallen backwards onto the trough.'

'Yes.'

Rachel looked at Jed. 'Will you go for the police, lad? They'll need to be told. Sergeant Irvin will be at home at this time of day on a Sunday. Do you know where he lives?'

Jed shook his head.

'No matter. I'll give you his address and directions. The sergeant is a crony of my husband's so are you both sure exactly what you are going to say to him?'

Cora stared at the woman she had come to think of as a friend. She knew. Mrs Burns knew, or had a pretty good idea of what had occurred, anyway. 'I was feeling bad so we came into the barn for a bit of privacy to say goodbye and – and we found him like this.'

Rachel nodded. And pigs fly. She looked down at the face of her husband. It was streaked with blood and his eyes were partly open. She felt not the slightest trace of pity. So, she thought grimly, you finally got what you deserve but not before you gave a bairn a baby and she died in the delivering of it. What a pity this hadn't happened years ago.

Her voice soft, she patted Cora's arm, saying, 'Are you all right, lass?'

The question was more than just about the scene in front of them and they both knew it. 'Yes, I'm fine, Mrs Burns. Just – just a bit bruised from the fall earlier but nothing else.'

Again Rachel nodded. 'Probably better if you don't mention that to the sergeant. It's only me who would notice your face is a bit swollen and we don't want to complicate things, do we?' Turning to Jed, she added, 'Come into the house and wash yourself before you leave, lad. Better to be clean and tidy, eh? It is a Sunday, after all. You can take the horse and cart – it won't take too long but in the meantime I'll keep Cora and the others in the house. Don't want Anna and Susan seeing this, do we? Well, funny how things turn out; we had the authorities here the other week asking if we wanted a couple of POWs from the Italian POW camp and Bernard wouldn't hear of it. Had a barney with them in the end when they went on about increasing production and the rest of it. Looks like that'll sort itself out now. I'll get in touch with them.'

Jed stared at Mrs Burns. Her husband was lying dead in a pool of blood and she was on about POWs. Was that normal? But then nothing had been normal at Stone Farm from what he could make out. And her present attitude certainly wasn't a bad thing in the circumstances. He didn't like the idea of Italian POWs around Cora, though; they had some working at the farm now and the men had already charmed his mother with their Latin ways.

The two of them followed Mrs Burns back into the house where Maria and the others had been helping the farmer's wife with some baking when Cora had rushed into the kitchen earlier. It was Mrs Burns who said quietly, 'There's been an accident in the old barn and Farmer Burns has been hurt. I don't want you going in there for the time being. Jed here is going to go and fetch Sergeant Irvin and he'll take care of things.'

Jed had hurried into the scullery to wash his hands before the girls noticed the blood, and when he emerged a few minutes later Mrs Burns motioned for him to follow her outside, leaving Cora with her sisters and Maud. Immediately they were alone, Maria said, 'What's happened? How bad is Farmer Burns?'

They had to know sooner or later. 'He's dead,' Cora said simply, not knowing how to dress it up. 'He had been drinking and he fell onto a broken trough in the barn and cut his neck so it just bled and bled.'

They stared at her and then Maud said timidly, 'He's definitely dead?'

'Definitely.'

Cora saw something lift from Maud's little face as though a veil had been taken away. When she glanced at Maria the same expression was on her sister's countenance. Even Maud's voice was different, lighter, when she said, 'I wish Enid was here so I could tell her she doesn't have to be frightened any more.'

Maud still had no idea of her sister's passing, and now Cora said gently, 'I'm sure she isn't frightened where she is, Maud. She's been well looked after, you can be sure of that.'

'I miss her.' Maud's lower lip quivered.

'We all miss her.'

'So what happens now?' Maria looked at Cora.

Cora shrugged. 'I would imagine the sergeant will arrange for Farmer Burns to be taken away first of all, and then, well, everything will carry on as normal. Mrs

Burns was on about having some POWs here so they'll do the work he did. The farm's hers now, I suppose.'

'She didn't seem very sad, did she?' little Susan piped up. 'I mean, about Farmer Burns.'

'No, well, he wasn't a very nice man, was he,' said Maria, glancing Cora's way and adding, 'No more looking over our shoulders all the time then, lass.' Maria had filled out considerably in the last year after starting her monthlies and her resemblance to the younger two was less marked. There was a gleam of red in her brown hair now and she was altogether prettier. They had both noticed the farmer watching her on many occasions and Cora had been ever more vigilant on her sister's behalf.

When Mrs Burns came back into the kitchen, she smiled at them. 'I'm going to make a pot of tea while we wait,' she said cheerfully, 'and I think we'll try some of these teacakes while they're warm. What say you?'

It wasn't only the girls who recognized that the badness had gone out of their life.

Jed's parents were anxiously waiting for him when he got back home later that night, his mother quite beside herself. He hadn't got in the door before she was, if not exactly shouting, then asking very loudly where on earth he thought he had been when he and Cora had been expected for their normal Sunday high tea at four o'clock. It was inconsiderate and rude not to let them know he wasn't bringing her as usual, and she, his mother, had been *so* worried but of course he hadn't considered that. Oh, no. Not when he'd been gallivanting, no doubt.

When Jed could get a word in edgeways and explain, his mother had put a hand to her chest, saying, 'Come into the sitting room and tell us everything,' and once in there, she had sat down very suddenly, looking white and shocked. Now, as Jed finished telling the tale, she said, 'Oh, my word, whatever next? Dear, oh, dear, poor Mrs Burns. We must go over tomorrow and see if we can do anything to help. And you say he'd been drinking and fell on an old trough in the barn? What are the chances of that?'

'One in a million, I'd say.' Wilfred had joined them a minute or two before, listening quietly as Jed had told them what happened, his eyes fixed on the farmer's son's face. He had left Horace asleep in the room they shared when he'd heard Jed return; he'd been on tenterhooks for hours.

'Perhaps not as much as you'd think,' Jed said quietly. 'Mrs Burns said he'd been drinking too much for years. She told the police he often took a bottle up with him at night and drank himself senseless.'

Wilfred said nothing but behind his blank facade his mind was racing. The cunning so-an'-so. He'd made it look like an accident, had he? Clever, very clever.

Mrs Croft went off to the kitchen to make them all a hot drink and as Wilfred sat listening to Jed talking to his father, he began to have an idea of what he was going to do. He knew without a shadow of a doubt that he had to make this whole thing with the farmer work for him; it was a gift from the gods and if he let the opportunity slip through his fingers nothing like this would come again. For months now he had been biding his time and suffering the torments of the damned when he saw Cora and Jed together. He couldn't go on like this, he knew he couldn't. He would do something stupid because he couldn't stand Jed thinking she was his. Just the other day he had been tempted to drive the tractor over Jed and he'd come as near as dammit to doing it, even though he knew Farmer Croft and the three POWs were about.

After a while he excused himself and went upstairs to the room he shared with Horace. Jed stayed talking to his parents for some time, but eventually Wilfred heard him come up to his room next door. Mr and Mrs Croft were at the far end of the landing and there was a spare bedroom between them and Jed.

Wilfred lay there, reliving the moment he'd brought the hoe down on Farmer Burns's neck. His only regret was that the man's dying had been over too soon. He would have liked him to suffer longer.

He waited a full hour before he quietly slid out of his bed, which was on the opposite side of the room to Horace's and by the door. Barefoot, he tiptoed onto the landing and stood for a minute in the darkness. He knew exactly what he was going to say.

Jed must have been awake because the moment Wilfred turned the door knob and entered the room, his voice came from the bed which was set under the window.

'Yes, who is it?'

'It's me, Wilfred.'

'What's the matter? Is Horace bad or something?'

Jed always slept with his curtains gaping wide and his window open. Moonlight was pouring in the room and Wilfred could easily make him out as he sat up in bed, raking back his hair. 'No, it's not Horace,' he said softly, walking across to stand by the bed. 'I want to talk to you about what happened this afternoon.'

'Oh, aye?' It was wary.

'Aye. Anything you want to add to what you told your mam an' da?'

There was a moment's hesitation. 'Such as?'

'Oh, just the trifling matter of you killing a man, something like that?'

'I don't know what you're talking about.' Jed stood up, towering over Wilfred as he added, 'And get out of my room.'

'Now, now, no need to be like that.' Wilfred found he was beginning to enjoy himself. Ever since Jed had taken Cora from him he had fantasized about having the other boy exactly where he wanted him, at his mercy. The fantasy had always ended with him leaving Jed in a crumpled heap somewhere, but what he now had in mind was so much better because no one, least of all Cora, could suspect him of having anything to do with what he proposed.

'I said, get out.'

'I'd suggest it's in your best interests and those of Cora to listen to what I have to say.' A shaft of moonlight was directly on Jed's face and Wilfred saw his eyes narrow. 'Unless, of course, you want her up before the beak as well. I know exactly what went on this afternoon so cut the flannel. You might as well know I followed you to Stone Farm. Fancied a walk myself.'

'Fancied a walk?' Jed's voice was scornful but Wilfred detected fear for the first time. 'And how often have you "fancied a walk" in the past? Cora's often felt uneasy. Have you made a habit of spying on us?'

'That's neither here nor there. The point is, you killed Farmer Burns and no court in the land would give you the benefit of self-defence, not now you and Cora have said what you've said to the law.'

Jed didn't deny the charge, but what he did say was, 'He was trying to rape her and then he intended to kill her. She's lived in terror of that man for a long time, as you well know. I'd have thought you were pleased he's where he can't hurt her.'

'Oh, I am pleased. Ecstatic, you might say. But that still doesn't negate the fact that you murdered him. And him getting on a bit and drunk into the bargain, and you a fine fit figure of a man without a mark on you. The police'll just love this, especially as they'll be a bit put out all their handouts have come to a halt. They'd like someone to pin this on – they must be feeling a bit aggrieved. It wouldn't take much to convince them it was no accident, Jed, not when I open their eyes. He was a bit bashed about, and besides that blow that killed him there'll be other bruises, no doubt. And if they start to snoop it wouldn't take the brain of Britain to know that trough was moved, not once they investigate. Like a dog with a bone, they'll be. A nice juicy bone.'

He watched as Jed squared his shoulders. 'I'll take my chance. My word against yours.'

'And you're prepared for Cora to have to take her chance too?'

Jed breathed in deeply. 'You wouldn't do that. You wouldn't involve Cora.'

Wilfred was well aware that the success of his plan depended on Jed believing he would do exactly that, and now he lied with a level voice and steady eyes. 'Oh, aye, I would. If it meant you keeping your dirty hands off her for good, I would. Besides –' he paused a moment for his words to sink in – 'your whole defence would be that you were protecting her. How could you put that forward unless she was there at the time of the assault? Like it or not she'd be dragged into it up to her eyes. And Cora being Cora, she wouldn't see you go down for murder without saying her bit anyway. You know what she's like. There's no half-measures with her where she loves.'

'So knowing that, that she loves me, why do you want to do this to her if you care anything at all about her? Why not just keep quiet?'

'*If* I care about her?' Wilfred's natural self had broken through, his control faltering for a moment. Then he said, his voice soft again, 'I love her in a way you could never achieve, not if you lived a hundred years. We're two of a kind, me and Cora, from the same background, the same streets. I've known her since I was born and I'm blowed if I'm going to let you take her from me. I can make her happy, I know it, and she already loves me. Maybe not in the way she loves you but that sort of love doesn't last, the romantic kind.'

'And you think she'd be with you if I was out of the way? Is that it? You don't know her very well, after all. If you sold me down the river she'd hate you for ever and a day, even if she wasn't implicated.'

'Which is why, to use your words, if you care anything at all about her you'll disappear and enlist. No goodbyes, no questions. You simply leave a letter for your mam an' da saying that the fact the Germans killed your brothers has been eating away at you and you want to go and do your bit. The alternative is staying here and dragging Cora down with you.'

'You're mad.'

Wilfred smiled. 'On the contrary, I'm as sane as you are.'

'You say you know I killed Farmer Burns?' Even in the shadows Wilfred could see the hate burning in Jed's eyes, and such was the twist in his nature that he found it gratifying. Anything was better than the faintly condescending, matey attitude Jed had displayed since he'd arrived at the farm. 'Then what's to stop me doing the same to you? According to you, I've got nothing to lose, have I?'

'Aye, I've thought of that.' Wilfred nodded, his voice almost conversational now. 'But I don't think you could kill someone in cold blood, Jed. That's the thing. It was in the heat of the moment with Farmer Burns and I don't think you intended him to die anyway. But you need a strong stomach for murder. Course, I'd say the opposite about you if you stay around, you can bank on that, but between us I'd say you haven't got the guts for it. Anyway, there it is. Your choice. Staying and seeing Cora brought down with you, or clearing off and acting the hero. It's up to you.'

'I couldn't leave here without saying goodbye to her. It'd break her heart, damn you. You know that.'

'I know nothing of the sort except you rate yourself pretty highly, but a clean break is for the best. It's the safest thing for her. Less messy. And it's not as if you're betrothed. There's no ring on her finger.'

'I was waiting till her birthday next month, when she's sixteen.'

'Very thoughtful. Stupid, but thoughtful.'

Jed swore, gripping Wilfred by the neck of his shirt as he ground out, 'I ought to bash your face in, you treacherous little swine.'

'Aye, but you won't, will you. No, I thought not.' As Jed let him go Wilfred took a step backwards before turning and walking to the door. And it was from there that he said very softly, 'You won't need to take much, not if you're enlisting and you can lie about your age. You look twenty-one or -two any day. And I'll back up your letter. Say you've been talking about your brothers all the time, wanting to get even, as you see it, with the

Germans. Of course, I never expected you to go and do something so daft as enlisting, not the blue-eyed boy who's always had the world at his feet, but there it is. We never really know anyone else, do we?'

'You must really hate me.'

'You've no idea . . .'

Chapter Thirteen

'Mr and Mrs Croft would like a word with you, Cora.' It was three days after Farmer Burns had died, and when she had seen Jed's parents arrive earlier Cora had assumed they were here to offer their condolences to the widow and had continued working in the dairy. Now she looked in surprise at Mrs Burns, not so much because Jed's parents had asked to see her – no doubt they wanted to express their concern for her in finding the farmer the way she and Jed had, according to their story – but because of the troubled note in the farmer's wife's voice. 'They – well, they have some news you might not be aware of.'

'News?'

'About Jed.'

'He's all right? Nothing's happened?'

'I think it's better they tell you themselves; there's a letter.'

Cora followed Rachel into the main part of the house and on into the parlour where Jed's parents were sitting, a tray holding cups of tea and a plate of teacakes on the low table in front of them. She saw immediately that Jed's mother had been crying and her heart jerked and then pounded at twice its speed.

'Cora, dear.' Mrs Croft had become fond of the girl that Jed had seemed so madly in love with. 'Come and sit by me. Mr Croft and I need to talk to you.'

Cora sat down on the sofa next to Jed's mother, his father being in a chair on the other side of the little table. She looked at Mrs Croft who said gently, 'Cora, we need to know. Has Jed spoken to you about what he intended to do?'

Cora didn't have any idea what Mrs Croft was referring to and it showed on her face.

'About – about enlisting in the army.'

'Jed wants to enlist?' Cora's voice was high. 'I don't believe it. He loves the farm, it's his whole life. He would never seriously consider leaving everything here.'

'I'm afraid that's exactly what he's done.' Jed's father leaned forward, his hands on his knees and his face grim. 'We can't understand it either but there's no doubt he's been thinking about it for a while. Wilfred's confirmed he's been talking about fighting the Germans for what they did to his brothers. Look, read this. He left a letter.'

'Left? You mean he's gone?'

'Yesterday, dear.' Mrs Croft was dabbing her eyes again. 'We were going to come to offer any help that's needed to Mrs Burns but then when we came down to breakfast we found this, and – well, I'm afraid I was in no fit state to visit anyone. It's very upsetting coming out of the blue. At least, it's out of the blue to us, and it appears to be to you too?'

Cora nodded numbly, taking the letter Mr Croft handed her. It was short and to the point.

Dear Mam and Da,

I'm sorry because I know this is not what you want but I have to do it. I'm going to enlist. Please don't try and stop me because my mind is made up and nothing will change that. Please try to understand and to forgive me for springing this on you but I feel it's for the best to slip away without long drawn out goodbyes. I'll write as soon as I know what's what, I promise. Cora knows nothing about this so I would be grateful if you would tell her yourselves. I know it will be a shock for you all but sometimes you just have to do something no matter how wrong it seems to everyone else. Just remember I love you very much.

Jed

'No.' It was a whisper. 'He wouldn't do this. Something's wrong.' She looked at Mrs Croft. 'He wouldn't go without saying goodbye.'

'I'm afraid he has, lass.' Mr Croft cleared his throat. 'It's a rum do, I agree with you, and right out of character for our Jed, but he's gone, no doubt about that.' His wife had tears trickling down her face and now he said, 'Come on, love. What's done's done. He'll come home again when the war is over, don't you fear. The Lord wouldn't take all three of 'em.'

But he didn't know that. Cora stared at him, her eyes dry, the shock too great for the relief of tears. 'I can't believe it,' she whispered. *He'd left her without even saying goodbye.*

'I know, lass, I'm the same.' Mrs Croft wiped her eyes and then blew her nose. 'It's Hitler, that's who I blame. Wrecking ordinary folks' lives just because he's power mad. I wish Jed had spoken to us about how he was feeling but he never gave an inkling. He mourned for his brothers, of course, but to join up? Never would I have thought it. He was so happy working on the farm and fair mad about you, and for him not even to tell you—' She stopped abruptly, realizing it was less than tactful in the circumstances. 'Well, I mean . . .' she finished lamely.

Jed's parents stayed another minute or so but everyone was struggling to make conversation. It was beyond Cora to say anything. She sat by Jed's mother, the pain of Jed's leaving freezing her body into numbness and clamping down on her emotions. She walked out with Rachel and Mr and Mrs Croft, standing by their horse and trap as goodbyes were said and trying to act normally while all the time she felt as though she was screaming inside now the shock was beginning to fade.

Rachel was well aware of how Cora was feeling; her voice was gentle as they watched the horse and trap disappear. 'You had no idea he was considering joining up?'

'None.' In the warm morning sunshine Cora shivered.

It was a beautiful day for the end of April and that in itself seemed wrong. It should be dark and cloudy and raining and cold – Jed was gone and she might never see him again. It seemed incredible, impossible, like a living nightmare. 'None at all.'

'That seems odd to me.' Rachel took her arm, leading Cora back into the farm kitchen where she sat her down at the table and made her a cup of strong, sweet tea. The girl was in shock, her face as white as lint and her eyes huge and strained. Only when Cora had finished every drop did Rachel say, 'Cora, I know this might seem a platitude in the circumstances when you're so upset but I have no doubt whatsoever that Jed loves you. I've never seen anyone look at someone the way he looks at you. I don't understand why he's done what he's done but I do know it's not because he's feeling any different about you. You must believe that. It's important.'

'I want to.' Cora's voice was a croak.

'I know, dear, I know.' Rachel patted her hand. She had umpteen things to do, not least taking refreshments to the four Italian POWs who had been brought to the farm that morning by the soldier assigned to guard them. They had seemed a jovial bunch, their young keeper laughing and joking with the POWs and telling Rachel in an aside that this was a cushy job all told. The Italians had assured Rachel that they all had farming backgrounds and indeed had had no trouble in harnessing the two shire horses and getting them out to the fields that needed ploughing. She had stood and watched them for a while in spite of all the work she had to do, faintly anxious that they wouldn't know what they were doing, but the beautifully straight furrows convinced her otherwise. She had walked back to the house smiling to herself, thinking how Bernard would have hated them handling his precious horses and even just setting foot on the farm. It had made their presence all the sweeter. It was Bernard's funeral the following day, and the soldier had assured her that she and Cora could leave the farm for a few hours, safe in the knowledge that all would carry on as normal.

'How could he just up and leave like this, Mrs Burns?' Cora swallowed hard before she stood up, also aware of the workload they had to get through. They both knew it was a rhetorical question and Rachel made no attempt to answer as they walked along to the dairy. Today was butter-making day, always hard work, and she needed to get Cora churning the cream in the end-over-end churn before she saw to the POWs.

Once she was alone, Cora allowed the tears to come although she didn't falter in churning the cream. It would be at least two hours before it was done and her arm always felt as though it was falling off long before she had finished, even though she and Mrs Burns took turns. But today she was hardly aware of what she was doing. Jed's going must be because of Farmer Burns – that was the only thing she could think of. He had said he was glad the farmer was dead and that was probably true, but now he'd had time to think about what he had done was his guilty conscience too much to bear? Was that why he had gone off to war and put himself in the way of goodness knows what? And she was tied up in his guilt, the cause of it. Had that made him feel differently about her, about the prospect of a life with her? It must have done. There was no other reason for him to have chosen to leave her, because the excuse he had made to his parents was rubbish. He was sad about his brothers – who wouldn't be – but he'd told her many times that he saw himself as his parents' solace; that he would hate to go to war; that his place was working on the land and providing towards the war effort in that way. And now he had enlisted; he had gone away to fight and if he was killed it would be her fault. She couldn't bear it, she couldn't. She would go mad.

All day she worked like a Trojan, refusing to eat at lunchtime despite Rachel's repeated requests and looking – as Rachel whispered to Maria when the other girls came home from school – like a walking corpse.

Maria found Cora cleaning out the fires in the bedrooms; a job, Rachel told Maria, she'd told Cora that Maud could do once she was back from school but which Cora had insisted needed to be done immediately so new fires could be lit and the rooms warming for bedtime. The April days were mild and sunny but the nights were still cold. The day after Farmer Burns had died, Rachel had told the five girls to collect their things from the attics because they would be moving into the main house with her. Between them they had cleaned the two bedrooms on the top floor and thoroughly aired them through, whereupon Maria and Cora had taken up residence in one, and Maud, Anna and Susan in the other. Both rooms were large, airy and comfortable and the height of luxury after the cramped attic, and each had held a double bed, a chest of drawers, a wardrobe and two easy chairs; they had taken the chairs out of Maud, Anna and Susan's room and put a single bed in their place in which Maud slept.

When Maria walked into the room she shared with Cora, Cora sat back on her heels and looked up at her sister. 'Mrs Burns has told you, hasn't she? About Jed enlisting?'

Maria nodded.

'It's because of me.'

'You?'

'He's gone to fight because of me.'

'Of course he hasn't.' Maria knelt down at the side of her. 'It's because of his brothers, Cora. What the Germans did to them. Mrs Burns said there was a letter.'

'It's not because of his brothers, Maria. Something happened.'

Cora's voice sounded tired and so unlike her that Maria's heart jumped in her chest. Something was wrong, even more wrong than Jed going off to war without telling her sister. Her voice low, she whispered, 'What do you mean?'

'Shut the door. You mustn't repeat to anyone what I tell you.'

Once she was back at Cora's side she sat down beside her on the clippy rug in front of the small fireplace and put her hand on Cora's. 'What is it?'

'Farmer Burns – he didn't fall and bang his head on the trough. Jed – Jed hit him with a hoe because Farmer Burns was attacking me. He was going to force himself on me and then kill me. He told me so. Put me in the river.'

Maria stared at her, wide-eyed. 'Oh, Cora.'

'Jed didn't mean to kill him, in fact we didn't even know he was that badly injured at first. He was drunk you see, Farmer Burns I mean. We – we went off to tell Jed's mam an' da what had happened but because we'd left him bleeding we changed our minds and came back to make sure he was all right. That's when – when we found him. And so we made it look like an accident. And it was, it was an accident really.'

'Of course it was.' Maria took both Cora's hands, her own eyes swimming with tears although Cora's now were dry. 'And he was a horrible man, evil, wicked.'

'But it's because of that, what – what he did, that Jed's gone. He said he was all right about it at first but he must have had second thoughts and started to feel bad, bad enough that he couldn't stay or even tell me he was going himself. Everything was fine before that and he would never have enlisted, Maria. Never. And now he's in the army and could be sent anywhere and if he dies—'

'He won't, he won't die, Cora.'

'He must hate me now. I'm the reason he's had to leave the farm and everything he loves.'

'Don't be daft, lass. Jed loves you. He'll always love you.'

'Then why didn't he at least come and say goodbye? If he still loved me he would have done that, wouldn't he? He blames me and he's right. It's all my fault.'

'If it's anybody's fault it's Farmer Burns's and to my mind he got what he deserved.'

'Jed said that, about it being Farmer Burns's fault and not mine.'

'There you are then.'

'But I don't think he can be thinking like that now. Actions speak louder than words, Maria.'

The two girls stared at each other, pain and desperation in one face and deep pity in the other.

'He'll come back, Cora. I know he will. Once the war's over. And then this will just be a bad memory. You two love each other too much not to be together.'

'He wouldn't have left like this unless it was over between us. I pray he'll come home after the war. I'll go mad if anything happens to him because of me, but I don't think there's a future for us now, not as far as he thinks. I'd – I'd just be a reminder of something he wants to forget.'

For the life of her Maria didn't know what to say. She loved her sister, perhaps more than anyone else in the world, but she didn't know how to help her. For the first time since she had found out that her mother had abandoned them all and run off with some man or other, she found her feelings to be on a par with Cora's where their mother was concerned and hated her for not visiting them or writing or just being at home where she should be. Cora needed their mam, she thought now. Their mam would have known what to say and how to comfort her. That's what mothers did, proper mothers.

Cora began to lay the fire and tidy the small hearth and Maria stood up. Once Cora joined her they left the room together and when Maria took her sister's ash-smeared hand as they walked downstairs, Cora squeezed her fingers in silent thanks for Maria's sympathy. Just before they joined the others, she said quietly, 'You can never say a word about this, Maria. You know that, don't you?'

'Of course, but I'm glad you told me. We'll get through this together, lass. We always have, haven't we? And I know it's not much comfort in the circumstances with Jed gone and everything, but you've always got me and always will have.'

Cora looked at her sister, her eyes full of sadness and her cheeks without colour, and forced a smile. 'It means more than you'll ever know,' she said softly. 'I love you, hinny.'

'And I love you.'

Later that night as she lay awake in the darkness with Maria breathing steadily beside her, Cora found herself thinking not of Jed, nor of Farmer Burns, but of her mother. How could you hate someone and love them at the same time? she asked herself bitterly. She didn't want to love her mother but she did, and she wanted to hate her but she couldn't do it wholeheartedly no matter how she tried. And she had tried over the last months, she really had. But right at this moment, in spite of all her mam had done, she wanted her. She felt like a little bairn again, small and all at sea, and she wanted her mam, it was as simple as that.

Scalding tears slid down her cheeks but now she didn't know if she was crying for Jed or her mam; perhaps both, she thought wearily, her head thudding with pain. Which just showed how stupid she was because she couldn't have either one. Maria had said she would always have her and that they would get through this together, and she was thankful for her sister, she really was, but she was frightened. Frightened she would go mad with how she was feeling, with the terror that Jed might be injured and badly hurt or worse, and all because he had stepped in and saved her from Farmer Burns. It wasn't fair, none of it was fair. Why hadn't Farmer Burns got himself killed some other way; why had Jed gone without coming to see her one last time, and why did her mother love some man called Ken more than her, than them all?

She lay still so as not to wake Maria, a stiffness in her muscles that had no connection with the exhaustion assailing her body and mind, and wondered how she was going to get through the next day and the ones after it.

Many miles away, in a dismal little room in a dismal house in a dismal street in Newcastle, Nancy Stubbs was asking herself the same question. She could hear Ken and his pals in the kitchen of the two-up two-down terrace and knew they were playing cards and drinking as they did most nights into the early hours. When she and Ken had arrived in Newcastle the morning after they'd fled from Sunderland, he had brought her straight to this same house close to the docks at the back of the saw mills. The North Eastern Railway ran almost at the bottom of the yard; there was a goods station and an oil works and a timber yard and other industry all around, and when she had protested that it was a prime target for Hitler's bombs Ken had told her shortly that this was where they were staying and that was that. His two pals rented the house and they had let her and Ken have the front room which had been filthy when they had first moved in. She had scrubbed it from top to bottom; ripped off the old bug-infested wallpaper and fumigated the walls, ceiling and floorboards; and thrown out the crumbling table and chairs that were full of woodworm holes. Apparently Ken's pals had used the front room for their gambling nights – which seemed to be every night as far as Nancy could tell – and these now took place in the kitchen, which she had also had to clean with bleach and disinfectant before she could cook any meals. She'd complained to Ken that his friends lived like pigs but he'd just laughed at her. The two bedrooms upstairs she'd never set foot in; she dreaded to think what they were like.

They had furnished the front room with a double bed and new bedding, two second-hand easy chairs and an old wardrobe, and she had bought a small thick rug for in front of the little fireplace, either side of which the chairs stood. She had also had a lock fitted to the door, something that had caused a huge row between herself and Ken when he'd said his pals would be offended, assuming he didn't trust them. She'd retorted that she was quite happy to take the blame and it wasn't that she didn't trust them, she merely wanted to be sure of her privacy and he could tell them so.

She turned over in the bed, as wide awake as when she had got into it an hour ago. Of course what she'd said to Ken wasn't true. She didn't trust Nat or Terence, and she didn't like them either. Nat in particular had a way of looking at her that always riled her, and in subtle little ways he had let her know that he thought she was no better than a common tart for leaving her husband and living with Ken. It didn't seem to matter that she contributed to the household with her wages for working in the local munitions factory – he still made her feel as though she was a kept woman at best, a whore at worse.

She sat up and plumped her pillow before lying down once more. All the women she worked with said they were asleep the minute their heads touched the pillow; twelve-hour days making piston rings for aircraft saw to that. She didn't mind the work except when bits of hot steel came flying out of the machine and stuck in your eyes, necessitating a trip to first aid where the factory nurse would put drops in and get the fragments of steel out with a magnet. Everyone complained about the unattractive uniform too

– navy blue overalls and hats with a snood to stop the operator's hair getting caught in the machines – but again, it didn't bother her. The pay of three pounds a week was more than twice what she had earned in the shipping office, after all, and the women she worked with were a friendly bunch on the whole. No, it wasn't the munitions factory that kept her awake at night, it was everything else in her life.

She bit down hard on her bottom lip, determined not to cry. She cried herself to sleep most nights, alone in the double bed while Ken drank and gambled with his cronies. Nat and Terence had got Ken set on at the docks with them as soon as they had arrived in Newcastle, and there was a group of men, the same lot who were in the kitchen playing cards at the moment, who were involved in the sort of black-market activities Ken had dabbled with in Sunderland.

She couldn't remember when she had first admitted to herself that she had made the biggest mistake of her life in leaving Gregory, along with her home and everything that was familiar. Perhaps it had been the night she had smelt cheap perfume on Ken's clothes when he had rolled in at midnight after supposedly doing a 'bit of business' with Nat and Terence at the docks, or yet again when he had slapped her round the face for objecting to him not coming home at all one night. Then there was the time he had thrown his dinner at her, plate and all. She only knew, when she had finally accepted that she had given everything up for a man who wasn't worthy to lick Gregory's boots, that it was far, far too late to do anything about it. She had lost her husband, her family and her home, but worse than that she had lost herself. She wasn't the same person any more and it frightened her. The old Nancy would have given back as good as she got but Ken had beaten her down, here, in her head, where it mattered.

She sat up again, reaching for the glass of water on the bedside table, and as she did so a guffaw of laughter reached her from the kitchen along with the sound of breaking glass. They were getting blind drunk in there, she told herself angrily, and in the morning the kitchen would be a mess of empty beer bottles and bottles of whisky, food, broken glass and debris. It was the same most mornings and if she didn't clear it up before she went to work it would still be in the same state when she came home at night. She was sick of it, she was so sick of it, but what could she do? She had confided in one of the girls at work a little while ago, a woman about her own age called Myra, and Myra had listened askance and then told her to walk out on Ken. But how could she? She had nowhere to go. And in spite of everything she kept hoping that Ken would change back into the old Ken, the one she had loved and adored. To leave him would be the final proof that she had made a terrible mess of her life, that she was a failure in every regard. She *had* to make it work with him.

The men in the kitchen began to sing a particularly foul dockside ditty at the tops of their voices, one so filthy it would make a sailor blush. For the first time in months,

Nancy felt her temper rise, sweeping away the misery and apathy she existed in from day to day. They knew she could hear every word; this was yet another way of Nat showing her how little he respected her. And this was her home too – she paid her bit towards the rent same as the three men and did more than her fair share, cooking the meals and cleaning and so on because those three wouldn't lift a finger. Oh, no, they deemed it far beneath them to so much as wash a cup and saucer. What was Ken doing letting this go on? She had long since stopped hoping he would ever want to marry her if she started divorce proceedings, but this, this was beyond the pale.

She slid out of bed and pulled on her dressing gown, jerking the belt tightly round her waist, her face blazing and her full mouth set tight. The neighbours either side had already complained umpteen times about the goings-on and she knew she had got a name for herself in living with three men, the more so because she was as sure as she could be that Nat had let it be known that she and Ken weren't married.

When she flung open the kitchen door she saw there were three other men besides Ken, Nat and Terence sitting round the table with cards in their hands. The place was a mess of beer bottles, whisky bottles and glasses, plates of chitterlings and other food mixed in with spills and debris. A beer bottle was lying smashed on the floor, fragments of glass swimming in a pool of liquid no one had even bothered to attempt to mop up.

Nancy ignored the other men, walking across to Ken

who was slumped in his chair, cards in one hand and a glass of whisky in the other. 'Isn't it time you called it a day? It's gone midnight and you told me you've got to be at the docks for six in the morning.'

The singing had stopped at her entrance, and now Nat said, his voice thick and slurred, 'Pushy with it, isn't she? Never thought I'd see the day when you put up with being henpecked, Ken.'

Ken sat up straighter, the silly smile that had been on his face disappearing. 'Get back to bed. *Now.*'

She should have left it there. For ever afterwards, when she thought of the events of that terrible night, she knew she should have turned on her heel and gone back to the room and locked the door. Instead the resurgence of the old Nancy caused her to stand her ground and say, 'Are you coming with me?'

'Oh, I get it.' Nat sniggered. 'She wants a bit, Ken. She's a brazen one, isn't she, treating you like a stallion at stud?' He grinned at the others. 'Her old man was no good in bed but then our Ken came along. Can't get enough of it, can you, Nancy, eh?'

'Shut up.' Nancy glared at him.

'Don't tell me to shut up in my own house.' Nat stood up, moving so that he was between Nancy and the door. 'You need to learn some manners, you do. You women think you're everything these days since the war started. Taking men's jobs right, left and centre in the factories and on the buses and what have you, even in the army and the air force. Whores most of 'em are, that's the truth of it, like you, doing the dirty on your man and running off and leaving him and your bairns.'

The atmosphere in the kitchen had changed. Nancy felt a trickle of fear run down her spine and she told herself she mustn't show she was frightened. Ken was still sitting in his chair, and now she said, 'Are you going to let him speak to me like that?'

Ken looked at her. Nancy had properly shown him up in front of his mates coming into the kitchen and ordering him about as though she owned him. Made him a laughing stock. And it wasn't the first time she'd presumed to try and tell him what to do. She was a lead weight round his neck, damn her, and he rued the day he'd taken up with her. He shrugged indifferently, the look on his face and the action speaking volumes to the men watching them.

Nat smiled. From the first time Nancy had entered the house she had grated on him, with her hoity-toity air and uppity ways. She'd made no secret of the fact that she considered it all beneath her and he'd longed to take her down a peg or two, but she was Ken's bit on the side and so he'd stayed his hand, biding his time. He was well aware Ken had got fed up with her, in fact he'd been amazed when Ken had arrived with a woman in tow – it wasn't his style – but Nancy had clung on and lasted far longer than he'd expected. But it seemed like tonight was the night he could scratch this particular itch. He looked straight at Ken.

'You got any objection if me and the lads teach her a few manners?'

Ken knew what Nat was asking. Years ago he'd watched a rape down at the dockside in Sunderland's East End; a couple of blokes had got a woman drunk and then had her on the cobbles of the pub's back yard. He had been as hard as a rock and found it difficult to walk home. Now he felt a shaft of excitement shoot through him. Nancy had brought this on herself, he told himself as he shrugged again – what decent woman would come into a room in her nightclothes knowing that several men were three sheets to the wind? It was asking for trouble. And maybe that's what she secretly wanted. She liked her sex, she always had.

'Be my guest,' he drawled.

'*Ken*?' She moved behind his chair, unable to believe he could mean it, and then, as a couple of the men laughed, kicking back their chairs as they stood up, her eyes shot to the back door that led into the yard.

She nearly made it before they were on her, and as she gave a despairing scream she heard Nat say, 'Shut her up,' and an arm seized her round her middle from behind as a hand clamped across her mouth. As she was turned round in the man's grip her eyes registered three images. Nat was sweeping everything on the table on to the floor, bottles and all. Two of the men were already obscenely unbuttoned and advancing towards her, and a third, she thought it was Terence, was saying, 'Gag her, gag her,' as he held out a filthy-looking piece of rag. Then blind, primitive panic had her struggling and kicking, but the more she fought the more she realized how helpless she was against iron arms and hands that bore her down onto the table.

The gag was stuffed into her mouth and her clothes ripped away and she heard them whoop and laugh at her nakedness. Her body was stretched out on the table while someone with hands like steel held her wrists above her head and others parted her legs and pushed down on her ankles. Their hands were on her breasts and all over her body, hard and pinching and kneading her soft flesh, obscene words and drunken laughter adding to her terror. She heard Nat say, 'Me first, me first, you'll all get your turn,' and then pain stabbed through her as he brutally forced himself into her, his stinking breath on her face as he called her vile names and bit at her lips against the gag. No sooner had he shuddered and expended himself than the next one entered her, laughing hysterically as the others urged him on with ribald obscenities.

She lost consciousness at some point, only to come round in the midst of more violation and defilement before once more the blackness overcame her. As she descended into it she knew she was going to die and she was glad . . .

She awoke in her own bed, the light through the thin curtains telling her it was morning. For a second she wondered why she was hurting so badly and then she remembered, trying to sit up as she groaned and whimpered. She was naked and surrounded by the smell and stickiness of them, her limbs so stiff and aching that she moaned and cried out as she flung back the covers and sat on the side of the bed, her head swimming.

They had raped her, on and on and on and Ken – Ken had had his turn. Again she moaned, like an animal, and it was the sound of her own voice that caused her to straighten and attempt to stand up.

She stood trembling and nauseous, looking down at herself. Blood and semen were caked on her legs, along with bruises and bite marks on her breasts and stomach. The remains of her nightclothes were lying on the floor next to the bed where they had been thrown. Had it been Ken who had carried her in here when they'd finished with her? It must have been. Had he calmly lain down and gone to sleep before getting up for work later?

She looked at the alarm clock next to the bed. It was seven o'clock. That meant she was alone in the house because the three men had been on an early shift at the docks.

She staggered to the wardrobe and took out her spare nightie, wincing as she pulled it over her head. She knew what she was going to do but first she had to wash the smell of them away. When she threw herself into the Tyne she wanted nothing of them on her.

She heated kettle after kettle of water on the range, pouring it into the tin bath until it was full to overflowing and almost scalding hot. When she lowered herself into it, scrubbing brush in hand, the heat almost overcame her but she welcomed it. She scrubbed herself for a long time and the water changed colour until it was red and quite cold before she stood up and dried herself.

Someone had brushed the debris from the night before into one corner of the kitchen and the table now held a few glasses and bottles but she didn't look at this. Instead she walked back into the front room and dressed herself before putting on her hat and coat and shoes. She looked at herself in the mirror on the inside of one of the wardrobe doors. Even clothed she looked bashed about, she thought dispassionately, a numbness having taken over her mind. Her lips were swollen and cut, one eye was almost closed and a great bruise stained her forehead. But it didn't matter. It wouldn't stop her doing what she needed to do. But first . . .

She carefully slid her fingers to the back of the stout mahogany wardrobe until she felt the package Ken had wedged in there between the wall and the wood. Drawing it out, she held it in her hand for a moment. Ken had called her stupid more than once lately, but she wasn't so stupid that she didn't know where he had his hoard of money hidden. He thought he was so clever, hiding it from her, but she'd known where his money was from almost the first day he'd secreted it there. She had never investigated to find out how much there was – it was his money and his business – but she had been disappointed he hadn't trusted her enough to be open about it. How strange, she thought now, that she had been bothered about something as trivial as that.

She walked over to the bed and emptied the contents of the parcel onto it, notes fluttering out. Even in the midst of the strange deadness in her senses her eyes widened. She knew Ken had a thing about banks and building societies; he didn't trust them, saying they were part of the establishment and as such no friend of the working man. Privately she'd always thought that the reason Ken was wary of depositing any cash he had into such institutions was because he thought they might ask awkward questions, like how did a docker manage to acquire and continue to acquire wealth beyond his means? But it suited her now that he had preferred to hide his money away, oh, yes. And there was a small fortune here, more than she could have imagined.

Fetching the box of matches from the small mantelpiece over the black-leaded fireplace which had the embers of yesterday's fire still glowing faintly in the grate, she lit a few of the notes, piling more on top once they were well alight and watching as the bedclothes began to smoulder and then burst into flames. Smoke was billowing out into the hallway when she left the room but she didn't hurry, walking through to the kitchen and fetching out the old rusty tin of paraffin that had been stored in one of the cupboards ever since she had come to live at the house. She had a little difficulty in unscrewing the lid but once it was off she sprinkled the paraffin over everything until the tin was empty. Throwing it on the floor, she lit the first match and then jumped back as the flames instantly took hold. She stood for a moment more and then opened the back door into the yard, shutting it carefully behind her and walking across the slabs to the gate into the back lane.

The Tyne with its deep black depths of fast-flowing water was beckoning . . .

PART FOUR

Hell Has Many Forms

1944

Chapter Fourteen

The morning was soft, bright yet ethereal, but the sun was already warming the air and Jed knew by midday it would be very pleasant. He had never given any thought to Italy, or to any other countries apart from Britain come to that, until he had been sent overseas not long before Italy completed her military about-face by declaring war on Germany in October the previous year. Germany had been her ally until little more than five weeks before this, but when the Italians had surrendered the wave of atrocities and looting that the Germans had engaged in had shocked new recruits like him. The old hands had been far more philosophical about the reign of terror by the Nazis.

Jed and his unit had been part of the Allied force trying to inch its way up the boot of Italy – 'like a bug on one leg' as Winston Churchill had put it – and they had run into stiff resistance north of the Volturno river. The Nazis had transformed the lovely Benedictine monastery at Monte Cassino into an almost impenetrable fortress, and at the time Jed had feared that every single British soldier would be wiped out. The Apennines made ideal shelter for Nazi machine-gun nests; there were few roads and the land was marshy. Fog had hampered Allied planes and winter was around the corner. That had probably been his lowest point since he'd joined up.

He stretched and his stiff limbs protested at the movement. He and several of his comrades had spent the night sleeping on the covered verandah of an Italian farmhouse, and although the long, low, stone building was beautiful on the outside it offered nothing in the way of luxuries. Not that they expected any. The area was full of crumbled ruins of buildings, and although it had become clear that Germany would lose the war, the Nazis were an enemy with whom you took tactical liberties at your peril. The German army was tenacious, ruthless, frugal and well led, and counter-attacked whenever the opportunity presented itself.

The area bristled with Italian partisans who, although mostly an undisciplined rabble, were brave and fought well. Many of them were clothed in rags without boots and were armed with antiquated Italian and Turkish weapons. They had passed one such column on the march the day before, and Jed had silently reflected that it was one of the most heterogeneous collections he'd ever seen or was likely to see. There had been mules, donkeys and horses; old men, young men and girls; and every conceivable garment from umbrellas to wooden shoes. The convoy had been singing and smoking, shouting and laughing in a fantastic moving caravan of humanity, and Jed had found himself wondering what they thought of him and his comrades. He and the others were making their way back to camp, having got separated from the rest of their patrol in an ambush two days ago. The patrol hadn't realized the village they'd been approaching was Nazi-held and had been hopelessly outnumbered. He and a few other men had escaped via the river which had been about two hundred yards wide with a very strong current. They'd been swept miles downstream but had finally managed to wade out in thick mud which had come to halfway up their calves, exhausted, soaked and disorientated.

The partisans had fed them and directed them to the farmhouse – a 'safe' house – for the night as well as giving them instructions on how to get back to their camp safely. Their leader had told Jed his convoy had passed the army camp some time before where they had been given medical supplies and food, along with several of their number who were sick and wounded being treated by the British MO.

'We help each other, si?' the rugged, bearded brute of a man had said cheerfully. 'We kill Germans. Filthy pigs.' And he'd spat on the ground.

Jed had been only too happy to agree.

He stood up, stepping over the rest of the men who were still asleep, and walked to the edge of the verandah where he stood looking out into the still morning. When they had arrived at the farmhouse the night before, they had found an elderly man and his wife working, the woman washing cans and the man carefully mending a cracked pipe stem with thin string. They looked an old couple, bent and grey-haired, but probably neither of them had yet reached sixty years of age because their youngest child, a boy of no more than ten or eleven, had been asleep on a bed in an alcove of the one main downstairs room of the farmhouse. The couple couldn't speak a word of English but when he had mentioned the name of the partisan leader as the man had told him to do, they had been all smiles and nods, feeding them bread and cheese washed down with red wine.

Jed breathed deeply of the morning air. The smell wasn't the same as England – it was more Mediterranean and carried a hint of olive groves and sun – but here, away from the camp and standing in this Italian farm, he missed home more. And then he caught the thought, mentally chiding himself – who was he kidding? It was Cora he missed. Cora. He closed his eyes. He rarely let himself think of her – it was too weakening, too painful, and most of the time it was enough to get through each day, hour by hour, minute by minute, never knowing if any moment could be his last. He had lost so many of his companions, so many friends. James Casey, who'd joined up the same day he had – a German Panzer had done for him. Dead and wounded from both sides were spread all around the battlefield and there was barely enough left of James to bury. But bury him they had, although there had been no ceremony, no ritual about it. James's death had hit him the hardest, not only because he had been the first of their group to die but because he had genuinely liked him. James had talked about his home, his family, his dog, things that mattered, and few soldiers, including him, did that.

Stop thinking. It was something he told himself all the time. He could get through each day if he didn't think, and in that regard being in the army was ideal. He just had to obey orders and get on with the business in hand, that of driving the Nazis out of Italy. Sounded simple when you put it like that. He smiled as he opened his eyes and then froze. Several German soldiers were standing no more than twenty yards away and they had their guns trained on the verandah.

It was instinct, not bravery and certainly not common sense, to reach for his gun, and as he did so he heard the shots a millisecond before they slammed into his body, catapulting him backwards. There was more shooting, noise, shouts, screams going on above him as he lay on the verandah but he must have banged his head because they were vague, as though through a thick fog, and then there was nothing at all.

He came to as he was carried into an advanced dressing station by two German stretcher-bearers where he was placed on a metal table. He wanted to speak, to ask after the others, but he felt sick and weak and the blackness was closing in again. This time, however, he didn't lose consciousness completely because he could still hear. There were German voices, one in particular barking orders, but he didn't speak the language so he had no idea of what was being said.

When he felt hands moving over his body he forced his lids open again to see a German surgeon with dispassionate eyes checking him. Realizing he was conscious, the man said coldly, 'You have been shot, yes? And lost a considerable amount of blood. I will do what I can.'

Jed licked his dry lips, his voice a croak as he said, 'The men who were with me?'

'Of them I know nothing.'

As something was placed over his nose and mouth he wanted to struggle, to object, but he had no strength. He was now a helpless prisoner dependent on an enemy doctor and it was a strange feeling. His last vision was of the heavy canvas roof of the bell tent and the surgeon speaking sharply to someone he couldn't see.

He came out of the unpleasant drugged sleep retching and coughing, and continued to vomit on and off for the next couple of days. He was in a bigger tent with several other wounded men but they all appeared to be German. He was in agony from two bullet wounds, one to his chest and one just below his navel, and felt so groggy he wouldn't have cared if he had died then and there. It was only when the nausea began to ease that the will to live kicked in again.

The surgeon or *Stabsarzt* – a surgeon with the rank of major – came to see him and told him he was lucky to be alive. All of his comrades had died on the verandah and he had lost so much blood, the surgeon said, that during the operation he had died twice. 'But back you came.' The *Stabsarzt* eyed him unsmilingly. 'And so I carried on.'

Jed didn't know what to say. After a moment, he mumbled, 'Thank you.'

The surgeon shrugged. 'It is my profession to save life. A patient is a patient, whatever his nationality, yes?'

Jed thought of the stories they'd heard about the Nazi death camps and the grisly experiments German doctors were doing. In spite of the man having undoubtedly saved his life he found he couldn't answer him.

For the next few days he lay in the tent suffering bouts of delirium in which he was sure Cora stood by the bed, crying and asking him why he had left without telling her and saying that she was going to marry Wilfred. Other times it was his mother's tearful, reproachful face he saw, or his father's grim one as he berated him for breaking his mother's heart. He would surface, drenched with sweat and as weak as a kitten, to find himself in the tent with the other men, two of whom died screaming as the time went on. There was no guard outside the tent; the medical staff knew he wasn't capable of escape. He could barely raise a cup to his lips.

He didn't know how long it was before he was moved, but eventually one morning two stretcher-bearers arrived at the side of his bed and unceremoniously carried him outside. After a few minutes he was loaded into the back of a small lorry, still lying down, along with two more wounded soldiers, both Italian. One of the soldiers was out of it and the other couldn't speak a word of English, and the guards ignored his questions as to where they were headed with blank indifference.

It was when the lorry started up and began to move that the pain seared through him, taking his breath away and making him gasp. It didn't get any better as the vehicle trundled along rough tracks and roads, hour after hour. By midday the soldier who had been unconscious had died, and as Jed looked at his body before the driver of the lorry and their guard carried it away – presumably to dump at the side of the road – he knew a sudden spasm of envy as he thought, his worries are all over now. No more pain, no more trying to survive in this hellish world. And why was he trying anyway? he asked himself bitterly. He had nothing to live for, not really.

He closed his eyes against the self-loathing that came when he let himself think of the past. He'd lost Cora through his own stupidity, that was the core of how he felt. Oh, Wilfred had played his part in it all, threatening to involve Cora and shop them both to the law, but he himself had been criminally weak and stupid to let Wilfred blackmail him. If he had known then what he knew now, he would have given Wilfred the hiding of his life and put the fear of God into the little runt.

But he hadn't.

He shifted slightly to ease the pain but it was more his regrets than the physical agony he was enduring. To his shame, he'd done what Wilfred had demanded and skedaddled. Admittedly to save Cora – oh, aye, he was clear about that – but he had regretted it the minute he'd enlisted. He wasn't a soldier, damn it, he was a farmer. All he'd ever wanted was to work the land he loved and live a peaceful life with Cora. That would have sufficed for him, heaven on earth. Wilfred had said that killing in cold blood was beyond him, Jed thought bitterly, but it wouldn't be now. To safeguard Cora and the life they should have had together, he could kill in cold blood now. But it was too late. He'd left, abandoned her, and she must hate him.

As the lorry started up again, he steeled himself to stand the pain of the journey. The remaining Italian said something to him he didn't understand, and then pointed to where his friend had lain and shook his head.

Jed nodded. 'I'm sorry,' he said awkwardly, hoping his tone would convey his sympathy. The Italian was young, probably no more than twenty, and he must have been good-looking before something, probably a German bomb or grenade, had mutilated half his face, taking most of his nose and upper lip and gashing his cheeks to ribbons so as they had healed he looked like an African tribal warrior.

The Italian pointed to himself. 'Leonardo.'

Jed nodded. 'Jed.' He reached out his hand and as Leonardo shook it he grinned, showing the remains of his broken teeth.

The guard who was sitting in the back of the lorry with them stared impassively. He was young too, fresh-faced and blue-eyed, and for a moment Jed thought how incongruous it all was – three lads of roughly the same age who didn't know each other from Adam, two of whom would kill the third – and he them – should the circumstances dictate. But that was the absurdity of war, he reflected wearily. And just months ago Leonardo would have been fighting on the Germans' side, which showed just how crazy it all was. Millions of men, women and children were merely pawns in a kind of horrific chess game that a few at the top of the governments of the world were playing.

He shut his eyes, wanting nothing more than to drift into oblivion which was of course impossible in the bumpy, jolting truck. Mid-morning, the guard had stopped the lorry to pin the door back as they'd been almost suffocating in the back of the vehicle, but now it was very dusty, causing him to sneeze and cough which was agony with his wounds.

They stopped a couple of times before nightfall which was spent in a small deserted building in the remains of what had been a German camp. Both the driver of the truck and their guard seemed agitated, and Jed and Leonardo got the impression that the men hadn't expected the camp to be deserted. It bore credence to what Jed had heard before he was captured, that it wasn't just his unit that was involved in fighting back the Germans in Italy, but that the Allies were launching a new assault on Cassino. Their sergeant, a gruff, plain-speaking Yorkshireman, had told them that by the end of April the Nazis would be on the run or he'd eat his hat. Not that that helped him much now, Jed thought, as he tried to sleep on the hard floor. And he was a little worried about what their guard might take it into his head to do to them if the man thought the Germans were retreating. It would be far easier for him and the driver to work their way out of Italy without dragging along two injured POWs.

The journey resumed at daybreak after the guard gave them a meagre breakfast of what looked and tasted like dog biscuits and water. The only consolation was that the two Germans ate the same food.

The hours merged as the day bumped on and Jed knew he was suffering from the delirium again because Cora was back, whispering that there was work to do on the farm and when was he coming home? His brothers came briefly too, telling him that he had been a fool to join up and he hadn't got the sense he was born with. He knew they were his brothers from their voices and what they said; their faces had been blown away and were red, gaping masses of blood and bone. He was glad when they left him.

He was barely aware of anything at all when he and Leonardo were loaded into a cattle truck at a railway siding, but when he came to himself as evening fell, he found himself crammed into the truck with other POWs, some of whom were British. He had been placed in a corner, and as he managed to struggle into a sitting position the man next to him said, 'All right, mate?' in a broad Scottish accent. 'Thought you were a goner there for a time.'

Jed could have cried to hear a British voice again.

Instead he nodded, his voice weak as he said, 'Where are we?'

'Your guess is as good as mine but I've a pretty good idea of where we'll finish up. I think this is the route the Nazis use to transport "enemies of the Reich" to their damn concentration camps,' his new friend said grimly. 'I'm Jock by the way.'

Jed looked round him. There was one window in the cattle truck which was a twelve-inch-square gap with barbed wire stretched across it, and no other ventilation or light. A bucket in the opposite corner to him was obviously their toilet, and a soldier was sitting on it straining and groaning.

Jock followed his gaze. 'Dysentery,' he said shortly. 'A number of the lads have it.'

'They can't keep us in here, can they?'

'Oh, aye, they can, laddie, and believe me this might be stinking and filthy but it's a damn sight better than the trucks they transport the Jews in. Them poor blighters can't sit or lie down they're packed in so tight, and they die standing. Imagine travelling to certain death with a corpse either side of you.'

Jed stared at him in horror. 'But the Geneva Convention?'

Jock shook his head. 'The Nazis don't regard them as people, just vermin, so what's the Geneva Convention got to do with it? We thought we'd had it bad in the camp we've been held in for the last months, but it's nothing compared to what them devils do to the Jews, even the little kiddies.'

'I had heard stories but you never know how much is propaganda, do you.'

'Whatever stories you've heard won't be as bad as the truth, laddie. Take it from me.'

The soldier who had been using the bucket finished, pulling up his trousers over a backside caked with diarrhoea. The smell in the cattle truck was overpowering and rancid, and no sooner had one man used the bucket than another took his place. Jed prayed he didn't catch dysentery, it would finish him off, but as it appeared that most of the lads were suffering with it he didn't hold out much hope.

After a few hours the train stopped and the door to the truck was slid open revealing several armed German guards standing outside. They allowed one of the POWs to empty the bucket but no one else could leave, and once the POW was back the guards gave them more of the tasteless biscuits and one container of water to share. The second the door slid back into place the train was off again in the darkness.

Jed had always imagined that hell was like the Bible described, a place of everlasting flames and fire and brimstone, but now he knew he had been mistaken. Hell had many forms, and this was one of them. And this conviction grew as the days passed and the train trundled on, the track eventually beginning to twist and climb. Jock had become a friend, along with several other of the

POWs including Neville, a little Welshman. It was he who first caught a glimpse of the Alps through the barbed wire of their window. 'Well, look at that now,' he said, turning and grinning. 'And here's me forgotten my skis.'

There were few moments like that. Three of their number had died from dysentery since the journey had begun and they were all wondering how much longer they could survive in the cattle truck. But then, at the next stop at a station somewhere, the train was shunted into a siding. German guards forced them and the occupants of the other trucks into covered lorries and then they were off again, driving through open countryside now which was wonderful after their incarceration in the trucks.

Jed sat with Jock and Neville in the back of one lorry, breathing in the fresh air. He didn't think he had ever smelt anything so beautiful, even if it was tainted by the odour of the POWs who were suffering with dysentery, but when they stopped in what seemed like the middle of nowhere in a forest glade that had a crystal-clear stream running through it, the German guards allowed them to get down and relieve themselves and wash in the water. The guards had set up a machine gun on a tripod before the POWs left the trucks, making it clear what would happen if anyone tried to escape, but most of them, including Jed, just wanted to get clean.

Jed's wounds had begun to heal in spite of the terrible conditions of the last days, and he joined the other POWs who stripped naked, bathing himself and then washing his clothes in the stream. It didn't matter that they put them on again soaking wet or that the men with dysentery would no doubt soil themselves if the lorries wouldn't stop when they were on the move once more; for the moment they felt like men again. Some of the POWs had scabies, tiny mites that had burrowed into their flesh and laid eggs causing a blotchy red rash that itched unbearably so they scratched until their skin was inflamed and bleeding, and they in particular lay in the water until the guards ordered them out. They were all, including him, a right motley crew, Jed thought, but never again would a bath feel so good.

It was the last time he would feel clean for a while. The lorries trundled on, and after a lengthy journey in which the days merged into a blur and the nights involved staying in a number of camps where the POWs were put in a compound separate from the resident inmates of whichever camp they were in, more of their number died. Some of these overnight camps had Russian POWs on the other side of barbed-wire fences and Jed could see that the prisoners were in a terrible state, frail and malnourished, with a ghastly stench drifting on the air which Jock told him came from decaying corpses.

'The Nazis like the Russians even less than they like us,' Jock said grimly. 'They're being worked and starved to death like the Jews, poor beggars. What state the world'll be in when this war's over is anyone's guess because some things can't be forgiven or forgotten.'

They were allowed no contact with the Russians, separated as they were by barbed-wire fences, but Jed and the others found that the rats had no respect for these fences. They were huge, the size of cats, and were feeding on the corpses of the Russian POWs. They would often come running through to their side of the camp once darkness fell. They knew the rats had been feasting on human flesh because of the smell of them, a smell Jed didn't want ever to experience again in the rest of his life.

Another train journey took the convoy of POWs into southern Poland, and here they were given over to a new and different batch of German guards. As soon as Jed looked at them he knew they were a different kettle of fish from the ones who had stopped and let the POWs bathe in the stream and wash their clothes. These were dead-eyed with hard faces. One of the Italians in their number stumbled as they were marched in line through huge gates into a slabbed yard surrounded by high walls, and by putting out a hand to save himself happened to brush against the arm of one of the guards. As the man righted himself the guard swung his nine-pound rifle at the side of the prisoner's head and there was the awful sound of crushing bone. The Italian fell like a stone, dead before he even reached the ground.

For a moment Jed stood stock-still, shocked to the core, before Jock nudged him to keep walking. The Italian had been a particular friend of Leonardo and they all heard the cry, something between a shriek and a roar, that Leonardo gave as he launched himself on the guard. It was a futile act; Leonardo had no hope of avenging the man's death. He was plucked off the guard immediately by two others while the original guard screamed something in his face, drew a revolver and shot him at point-blank range. The whole episode had lasted no longer than thirty seconds.

Again it was Jock prodding him violently in the back that prompted Jed to move, his voice low as he murmured, 'Don't even think about it. Keep walking, these are SS.'

Sure now that they were all going to die, Jed walked in line into the long concrete building in the yard. His thoughts full of Cora, he willed her to know that he loved her, that somehow over the miles separating them she would know he loved her. The guards lined up in front of them and they were told to strip while several Germans in white coats came in the door. Once they were as naked as the day they were born, the POWs had a pungent white powder puffed over them by a couple of the white-coated men, between their legs, under their arms and over their feet while their clothes were sprayed with something eye-watering.

Jed glanced at Jock and Neville. They were nothing but skin and bone like him; now they resembled some kind of strange white wraiths.

One by one the men, still naked, had their hair cropped short and then were told to put their clothes on once more, after which they were walked out into the yard. They had no idea what day it was, merely that it was late May or maybe June. The air in the yard was warm and faintly scented by the fir trees they had passed;

all Jed could think about was Leonardo. One moment the man he thought of as a friend had been alive, the next his brains had splattered the ground.

'All right?' Jock was standing at the side of him, hands thrust in his trouser pockets. 'You couldn't have done anything, laddie. Better to live to fight another day. Our time'll come.'

Jed nodded. He didn't believe it and he doubted if Jock did either, but the alternative, to give up, wasn't an option. Once again the words Wilfred had said to him came into his mind and his eyes narrowed. Couldn't kill in cold blood? Just give him the chance.

Come nightfall they were given a kind of watery green soup that smelt disgusting and tasted worse, along with lumps of hard grainy bread, and told to sleep in the yard on the slabs.

The next morning they boarded a train again and the reason for the previous day's fumigation became clear. This time they were in normal rail carriages with a corridor down one side and small compartments, the sort of train ordinary civilians might travel on. Clearly the Germans wanted to cut down the possibility of the train being infected with lice and fleas and anything else the POWs might be carrying.

Mentally and physically exhausted, Jed sat between Jock and Neville as the train rolled through quite pleasant countryside. He'd lain awake all night on the cold slabs thinking of Cora and home, of Leonardo and the other Italian, of the misery of the Russians in their foul camps and of the terrible things he'd seen and heard about over the last weeks. Now he was too tired to think and it was a blessed relief.

When the train stopped it was at a small station seemingly in the middle of nowhere. The guards marched them off down a wide track and birds were singing in the trees either side of the trail. Jed had always loved to hear the birds, even the calling of the wood pigeons that were such a pest with the crops – it was part of what made the farm home – but now the sound was a subtle and cruel mockery of what they were having to endure. Nature was oblivious to their misery and was continuing on regardless. The sun still came up and went down, night followed day, and underneath the blue sky there were unspeakably evil things happening. He could go mad if he thought about it too long.

They must have walked through fields and woods for nearly four miles before the countryside suddenly vanished. Ahead was a POW camp with armed guards on a watchtower but beyond that, in the distance, was what looked like a massive building site stretching as far as the eye could see. Smoke plumed from chimneys and steam cranes and the framework of what looked like a huge factory was in place.

They were marched into the camp which was situated on the southern edge of the building work, and found the compound to consist of rows of barracks in which there were no mattresses but just bare timber bunks. The latrines were basic, each merely a row of holes in a plank over a pit, and they stank to high heaven. It wasn't until other Allied prisoners returned from working at the site they had seen in the distance that Jed found out what it was all about and where they were.

The gigantic factory was being built to manufacture synthetic rubber for Hitler's war effort, as well as methanol for fuel. It was even larger than Jed and the others had thought, being two miles long and a mile deep, and was laid out like a huge grid with many buildings, towers, chimneys and gantries everywhere and narrow railway lines connecting each block, the whole thing being dominated by a large industrial plant with four chimneys.

'So it's a labour camp?' Jock asked their informant.

The man looked at the newcomers and shrugged. 'In a manner of speaking. You'll see soon enough tomorrow.'

'What do you mean, in a manner of speaking?' Neville wasn't one for prevarication.

'Well, it might be a labour camp for us, but not for the stripeys.'

'The stripeys?'

'The Jews. There's thousands of them, all starving, all dying, all being worked to death. They die by the dozens every day in their zebra uniforms and the Kapos beat and kick them to death where they fall, straight in front of us. They don't even waste a bullet on the poor beggars. Did you notice that sickly-sweet smell when you were marched in? It's coming from the chimneys in the original brick-built camp where they burn the Jews, dead or alive. That's where the gas chambers are. The SS and the Kapos – they're German criminals recruited as guards and every bit as bad as the SS – they have a field day over there. It's hell on earth, plain and simple.'

Jed felt sick. 'Where are we? What's this place called?'

'The Polish name is Oświęcim. The Nazis call it Auschwitz.'

Chapter Fifteen

Cora stared at Jed's mother. She knew, even before Mrs Croft spoke, what she was going to say. It was written all over her face. 'We . . . we had a telegram, lass. Missing presumed dead.'

Mr and Mrs Croft had just drawn up in their horse and trap and Cora had gone to meet them, having been walking across from one of the barns. Now she was aware of Rachel hurrying from the house, saying, 'Is everything all right?' as she came wiping floury hands on her apron. 'Is it news of Jed?'

Cora turned and said simply, 'Missing presumed dead.'

'Oh, lass, lass.' Rachel squeezed her shoulder before looking up at Jed's parents sitting in the trap. 'I'm so sorry, so very sorry, but missing . . . There's still hope. Only last week Mrs Newton heard her Luke's alive and he's been missing since before Christmas. Come in for a cup of tea, won't you? The kettle's on.'

'Thanks all the same but we'll get back. We just

wanted to let Cora know ourselves.' Mr Croft cleared his throat. 'He thought the world of you, lass,' he said awkwardly, his blue eyes resting on Cora's stricken face. 'I don't understand why he went off like he did, I'll never understand it, but I do know you were the only lass in the world for him.'

'Thank you, Mr Croft.' She felt sick with guilt. What would Jed's parents say if they knew the truth? That she had been responsible for him leaving without a word and enlisting? That he had killed a man to protect her and then hadn't been able to stay where he would be constantly reminded of what he had done?

Rachel had moved round the trap and was patting Mrs Croft's hand. 'Don't give up hope, lass,' she murmured, looking into Jed's mother's swollen, pink-rimmed eyes. 'I've a feeling your lad's all right and I'm not given to fancies.'

Cora's eyes shot to Rachel's face. Was she just saying that to comfort Jed's mother or did she really believe it? She would give anything for it to be true, anything.

They stood together as the trap disappeared in a cloud of dust. The August day was baking hot like the ones before it and the month had been a good one for the Allies. In the middle of August a massive Allied force had landed on a hundred-mile coastal strip from Nice to Marseilles, and days later they had taken back Florence, Marseilles and Grenoble from the Nazis. Then, after four years of brutal German occupation, the population of Paris had celebrated as French tanks led the Allies into the city. The Nazi swastika was gone from the Eiffel Tower and the Tricolour flew once again for the Parisians. General de Gaulle had returned and the people of Paris could move freely again.

All this ran through Rachel's mind as she stood with Cora wondering how to comfort the girl. She knew that every time there had been a positive report about the war since Jed had gone Cora had been buoyed up, hoping it signalled a step nearer to the Nazis being defeated and Jed coming home safe and sound. And now this. Missing presumed dead. Quietly she said, 'Lass, they say "missing presumed dead" when they don't know, that's the truth of it.'

'Did you mean what you said to Jed's mam? About him being all right?'

Rachel nodded. 'You know me well enough by now to know I'm not one for soft soap, Cora. I've felt all along, right from day one, that Jed'll come home.' She cleared her throat. The hope in Cora's eyes was painful to witness. 'And when he does, you two'll get together again, you mark my words.'

'I doubt that but it won't matter as long as he comes back. He's never written, has he? But he's sent letters to his mam.' Cora drew in her breath. 'And he's made no mention of me.'

'Jed's mother told you that?'

'No, no, but she's mentioned to Wilfred she thinks it's odd and he's told me.'

'Right.' Rachel had her own opinion about Wilfred.

She could see he was besotted with Cora and always had been, and of course the lad couldn't help how he felt, but there was something about him she couldn't put her finger on. He was always very polite and helpful when he came to the farm which he'd taken to doing on a Sunday afternoon since Jed had joined up, ostensibly to 'take Cora out of herself for a bit' as he'd put it, but there was something, perhaps the way he looked at Cora, that was . . . Rachel couldn't find a word to describe what she meant, she just knew it gave her the creeps. 'Well, personally, considering Wilfred's supposed to be such a good friend, I think that was unhelpful of him to say the least.'

'Oh, it just slipped out, he didn't mean anything by it.' Both Cora's voice and attitude were on the defensive. She didn't know what she would have done without Wilfred over the last months. He had been sympathetic and supportive without making any demands on her, regularly providing a shoulder to cry on and offering unconditional friendship. And he hadn't been nasty about Jed either. She had appreciated that, not judging him for disappearing without a word to anyone and joining up, which she had expected. It would have been hard if Wilfred had taken that tack. She felt guilty enough as it was. But Wilfred had just said that although he didn't understand how Jed could have left her the way he had he assumed Jed must have his reasons, and as Jed had grown to be a friend he wouldn't speak ill of him.

'No? Well, you know Wilfred better than me but still

waters run deep, that's all I'd say.' And then Rachel's voice softened as she said, 'Come on in and I'll make us a cuppa, lass.'

As it was the last week of August Maria and the others were still on holiday from school and at present out in the fields helping the POWs and a couple of soldiers bring in the harvest. It had been a hot summer but Rachel, like many other farmers, had been on edge for the last week or two. It just needed a spell of bad weather, with wind and rain battering down the grain fields and lodging the heads and shedding the corn, and a whole year's work could be sabotaged at the whim of nature. But today, like the ones before it, was dry and sunny, and everyone had been in the fields since daylight except for Cora and Rachel who were seeing to the other jobs that needed doing around the farm, as well as bringing the workers' food and drink to them at regular intervals. Breakfast at six once the POWs and soldiers arrived at the farm and before they began work, lunch at ten o'clock, dinner at one, afternoon tea at four and supper at seven. It was a full-time job in itself.

Once in the kitchen they drank their tea as they prepared dinner for the workers in the fields, but when Rachel offered Cora a warm teacake she shook her head. If she tried to eat anything it would choke her; the lump in her throat was too big. *Missing presumed dead.* The three words were pounding in her head like a sledgehammer, an embodiment of all her worst fears come true, and she longed to talk to Wilfred. He would understand, he always did, but she knew he would be working on the harvest at Appletree Farm along with Horace and wouldn't finish until dusk. No doubt all he would want then was his bed.

The day dragged on. Maria and Maud were all sympathy when they heard the news, coming out with the usual platitudes that folk said at times like this and looking at her with concerned faces. Cora wanted to ask them to say nothing at all because banalities like 'It will be all right, lass, you wait and see' and 'You don't know for sure, don't give up hope' were well meant but made her want to scream. But of course she said nothing to upset them, it wouldn't be fair. She returned Maria's hug, fighting back the tears when Maria whispered, 'Like I said before, we'll get through this together, lass, and don't forget you've always got me,' but knowing she was really on her own because no one could truly understand how she felt. The weight of her guilt seemed impossible to bear but she had to bear it, it was as simple as that. Somehow, for the rest of her life, she had to shoulder this burden alone and she didn't know how she was going to do it.

It was almost dark when there was a knock at the back door just as they were all drinking their last cup of milky cocoa before going to bed. When Wilfred walked into the kitchen, Cora was aware that she had known deep down he would come once he heard about Jed. He would know she needed him and Wilfred had never let her down.

She jumped up, taking his arm as he nodded to the

others, and saying, 'Come for a walk,' before turning to Rachel and adding, 'I won't be long.'

He didn't speak until they were outside, and then he put his arms round her as he said softly, 'I'm so sorry, lass. I'm so, so sorry.'

For a moment she stiffened – it was the first time he had taken her in his arms – but then she relaxed against him and the tears she had been holding in all day spilled over. Wilfred was the same height as her, non-threatening, comforting, and just Wilfred, and she had never needed his brotherly love so much.

For a full minute they stood quietly, Wilfred letting her cry, and then as she pulled away, wiping her face with the back of her hand, he pulled out his handkerchief.

'Here,' he said very gently, adding with a small smile, 'And it is freshly laundered, don't worry.'

She managed a small smile back.

'Come on, let's go for that walk you mentioned.' He took her hand before she could protest but then she didn't really want to object. She knew she wouldn't sleep a wink.

He led her away from the farm and once they were in the dusty lane beyond, the scent of trees and flowers was sweet on the still night air, the smells of the farmyard behind them. The birds had already put themselves to bed but the occasional one still called or sang in the thick twilight. It was peaceful, timeless, and all at odds with how she was feeling inside.

As though he had heard her thoughts, Wilfred

murmured, 'I'm not going to say time's a great healer because you don't need that now, but what I would say is, take each day a minute at a time, Cora. Don't try and look beyond the immediate moment. The future will take care of itself. And you're not alone, however much it may feel like it. You come first with me, you always have and you always will.'

Cora swallowed hard. She felt sick with remorse but she couldn't betray Jed by telling Wilfred that Jed had killed a man for her. Instead she whispered, 'There's . . . there's things to do with me you don't know about, things I'd give anything to change.'

She had pulled her hand from his, her head bowed, and now Wilfred lifted up her chin with one finger. 'Nothing you could do or say would make me think any the less of you, lass, and I'm here for you, all right? Always.' His hazel eyes held hers. 'You know that, don't you?'

She nodded. Yes, she did know that and in spite of her misery Wilfred's presence here tonight was balm to her sore heart. Her mam had abandoned her, her da too in a way, and then Jed, but Wilfred remained constant. Some lads with a mam and da like he'd got would have grown hard and bitter but Wilfred wasn't like that. She smiled a little shakily, and then slipped her arm through his as they began to walk again. Echoing what she had thought earlier in the day, she said softly, 'I don't know what I'd do without you, Wilfred.'

Her words and the pressure of her arm in his caused

a feeling that was akin to pain to assail Wilfred. Physically he wanted her so much that most nights, exhausted though he was after a day's hard grind on the farm, he couldn't fall asleep until the early hours, the burning in his loins causing him to toss and turn in his bed across the room from Horace. But it was his great love for her, which was a thing apart from physical desire, that kept the craving in check when he was with her. He knew if he was to bring his plan of making Cora his wife to fruition it was essential he trod carefully. And so that was exactly what he had done since Jed had left.

Good old Wilfred, reliable old Wilfred. Mentally he smiled derisively. But it was working. He knew it was. He had won back all the ground which had been lost when Jed had been around, and more. Aye, and more. The love she felt for him had changed even though he knew Cora wasn't aware of it, but she needed him now. Her face had lit up when he had walked into the kitchen earlier.

Following on from this thought, he said quietly, 'You knew I'd come to see you tonight, didn't you?'

'I hoped you would.' She paused. 'How is Jed's mam?'

'Upset as you'd expect.' He felt sorry for Mr and Mrs Croft, they'd been good to him, but he did not hold himself responsible for their grief. If Jed hadn't tried to take Cora away from him he would still be here with his parents on the farm. Jed had brought it all on himself, and them. The golden boy, who'd always had everything he wanted – well, he'd showed him, hadn't he.

'Poor things.' The guilt was a ton weight on her soul.

Their three sons gone now. However would Mrs Croft bear it?

Knowing what she needed to hear, Wilfred said, 'Actually, they're coping far better than you'd expect. They've got a strong marriage, you see, and they draw on each other. Rumour has it that Jed's da got Mrs Croft on the rebound. She'd been engaged to someone else and he skedaddled, but she absolutely thinks the world of Jed's da now.' This had the advantage of being true. He'd heard the story from one of the old timers in the village and had mentally stored it away for a suitable moment to repeat to Cora. A seed in her mind, if you like.

'I didn't know that.' Cora looked at him in surprise. She, too, had noticed how happy Mr and Mrs Croft seemed together on the Sundays she'd had tea at the farm.

'Oh, aye.' Wilfred kept his voice airy and conversational with some effort. He wanted to say more but to labour the point tonight wouldn't be appropriate.

'Mrs Burns feels Jed's still alive,' Cora said suddenly.

Wilfred faltered in his step but then continued on, and his voice came level and untroubled when he said, 'What do you feel? You were close to him, after all.'

There was a long pause. 'I don't know. I – I want to believe he is and I do in a way, but then I think it's only that I want to believe it and not the truth. That if I keep willing him to live, he will. Does that sound barmy?'

'No, not barmy, but . . .'

'What?'

'It's just that . . .'

'What? Tell me, Wilfred.' Cora stopped, taking her arm from his and searching his face in the darkness. 'Please, say what you're thinking.'

'You know I care about you, right? And I don't want to see you driving yourself crazy. Sometimes it's better to face the truth and accept something, however horrible, than go on living in hope. Maybe, just maybe, it's time to let go, lass? After all, he chose to leave, didn't he?'

'You mean he left me.' It was flat.

'No, not just you, everyone. And that being the case, whether he is still alive or not, perhaps you ought to get on with your life. Look . . .' Wilfred allowed a moment to expand, become tension-filled. 'Maybe Jed doesn't want what you want, what you imagined he wanted. No one really knows someone else.'

'*No.*' Cora took a step backwards, away from him. 'You don't understand. It's not as simple as it looks. It's difficult, complicated . . .' She left the sentence unfinished because it was impossible to finish.

'Complicated or not, I know one thing, Cora.' He wanted desperately to take her in his arms again, even though it had called on resources of resolve he hadn't known he was capable of. 'I would never have gone away and left you.'

'Oh, Wilfred.' She shook her head.

'No.' His voice came deep, thick. 'Don't "oh, Wilfred" me. I wouldn't have left you, Cora. Believe that if nothing else. The devil himself couldn't have made me.'

She stared at him, a mixture of emotions washing across her face, but it was the flash of uncertainty, almost fear, that enabled him to take on the persona he had given himself, the one she was comfortable with, and say steadily, 'I happen to believe in family, although with *my* mam an' da that might sound strange. But you and Horace and the others, you're my family – and family, real family, is worth dying for. It's nothing to do with blood being thicker than water, in fact blood has nothing to do with it. It's about folk being there for you, caring, no matter if your surname is different to theirs. Am I making sense, lass?'

He was relieved to see her nod as her face relaxed. It was too soon to declare himself, much too soon.

'I know you're at odds with your mam but she was more of a mam to me all my life than my own and I appreciate that, more than she'll ever know. How many times did she feed me, eh? A poor little waif and stray covered in bruises with his backside hanging out?'

He continued to talk in the same vein, keeping it general with comments about her parents, Horace, Maria and the little ones, claiming himself all the time as part of them. His reward was her arm slipping through his again as they began to retrace their footsteps.

His time would come. It was a promise to himself. From when he could remember he had had their future mapped out and nothing and no one would stand in the way of it. They were bound together, him and Cora; no one could love her as she deserved to be loved but him. It didn't matter that he would always care for her more than she cared for him. All he wanted in life was her but her needs were greater, it was part of what made her Cora. Her energy, her intelligence, her vivacity and strength; she was in love with life and it would always be so.

Just for a moment a little voice at the back of his mind said, 'In love with life? She might have been before Jed went away but she's lost her sparkle and you know it,' but he brushed the thought aside. He only wanted the best for Cora and *he* was the best because no one could love her the way he did. He could make her happy, he knew he could. Once they were back in Sunderland and he got a job he'd work his socks off for her and provide them with a home, a nice little place where it could be just the two of them until the bairns came along. And he was in no rush for bairns. He knew lassies always wanted their own babies, it was natural, but if it was just him and Cora for the rest of their lives that would suit him down to the ground. Not that a little Cora with red hair and brown eyes like her mam wouldn't be the icing on the cake.

When they reached the farm, Cora reached up and kissed his cheek. 'Thank you for coming,' she said softly.

'Of course I came.' The kiss meant nothing beyond a sisterly caress, he knew that, but it had sent the blood singing through his veins.

'I'd better go in.'

'Of course, go on. I'll watch till you're in so I know you're safe.'

Just a day or two ago his proprietorial attitude might have slightly jarred; tonight she was grateful he cared so much about her well-being. 'See you Sunday?' she said quietly.

'I'll be here.' It was the first time she had asked him; normally it was he who said it, or sometimes he would just arrive at the farm. There had been times, shortly after Jed had gone, that Cora had merely humoured him by going for a walk on a Sunday, he knew that. She would never have hurt his feelings by refusing to accompany him or asking him not to come, but he had known she would rather be by herself. He had felt it was essential that he set the pattern for Sundays straight away though, because he intended to stay at the forefront of her life. Initially he had sometimes persuaded Horace to come with him and suggested to Cora that Maria and the others join them too, but gradually he had done this less and less and Cora had accepted that it would be just the two of them.

A steady drip-drip. As he watched Cora walk across to the house, he nodded mentally at the thought. They already had the foundations of what could be a good marriage although she didn't realize it yet, but one day she would. He would make sure of it.

She turned and waved before opening the back door and he waved back, and once she had gone inside, his shoulders went back and he exhaled in satisfaction.

Progress had been made tonight and it was all turning out as he had planned. Thousands, millions, had died and were still dying in this war, so why not Jed? Missing presumed dead. They were beautiful words.

Chapter Sixteen

'Oh, come on, lad, you don't want to be seeing the New Year in all by yourself, now then. Come round to mine and we'll have a bevvy together, eh? I dare say Patrick and Kitty'll be popping in and Mrs McKenzie now she's on her own, and likely Mr Johnson from thirty-two. He drops in for a chat now and again.'

This last was pointed and Gregory knew why. Beryl was hoping Ronald Johnson's interest towards her might prompt him to come up to scratch, as no doubt she'd put it, but he had no intention of taking the arrangement they'd begun when he'd first come back to Sunderland to the next level. Beryl was a nice enough woman and a good cook, but there it ended for him. She, on the other hand, had been dropping broad hints for some time that she would be quite prepared to warm his bed as well as see to his washing and ironing and the rest of it. He'd managed to bring into the conversation several times in a roundabout way that he was still a married man and content for things to remain as they were, but Beryl being Beryl wouldn't give up. Short of saying he would rather be hung, drawn and quartered than make the woman his common-law wife, he didn't know what else to do.

'I'll see how I feel, Beryl, all right?' His tone was purposely abrupt but he knew it'd have no effect. The woman had a hide like a rhinoceros when it suited.

'Aye, you do that, but I'll nip round later and make sure you haven't dozed off in the chair like last year.'

Gregory would have smiled if he wasn't so irritated. That was the excuse he had given the year before for not joining her and she had never let him forget it. Several times he had tried to pull out of their arrangement, saying now that he was better he was quite capable of seeing to the house and the meals himself, but she'd brushed it aside as only Beryl could. Of course, it didn't help that some days he still didn't feel too good. The doctors had said it would be a long recovery – the blast that had taken his eye and mangled his arm had done a bit of damage to his chest too – but he was getting there. Aye, he was getting there.

Once Beryl had bustled out and he was alone, Gregory sat back in his chair in front of the glowing fire in the range and sighed deeply. The woman would drive him mad before she was finished. He only hoped that when Archie came back from where he had been evacuated, Beryl would turn her attention to her son. But then she wasn't too pleased with Archie. Apparently the lad had settled into where he was living in the country like a duck to water and had resisted his mother's efforts to get him to come home for some months. Quite a few of the parents he knew had brought their bairns home in the last year or so after no bombs had fallen in that time, but much as he'd like to have Cora and the other bairns home, he wasn't about to risk it. The Nazis had bombed the hell out of London with their V-1s and V-2s this year; who was to say they wouldn't begin bombing the north-east again? Just because Sunderland had been enjoying a break in the bombing thus far it didn't mean old Hitler was finished with them yet.

He reached for yesterday's paper. It was still full of the news that the Allies had been caught on the hop by the Germans' surprise attack through the Ardennes forest towards the Allied front in Belgium. A spokesman at the Allied HQ in Paris was maintaining that the offensive was merely a desperate attempt by Hitler to delay the inevitable, which was probably true, but it convinced him further that it was right to leave Cora and the others where they were. A dying scorpion was a darn sight more dangerous and unpredictable than a healthy one in his opinion and he wouldn't be surprised if the Nazis had a sting in their tail yet.

There was also a short paragraph on the third page about the search being called off for Glenn Miller who had gone missing over the Channel two weeks before. He had been sad when he'd read about the band leader's probable demise. Nancy had always liked Glenn Miller and Duke Ellington and the other masters of jazz and big-band swing, and he could still picture her dancing in this very kitchen to one of Miller's records on the wireless. It didn't seem right that a man who had taken the Miller Orchestra all over the world in war zones like the Pacific and Europe and the UK should have been killed when his plane was lost on a routine flight to France so late in the war. But then this damn war had destroyed so many lives in one way or another.

He sat up straighter in his chair. He'd allow himself a couple of drinks tonight; it was New Year's Eve after all. He rarely drank these days – he'd drunk enough to last the rest of his life when he'd first come back from the war and Nancy had left him, but it had got him through those first hellish months. Once he'd begun to pull himself together it had been surprisingly easy to quit the booze, but then he'd never been one for drinking or smoking or gambling. Nancy had been his only addiction. He grimaced to himself.

Levering himself up by his good arm he walked across to the kitchen cupboard and took out a half-full bottle of whisky that had been sitting there since the previous New Year's Eve. He glanced at the clock. Six o'clock. Not too early. He'd have a couple of quiet drinks, listen to the wireless for a bit and then go to bed after he'd locked up. Beryl wouldn't like it if she did what she'd threatened and popped back later only to find the door bolted, but that was all to the good.

Before sitting down again he drew the curtains at the kitchen window. It was snowing heavily and a wind was getting up. Pity any poor blighter out tonight, he thought, taking his glass and resuming his seat in front of the fire. Beryl had cooked a nice piece of brisket earlier, it being a Sunday, and he was still comfortably replete, and what with the foul weather outside and it being warm and snug in the kitchen he experienced a rare moment of contentment verging on happiness.

He had barely settled himself in the chair when he heard a knock at the front door which made him frown in surprise. No one round these parts used the front door and even if someone had taken it into their heads to be first-footing, it was far too early. Of course, it could be bairns larking about – knocking on the door or ringing a doorbell and then disappearing was a great prank when you were knee high to a grasshopper – but with the snow coming down the way it was he'd have thought any bairns would be indoors.

The knock came again before he reached the front door and on opening it he found a woman he didn't know peering up at him, her hat and the shoulders of her coat covered in snow. 'Sorry to bother you,' she said, 'but you wouldn't be Mr Stubbs by any chance? Gregory Stubbs?'

'Aye, that's me.' She looked a respectable enough little body, he thought, but what the dickens did she want with him?

'You don't know me,' she carried on, stating the obvious, 'but I run a boarding house in Woodbine Street near Hendon Junction, and, well, it's about one of me lodgers that I've come. I've always known her as Nancy Wright but it appears her name is Stubbs. I only found that out this afternoon, mind you. I didn't know she was married, she's always passed herself off as a widow.'

He stared at the woman, his eyes unblinking and his mouth closed, and it was only when she brushed at her coat with a gloved hand that he came out of his shock enough to say, 'You'd better come in for a minute.'

'No, I won't come in, thanks all the same.' She stared up at him from the pavement, and now there was definite condemnation in her tone when she said, 'She's poorly, Nancy, right poorly and I thought you ought to know. She don't know I'm here but I thought it only right. When I married my Eustace we took each other on for better 'n' worse and I'm old-fashioned enough to think that's the way it should be. He wouldn't have had me living in one room while he was in clover, no matter what we'd fallen out about. Of course it's none of my business –' her tone made it quite clear she thought exactly the opposite and moreover where she deposited the blame for their marriage breakdown – 'and I don't know what's gone on, but I thought you ought to know she's bad.'

He gathered himself together enough to ask, 'What's the matter with her?'

'The flu. We all had it over Christmas, all of us in the house, I mean, but Nancy didn't throw it off like me an' my other lady. They sent her home from Blackett's yesterday morning, that's where she works. Did you know? Well, she does, and I insisted on calling the doctor although she wouldn't have it at first. He said she's got pleurisy and he's given her some medicine but she's been coughing fit to wake the dead. I sat with her this afternoon and that's when she told me about you and her bairns and the lovely little house she used to have. I think it comforted her to talk about it because—' The woman stopped abruptly.

'What?'

'Well, I reckon she thinks she's not long for this world.'

'She's as bad as that?'

'I think so, aye.'

What had happened to this fella she'd run off with and why wasn't she still in Newcastle? She'd written to him shortly after she'd left him, but he had never replied and since then there had been nothing. 'How long has she been living with you, Mrs . . . ?'

'Duffy. Barbara Duffy. How long? Good few months now.' Barbara Duffy didn't add here that when the woman she now knew as Nancy Stubbs had arrived on her doorstep asking about a room, she'd thought she must have the consumption or something. Thin as a rake, Nancy had been, still was, but when she'd questioned her before letting her lodge with them Nancy had told her she'd been in hospital for a while. Caught in a bomb blast, Nancy had said, but she'd wondered then and she wondered now if that was the truth. There had been no visible signs of injury, not that there had to be, she supposed. Still, there had been something about Nancy that had bothered her from day one. Not that the lass had been any trouble, far from it. Nancy always paid her rent on time and was quiet and clean and polite. Perhaps too quiet and polite? As though something was missing inside, like the main spring was broken?

'Could I come and see her?' Gregory's voice was flat but inside he was in turmoil now the shock was wearing off. 'I mean, do you think she would want me to?'

'You probably know best about that, being her husband –' again the disapproval was overt – 'but if you're asking my opinion, from the way she spoke about you this afternoon I think she'd want to see you, aye.' Round bright eyes, like a robin's, fixed Gregory's in a piercing gaze. 'But if she gets over this she'll need looking after properly. She's nowt but skin and bone as it is, but she'll be worse after the pleurisy. That's what did for my Eustace years ago and he was a big strong bloke at the time, not like your wife, Mr Stubbs. A breath of wind could blow Nancy away.'

She wasn't describing the Nancy he had known. She had never been fat but her hour-glass figure had been beautiful. Gregory cleared his throat. 'Could I accompany you back now?'

'Aye.' Barbara Duffy gave no sign of relenting in her stance of measured hostility. 'You could.'

'Would you come in a moment while I change out of my slippers and get my hat and coat?'

This time she accepted the invitation, stepping into the hall, whereupon Gregory closed the front door and then as he led the way she followed him down the hall and into the kitchen. He bolted the back door – he didn't want Beryl in the house while he was gone – and then sat down to change into his boots. This was always a fumbling procedure – he had been right-handed before the injuries – and he was aware of her eyes on him although she did not speak. His cap and overcoat were hanging on a row of pegs to one side of the range – it was always warmer in the kitchen than the rest of the house which often resembled an icebox – and as he donned these, she said, 'Cop it in the war, did you?'

'Aye, Tobruk, but I was luckier than most of my pals.'

Her tone softening for the first time, she said, 'There's plenty who didn't come back from them parts, isn't there.'

'Aye.' He nodded. 'If Rommel had been on our side the war'd be over by now.'

Softening further, she nodded to his muffler still hanging on one of the pegs. 'I'd put that on, lad. It's bitter out.'

He left the house by the front door, the first time he had done so for a long time. The snow was thick and still falling steadily and in spite of it being New Year's Eve and a time when the north-east celebrated, war or no war, the streets were hushed. They walked in silence and Gregory was concentrating so hard on not going headlong that the impending meeting with Nancy was of necessity pushed to the back of his mind, for which he was grateful. The pavements and roads were lethal, ice and snow providing a combination that made it impossible to hurry, and as they passed lighted windows glowing warmly in the darkness he reflected that since the blackout restrictions were lifted in September it had made the end of the war seem within reach at last.

Once, when Mrs Duffy slipped, he grabbed her arm and righted her, and after she'd thanked him, she said, 'What happened between you and Nancy, if you don't mind me asking?'

He did mind her asking. 'It's a long story.'

'She said she was to blame but to my mind it always takes two.'

'Aye, you're right there.' He had dissected his marriage over and over again since Nancy had run off, and one of the unpleasant home truths it had thrown up was that he had smothered his wife with a love that must have been stifling to someone like Nancy. He no longer asked himself the question as to whether it was possible to love someone too much – he knew the answer only too well – but at the same time it didn't excuse Nancy for doing the dirty on him and on this point he was clear. But it was water under the bridge. When she had chosen her fancy man over him, and at a time when he had never needed her more, it had been the death knell on his love. Admittedly it had taken time to wither and die completely – you couldn't just change your feelings overnight – but there were days when he didn't think about her at all. Well, hardly at all. Certainly not as much as he used to.

He wondered if he was doing the right thing in going to see her but at the same time he knew it was the only thing he could do, especially if Nancy was as ill as her landlady alleged. He felt a sick churning in his stomach and immediately told himself, no, none of that, he was past all that. For weeks, months, after she'd skedaddled, he'd been unable to eat more than a few mouthfuls at a time, such had been the state of his insides. His heartache and misery had made him feel as though his stomach was full of a lead weight, and when he had tried to force himself to swallow food he had actually vomited more than once.

But he was better now. He repeated the thought to himself. Whatever transpired this night, he was better, he was his own man. Nancy had done him a favour in a way because he was far tougher mentally than he'd ever been, it was just his body that let him down now and again. In throwing off his love for her and determining to go on and make the best of life, he'd developed a resilience he would never have believed himself capable of.

By the time they approached Woodbine Street off Moor Street he felt himself fully prepared for seeing Nancy again. 'We'll go in the front way,' said Mrs Duffy as they turned the corner. 'The bairns have made the back lane treacherous with their slides.'

Halfway down the street she stopped outside the two-up two-down terrace and took out her key. The door was painted a dark blue and the brass knocker in the shape of a grinning goblin was well polished, and as soon as the door opened Gregory was greeted with the smell of furniture polish.

'Nancy has the back bedroom,' said Mrs Duffy, and as though on cue Gregory heard the sound of a racking cough from upstairs.

He winced, he couldn't help it. It sounded painful. Mrs Duffy was staring at him and now he said, 'Should – should I go up?' He had expected her to lead the way.

'Aye.' Still the landlady didn't move.

'Do you want to go first? To make sure –' he had been going to say to make sure she is decent but that sounded ridiculous, him being her husband, so he changed it to – 'she wants to see me?' Nancy had no idea he was coming, after all.

'Whether she wants to see you or not you're here now. Besides, like I said, the way she spoke about you she'll want to see you.' It was unequivocal. He was on his own.

'Right.' He looked at her helplessly for a moment more and then began climbing the steep stairs. He was almost at the top when Mrs Duffy said from the hallway, 'She's in the back, like I said. The door's right in front of you when you step onto the landing. It won't be locked 'cause I've been in and out.'

The landing was in darkness but enough light had filtered up from the hall to see clearly enough. He was about to knock on the door when another bout of coughing from the occupant inside stilled his hand. Instead he paused for a moment and then opened the door. The light was on and it showed the skeletal figure lying in the single bed under the window in stark sharpness. She had changed so much that she was almost unrecognizable.

Shocked beyond words, he stared at Nancy. He knew he ought to speak but he was unable to say anything. It wasn't just that she was thin to the point of emaciation so that her eyes looked huge in their sunken sockets and her cheekbones stuck out like blades, but her hair, her glorious hair that he had once thought the colour of fire, was sparse and faded and she looked old, old enough to be his mother. But even more than that, it was the look in her eyes as she stared at him. There was no sparkle, no life, no dignity or hauteur, nothing that had made Nancy her, just an unearthly sadness and hopelessness that brought him across the room to kneel by the bed as he whispered, 'Oh, love, love, what have you done to yourself?' as he took the woman he loved, the woman he would always love, into his embrace.

It was several hours later. Outside the house the New Year had been welcomed in a little while earlier with frenzied hoots and whistles from the ships in the docks, the sound of folk shouting and laughing and calling to each other, dogs barking, along with people singing in the distance, but here, in Nancy's room, all was quiet. Gregory was sitting in front of the small fireplace toasting his feet by the embers of the fire, a blanket round his shoulders. The little armchair the room held was more comfortable than it looked but he had no desire to sleep. Every other moment or so his gaze would fall on the woman sleeping in the bed and when it did, he'd pray another silent prayer: Let her get well. Please, God, let her get well.

Mrs Duffy had waited a full hour before she had brought a tray of tea up after he had first entered the room, but in that time Nancy had done little more than to cry in his arms, incoherently and painfully, her sobs interspersed with coughing so tortured that Gregory had found himself hunching his shoulders against it. It was only after he had persuaded her to drink the tea laced with the little tot of brandy Mrs Duffy had put on the tray for him – 'After that walk in the snow you need something to warm you up, lad' – that the coughing eased somewhat and she was quieter.

She had finished the tea and leaned back against the pillows he had plumped up behind her when her voice came, soft and husky: 'She shouldn't have fetched you.'

'Mrs Duffy didn't fetch me. She told me about your condition and I asked if I could see you.'

'It's not fair, not after what I did.'

'Don't talk daft, woman.' He chose brusqueness to hide what the state of her had done to him – in reality he wanted to bawl his head off like a bairn. 'You're my wife, of course I should know you're bad.'

'Bad in more ways than one.'

'Don't, Nancy.' He was sitting on the edge of the bed and he reached out and took her hand. The skin was transparent, paper thin. 'Don't talk like that.'

'I must. To tell you I'm sorry doesn't even begin to cover how I feel about what I did. I look back on that time and I think I must have been crazy, deranged.'

Another spasm of coughing brought her leaning forward,

her chest heaving. He brushed the hair back from her forehead and was startled at how hot her skin was because her hands were icy cold. 'Don't try to talk, just lay quiet, lass. It's all right, everything is going to be all right.'

She pointed to her medicine and he poured a little into the spoon and gave it to her. After a moment or two, she whispered, 'He – he was not a nice man, Ken. I didn't realize it at first or perhaps I did and wouldn't admit it to myself, I don't know, but he wasn't worthy to lick your boots, Greg. I – I was infatuated with him, like a silly schoolgirl, and he was there and you were gone . . .'

'I know, I know.' She ought to be in hospital. He had said this earlier to Mrs Duffy on the landing when she had come to retrieve the tray, and she had told him the doctor had thought the same but Nancy had refused to go.

'And then, even when I knew I'd made the biggest mistake of my life, I wouldn't eat humble pie. Stubborn. You always said I was stubborn, didn't you.'

'Oh . . .' He made a sound in his throat and shook his head. 'I said a lot of things and half of them were rubbish.'

'That wasn't.' She had shut her eyes at that point, he remembered now, and it was only when she'd said what followed that he realized she had needed to shut out what his face might show. 'I paid for my stubbornness and stupidity, Greg. I want you to – to know. Ken and some of his pals, one night they – they were drunk and they –' she drew in a deep breath – 'they raped me, over and over, and did things, vile, degrading things.'

He had frozen. He knew he ought to say something but it was beyond him.

Her eyes still closed, she whispered, 'The next morning, before I left, I set fire to the house and his money and clothes, everything, and – and I went to the river. The house went up like a tinderbox – I could see the smoke when I threw myself in. I came to in hospital. Some fishermen had jumped in the water and pulled me into their boat. I hated them for that. I pretended to the doctors and nurses that I couldn't remember my name, couldn't remember anything, and for a while I was so ill they thought I was going to die anyway. When I was well enough they sent me to the asylum. They didn't call it that, they said it was a special hospital for people like me whose minds needed rest and healing. They were nice, kind, the doctors and nurses, but the poor people in there, the patients . . .' She shuddered. 'I put up with it as long as I could and then made out my memory was coming back. They counted me as one of their successes.'

He'd found his voice and it was quiet when he said, 'I'll find him and kill him.'

'No.' Her eyes had flown open at this. 'No, please, Greg. That's the last thing I want. You'd get into trouble. Promise me, promise me you won't look for him.' She had begun to cough again and through her struggling for breath had continued to plead with him until he had promised.

She had been quiet for a few minutes after this, lying with her eyes closed, and he thought she had fallen asleep. Then her lids rose and she had looked straight at him. 'I disgust you now, don't I,' she stated softly. 'I'm dirty, soiled.'

'*What*?' Lowering his voice, he said, 'Don't you ever, *ever* say that to me again.'

Her lips began to tremble and he'd leaned down, gathering her against his chest with his good arm as she began to weep again. After a while her sobs had lessened and then ceased altogether, and again he thought she had fallen asleep. He was just about to lay her back against the pillows once more when her voice came in the breath of a whisper, 'I love you, Greg.'

He shut his eyes tightly. He had been married to her for umpteen-odd years and every day before he had gone to war he had told her he loved her, but never once in that time had she told him she loved him unless he had said it first and she'd felt obliged to reply. In a moment of acute sadness and fierce joy he knew the old Nancy had gone for ever, and for however long they had together from this point she would love him and need him in the way he had dreamed about in the past but accepted would never happen. But the cost for him to hear those words had been high. Softly, he murmured, 'I love you, lass. I love you.'

She had slept deeply after that, the noise at midnight from the celebrations outside not causing her to even stir. Twice he had risen from his armchair to check she was still breathing, panicking that now they had found each other again Nancy would leave him once more, but in a way from which there was no coming back.

Mrs Duffy and the third occupant of the house, a tall, plain woman called Miss Franklin, had tiptoed into the room just before midnight with a glass of brandy for him, and both had wished him a happy New Year as they'd toasted 1945 to the belting out of the ships' sirens. He had told the landlady that Nancy would be coming home with him as soon as she was well enough to be moved, at which news the good lady had beamed and said she couldn't have wished for a better start to the New Year, and Miss Franklin had remarked that she was pleased for them but would be sorry to see Nancy go as she had become fond of her.

He didn't know what the bairns would make of this turn of events, Gregory thought, as his eyelids began to grow heavy at last. Likely Horace and the two younger lassies would take it in their stride, but Maria, and especially Cora, were old enough to have their own opinions about such matters. He'd write and explain that he and their mam had got back together again and warn them to go steady with her, he wasn't having Nancy upset, besides which Nancy leaving the way she had hadn't really impacted on the bairns' lives where they were.

Everything would be all right. He echoed the words he'd said to Nancy earlier. He would make sure it was all right. But for now his prime concern was Nancy and he intended to get her well. Everything and everyone else was secondary to that.

Chapter Seventeen

'He's taken her back.' Cora flung the letter she had been reading at Maria, her voice flat but her eyes blazing. She looked at Rachel who was sitting eating her lunch at the kitchen table, along with Maud and Anna and Susan, and repeated, 'He's taken her back after what she did. Is he mad?'

'I take it you mean your father?' said Rachel calmly, continuing to eat the baked jam roll she'd cooked for their pudding.

'She's been *living* with another man.' Cora was beside herself. 'And now she's got fed up with him, or he's got fed up with her, I don't know, she thinks she can just come back and take up where she left off as our mam?'

'She's first and foremost a wife.' Rachel's voice was quiet. 'And what they've worked out and decided to do is between the two of them, don't you think?'

'No, I don't.' Cora breathed in deeply. 'I love my da and what she's done once she'll do again and then where does that leave him?'

'You don't know that, Cora.'

Cora stared at the woman she now counted as a dear friend, her hurt evident when she said, 'Why are you taking her side?'

'It's not a question of taking sides, lass.' Rachel looked at Maud. 'Take Anna and Susan to collect the eggs, please, before you three clean the coop out,' she said, her tone brooking no argument although Maud hadn't quite finished her second helping of pudding. 'Maria, you stay here with Cora.'

When the other children had left, Rachel said, 'May I?' as she pointed to the letter Maria was still holding. She read it in silence but it conveyed little in the way of information:

Dear Cora,

I'm writing to you as the eldest but I want you to explain what I have to say to Maria, Horace, Anna and Susan in your own words. Your mam is back home and everything is all right between us. She realizes her leaving was a mistake and one she very much regrets, and the pair of us want nothing more than for things to return to normal now. I know you'll be pleased we can be a family again once the war is over and you bairns are back home where you belong. Hopefully that won't be too long now.

Your loving Da xxx

Rachel read the letter through twice before she raised her head. It seemed curiously stilted to her in the circumstances but maybe Cora's father was no letter writer. Some folk found it hard to put pen to paper. That would explain the lack of details too, because in spite of what she had said to Cora she felt that at Cora's age she was entitled to some sort of explanation regarding how the reconciliation between her parents had come about. But then perhaps Cora's father saw her not as a young woman who would be eighteen years old in May, but as the bairn he had referred to in the letter, the young bairn she had been when he had left for the war. He wouldn't be the first to make that mistake, nor the last. Families that had been separated for four or five years were going to have to make huge adjustments; it wasn't just difficulties between husbands and wives that were already being reported in the newspapers, but problems with children who'd been evacuated and their parents, and the war wasn't even over yet. These situations would escalate alarmingly once it was. But for now she had to try to pour oil on troubled waters if she could.

Cora and Maria were sitting facing her and their eyes were on her face. Cora said exactly what Rachel had thought: 'He said he wants me to explain things to the others but how can I when he hasn't said anything except that she's back?'

It was noticeable to Rachel that Cora didn't refer to her mother as 'Mam' but as 'she' and it had been like that for a long time.

'In things of this nature it's very difficult to make anyone understand all the whys and wherefores if you're not speaking face to face. I would imagine your da thinks it's better to wait until you're home and you can speak to your mother yourselves.'

There was silence for a moment, and when Cora broke it her voice held a tremor. 'I can't believe he expects us to be pleased about it. She doesn't care about us, any of us. All she was bothered about was this man she went off with. She'll hurt Da again, I know she will.'

'No, you don't know that and it's clear from what he *has* written that he's counting on you all giving your mother a chance to make amends. I can understand how you're feeling, Cora, I really can, but for his sake I think you've got to – if not exactly appear happy about this, then agree to be open-minded.'

Again there was silence until Maria whispered, 'I think that is the only way, Cora.' She laid her hand on her sister's arm. She knew their mother's defection had hurt Cora more than any of them. Horace was so absorbed in his new life at Appletree Farm and so happy in the country that his mother was part of the old life he had no wish to go back to, and this had enabled him to shrug off her leaving them fairly easily. Anna and Susan didn't really understand and barely remembered their mam or da anyway, and although she, herself, had been upset, she had Cora, and Cora had always been more of a mam than a big sister to her, to them all really. In a strange way, because Cora was so like their mam it had made the pair of them closer even though it had also meant they rubbed each other up the wrong way, so sparks flew. She could still remember times before the war when they had all been together and happy, and Cora and their mam had fallen about laughing about something or other while the rest of them, including her da, had looked on bemused.

When Cora didn't respond, Maria said apologetically, 'I feel the same as you, lass, and I'm worried what Da would do if she went off again, but, well, it's up to them, isn't it?'

Cora stared at her sister and then sighed. They were right, of course they were right, she just didn't want to hear it. And for her mam to be able to simply swan back and take up where she had left off with everyone's blessing seemed so *unfair*. Her da had always been putty in her mam's hands, that was the trouble. She had thought that was quite sweet at one time but she didn't any more. But *if* her mam was really going to stay put, and *if* she'd settle into being a mam to Horace and the little ones and Maria, and *if* she made their da happy, then she could see that her coming home would be for the best for everyone. But that was a lot of 'if's in her opinion.

She squeezed Maria's hand before standing up. 'All right, I'll write back and say we're all over the moon and jumping for joy,' she said, tongue in cheek, before managing a wry smile. 'And I'll be positive about it with Horace and Anna and Susan, I promise. Come on, we'd better get back to cleaning out the cowshed.' The POWs were out in the fields with the horses doing the ploughing, turning the ground over so that in the spring the furrows could be cultivated and the crops sown. January had been a bitterly cold month with snow and ice but now, in the middle of February, the snow had cleared to a large extent and sleet and slush were the order of the day. Cora was longing for the spring when they could let the cows out to pasture and the animals could forage for themselves; the herd took up a great deal of her time in the winter months.

As they walked to the cowshed, Maria said, 'I wonder when Mam came back. He didn't say, did he?'

'He didn't say much at all.'

'No, but then Da has never been one for writing letters, has he? Mam neither, come to it.' Maria stopped at the door to the shippon. 'I feel unsettled,' she said suddenly, 'and a bit scared at the thought of the war ending and going home. I hated it here when we first came but now it's different. Do you know what I mean?'

Yes, she knew what Maria meant, and if Jed had still been alive and their plans for the future were in place Appletree Farm would have become her home. She might even have been married by now, certainly engaged and looking forward to a blissful life as a farmer's wife. Wild horses wouldn't have been able to drag her back to Sunderland, whereas now, now she wouldn't be sorry to leave, much as she liked Rachel and working on the farm. Perhaps in Sunderland the ever constant thoughts of Jed, the painful ache in her heart and the knowledge that she had sent the man she loved to his death would ease. She hoped so. Oh, she did so hope so because there were times when the future appeared like a big black hole with nothing but emptiness and loneliness in front of her.

One thing was for sure: the war was definitely drawing to a close. It seemed as though every day there were more reports of the Allies taking ground, and even in their little backwater here the talk was of nothing else. The latest was that in a couple of days of relentless bombardment the RAF and the US Air Force had reduced Dresden to a smoking ruin with tens of thousands of people reported to have lost their lives. They had been taught a little about Dresden at school in geography by Mr Travis who had apparently visited the city on his honeymoon years before and didn't let anyone forget the fact that he had travelled. He had told them Dresden was famed for its seventeenth- and eighteenth-century baroque and rococo art and architecture, and Dutch and Flemish paintings, and was comparable to Florence. The city had looked beautiful from the pictures he had shown them, but then, Cora reflected, so had Coventry before the Germans had turned it into an inferno. Could two wrongs make a right? It was a question she had asked herself more than once as the war had progressed and she was no nearer an answer. One thing she did know was that Hitler had had to be stopped, and the occasional doubt she'd had in the past about whether it had been right for Britain to oppose him had been put to rest when the horrors of the Nazi death camps had begun to be exposed.

As she and Maria entered the cowshed which was a few degrees warmer than the cold and overcast day outside, a few of the cows gave a soft bellow of welcome, hoping that the girls' appearance meant they were going to be fed. As ever, the big, gentle animals worked their magic on Cora, and she said hello to a couple of her favourites, scratching their great heads as she passed.

This was real life, she thought to herself as she and Maria began to muck out with shovel and brush, and this was how things were meant to be. And most folk were content with ordinary, even humdrum, lives, weren't they? So how come the Nazis had got so twisted and evil as to set about a cold-blooded and systematic attempt to destroy an entire section of the human race? Of course there had been talk about the existence of the concentration camps for years, but no one could have guessed at the truth of what had gone on. She still found it hard to believe. The newspapers had reported that the Allies were experiencing a glimpse of hell as the Nazi death camps fell, hardened soldiers weeping at what they had discovered.

The reports that Cora and the others had read about lately, like them finding lampshades made from tattooed human skin and even shrunken heads, had made her physically sick. She and Rachel had made the decision that any newspapers and magazines should be kept away from Anna and Susan. Undoubtedly they'd hear talk at school from their friends, but it wasn't the same as reading it in black and white. And she didn't want their heads filled with such terrible things, not at their age. Wilfred had said the same about Horace but unfortunately her brother, macabre little wretch that he was, had managed to ferret out every gruesome detail that had been reported thus far, but Wilfred had warned him not to say a word to the girls, threatening him with dire consequences if he disobeyed. Dear Wilfred . . .

As she fetched the cows' fresh bedding of wheat straw, which they invariably ate given half a chance, she thought again of what Wilfred had told her a few days ago. It had been a day of icy rain and sleet showers, cold and miserable and bone-chilling, and when he had turned up at the farm after the day's work was done she had been surprised to see him on such a night. When Jed had gone off to war his parents had extended an open invitation for her to come for Sunday tea as had been the pattern when their son was at home, but she hadn't taken them up on it. After a month or two they had sent a specific invitation through Wilfred which he had persuaded her to accept, and since then she had gone for Sunday tea every so often, not so much because she wanted to – it was too painful to be pleasurable – but because she knew it pleased Jed's parents. That night she and Wilfred had sat in the kitchen, the rest of the household being in the parlour in front of a roaring fire, as had become the norm since Farmer Burns's death.

'I've some news.' Wilfred had been excited, she could tell, and for a blindingly hopeful moment she had thought that Mr and Mrs Croft had had news about Jed. 'The

Crofts want me to stay on at the farm when the war finishes and begin to learn more about the financial side of running the farm as well as the physical work. Mr Croft wants me to start going into town with him, to the markets and all that, to see how things are done there, as well as accompanying him to the bank. He said he'd like me to become familiar with the accounts, with everything connected with the farm really. You know what this means, don't you?'

She stared at him. Her disappointment that this wasn't about Jed was so acute she couldn't speak.

'They're looking to me to take over eventually, now that—' He stopped abruptly.

'Now that Jed's dead,' she finished flatly.

'Well, aye, yes.' Wilfred had the grace to look slightly awkward. 'With all three sons gone, there's no heir, is there, but they both said they look on me more and more as family. They know what things are like back in Sunderland with my mam an' da.'

'Do they?' This surprised her. Wilfred never talked about his home situation to anyone but her, and for a brief moment she had the unworthy thought that there had been an element of manipulation in him speaking out to Jed's parents, but immediately dismissed it. Wilfred wasn't like that, and it was his business after all.

'So they know I've got nothing to hold me in Sunderland. And you like it here, don't you? You could see yourself staying on? Living in these parts permanently, I mean?'

'No, not really.' She got up and busied herself making a pot of tea, her back to him. 'Wilfred, I'm glad for you, I really am, and of course you should stay – it's a wonderful opportunity. But when the war ends I shall go home. There's too many memories here for me.'

'Of him, you mean.'

She had turned round then; there had been something in his voice that had disturbed her, but his face was expressionless. 'Of Jed, yes.' She finished making the tea and brought the teapot to the table with the milk jug; they'd used up their sugar ration. 'I can't help it but I could never settle here now, not and be happy, but I meant what I said. You should stay.'

'I wouldn't stay without you, there's no point.'

'Of course there is.' It flashed across her mind that Wilfred was seriously considering stepping into a dead man's shoes but that was his concern. 'You've got friends here and now this chance to make a new life. It's – it's great,' she finished lamely.

He took the mug of tea she poured him and she knew he was upset at her response. For a moment she felt guilty, but then she asked herself what he had expected? He knew full well how she had felt about Jed so why on earth would he think she would be prepared to stay in the district where everything, every single thing, reminded her of what she had lost? If he wanted to take on the role Jed would have performed that was up to him, but she couldn't be party to it.

And then Wilfred himself answered the question when

he said, 'I thought you were getting over him – Jed, I mean. It's been months.'

Oh, she knew how long it had been, to the day, the hour. Warning herself not to snap at him because he couldn't understand – he had never fallen in love with a lass, after all – she said quietly, 'I don't wear my heart on my sleeve, if that's what you mean. It doesn't help anyone.'

'I see.'

'But you must do what's right for *you*, Wilfred.'

'I thought you liked Mr and Mrs Croft.'

'I do, very much, but that's got nothing to do with it.'

They had finished their tea in silence and Wilfred had gone shortly afterwards, but before leaving he had said flatly, 'I'll put off saying anything to Mr and Mrs Croft for a while in case you reconsider staying around, but otherwise I shall come back to Sunderland with you and the others. You're all my family and you don't know what you're going to find back home what with your da being poorly and all this with your mam. I'd – I'd worry about you.'

'Oh, Wilfred.' She had hugged him. 'You don't have to concern yourself about that.'

'Of course I do. I know Horace likes it here and isn't looking forward to going home, and Maria too to some extent, so I thought if you stayed it would probably just be Anna and Susan who'd choose to go back. Appletree Farm would be big enough for all of you and the Crofts wouldn't mind.'

Her brow wrinkled. 'But if I stayed, Maria and I would be here, with Mrs Burns.'

He didn't say anything for a moment, then opened his mouth to speak, stared at her for a few seconds, and shut it again, before nodding and turning away. She watched him on the kitchen doorstep as he walked off, only to come to a halt after a few steps and turn.

'I want the best for you, Cora. I always have. You know that, don't you? I don't want to sound hard but Jed's gone and life has to go on.'

'I know that, Wilfred.'

'Just keep an open mind about what I've said, that's all I ask. Horace loves it here and if you stayed I'm sure your mam an' da would agree to him and Maria staying too. But I'll do whatever you want.'

'This isn't about me.'

The night was pitch black and it was sleeting again and she couldn't see him clearly, but she heard the sigh he gave.

'Goodnight, lass.'

There had been something in his voice she couldn't pin down, she thought now, as she finished sorting the cows' fresh bedding and lifted the handles of the wheelbarrow to cart the old manured straw to the midden. Something more than disappointment that she hadn't seen things the way he had. But bless him, she didn't want Wilfred feeling responsible for them all. It was wonderful having him as a support but perhaps it wasn't fair to him? Not if this sense of duty he had towards them kept him from taking up the Crofts' offer? Somehow – and she knew she would have to pick her words so she didn't offend or hurt him, which was the last thing she wanted – somehow she would have to make it clear that it wasn't his role in life to look after Horace or her or any of them. She would face what she found at home in Sunderland when the time came and deal with it. She wasn't a bairn any more.

Of a sudden she felt weary, though the weariness was not a physical thing but more a state of mind. She missed Jed more than she could ever have expressed to a living soul, and if she allowed herself to think of how she felt, it frightened her, because it wasn't getting any better as time went on. And then bizarrely, and as clearly as if she was standing right in front of her, she heard her mother say, 'So don't think of it then, lass, all right? Get on with what needs to be done and keep your mind from wandering.'

Cora stood stock-still, and so real had the voice been that she found herself glancing round before she told herself not to be so daft. Her mam was miles away in Sunderland and furthermore she was the last person in the world she would unburden herself to or take advice from.

Nevertheless, and in spite of the very real anger and resentment she felt towards her mother, her back straightened and her head lifted. She gave a little 'huh' to herself, at the same time as thinking she would end up in the loony bin if this carried on; but the strange episode had been oddly comforting, much as she didn't want to admit it.

Chapter Eighteen

'This is it, lads. The Russians are closing in.' Jed glanced round the construction site where they had all just assembled, expecting to work as usual. Instead the site was eerily quiet, not one striped figure to be seen. They had been hearing gunfire and artillery in the distance for days and knew that the camp's days were numbered. None of them knew whether that meant slaughter at the hands of the Germans before they could be liberated, or whether they were going to be marched further into German-held territory. They had passed the Jews' camp, a few hundred yards down the track from their own, on their way to the site but it had been empty. Someone had heard a rumour that the Jews had been marched at gunpoint out of the camp early that morning, but rumours had been flying about for days and no one knew what was what. They did know, because they could see and smell it for themselves, that the brutal extermination camps to the west of the complex, Auschwitz I and Auschwitz-Birkenau, had been working full-time burning bodies in their crematoria, the sickly stench of the smoke permeating every nook and cranny.

'Getting rid of the evidence,' Jock had said grimly a few days earlier. It had been then, in their hut, that Jed and the others had made a pact that if any of them survived they would make sure that the world knew what had gone on in Auschwitz.

It had snowed during the night, the fresh snow falling on frozen ground and ice and deep ridges, so that wherever they walked on the site they were in danger of falling over or breaking a limb. It had been a common sight to see the Jews fall, either tripping or collapsing and dying of exhaustion and starvation. They weren't being fed enough to survive. When the Nazis had extracted the last ounce of labour from each dying prisoner they were sent to the gas chambers. Now the hundreds of striped walking skeletons who had swarmed over the site like ants on an anthill were gone but over to the west of them the chimneys were still belching their foul smoke as much as ever.

Jed and the others set about their work as instructed but it was clear the guards were on edge, and although their brutality was normally reserved for the Jews the POWs were careful not to upset them. Not now, when it looked as though liberation might be within reach. There was no doubt the Russians were advancing.

Later that day they were marched back to their barracks and fed the stinking liquid that went under the name of cabbage soup. It had made Jed gag when he had first arrived at Auschwitz but since then he had learned that you could get used to anything if it was the difference between life and death, and compared to the filth the Jews were given it was the finest cuisine.

There had been several Russian air raids in the last days, but Jed and the others had no sooner settled in their bunks than the mother of all raids began. Every last man fled the huts for the field behind them that was full of small humps and depressions, most of the men, including Jed, swearing at their 'liberators'.

'Funny way to rescue us,' Neville said in his broad Welsh accent, calling the Russians every name under the sun a moment later as a bomb fell so close that he was covered in dirt and stones and grime. 'There won't be any beggar left to liberate the way they're carrying on. I'm all for knocking ten bells out of the Germans but what about us?'

'They're not bothered about us, matey,' Jock yelled from his dent in the ground. 'Haven't you cottoned on to that yet? All that matters is moving forward and taking ground from the Germans. If we get in the way of that, that's our funeral.'

'There won't be enough left of us to give a funeral to,' Neville yelled back. 'The mad blighters. And where's the damn Luftwaffe when you want them?'

It would be just their luck to be killed by the Russians on the eve of the war ending, Jed thought to himself in his shallow hollow in the ground, keeping his head down and wincing every time a shell came close. Irony didn't even begin to cover it. But then this just about summed up what war was about – madness and mayhem. There was no sense to it, no reason, just blind slaughter and annihilation. He felt Jock, lying to the side of him, dig him in the ribs, and as he said, 'What?' the older man shouted above the noise of the bombing, 'Just checking you're still in the land of the living, laddie. You've gone a bit quiet.'

'Funny, but I didn't think this was the time for a cosy little chat,' he yelled back, hearing Jock chuckle appreciatively. And in spite of the bombs raining down on the camp just a short distance away, Jed smiled. This was what enabled you to live and survive in hell, he thought as a shower of dirt sprinkled over him, this looking out for each other. He thought he'd had pals before he had joined up but the comradeship that had been forged under fire with Jock and Neville and the others was beyond anything he'd experienced before or was likely to experience again. He'd seen starving men giving up their rations for a sick friend, or put themselves in the way of a brutal beating to protect a weaker individual who wouldn't survive more ill treatment. Amongst all the senseless murder, the cruelty, the bestial acts that defied belief, there were bonds the Nazis couldn't break. Which in the face of unimaginable suffering was an incredible accolade to the human spirit; this defining choice men made of refusing to become mindless autonomous beings just looking out for themselves.

The bombing continued for a long time. It was freezing cold on the snow-covered ground and many of the men curled themselves into a foetal position to try and keep as warm as they could, along with cursing the Nazis and the Russians in equal measure. In spite of the noise and imminent danger Jed dozed once or twice, a mixture of starvation and exhaustion being a powerful sedative. Jock was actually snoring at the side of him.

It was still dark when the raid finished. Jed and the others emerged from their dents in the ground to find that their barracks had been blown to bits although several other blocks were still intact. They stood shivering in the icy air, listening to the Russian guns in the distance that were getting louder. The sound was heartening and terrifying at the same time.

A couple of the watchtowers had been destroyed during the night and the German guards were in a foul mood, ordering the POWs into two columns and telling them they were leaving the camp. Jed looked at Jock and Neville. Did that mean they were going to be led away into the countryside and shot? Anything was possible. Short of getting shot right now, however, they had no other choice but to do what the guards demanded. The Germans were well wrapped up against the sub-zero temperatures in their thick uniforms and greatcoats, but not so the POWs, and as Jed looked down the columns of men there were some who looked as though they could barely stand, let alone march. Nevertheless, at first light they were taken out through the gates of the camp that like the fences were laced with heavy twists of vicious barbed wire, and towards the south-west. Jed wondered if there were any

Jews left in Auschwitz after the orgy of killing and burning that had gone on in the last weeks as the Allies had advanced, or whether the SS had managed to destroy them all in the gas chambers.

They'd only gone a short distance when Neville nudged him and pointed to a striped mound at the side of the track. It was one of the Jewish POWs, covered with a dusting of snow and frozen solid by the heavy frost. The Wehrmacht guards barked for them to keep walking and indeed there was no point in stopping, since it was clear the man was long dead. One of the crude wooden clogs the Jews had worn was lying a foot or so away from the body and seemed infinitely pathetic, summing up the impossibility of any of the men surviving in their thin rags and practically bare feet.

'They've taken the poor blighters on a death march,' Neville murmured as within a minute or so they came across the stiffened corpses of more people, some of whom had been shot where they'd fallen and left, and a number of others dumped in ditches at the side of the track.

'What do you think this is then?' said Jock behind them. 'A Sunday-school picnic?'

That first day as they walked they came across more and more striped bodies, so many that it soon became horrifically commonplace. By the time night fell Jed wondered if any of the Jewish prisoners would survive their march to who knew where. And would he and the others? One of their number, a young thin strip of a lad called

Charley, had already collapsed through fatigue and cold. He had been unable to get up when the guards had ordered him to, but when they'd pointed their rifles at him two of his pals had hoisted him to his feet, telling the Germans they would take turns in carrying him piggy-back fashion. They had all wondered if the three would be shot on the spot, but the guards were not the SS and had merely shrugged uninterestedly and let them do as they wanted.

When they stopped for the night the guards set up their machine guns on tripods, whether as a warning to anyone who had ideas of trying to escape or because they were worried about the Russians, Jed didn't know, but it made everyone jumpy. They had no idea where they were headed or what was planned for them, and after the things they had witnessed at Auschwitz no one had any faith in the rules of the Geneva Convention being adhered to by the Nazis. They had come to a kind of clearing in thick woodland that made it easier for the guards to watch them during the night but which gave no shelter from the bitter cold and snow. Dressed as they were, to sleep was to die, and so, exhausted though Jed was, he merely dozed along with everyone else, and if anyone appeared to be going into a deeper sleep he was woken up by those nearest him.

The guards had doled out a few hard biscuits once the POWs were sitting in the clearing and Jed ate his so quickly he almost choked. The long march over snow and ice in the bitter cold, and not least the increasing number of frozen corpses in their striped rags, had taken its toll on everyone and there was little talk among the men. Even Jock, the undisputed joker of their hut, was subdued. It had become clear that the Germans had rounded up all the Jewish prisoners who were capable of walking for the march, no doubt hoping to wring some more work out of them, but that few would survive. Jed glanced round the POWs as the first faint light of morning streaked the night sky. Even among their own number there were those who weren't going to make it. Starvation and numbing cold had been bad enough to cope with back at the camp, but now they were expected to march miles at a brisk pace and some of the lads weren't up to it, like young Charley for instance. He'd been severely beaten some months before by one of the guards when he'd tried to prevent a young Jewish boy from being kicked to death, and had never really recovered.

The guards had a truck holding their equipment and supplies and the day before a couple of them had ridden in the vehicle with the driver for two or three hours, before alternating with those walking with the column of prisoners. Jed watched as one of the guards brought out more of the cardboard-tasting biscuits from the back of the truck and distributed them among the POWs.

Charley's pals had to feed him his quota, persuading him to eat when he tried to refuse, but when it came to the time the prisoners were told to stand up and form a line, it became apparent Charley hadn't the strength. His friends lifted him, hoisting him onto the back of one of them as the guards watched dispassionately. Filled with a sudden fury, Jed called to the nearest German, 'Your truck – can't he ride in the back of your truck?'

Cold blue eyes stared back at him and for an answer the guard walked over until they were eyeball to eyeball and then drove his rifle butt into Jed's stomach with enough force to send him keeling over. For a moment he couldn't breathe through the pain. He was vaguely aware of Jock and Neville dragging him to his feet, much as Charley's pals had done, and Jock muttering, 'That's enough of the heroics, laddie,' and then the column began moving. He stumbled along between Jock and Neville, practically doubled up and feeling as sick as a dog, but after some hundreds of yards the pain lessened and he was able to straighten himself although his stomach muscles were screaming.

Within minutes the procession was walking alongside more frozen bodies, and so it continued all day. A couple of guards rode in the truck, taking turns with their comrades as they had done the day before, but apart from the occasional brief stop for the prisoners to relieve themselves they marched all that day. It was four o'clock in the afternoon and snowing in the wind when Charley dropped off the back of the man who was carrying him. At what point the boy had died no one knew, but he was quite dead when he hit the ground.

One of the two guards who strode over to inspect what was going on was the German who'd punched Jed in the stomach with his rifle earlier, and he stared at Charley without the slightest flicker of feeling on his young face. He couldn't have been more than Charley's age himself and had probably been one of the Hitler Youth, indoctrinated from childhood as to his place in the 'master race'. He saw Jed staring at him, and in spite of Jock hissing, 'Look away,' Jed continued to let his face express his hatred and revulsion.

When the guard motioned for Jed to go forward, he did so, stopping in front of the German without veiling his expression. 'You, and you –' the guard pointed to the man who had been carrying Charley – 'put him in zhere.' He flicked his gloved hand towards the ditch running at the side of the track.

Jed stared at the Nazi. He knew what the German wanted him to do and that was to refuse to dump Charley's body into the ditch as though it was a sack of rubbish. It would give the guard the excuse he needed to shoot him. For a moment he considered doing just that. Then he crouched over with the other man and together they tenderly lifted Charley between them, stepping down into the four feet of snow and laying the body to rest as gently as though they were settling Charley into a soft comfortable bed. Jed heard the guard say something, contempt in his voice, but he didn't look at him as he climbed out of the ditch, walking back to his place in the column. He was aware of Jock letting out his breath in a deep sigh of relief.

In an aside, Jed muttered, 'I'll kill him before this is over if I get half a chance. I swear it, Jock. I'll squeeze the life out of him with my bare hands.'

'You and me both, laddie. You and me both.'

A half-mile or so along the track from where they'd left Charley, the column came to a burned-out farmhouse that looked as though it had been deserted for some time. There was a large barn at the back of it that was still intact, however, and the guards marshalled them into it. Bedding down in the straw it contained was infinitely preferable to the previous night, and although Jed went to sleep with his stomach growling, it was a relief to be able to give in to the exhaustion knowing he was in no fear of freezing to death while he slept.

In the morning the column continued to head west, and so it was in the days ahead. Frozen striped bodies by the wayside; nights spent sleeping out in the snow when no shelter of any kind was available; constant gnawing hunger as even the biscuits became fewer, and still no idea where they were ultimately bound for.

It was on the seventh day of the march, around midday, that Jed suddenly realized they hadn't come across any Auschwitz victims for a couple of hours. The corpses hadn't gradually become less but had stopped abruptly, and it was this that told him that the convoy was now on a different route from that which the Jews had taken. On that day too, with food now very scarce, he and the other POWs – under the guards' watchful eye – stole what they could carry of a crop of winter vegetables from the fields either side of the road. That night the guards lit a fire and they cooked the lot and for once prisoners and Germans alike went to sleep with full stomachs. From that point on most of what they ate was of necessity stolen from fields, barns and even cottage gardens, but still they were hungry all the time.

It wasn't the hunger or exhaustion or even the aches and pains in his frail body that was the hardest to bear, though, Jed thought one night as he lay awake between Jock and Neville on the frozen ground. It was Cora flitting into his mind if he allowed himself to sleep on the nights they were under some kind of shelter. Each time he awoke after dreaming about her, the pain of losing her was as raw as the first day he had left the farm. If, by some miracle, he made it through to the end of the war, he would still be facing a life without her because she must hate him now. Had she turned to Wilfred for comfort? His guts twisted. But why ask the road you know? Wilfred would have made sure of it. Damn it, he'd been such a fool.

He must have dropped into a light doze eventually because although he could hear Neville rousing him and Jock it was on the perimeter of his consciousness. Somehow he made himself sit up, shaking his head to dispel the fogginess in his mind and taking a couple of the raw carrots Neville had given him as his share from what the convoy had stolen the day before.

That day they saw mountains in the distance and the track steepened. The further they climbed the colder it got, the snow whipping skin and turning into little ice balls in beards and hair. Jed noticed that the guards rotated who rode in the truck and who walked with the prisoners more often now, the Germans marching for no more than an hour or so without a break, but the punishing pace didn't lessen in spite of the conditions. Several more POWs succumbed to exhaustion and the weather, each of the four men who died falling to sleep at night in the snow and not waking up. Jed, Jock and Neville took turns each night to sit up for a couple of hours, ensuring that the two who were dozing didn't go into that deeper sleep from which there was no awakening.

After a few days the route began to slowly level out and then they found themselves beginning to descend. It made walking easier and the further they went the less cold it became, although on the third day of the descent when they spent the night in a ramshackle outbuilding attached to an abandoned and derelict farmhouse, when Jock pulled off one of his boots he left part of a toe behind. Jed had lost the sensation in his feet more than once, causing him to stamp and jump in spite of his exhaustion in an attempt to stave off frostbite, and after staring aghast at Jock he took off his own boots in fear and trepidation, immensely relieved when ten very dirty and very smelly toes still firmly attached to his feet greeted him.

Jock took the loss of the toe in his usual pragmatic way. 'Could have been worse,' he said wryly. 'A toe or two I can do without as long as my wedding tackle's in place. The wife wouldn't be too impressed if I left that halfway up a mountain.'

They were tending to march about twenty miles or so

each day, and once they had left the mountains and were back in open country again, they all noticed that the guards were a lot more jumpy. They were in partisan territory and the Germans clearly were edgy about an attack. Each night they set up their machine guns on tripods facing away from the circle of POWs and into the darkness beyond, and once or twice in the middle of the night one guard or another fired off a volley into the blackness thinking he had seen something, causing hope and consternation in equal measure in the POWs. Jed knew they couldn't escape without outside help – they were under armed guard all the time and the Nazis wouldn't hesitate to shoot first and ask questions later – but in a shoot-out with the Germans and the partisans it was likely a good number of the prisoners would be killed. Jed had already decided, however, that anything would be better than this march and slowly being starved to death. If a chance to escape occurred he'd take it, whether he ended up with a bullet through his head or not. The convoy was now mostly surviving on mangel-wurzels stolen from the fields, any remaining supplies in the truck being reserved for the guards.

Jed had ceased wondering where their eventual destination was. Days had turned into weeks and the Germans had taken them through Ratibor in Silesia and on into Czechoslovakia, passing through Pardubice on the river Elbe and then Prague. More of their number had died but now with each death the guards did at least let the POWs dig a grave by the wayside and bury their comrades with the dignity they hadn't been afforded in life. It seemed the Nazis were getting as weary as they were, and disillusioned with the war in general. Not that Jed doubted for a moment that they would execute a POW at the drop of a hat, but the ferocious arrogance that had characterized every last one of the guards was not so much in evidence. When they passed through the outskirts of villages and towns and the local people – Czechs rather than ethnic Germans – gave the POWs bread or lumps of cheese or anything they had to hand, the guards didn't try to prevent it as at one time they would have done. Jed didn't think it was out of pity or any feeling for their fellow man but simply that they didn't care any more. They were beaten – they had lost the war and they knew it – but the motions still had to be gone through. The glorious future that Hitler had promised each and every one of them was crumbling about their ears but orders still had to be obeyed and they would deliver the POWs to their destination even if they died doing so.

Jock was struggling by the time the column came to the outskirts of Cheb. His damaged foot had become infected and was oozing pus. The thick greenish-yellow liquid stank to high heaven and his ankle was so swollen that the skin looked as though it was ready to burst open. Jed knew the guards would do nothing to help; another POW buried at the wayside meant little to them except for the inconvenience of having to delay the march for a while.

The column stopped for the night in a huge barn full of straw and to their delight, in a corner of the building and covered with dirty sacks, were piles of potatoes, obviously stored away and hidden by the owner of the farm. Within minutes the POWs had gathered wood and lit a fire just outside the barn to cook the lot, the guards making sure they had their share first. Jed and Neville carried their potatoes and Jock's over to where their friend was sitting, his face grey and tight with pain from his injured foot. Jed waited until they'd all eaten their fill. It was the first time in weeks their stomachs had been full and for what he had to say it was better received when replete.

He looked straight at Jock and said, 'You know that infection's going to spread and at the very least you're likely to lose your leg.'

Jock stared at him, taken aback. 'If you're trying to cheer me up you're doing a miserable job.'

'No, I'm not trying to cheer you up, I'm facing facts. If you've got any chance of keeping your leg and your life along with it, we have to get medical help. You've got nothing in you to fight infection – none of us have, we're all half dead as it is.'

Neville shook his head. 'The guards will never agree to it, you know that.'

'Aye, I do, that's why the three of us have got to escape and tonight's as good as any other. Better, in fact. The guards are full of potatoes and whatever else they've still got in their truck. They're more relaxed than usual and that means they're less on the ball. Why do you think I got us three sitting here, at the back of the barn?'

'Enlighten us, laddie.'

'There's a damn great hole, well, a hole at least, behind the bales of hay you're leaning against, Jock. Big enough for us to crawl through at a pinch. We'll wait till everyone's asleep and the guards have just done one of their patrols, and then we'll make a run for it. Or in Jock's case, a hobble.' He grinned. 'Piece of cake.'

'A cake with too many holes in it for my liking.' Jock's voice was grim. 'And I'm not letting you two get killed because of my foot. Even if we manage to crawl through the gap and get outside we've no idea where to go. We've got no weapons and we can't trust the locals, added to which I'd slow you down too much. You two go but I'd be a liability.'

'We either go together or not at all and I, for one, am not prepared to watch you die slowly like poor old Ralph or that young London lad.' Both of these men had contracted infections through open wounds; one, Ralph, had died of gangrene and the other of septicaemia. Both deaths had been chilling.

'One of the lads is sure we're going to cross the border into Germany in the next twenty-four hours or so. You know who I mean? Walt, the lad with a smattering of German. He heard the guards talking. Who knows what'll happen then. What with our lot bombing the hell out of the Nazis and then us turning up to one of their damn camps, seems to me we're piggies in the middle. If we're not shot on sight by the Germans, the Allies might do the job for 'em with a damn great bomb. If we get away tonight we'll have a chance, and we'll find someone to look at your leg, Jock. If I have to steal a weapon and shoot someone to do it, I will.'

'If you shoot 'em make sure it's after they've treated me leg and not before.'

'So you're up for it?'

'You've painted such an attractive picture of what'll happen if I don't, I can't see I've any choice.'

Jed looked at Neville. 'All right with you?'

Neville nodded. He could see that Jock needed help and fast. Jock had three young children at home who hadn't seen their father for some years; he didn't want it to end for their mate like this with his flesh slowly going bad.

'Once it's quiet then.' Jed's voice held a thread of excitement. For weeks, months, he had been longing to *do* something, and the longer the march had gone on the more he had been determined not to be shot at the end of it. When the Nazis knew they had lost for sure, when it was official, he wouldn't put it past them to slaughter any POWs in their care. The fewer witnesses to accuse them of war crimes the better. As far as they were concerned the Geneva Convention boiled down to their trigger fingers on a machine gun or a Luger pistol. Life was cheap. Suddenly the terrified face of a young, beautiful girl flashed into his mind. She had been in the back of a lorry with other female POWs that had passed them as they'd walked back to their camp one night from the site in Auschwitz, and he had noticed her because there was something about her that reminded him of Cora. He had gazed after the lorry for a moment, and the man next to him in line had muttered, 'Poor devils, they've been picked to go in the brothel. The Kapos need a constant fresh supply with what they inflict on the women. They don't last long.' He'd stared aghast at the man and for some time after that he'd tormented himself with what she might be going through.

With the image of her clear in his mind now, he whispered, 'Tonight then, for better or worse.'

Jock gave a weak chuckle. 'I'm not marrying you, laddie, bonny though you might be with them big blue eyes of yours.'

In the event, the escape went like clockwork. The rest of the prisoners were snoring loudly and the guards on duty at the doors of the barn had settled down with a hot drink and were talking amongst themselves when Jed nudged Jock and Neville awake.

Neville went first, slowly manoeuvring himself into the thin narrow space between the wall of the barn and the bales of hay by shuffling an inch at a time until he was hidden from view. Jed gave him a minute or two and then it was Jock's turn. Jed and Neville had decided they needed one of them on the outside of the barn to help Jock through the hole, and after Jock had inched out of sight Jed was glad of the chorus of snores from their fellow POWs as he heard muffled cursing behind him and a good deal of rustling. Clearly Jock, who was a big man at six foot four, had got wedged in the hole in the wall of the hut. Jed had to trust that Neville could ease Jock out because there wasn't enough room for him to duck down behind the bales and help. After a few moments it was quiet, and now he followed the others, careful not to dislodge the bales or make any noise. He slid through the hole fairly easily to find Neville and Jock lying flat on their stomachs waiting for him.

Leaving the bulk of the hut for the field beyond was scary, and any moment Jed expected shouts or warning shots in the air, but the night was dark and quiet. They crossed the field and the scrubland beyond, their hearts pounding fit to burst and Jock swearing every so often from the pain in his foot, but then they were in a second field with high thick hedgerows surrounding it which obscured them from view.

They walked for a couple of hours but slowly; Jock was finding it hard. When Jed was satisfied they had put enough miles between themselves and the German guards, they crawled deep into thick hedgerow that had space enough in the middle for them to lie down as well as giving a surprising amount of shelter from the cold wind. It wasn't as warm as the barn they had left but the fact that they were free, that they had escaped their captors, made the accommodation like that of a first-class hotel.

Jed awoke at first light. Jock and Neville were still sleeping soundly and he let them. He needed time to think. The first thing they had to do was to find some kind of help for Jock, but he didn't have the faintest idea of where they were or how that could be accomplished. The three of them were dressed in what remained of their battledress and there was no way they could venture forth into a town or village in daylight. Some of the locals the column had passed on their journey had been friendly enough; others had spat at them or shouted insults. A few times, when someone had thrown food to them, other folk had remonstrated with the benefactor and even come to blows. Nevertheless, they would have to take the risk of being captured and shot if Jock was to avoid losing his leg.

Once the others were awake, they set off in a south-westerly direction. Jock had a little compass on him that had been his father's and which he'd kept safe all through the war; it now came into its own. It was around three or four in the afternoon when they came across a brick-built house with a neat front and back garden. They had skirted a village shortly before, taking care not to be seen, but the house was a good mile or two from the settlement and set on its own in countryside with fields behind and to the sides of it.

They were hungry and tired, and it had become clear in the last hour that Jock couldn't walk for much longer that day. As Jed surveyed the house, it came to him that he had little option but to try and get food, and maybe hot water and disinfectant for Jock's foot. It was agreed Jock would remain out of sight while he and Neville approached the house. They both knew what it might mean. If the householder was hostile it would be kill or get killed but as Neville, a churchgoer back home in his native Wales, said, 'It's in God's hands, boyos. It's in God's hands.'

They left the cover of the hedgerow that bordered the lane off which the house was situated, crossing the road and opening the little wicker gate into the front garden which had been planted with row upon row of vegetables. Walking round the side of the house they came to the back door where a large black-and-white cat was busy cleaning itself on the doorstep. It eyed them lazily through bright green eyes and then miaowed loudly, standing up and rubbing round their legs.

'Well, the cat's friendly enough,' Neville whispered, just a moment before the door opened a crack and a rifle poked out of the gap.

It was one of those moments in life where time seemed suspended. They stood frozen, the cat continuing to wind round them, purring now, and then the door opened further to reveal a little gnarled old woman with a crab-apple face and thin white hair pulled into a tight bun on top of her head. They stared at her and she stared back, and it was only afterwards that Jed reflected the sensible thing to have done would be to put their hands in the air. She eyed them up and down before saying, 'English?'

Totally taken aback, Jed nodded. 'We – we mean you no harm. We're not armed,' he stammered, hoping she understood. Certainly her pronunciation of the word 'English' had been good. 'But we have a friend who needs help. His foot's infected.' He lifted up his own foot and pointed to it. 'Infected.'

The woman surveyed them for a moment more before saying in perfectly good English, 'There is no need to labour the point. I am in full possession of my mental faculties. Where is he?'

Jed turned and pointed. 'In the lane.'

'Fetch him.'

Jed blinked. Of all the possible scenarios that he had considered first thing that morning when the other two had still been sleeping, coming across a little granny who spoke English and seemed friendly had not been one of them. Mind you, she still had the rifle pointing at them.

'Thank you. If we could just have some hot water and disinfectant if you have any?'

'Fetch him. And my name is Etta, Etta Mieser.'

An hour later Jed was reflecting that God must be on their side. When they'd got Jock into the house, Etta already had a kettle full of boiling water ready and had fetched a tin box from a cupboard which contained bandages and other medical bits and pieces. The rifle had disappeared – she obviously didn't trust them enough to leave it in view – and she had told them to sit at the kitchen table while she eased Jock's boot off his foot, drawing in her breath in a sharp whoosh when she saw the state of it.

She had left the kitchen for a moment, returning with a small framed photograph which she had shown to Jock.

'This is me,' she said quietly. 'I used to be a nurse so I know what I am about.' The photograph showed a young smiling girl in nurse's uniform.

She had the slightest of accents, and Jock had said, 'Are you English?'

'Swiss. My husband is German – was German. He has been dead for many years but I think that is good now. He would not have wanted to see what Hitler has done to the country he loved.'

This boded well. Heartened, Jed ventured, 'You're not in favour of Hitler?'

She looked at him. 'I had friends who were Jewish,' she said simply before turning away and mixing hot and cold water along with a considerable amount of salt into a bowl which she set on the floor at Jock's feet. 'First we soak, then we see better.'

Over the next little while as Jock's foot continued to soak, Etta fed them a meal of fried potatoes and a strong-smelling sausage that tasted as if it had fallen straight from heaven, along with a home-made loaf of grainy bread that she cut into slices and daubed with dripping. As they ate she told them how her family had moved from Switzerland to England towards the end of the last century when she had been verging on womanhood, and then back to Switzerland in the mid-twenties where she had met her husband, Hans, a doctor. The pair of them had married and transferred to a hospital in Hans's home town of Marktredwitz when Hans's aged parents had become frail, and once the old couple had died had made their home just across the German border in Cheb, initially in the town itself before moving out into the country to this present house. They had never had children, having married relatively late in life and both being dedicated to their careers, something, Etta had told them, she again gave thanks for now.

'So many young men dead,' she said with a shake of her head. 'So many mothers' hearts broken.'

Jock's foot had been in the bowl for an hour and Etta had changed the water twice, making it as hot as he could bear. She now dried it with a towel and looked at her patient.

'This will not be comfortable,' she said quietly, 'but it needs to be done.'

Jock stared at her. 'The last time a doctor said that I had a damn great needle stuck in my backside.'

Etta smiled. 'You men,' she murmured. 'Such babies, yes? But I have no needle so that is good.' She unfolded the towel to reveal a nasty great open wound that had spread across most of his foot under his remaining toes and which was oozing gently. His ankle had ballooned and was red and angry, and there were signs that the infection was beginning to spread up his leg. His foot was resting on a towel on Etta's lap and as she placed her fingers either side of the wound, she said, 'If you want to swear and shout, please do so. No one will hear but your friends here. In my time I have heard it all, I assure you, young man.'

Jock didn't swear or shout but after she had finished

draining as much of the pus as she could, he gave a long shuddering sigh of relief. His forehead was wet with sweat.

'We now clean again with my olive-leaf extract.' Etta smiled at Jock. 'The leaves are soaked in vodka for five weeks. You would like to drink this, yes? But not today. Today your foot benefits.'

Jock raised his eyebrows at Jed and Neville. Etta caught the look and said, 'Trust me. This will help fight the bacteria and inflammation and it is natural. My husband was a clever man and did much research into the way the body heals. Sometimes when we try to beat Nature at her own game we do more harm than good. We do not want to interfere with the process of wound healing if we can help it but merely assist.'

'I'm in your hands.'

'Yes, you are.' It was firm. 'Now the wound is deep, too deep, but as we cannot take you to the hospital I will do the best I can. This wound needs to heal from the inside out and be kept moist. No scab, you understand?'

'What? But . . .' Jock stared at her helplessly. 'I need you to bandage me up so we can be on our way.'

Etta shook her head. 'This will not be possible for a while.'

'But a scab under the bandage'll protect the foot, won't it? Everyone knows that.'

'I am not everyone.' Suddenly Etta was every bit the nurse, in fact she reminded Jed of a matron he'd seen in action in a hospital in England when he had visited a sick pal. She'd scared the living daylights out of patients and doctors alike, and her nurses were absolutely terrified of her. But the hospital had run like clockwork. 'We need new cells to colonize the wound area and as you are far from healthy your body will need all the help it can get.' She had finished dousing the foot with her concoction which she allowed to dry naturally before glancing at Jed. 'That jar of honey there, pass it to me.'

Jed was past asking questions. He watched as Etta opened the jar and slathered the honey over Jock's foot, after which she took a thin gauze strip that she'd soaked in the olive-leaf extract and laid it over the wound. Once Jock's foot was resting on the towel on the chair, she smiled at them. 'My bees produce the finest honey in Czechoslovakia.'

'I'm sure they do,' Jock said, humbly, 'but—'

'No buts. You will stay here until your foot is healed sufficiently. We will keep it clean and moist and you will eat good food with lots of garlic and honey to help the process.'

'But we can't take your food and if you are caught helping us—'

Etta made a sound in her throat. 'I am not afraid,' she said, her voice suddenly soft. 'I am an old woman and often I think I have lived too long as it is. To see what I see these days is painful beyond words. My Hans would be distraught. I have seen neighbours, friends, delivering other neighbours and friends up to the Nazis, knowing that they will be sent to the death camps, and simply because they are Jews. Little children, babies . . .' She shook her head. Looking at Jed, she said, 'The three of you will be as safe as it is possible to be in these times here. No one comes, not any more. I grow my own vegetables, I keep my chickens and I have Oriel, my cow, for milk and cheese. I have plenty to share. Saxon and I want for nothing.'

'Saxon?'

'You met him on the doorstep.' Etta smiled. 'Now, I will clear away and then I will put the kettle on, yes? It will be good to have company for a while. And then we will see about where you will sleep, and you –' she turned to Jock – 'will be still and keep your foot on the chair like a good boy.'

Jed looked at the small figure and found to his embarrassment that he was fighting back tears. After all the brutality, the vileness, the unbelievable atrocities of the last years, here was this tiny woman with snow-white hair and a flowered pinny offering them not just the hand of friendship in an alien environment but help and succour, despite the danger to herself. He swallowed hard and glancing at Neville and Jock he saw his feelings reflected in their faces too. Here, in this little kitchen, there was more healing going on than just Jock's foot.

PART FIVE

Births, Marriages and Deaths

1945

Chapter Nineteen

'So, lass, there were times when we thought it was never going to happen but it's over. There's just the Japs to beat now but they're as good as finished, from all accounts.'

Cora nodded. She and Rachel were setting the table for breakfast and Maria and the others had gone to the hen coop to let the birds out after being confined during the night, and to bring any fresh eggs back with them. The schools were closed for two days and in the village closest to the farm, bunting and flags of the victorious countries had been up for days. A street party, to which the inhabitants of the nearby farms were invited, was planned for that afternoon.

Rachel stopped what she was doing and came over to Cora, patting her arm as she said, 'I know this is a day of mixed blessing for you, dear.'

It was rare for Rachel to use any form of endearment and this, more than her words, touched Cora. She was determined, however, that she wasn't going to be a wet blanket on the air of excitement that was pervading the house on this special day, VE Day, and so she blinked away the moisture at the back of her eyes and forced a smile. 'Me and countless others.'

'Aye, that's true, but each of us has to carry our own burden, lass, and it doesn't make it any the less heavy by being aware of others doing the same.'

As Rachel walked over to the range and stirred the porridge, Cora looked out of the kitchen window. It was raining, but that suited her mood. She didn't want blue skies and bright sunshine, selfish though that was in view of the celebrations planned for the day. And it wasn't just Jed she was thinking of, who had lost his life in a foreign land so far away from everything he had loved, but the men fighting in the Far East. It didn't seem right to be rejoicing when British soldiers were still being killed every hour of every day. Rachel had said the Japs were as good as finished, but they *weren't* finished, that was the point, however much the newspapers went on about the Allied victories, and all the flag-waving today wouldn't change that fact for the families here still living in dread of receiving an official telegram. And she couldn't get it out of her head, no matter how much she told herself it was pointless to think this way now, that if Chamberlain and the rest of his cronies hadn't imagined that they could meekly pacify Hitler but had called his bluff and shown that Britain was prepared to defend herself in 1938, the war might not have happened anyway.

But all that was speculation, and however she felt, the rest of the country were apparently going to go all out with parties and teas and what-have-you. Anna and Susan had come home with stories that some of the mothers in the village had gone to great trouble to cut up any pieces of material they had available to make red, white and blue dresses for their offspring, and at the very least the girls were going to have hair bands of the same colours, little lads bow ties, older folk rosettes; and one of Anna's friends had told her their mother had sewn a coat for their dog from a flag she had bought. It was as though after all the drabness and privation of the last few years, people were determined to go mad. Cora sighed. And she couldn't blame them. If Jed was alive and well she'd probably be the same. As it was, she would have preferred to just go about her work on the farm quietly and thank God it was all over.

The four girls came back with a basket of eggs in the next moment, full of chatter and squeals and laughter, and again Cora inwardly sighed. It was going to be a long day.

At just after two when Wilfred and Horace arrived at the farm as had been arranged the previous Sunday, the weather was proving mercurial. The heavy rain first thing that morning had given way to blue skies and sunshine later, before more clouds and a cold drizzle as Cora had eaten lunch. Now it was merely dull and overcast but Cora, whose emotions had fluctuated wildly all day, felt perfectly in tune with Mother Nature.

They were riding to the village with Rachel in the horse and cart, Cora sitting beside the farmer's wife on the plank seat and the others perched in the back of the cart on a number of sacks filled with straw. Maria and Maud and the three younger ones could barely sit still, they were so excited about the street party, chattering away and chirruping like a small flock of sparrows. Cora turned round to Wilfred who was sitting just behind her.

'Are Jed's parents coming today?' she asked quietly. She hadn't been to Appletree Farm for some weeks. Strangely, the closer the end of the war had seemed, the harder it had been to see them on a Sunday afternoon. She couldn't rationalize why and she didn't try.

Wilfred shook his head. 'They're staying at the farm. Mr Croft said they'll have a glass of sherry and listen to Churchill's broadcast at three.'

Cora could understand that. She would have liked to sit quietly at home and toast the fallen. It was more appropriate than fun and frivolity and she knew they would be thinking of their three sons. Many times in the night when she couldn't sleep for thoughts of Jed, she had considered how his mother must feel. She had lost her three precious boys to this war, and yet she made herself get up each morning and get on with the day. Jed's mother didn't know it, but she was remarkable, like so many others.

When they arrived at the village they found the main street had been decorated to within an inch of its life. Tables and benches and chairs lined the road, and large flags, small flags and bunting stored from the Coronation turned the street into a rainbow-like world, along with

Christmas decorations and coloured lights. Someone had rigged up a loudspeaker in readiness for the Prime Minister's broadcast at three, and when it began even the most excited of the children became silent. As Churchill began to speak Cora couldn't hold back the tears, but then every other woman around her was the same. There was barely a family represented here today who hadn't lost a loved one.

The familiar voice began: '*Yesterday at 2.41 a.m. at General Eisenhower's headquarters, General Jodl, representative of the German High Command and Admiral Doenitz, designated head of the German state, signed the act of unconditional surrender of all German land, sea and air forces, in Europe, to the Allied Expeditionary Force and simultaneously to the Soviet High Command. Today, this agreement will be ratified and confirmed at Berlin. Hostilities will end officially at one minute after midnight tonight, Tuesday 8 May, but in the interest of saving lives, the "Cease Fire" began yesterday to be sounded all along the fronts.*'

Next to Cora, Mrs Armstrong, the butcher's wife, gave a choked gasp, the tears pouring down her face, and her husband put his arm round her. They had lost two boys at Dunkirk but had twenty-two-year-old twins, Toby and Lonnie, still at the front somewhere in Germany, and their mother was terrified one or both of them would be killed in the last hours of the war.

Apart from stifled weeping there was not a sound to be heard in the village as the Prime Minister continued,

'I should not forget to mention that our dear Channel Islands, the only part of His Majesty's Dominions that has been in the hands of the German foe, are also to be freed today. The Germans are still in places resisting the Russian troops, but, should they continue to do so after midnight, they will, of course, deprive themselves of the protection of the laws of war, and will be attacked from all quarters by the Allied troops. It is not surprising that on such long fronts and in the existing disorder of the enemy, the commands of the German High Command should not, in every case, be obeyed immediately.'

Mrs Armstrong gave a little muffled cry and Cora heard her husband say, 'They'll be all right, Beth, they'll be all right. I know you're worried but stop torturing yourself, lass. Let the day's troubles be sufficient unto the day, that's what the Good Book says. The lads'll be home before you know it, I feel it in me water.'

Cora had missed a little of Churchill's speech but now she concentrated again as the loudspeaker crackled and whined for a moment in the cold north-east wind.

'After years of intense preparation, Germany hurled herself on Poland at the beginning of September, 1939, and, in pursuance of our guarantee to Poland and in agreement with the French Republic, Great Britain, the British Empire and Commonwealth of Nations declared war upon this foul aggression. After gallant France had been struck down we, from this island, and from our United Empire maintained the struggle single-handedly for a whole year until we were joined by the military

might of the Soviet Union and later by the overwhelming power and resources of the United States of America.'

There was a wave of muted muttering at this point; some of the men present making their feelings known, albeit quietly, about the lateness of America's arrival into the war. They hadn't seen too many GIs hereabouts but that didn't stop the menfolk from objecting to the young, dashing strangers who had swarmed into the country and straight into the affections of innumerable British women. The catchphrase of 'overpaid, oversexed and over here' was also, according to many women, overdone by their resentful menfolk.

'*Finally*,' the Prime Minister went on, '*almost the whole world was combined against the evil doers who are now prostrate before us. Our gratitude to all our splendid Allies goes forth from all our hearts in this island and throughout the British Empire. We may allow ourselves a brief period of rejoicing, but let us not forget for a moment the toils and efforts that lie ahead. Japan, with all her treachery and greed, remains unsubdued. The injustice she has inflicted on Great Britain and the United States, and other countries, and her detestable cruelties call for justice and retribution. We must now devote all our strength and resources to the completion of our task both at home and abroad.*'

There was a moment's pause, then, '*Advance Britannia! Long live the cause of freedom! God save the King!*'

Everyone in the street had hung on to every word Churchill had said and now there were loud cheers and a waving of hats and flags. People were laughing and crying, and the children, released from their enforced solemnity and knowing that the promised high tea with jellies and cakes and sweets was about to begin, went mad with excitement, squealing and dashing about and getting in everyone's way.

Cora felt as though she was on the outside looking in as the afternoon progressed, and had she but known it plenty of other women, behind their cheerful expressions, felt the same. But the celebrations were in essence for the bairns, as one housewife murmured to her after the tea had finished and the planned games began.

'Today doesn't really mark the first day of peace, not the way we knew it before the war anyway,' the middle-aged woman said sadly. 'Japan's still fighting, the wicked so-an'-sos, and we've still got all the wartime restrictions after all. Mind, there's some who are only too pleased to make merry.' She cast a grim and meaningful glance at her husband who was on his umpteenth glass of beer.

He ignored her, winking at Cora who was standing with Wilfred, keeping an eye on Horace and the younger two girls who were engaged in a game of musical statues, a piano having been hauled out of someone's house onto the pavement.

'I keep telling her a glass of something or other would do her the world of good,' he said in a stage whisper so his wife could hear every word. 'Got a face like a battered pluck half the time, she has. Here, lad,' he added, reaching for a jug on the table and filling up Wilfred's empty glass with foaming beer, 'get that down you. Nothing like home-brew for putting hair on your chest.'

Cora looked a trifle anxiously at Wilfred. He'd already had three glasses of beer to her knowledge and it showed. Rachel had warned them on the way that most of the home-made beer and wine that would be on the tables that day was strong enough to knock a mule out.

'Mrs O'Leary's blackberry wine is the worst,' she'd murmured so the younger ones didn't hear. 'When the vicar went round to discuss their youngest daughter's wedding last year they had to carry him home to the vicarage and he swore he'd only had two glasses. Mind, knowing the O'Learys, I bet it was pint glasses they gave to the poor man. Took him ages to live it down in spite of him insisting he thought it was blackberry cordial rather than wine. We certainly haven't had any sermons about the demon drink since which is a blessing. He was hot on that at one time.'

Wilfred caught Cora's look and grinned at her. She had had one small glass of wine at the end of Winston Churchill's speech when one of the local farmers had taken it upon himself to raise a toast to the Prime Minister, the fallen and the brave lads who were still fighting, but since then had drunk only cups of tea. He drank half the glass of beer straight down before he wiped his mouth on the back of his hand and said, 'I agree with that fella, lass. It's a day for celebrating and we've waited for it long enough.'

She smiled back but said nothing. He was right, of

course he was right, but she just didn't feel the way he did.

Although the afternoon was cloudy and overcast the rain held off, and after the games for the children had finished, the red-cheeked buxom matron at the piano struck up song after song for the dancing which went on until twilight. Wilfred had tried to persuade her to dance several times but Cora had refused, using the excuse that she needed to keep an eye on Maria and the others. She was finding she didn't like the Wilfred who drank. He was over-loud and despite her encouraging him to ask one of the girls waiting for a dance to take the floor, he remained glued to her side. When a couple of the local lads asked her to dance at different times during the evening he was quite rude to them, and although she took him to task and said she was quite capable of refusing their attentions without his help he just laughed and said it didn't hurt for them to know the score. Quite what the score was she didn't know, and she wasn't about to ask Wilfred in his present state of intoxication.

By the time it was dark enough to light the huge bonfire on the common which had been added to for days, Cora had a thudding headache and was longing for the time when she could collect Maria and the others together and they could go home. Rachel had been sitting with a group of villagers all evening and Cora had noticed that one man, who seemed unattached, had paid her marked attention. Rachel looked flushed and bright-eyed and twice had danced with him; she certainly seemed in no hurry to leave the festivities, and Cora had resigned herself to staying at the celebrations until the bitter end.

A life-sized image of Hitler, stuffed with straw, had been suspended by the neck in the middle of the main village street on a rope stretched from one bedroom window across to another on the opposite side of the road. Now that the bonfire was going to be lit, it was brought down and the effigy was placed on two planks to be carried to its funeral. The 'bearers' led the way to the common at the head of a procession of all the residents of the village and other merrymakers, whereupon 'Hitler' was hoisted to the top of the bonfire and the fire was lit. There was much cheering and yelling as the effigy was consumed by the flames, children shrieking with glee without really having the faintest idea of what was going on besides the fact that after five years of blackout, illumination had returned to their world.

As folk began to dwindle back to the street and the piano for more dancing, Wilfred caught hold of Cora's arm, his eyes glittering in the glow of the dying bonfire. 'This is a new beginning for everyone, do you feel that?' he said thickly, stumbling a little over his words. 'The past is behind us, we have to look to the future now. Do you see that? Do you?'

Taken aback by his manner and his grip on her arm but thinking it was the drink talking and aiming to placate him, she murmured, 'Yes, yes, Wilfred. The war is over for most folk and things will get better now.'

Pulling her away from the bonfire and into the

surrounding shadows, he ignored her attempts to extricate herself. 'I need to talk to you, to tell you,' he muttered, almost to himself. 'That's what I need to do.'

Cora suddenly had the feeling she didn't want to hear what he had to tell her. 'Not now,' she said quickly. 'I need to see where Maria and Maud are, and the others. You can't trust Horace near bonfires, he's liable to fall in.'

'He's not a bairn any more, Cora. He's fourteen, for goodness' sake.' The thickness was gone and his tone was sharp, irritable. 'We're all a lot older than when we first came here.'

'I know that.' She jerked her arm free with enough force to make him let go of her. 'What's the matter with you?'

She watched him draw in a deep breath and his voice was quieter when he said, 'I'm sorry, I'm sorry. Look, I don't want to argue, it's the last thing I want. Just listen a minute, will you? Properly listen. You never really *hear* me, Cora.'

She stared at him. The smell of beer was strong on his breath and he was swaying slightly. She would have liked to walk away but sensed that the mood he was in he was capable of causing a scene. Without enthusiasm, she said coolly, 'What is it you have to tell me, Wilfred?'

Wilfred stared back at her, frustration paramount. This isn't how he wanted it to be. He'd got her back up now, damn it. But he was sick of pussy-footing about. He'd been patient, more patient than most would have been in the same circumstances. He'd listened to her go on about Jed in the first months after he had gone, comforted her when they'd heard Jed was missing presumed dead, and continued to be good old Wilfred, always ready with a shoulder for her to cry on. Soon they'd be returning to Sunderland and he wanted things in place before they left here. Or if not in place as such, he wanted her to start thinking about him as something other than a big brother. He knew it was Dutch courage prompting him to speak tonight, but he also knew that without the alcohol he'd chicken out before he said anything. He had tried before, hadn't he? And then, always at the last moment, had bitten his tongue for fear of spoiling what they had. But what they had wasn't enough and it was driving him stark staring mad. Keeping his eyes on her face, he cleared his throat.

'I want to tell you I love you, like a lad loves a lass, I mean, and before you say anything I know you don't feel the same.' He held up his hand as she went to speak. She had taken a step backwards away from him, and now he said, 'Like I said, I know you don't feel that way about me, not yet, but don't close your mind to it, that's all I'm asking.'

She had known, she'd always known, hadn't she, deep down somewhere inside where she had buried the knowledge, not wanting to face it? And now he had forced the issue and she didn't want to hurt him, not Wilfred.

'But you know how I feel about Jed. I've never hidden it.'

Quietly now, even gently, he said, 'Felt about Jed, Cora. Felt. He's gone.'

'I know that but it doesn't change how I feel.'

'It doesn't have to. You can remember him as much as you like but whether you let it give you a barren future is up to you. I know you care about me –' again he held up his hand as she went to speak – 'and I know it's not the same feeling you had for him, but that's all right. The best marriages are built on friendship first and foremost. Remember what I told you about Jed's mam and da? And we are best friends, lass. We've always been best friends, but, well, I love you in every way there is to love, that's all. If you married me you would always come first and I would take care of you to my dying day, lass. Nothing would be too much for you—'

'Don't, Wilfred.' She interrupted him shakily. 'I can't—'

'No, don't say can't when I know you can and will.' He aimed to appear cool and in control when inside he was trembling. But it had to be done. He couldn't have gone on without speaking. 'You're the sort of lass who is meant to get married and have a home and family, and I could give you all that. And you'd grow to love me in that way, I'd make sure of it. Not as much as I love you because that would be impossible, but enough that you would be at peace and contented and happy. I'd never ask anything of you that you can't give.'

But he was, right now, she thought frantically.

And then as though he'd heard the thought, he said,

'All that would take time, I know that. Lots of time. But I can wait. For you I can wait, lass. We're young and being best friends, being together, is all I ask. No one could love you more than I do, Cora. You have to believe that.'

She did believe it but it gave her no pleasure. She moved her head slowly from side to side, then bit down hard on her lip as she looked at him again and read what was in his face. 'It wouldn't be fair,' she whispered. 'You deserve someone who loves you.'

'You do love me,' he said softly. 'And I will make sure you love me more and more.'

She felt helpless. Wilfred hadn't been listening to a word she'd said; he was like a human bulldozer. His gaze was tight on her face and she saw now tiny beads of sweat on the faint line of stubble on his upper lip and the way his Adam's apple jerked up under his chin and then fell again when he swallowed deeply. Tenderness replaced the exasperation that his doggedness had caused. He wasn't as sure of himself as he was making out, she told herself, and it must have cost him a lot to bare his soul to her today, knowing how she felt about Jed. And she *did* love Wilfred, she couldn't imagine him not being in her life. He had been wonderful over the last months since Jed had left. Left *her*. That's what she had to remember. Jed had left her without so much as a goodbye. Wilfred would never do that.

Again she whispered, 'It wouldn't be fair to keep you hanging on, just in case. I can't promise anything, Wilfred.'

'I know that.' He had read her thoughts as though she had spoken them – her face had always been an open book – and he aimed to keep the exultation out of his voice as he murmured, 'Just trust me, that's all I ask, because I know you better than you know yourself. And don't look so worried, else everyone will be asking why.' He grinned at her, taking her hand and slipping it through his arm as they began to walk back towards the street. 'And I promise you no more beer tonight, all right? I'm like a henpecked husband already, aren't I?'

'Wilfred—'

'I know, I know, no promises.' But the lilt in his voice told her that he was thinking the opposite. 'And like I said, lass, I don't need any, not where you and I are concerned. The war's over and time's on our side. Now, come and have at least one dance with me so I know you're not mad at me? Please? And then we'll round up the bairns ready for home and drag Mrs Burns away from her admirer.'

It was indeed as though they were already married, she thought with a flash of panic, before she told herself to calm down and take a breath. This was Wilfred and she could trust him. He would never do anything to hurt her. They would be going home within the next few weeks and even in that he had proved his depth of love for her. Most lads would have jumped at the chance Jed's parents had offered Wilfred, but because she hadn't been for staying around these parts he had turned his back on what was a golden opportunity, even though she had tried to persuade him to reconsider several times.

He was a good person. She nodded mentally to herself. An exceptional person, especially in the way he loved her, and bruised and sore as she felt about Jed's rejection and her guilt that she had been the means of causing him to go to war, she had to acknowledge it was comforting to be loved the way Wilfred loved her. To know that she could trust him to always do what was best for her.

Chapter Twenty

'Oh, Gregory, they'll be here soon. However are we going to tell them? What'll they think? Especially Cora?' Nancy shook her head as she added, 'But then I know what she'll think. Of me, at least. She's made it quite clear in the couple of letters she's written this year exactly how she views me coming home, and I can't blame her.' Nancy looked at her husband, at this dear kind man she had come to love in a way she wouldn't have dreamed was possible before they'd become reunited. '*I* don't understand how you could take me back and love me either.'

'Don't be daft, woman.' It was a constant source of amazement to Gregory, this reassurance Nancy needed from him day in and day out. 'There's nowt *to* understand. I love you an' I'll die loving you and that's that. As for our Cora, don't forget she loves you, lass.' And as Nancy shook her head, he said, 'Oh, aye, she does, she does. And her letters have been all right, haven't they?'

Nancy had to smile. Only Gregory could fail to read behind the lines Cora had penned. Stilted, very correct lines. True, their daughter had said nothing out of place but it was more what she *hadn't* written, than what she had, that stated Cora's opinion about her mother's behaviour very clearly. But like she'd said to Gregory, she couldn't blame Cora.

'I'll just have to prove myself, won't I?' she said now.

'No, you damn well won't.' Gregory reared up in his chair, nearly spilling the cup of tea she'd given him a minute or two earlier. 'This is *our* house and what we decide is *our* business and if Cora, or anyone else for that matter, doesn't understand it's too bad. You have nothing to prove to anyone, lass, and I won't have you thinking that way. We're all right together, that's all that matters.'

It was a nice way of looking at things, but Nancy knew that once the children were home the dynamics of their going-on would change radically. Cora and Maria were essentially young women now as she had tried to impress on Greg, and Horace had been a little boy in short trousers when he had left Sunderland. She knew she and Greg would see a huge difference in all the bairns and already they'd had to rethink the sleeping arrangements. She had persuaded Greg that they must move into the front room so Cora and Maria had one bedroom and Susan and Anna the other, rather than the four girls top and tailing in one double bed as they had done in the past, with Horace on a pallet bed at the foot of it. Horace was now destined for a camp bed in the kitchen; it was the best they could do.

Nancy sighed. It wasn't the lack of accommodation

that worried her but the prospect of the tension and difficulties that would arrive with the children. Of course families all over the country were facing the same problem – look at poor Beryl. Beryl Johnson as she was now, having married Ronald in the spring. When Archie had come home a few weeks ago there had been ructions, and the latest news was that Archie had run off in the middle of the night and had been brought home by a constable who'd told Beryl the lad was on his way back to the foster family he'd spent the war with. Beryl had been distraught, and when Ronald had attempted to reprimand the boy, Archie had punched him in the face. Nice things *he'd* learned while he'd been away.

Nancy walked across to her husband and sat down beside him at the kitchen table. And now she and Greg were going to have another baby. At *their* age! Greg insisted she was still young at thirty-six but she didn't feel it, and she'd thought her childbearing days were over but no. Whatever would Cora say? It certainly wouldn't help things. And yet, at the bottom of her, she had to admit she was thrilled. She'd felt she'd been given a second chance in life and this baby set the seal on it. How they would manage she wasn't quite sure, but they would muddle through. Everyone was going on about the call for a period of austerity as the government encouraged folk to put up and make do, and there was no doubt the rationing was getting worse and not better despite the fact that they'd won the war, but none of that bothered her. What did worry her was the prospect of how the family would rub along together once they were living under the same roof again.

'Penny for them?' Gregory put his hand on hers. 'You're not still whittling about how Cora will react to this baby, are you? I've told you that you don't have to tell her straight off. You can wait a while, pick your moment.'

'I'll still have to tell her, though.'

He grinned. 'Well, obviously. Nature has a way of showing these things up eventually.'

'Oh, you.' She pushed at him with her hand. 'You're not a bit embarrassed, are you? I mean about the fact we've fallen again, and us old enough to be grandparents.'

'Very young grandparents,' he said, laughing now. 'Especially you. But no, I'm not embarrassed. I'm tickled pink, to tell you the truth.'

She smiled. He had been over the moon when she had told him she was pregnant which had been a relief as she hadn't been sure how he'd feel. A baby meant sleepless nights and more responsibility just when the other bairns were getting to an age when they were more independent.

'Cora will be fine,' Gregory said now. 'You'll see.'

'I hope so.' Things were going to be difficult enough with her eldest, she knew that.

Still, she told herself, the waiting was nearly over now and the bairns would be home today, thank goodness. She always thought waiting for anything – good or bad – was the worst part. She had written to Cora offering to meet the train if her daughter would let her know the time, but Cora had written back saying they preferred to make their own way from the station and it would be late afternoon or evening. It was now six o'clock so surely their arrival must be imminent?

She glanced across to the kitchen window as she sipped her tea, Gregory having picked up his paper. It was a lovely June evening and the day had been a hot one. She had worked all day cleaning and polishing until the house was sparkling, not so much because she was concerned what it looked like but because she simply hadn't been able to sit and relax. Her nerves were stretched as tight as piano wire, the more so because she had been trying not to let Gregory see what a state she was in. She so wanted them to be a family once more, and she wasn't daft enough to think it would be plain sailing, whatever Greg might say.

She let her gaze wander round the kitchen now, and as she had done many times in the last months, she marvelled that she was in her own home again, safe and secure. The time between coming round in the hospital in Newcastle and Gregory finding her was seared on her memory, a time of pain and aloneness and terror. She would never take the smallest thing about her home for granted again.

The opening of the gate in the back yard brought her stiffening. Cora and the others walked towards the house, but as Gregory stood up, Nancy found she couldn't move. She sat holding her breath, staring at the five strangers who came into the kitchen. She hadn't expected Cora to express any gladness about being home, probably not Maria either because she had always followed her sister's lead, but she noticed Horace was keeping to the back of the group and Anna and Susan were standing together, half-hidden behind their big sisters.

Gregory's voice broke the moment of acute silence, his tone over-hearty when he said, 'Well, what's this then? And about time too. Come and give your old da a hug then, your mam an' all. We've been waiting for you. The kettle's on and your mam's got a fine tea ready.'

Nancy watched as Cora pushed Anna and Susan forward, Anna coming hesitantly to her and Susan to her da, and she forced herself to say, 'My, my, you've grown, you've all grown, and Horace, you're a young man now. Are you too grown up to give your mam an' da a kiss then?'

Her words seemed to break something and in the next moment they were all kissing and hugging, all except Cora.

Cora watched the others and it was with some effort that she kept her face expressionless. She wanted to turn round and run out of the kitchen, out of the yard, out of these mean little streets that seemed so closed in and confining after the wide open spaces she had come from. She wanted to keep on running until she found her way back to Rachel and the farm she now thought of as her home. Rachel had cried when they had left her at the train station, and even though Cora knew her friend now had Jack, the man she had met at the VE Day street party who had become a regular visitor to the farm, she had felt guilty at leaving her, partly because she had *wanted* to leave. Not because she'd desired to come home, to this house and to the two strangers looking at her over the others' heads, but simply because she wanted to put as much space between her memories of Jed and what might have been as she could.

She was shocked at the change in her mother now she really looked at her. The mam she remembered had always been young and vibrant and pretty; this woman was much, much older, far older than her actual years although still pretty in a sort of faded way. Her da, too, looked older but not in the same way her mam did, not even with his poor scarred face and eye patch.

She held herself very straight as her father gently pushed the others away and walked round the table to where she was standing, still just inside the door. He stopped in front of her, his voice holding the tender note she remembered from old when he said quietly, 'By, lass, but you've turned into a beauty, all right, but then I knew you would. Bonny as a summer's day, my little lassie, eh?'

It was something he had been in the habit of saying in those long lost days before the war, and as she felt the sorrow rising up in her she told herself she couldn't, she mustn't cry. And then as he pulled her in to him it was with just the one arm and she was choked with her love for him, for the fact that he had been so badly hurt and broken.

As her arms went round him Gregory breathed a silent

sigh of relief. For a moment or two there Cora had looked as though she was going to bolt and what would they have done then? Fine start to the homecoming that would have been. He held her to him with his good arm, letting her cry with her face in his shirt front, and his own eyes were wet when eventually she straightened away, fumbling for her handkerchief and dabbing at her face as she said shakily, 'Sorry, Da.'

'Don't be daft, lass.' He wiped his eyes with the back of his hand. 'Come an' say hello to your mam then,' he added, as though she had just been out for the day and was returning after a few hours away from the house. 'She's been a-cleaning and doing-on all day, barely sat down for more than a minute. Couldn't have made more of a to-do if we'd had royalty coming, I tell you.' He stopped abruptly, aware that he was gabbling.

Cora stared at her mother and Nancy stared back. 'Hello, lass,' Nancy said softly.

'Hello, Mam.' It was cool, expressionless.

Nancy stared at her daughter for one moment more, then she walked to the range, saying, 'I'll mash a fresh pot of tea and then we can eat. Go and wash your hands and tidy up the lot of you, and take your things up to your rooms. You girls have the two bedrooms, and Horace, you'll be sleeping in here on that.' She pointed to the camp bed propped against one wall. 'I've cleared out a cupboard for you to put your things in, lad. I know it's not the same as sleeping upstairs, but it'll have to do for now.'

Horace scowled, thinking of the comfortable bedroom

he had shared with Wilfred at Appletree Farm. 'What if I want to go to bed before anyone else?'

It was Cora who answered, and sharply. 'You never want to go to bed so don't come that. And the kitchen will be lovely and warm in the winter, and cosy with the range.'

Horace's scowl deepened. 'You sleep in here then.'

'Don't start, Horace.'

Don't start! Horace had never felt more aggrieved. He hadn't wanted to come home. He liked farm work and he knew he was good at it. He'd asked Mr Croft if he could return to the farm when he'd left school, and he'd said he'd see. The painful feeling of homesickness for Appletree Farm which had been with him all day and which had grown stronger the further he had travelled overwhelmed him. He didn't want to be here and he didn't see why he had to be, but as one of his pals had said to him before he'd left Northumberland, once he was finished with school for good he'd have more clout for the argument of returning to Appletree Farm. For now he would have to bide his time.

Tea was a somewhat stilted affair, not least because Horace, with a spectacular lack of tact, spread a slice of bread with what he thought was butter, took a bite and made a face as he said, 'Yuk, what's that?' earning himself a swift kick from Cora under the table.

'It's margarine,' said Nancy quietly, aiming to show no reaction. 'I suppose you've been used to butter where you were staying?'

Horace nodded sulkily, his shin stinging.

'You too?' said Nancy, looking at the girls.

When Cora didn't answer, Maria said uncomfortably, 'It was a farm so . . .'

'We had cream and butter and Mrs Burns made her own cheese—' Susan stopped abruptly as Cora shook her head at her sister.

'No, it's all right.' Nancy looked from one to another of her children. 'I know it's been very different where you have been living in many ways, your da and I understand that, but now we have to settle in together, don't we?' She forced a smile at the sea of doubtful faces. 'We'll all do our best.'

Horace looked at the table. Tea at Appletree Farm had meant slices of ham, hard-boiled eggs, butter, cheese, crusty bread, Mrs Croft's home-made preserves, warm scones . . .

His face said it all and quickly Cora said, 'This is a lovely tea. Thank you for going to so much trouble,' but she didn't look directly at her mother as she spoke. In truth, it was paining her to see the change in her mam. The last thing she had expected was to feel sorry for the woman who had let her da down so badly, and who had virtually cut herself off from them all in choosing to run off with this other man. She didn't *want* to feel sorry for her any more than she wanted to let bygones be bygones as her da had apparently done. It wasn't fair; it let her mam get away with what she'd done. Her thoughts racing, she forced down a slice of bread and margarine spread thinly with jam and a small piece of the eggless sponge cake her mother had baked. It was absolutely nothing like Rachel's delicious fare.

Once the meal was finished, the girls went upstairs to unpack and Horace put his things away in his designated cupboard in the kitchen before going upstairs to Cora and Maria's room. He sat down heavily on Cora's bed, his face a picture of misery. Cora glanced at him. She had never seen him look so glum.

'Cheer up,' she said softly. 'It's not as bad as all that.'

'It's worse.' He sucked his lips in between his teeth, then looked at her. 'Wilfred said they wanted him to stay on at the farm. He said Mr Croft was all for making him like one of the family.'

'So?'

'If he'd have stayed, I bet Mam an' Da would have let me, but he wouldn't stay without you and he said you wanted to come back. Why did you want to come back to – to this?'

'It's our home, Horace. And there's Gran and Granda, don't forget. And Auntie Ada and Uncle Cyril and everyone. We haven't seen them for a long time. Don't you want to visit them and—'

'No.' Horace glared at her. 'I don't know them now. I want to live on the farm with Mr and Mrs Croft. I hate it here.'

'You can't say that, you've only just got back. You have to give it a chance. And what about Mam an' Da? How do you think they'd feel if they heard you now?' She sat down beside him, her lips pursing as he purposely moved a few inches along the bed. 'You'll be fine once you meet up with all your old friends again, I know you will. Be reasonable, Horace.'

'Huh!' He jumped up. 'You think you know everything. Wilfred didn't want to come back and you made him and that's not fair. That's not *reasonable*. None of us wanted to come back except you. You always have to have your own way, Cora.'

'Horace—'

But he had gone, slamming the bedroom door behind him. Cora looked helplessly at Maria who shook her head. 'Little toad,' she said with sisterly disgust. 'Take no notice. Within a day or two he'll be as right as rain.'

'He's right though,' Cora murmured. 'Wilfred had a wonderful opportunity with the Crofts and I ruined it for him.'

'Oh, for goodness' sake, lass, don't start feeling guilty about Wilfred. He's big enough and ugly enough to make his own mind up about what he wants to do.'

Cora stared at her sister. She hadn't told anyone about what Wilfred had said on VE Day, feeling it would be a betrayal somehow, but now she whispered, 'Wilfred *did* come back because of me, Maria. He – well, he asked me to be his lass, you know, properly, with a view to marriage eventually. He said he loved me and if I wouldn't stay in Northumberland, then he wouldn't either. But I couldn't have stayed, not with Jed gone and everything, and if Wilfred had taken Jed's place at the farm it would have been even worse.'

'I see that.' Maria came and knelt in front of her. 'I absolutely see that, and I'm surprised Wilfred could expect anything different knowing how you felt about Jed. What did you say, when he asked you to be his lass?'

'I said no, of course. But I don't think he really listened.'

Maria was silent for a moment. Then she said, very softly, 'It wouldn't be right for you even to consider Wilfred, lass. Some day there might be someone, in the future I mean, and I know you wouldn't feel the same as you felt for Jed, I understand that, but you're still young and time does heal – but Wilfred? No. A marriage out of pity wouldn't work for you, and that's what it would be on your part. You've always felt sorry for him, haven't you? Right from when we were little bairns playing in the back lane. And while we're talking like this I have to say something more. The way Wilfred is with you? It's not quite right. I can't explain it, but Mrs Burns noticed it and said something to me.'

'Rachel?' Cora and the farmer's wife had been on first-name terms for some time, and now Cora said, 'But she never intimated anything to me. No –' she paused – 'that's not quite true, thinking about it. When we found out Jed was missing she said something about still waters running deep in regard to Wilfred, I remember now.'

Maria nodded. 'I wouldn't say she disliked him but

she was wary of him where you're concerned, and to tell you the truth, lass, I agree with her.'

Maria's face wore a sober look, her pale blue eyes anxious, and now Cora felt obliged to say, and lightly, 'Oh, Wilfred's all right, don't worry about that. He is, Maria, really. And when you think about everything he's had to put up with, his mam an' da and all, it's a wonder he's such a good person.'

'There, you're doing it again. Feeling sorry for him.'

'No, I'm just saying . . .' Cora's voice trailed away. And then she went on more firmly, 'I'm just saying I can understand why we're all so important to him. We're the only family he's ever had, proper family, that is, because his own is a nightmare.'

'All right.' Maria sighed. 'Have it your own way, but you wouldn't let him persuade you to start courting one day, would you? You wouldn't let him wear you down?'

Cora shook her head. She didn't know how to put it into words, but since Wilfred had spoken about the future, deep inside her a sadness had settled. Maria had said there might be someone in the years ahead and that time heals, and she knew her sister was speaking out of love, but she also knew now with a quiet certainty that it wouldn't be that way for her. What she'd had with Jed had been so special, so perfect, nothing else would do. And so she had to start thinking about what she was going to do with her life now the war was over, once she let the dust settle, so to speak. But marriage wouldn't be an option, not to Wilfred and not to any man. She reached out and hugged Maria.

'I promise you, Maria Stubbs, that I, Cora Stubbs, will not enter into marriage with one Wilfred Hutton. Will that do?' She smiled. 'And you know I don't go back on my promises.'

Maria laughed quietly. 'It'll do, lass. It'll do.'

'Now, hand me your ration book and I'll collect the others and take them down to Mam,' Cora said briskly, but once she had the books she stood for a moment on the landing, looking down the stairs. This had been her home for a good part of her life and yet it felt alien. She didn't belong here any more; she didn't belong anywhere and it was a strange feeling. Then she squared her shoulders. It was no good feeling sorry for herself. She had to get on with things because there was the rest of her life in front of her and it couldn't be faced looking backwards even though, if she had the choice, she would give up all the time allotted to her for one day, one hour with Jed.

It was two o'clock in the morning and Cora still hadn't gone to sleep. Her mind was churning round and round, reviewing the events of the day in an endless cycle until she felt like screaming. Instead she slid out of bed, pulling her dressing gown over her nightie although she didn't really need it, and taking care not to wake Maria. Quietly padding downstairs on bare feet, she went silently into the kitchen where Horace was snoring loud enough to wake the dead, and then out through the back door into the yard. And there she nearly *did* scream, putting both hands over her mouth to prevent any sound emerging.

The shadow she had recognized as her mother a split second after she had seen it sitting on one of the two old wooden chairs in the yard said softly, 'Hello, lass. Can't you sleep neither?'

Cora stood for a moment, hesitating, and then walked over to the other chair and sat down. It was a beautiful night, still, with no breeze, but a faint smell from one of the neighbours' privies hung on the air. Her mother had always kept theirs so clean her da used to say you could eat your dinner in there, but not everyone was so particular.

As softly as her mother had spoken, Cora said, 'You'd think that a farmyard would smell worse than anything but after a while you don't notice it. It's natural, I suppose, with the animals and everything, but here . . . I never got used to the privies stinking and I don't think I ever will. It's different with humans.'

'Aye, I know what you mean.' Nancy paused. 'Were you happy at the farm?'

It took all of Cora's willpower not to snap back and say, 'Bit late to ask now, isn't it?' as a flood of feeling – rejection, hurt, grief, pain – caused her to tense. Before she had left for Northumberland she had thought their mam loved them, that she was the best mam in the world despite the spats they used to have, but she had been stupid. Her mam hadn't cared about her or their da or any of them the way she thought she had.

After a moment or two, she said quietly, 'Not at first, no. The farmer, he was a pervert, a horrible man. He'd been molesting one of the girls who was there when we arrived.'

'*Cora, no.*' Nancy's voice was high and she lowered it as she said, 'Oh, lass, lass. Why didn't you write and tell me? I'd have come and taken you all out of there.'

'We didn't know at first, not properly. We knew there was something funny going on but well, you don't expect that, do you? We were bairns, just bairns. And when it all came to light . . . Well, you weren't interested in us, were you?'

The silence stretched, and at first Cora didn't realize her mother was crying, not until she said, 'I'll never forgive myself for what I've done, never. How your da took me back I'll never know, and I can't make it right with you, I know that, but one thing I will say – I never stopped loving you bairns. I was like someone else for a time, that's the only way I can explain it, and – and besotted, that's the only word I can use, besotted with a man who wasn't worthy to lick your da's boots. I know you can't forgive me, lass, and I wouldn't ask you to. What I've done is unforgivable.'

She had to ask. Through the pounding of her heart, Cora said, 'You aren't going to go off again, are you? Leave Da again? If – if this man should turn up and ask you?'

Nancy was wiping her face and trying to pull herself together. The canker of shame and humiliation she felt about the night of the rape would be with her to her dying day, she knew that, and the fact that only Gregory knew about it had been a kind of comfort. Even now she felt so dirty, so soiled and defiled that at times, despite how happy she was with Gregory, she still had the desire to put an end to it all. Some nights she would lie awake for hours, fighting her thoughts and unwilling to sleep because of the nightmares that plagued her. But something was telling her that unless she explained it all to Cora, from the very beginning to the bitter end, her relationship with her daughter would never be mended. Her lass was eighteen years old now, a young woman, but a distant, hostile young woman, and she couldn't bear that to continue without at least making the effort to set things straight between them. It was selfish in a way, she knew that, and perhaps she shouldn't burden Cora with the knowledge of what had happened, but Cora was strong enough to bear it. Her lass was just as she herself had been once.

Nancy cleared her throat. 'Lass, I'm going to talk to you like I never have before and never will again, not so much as a mam but as woman to woman, you know? And I want you to listen till I'm through without saying anything. It won't be easy to hear but it's the truth. And it won't explain what I did because that's impossible. Your da's the only person who knows about what I'm going to tell you and he's been . . .' Nancy shook her head. 'There's no words to describe how he's been.'

Cora stared at her mother in the darkness. 'You don't have to tell me anything.'

'I think I do, hinny.'

The old northern term of affection silenced further protest from Cora because it brought a lump into her throat that made it impossible to speak.

'I'll start from when I first met Ken. It was like this . . .'

There were a couple of times when Cora murmured, 'Oh, Mam, Mam,' through her tears but apart from that she said nothing until Nancy finished speaking. Nancy was holding her tight and Cora's head was on her mother's shoulder when Cora whispered, 'I want to kill him. I want to kill them all.'

'Your da said the same thing and I'll tell you what I told him – that's the last thing I want. Ken would never dare come back to these parts knowing Dan Vickers would be waiting for him, so at least it's over with. Finished.'

'I hope he gets what he deserves. I hope they all do.'

'Me too, lass. Me too. Of course, some folk would say *I* got exactly what I deserved.'

Cora reared up as though she had been prodded with a stick. 'No, Mam, no one would say that, no one with a grain of human decency.'

'Thank you for that, hinny. In the first days and weeks I thought it was a punishment from God, judgement for my sin, you know? But I don't believe that any more. God doesn't work like that. What happened was because of my own actions in putting myself into a position where it *could* happen, nothing more and nothing less. One thing's for sure, if it wasn't for your da I wouldn't be here now. As for ever leaving him again, only death'll part us and not for a long, long time I hope. I don't just love him, Cora, I adore him, worship him, and the rest of you too. I've been given a second chance to see what is right in front of my nose, what's always been there. And there's something else.'

'What?' Cora didn't feel she could take much more. She had never stopped loving her mother, she knew that, but she had stopped liking her. Her mother had talked about being judged for her sin and Cora knew she had been guilty of doing just that. She had wanted her mam to be crushed and humbled for what she had done rather than, as she had thought, her da welcoming her mam back with open arms. Now she felt sick with remorse. Her mam had been crushed all right and all the time she, her daughter, had been on her high horse, dripping self-righteousness with her holier-than-thou attitude. When would she ever learn? she asked herself passionately.

'Your da and I . . .' Her mam paused.

Cora stared at her, at the dear face that looked so much older than she remembered and for good reason. 'What?' she said again, willing that one of them wasn't ill with an incurable disease or something. After the last hour nothing would surprise her.

'We're gonna have another bairn,' Nancy said in a rush.

For the third time, Cora said, '*What*?' but then as her daughter's face lit up Nancy knew it was going to be all right. She felt herself enfolded in Cora's embrace, her daughter half-laughing and half-crying as she hugged her. 'Oh, Mam, a war baby that will grow up in peacetime, a proper new beginning.' And then grinning, she added, 'This'll get the neighbours going, you know that, don't you? You'll be the talk of the back yards, the pair of you. I can just hear them now – Have you heard about Mr and Mrs Stubbs? Expecting again, and their youngest all of eleven. That Mr Stubbs is a sly one but there's life in the old dog yet.'

'Oh, go on with you,' said Nancy, giggling, and then they were both laughing helplessly as they had done in the old days, the way they only did with each other, trying to stifle their mirth so they didn't wake anyone, which only made it funnier.

Some time later, as a pale pink dawn began to creep across the night sky, Cora still hadn't been to sleep but her mind was at rest now. She and her mother had talked for a little while after Nancy had told her about the baby, and then they had crept indoors so as not to wake Horace who was still vibrating the kitchen with his snores. She had thought about telling her mam about Jed but had decided it wasn't the right moment – there had been enough emotion and revelations for one night. When she told her it would have to be the whole story, including the part about Farmer Burns and why Jed had left to go to war, and for that reason it would be better another day. The immediate thing now was for her to look for a job although she didn't have the faintest idea what she wanted to do, but anything would be all right short-term. Long-term? Her brow wrinkled. Not a factory or a shop, she'd feel buried alive. Maybe nursing? Something that would grow into a career? Something to fill the empty days of the future that weren't going to be at all as she had thought before Jed had gone.

She looked towards the window as the sky began to turn pink, the thin curtains doing little to keep the light at bay. At the farm the dawn chorus would be in full throttle, the cows would be mooing to be milked and there would be fresh eggs to collect from the coop. She would already have been up for at least half an hour and looking forward to one of Rachel's breakfasts, after which they'd work in the dairy or in the fields or at another of the hundred and one jobs that needed doing.

A physical ache cramped her chest. She'd felt she had been born to be a farmer's wife after she'd met Jed, but it wasn't to be and she had to accept that. She knew she had to accept it – in her head. Her heart was another matter.

Chapter Twenty-One

Wilfred was sitting in the bedroom he'd shared with his brothers before they had left home. He, too, had been awake all night. The room was filthy and the two beds it held stank. Apparently his parents had had a succession of lodgers since he had been away, the last two doing a moonlight flit just a day or so ago owing a couple of weeks' rent. He didn't blame them. He'd resent paying good money to live in such a rathole.

He was sitting on the hard-backed chair the room contained. He didn't want to touch the beds with their soiled covers, let alone lie in one. In his mind's eye he was seeing the scene in the kitchen when he'd walked in the evening before. His parents had been slumped in their greasy, grimy armchairs in front of the range. It didn't look as though it had been cleaned since he'd been gone and the smell of the kitchen had nearly knocked him backwards. It was the stink of his childhood; unwashed bodies and stale sweat, food that had gone bad, dirt and decay. It was a smell that permeated flesh and bones, the very pores of the skin.

The pair of them had been three sheets to the wind, his mother surveying him through bleary eyes, her slack mouth half-open. It had been his father who had said, 'Well, as I live an' breathe. Look what the wind's blown in.'

'Hello, Da.'

His mother had attempted to straighten herself before flopping back in the armchair. 'Who is it? Wh – what's goin' on?'

'It's Wilfred,' he'd said shortly, his spirit recoiling.

'What? Who?'

His father had cursed, his voice rough as he'd said, 'Wilfred, the youngest, woman.'

Wilfred doubted his mother had heard; she'd already shut her eyes and to all intents and purposes dozed off.

His father had stared at him. 'You're back then? An' lookin' chipper. Had a comfortable war, did you? Not like us here in the thick of it, times we thought our number was up.' He belched loudly, the sound glutinous and sticky, before wiping his mouth with the back of his hand. 'Well, you're in luck, boy. The room's vacant upstairs so you'd better take your things up. We'll talk rent when you come down – there's no free rides here.'

Wilfred had looked at his father and he remembered just how much he hated him. He had little option but to stay the night but come morning he'd be on the hunt for a room somewhere else.

And now it was morning. He stood up, walking over to the window. The only good thing about living here had been that he was next door to Cora, but he'd look for a place close by and at least he had a bit of money behind him. The Crofts had paid him a decent wage along with his free board and lodging; they'd been more than fair. He'd been able to salt away most of what he had earned which stood him in good stead now.

He'd miss the Crofts. His eyes narrowed. But he hadn't completely given up on the idea of going back one day, with Cora of course. He'd given little hints to Jed's mother that he was interested in her now Jed was gone, skirting round the subject, until one day she'd asked him outright if they were courting. He'd acted embarrassed, asking her if she would mind, and when she'd said that they thought the world of Cora and of him too, he had smiled and said if he had their approval then nothing else was holding them back.

'We'll invite you to the wedding,' he'd said, kissing her cheek, 'but we'll come and see you before then, I promise.'

He continued to stand at the window for a while as the street below woke up, men going off to work, housewives cleaning their doorsteps and bairns coming out to play. Just outside his window was a lamp post and two lads, no more than five or six years old, began to swing on a rope an older lad had tied to it.

Wilfred smiled to himself. Some things never changed. Hitler had dropped his bombs and Sunderland, like so many towns and cities throughout the land, had had large areas flattened with ordinary folk killed and injured, but bairns went on playing their games. Life went on. It was only right and proper. And his life was all about Cora. Nothing mattered but her.

He heard his parents' muted voices from the room across the landing and after a while the sound of them going downstairs, but he was in no rush to join them. A few minutes later there was a knock at his door and then his father opened it and poked his head round to say, 'Your mam's made a brew. You comin' down?'

Wilfred tried to hide his surprise. He couldn't remember when his parents had offered him a cup of tea in the past. It had always been his brothers who had made sure he had something to eat or drink, and when they'd left home he'd had to fend for himself like a feral cat. Without Cora and her mam he doubted he'd have made it through his childhood. Still, he might as well keep things friendly until he found somewhere else, hopefully later today. His da was a nasty piece of work at the best of times. Nodding, he said, 'Aye, I'll be down in a minute or two.'

Alone again, he pulled a clean shirt out of his holdall and changed into it, sniffing it once it was on. The smell of the house had got up his nose and it felt as though everything was foul. He had visited the privy last night before retiring but he'd only got as far as opening the door. That had been enough to make him retch. Because it had been dark he had used a corner of the yard to relieve himself before going upstairs, but he'd just have to hold it in this morning. Once he was out of the house he'd find somewhere to go. He shook his head. They were a pair of dirty so-an'-sos all right.

When he entered the kitchen his parents were sitting at the table. He noticed that the debris that had cluttered it the night before had been cleared, but it was still crusty with a layer of goodness knows what.

His mother got up, saying, 'I'll get you a sup, lad. Sit yourself down.'

He sat down because there was little else he could do and as she placed the cup of tea in front of him he noticed that the folds of her neck were engrained with dirt. It turned his stomach, that and the smell of her.

'So.' His father stared at him. 'I daresay you'll be out lookin' for work later then? Got anything in mind?'

Wilfred shrugged. 'Not really.'

'Well, think on. Can't sit on your backside all day, boy.'

It was on the tip of Wilfred's tongue to say he didn't see why not – his father had done a pretty good job of it for years – but he kept himself in check. With any luck he'd be out of here today once he found himself a room, and that'd be the last of them he'd see because he had no intention of ever coming back. His brothers had done it and so could he now he was of an age to work.

After a minute or two when Wilfred didn't speak but sat quietly drinking his tea, his father got up and walked out of the kitchen and up the stairs. His mother had been standing with her back to them, stirring something or other in a black saucepan on the range, but now she turned and said, 'Well, lad, it's a stranger you are and no mistake. You've grown since you've been gone. What have you been doing with yourself since you left school? Working on that farm where you were placed, I suppose? Good to you, were they?'

'Aye, they were.'

She nodded, her flabby face wobbling. 'Don't suppose they paid much, not for farm work, eh?'

Wilfred stared at the woman who had given birth to him. But that was all she had done, he thought flatly. Given birth to him, suckled him for a couple of years and then left him to fend for himself. Animals treated their young better.

As he looked at her, it suddenly dawned on him why his father had gone upstairs leaving her to engage him in conversation down here.

He was out of his chair like a shot, taking the stairs two at a time, and as he burst into his bedroom his father was bending over the holdall he'd left on the chair. Wilfred looked at the wad of notes tied with an elastic band in his father's hand. 'Put that back,' he said softly.

'Put it back? The hell I will.' His father straightened, glaring at him. 'Me an' your mam weren't going to see a penny of this lot, were we? Oh, I know your game, boy. I saw the look on your face when you walked in last night. Not good enough for the likes of you now, are we? I can read you like a book. You weren't gonna stick here for more than a day or two afore you skedaddled like your brothers. Well, you do that, go and be damned, but I'm keeping this for all the years we fed and clothed you afore the war.'

'I said, put it back.'

'You gonna make me?'

'Aye, if I have to.'

'Oh, we're the big man now, are we?' His father gave a growl of a laugh. 'I could lick you with one hand tied behind me back, boy.'

Wilfred stared at the man who had terrified him all his life. There had been occasions when he was a bairn when just hearing his da's voice or his heavy footsteps had caused him to wet himself. But not any more. No, not any more.

His father gave a 'huh' of contempt as he made to push past him, but Wilfred grabbed his arm and swung him round. As his father's fist shot out, aiming full in his face, Wilfred ducked. He had been expecting the blow. And although he would always be small and wiry, he wasn't the weak, puny boy of yesteryear. He twisted one of his father's arms behind his back with enough force to bring him to his knees shouting in pain. Prising the wad of notes from his hand, Wilfred dragged him across the landing to the top of the stairs where he pulled his father to his feet, and he actually heard his arm break in the process.

'This is for all the years of misery,' he said, his voice low but hate-filled. 'Rot in hell, Da.' And with that he threw his father down the stairs with the force of a stone from a catapult. There was one high-pitched scream as the body plummeted through the air before hitting a step almost at the bottom of the stairs and turning a rag-doll somersault, landing with a crash in the hall.

Wilfred stood quite still, elation that he had finally done what he had dreamed of doing for years filling his chest and making his head buzz. His mother came into the hall and when she screamed, he said, 'Shut up. Do you hear me? Shut up,' as he walked down the stairs. He didn't need to check the twisted body to make sure his father was dead; the head was at such an unnatural angle, practically back to front, and it was clear the neck had snapped.

Nevertheless, his mother said, 'Is he dead? What did you do? You've killed him.'

She couldn't have seen anything, she had been in the kitchen, and knowing this Wilfred said, 'He fell. It's obvious, isn't it? He fell, probably because he was still drunk from last night.'

Her hands pressed to her face, his mother said, 'He wouldn't fall, not Abe. He's bin up and down them stairs with a load on more times than I've had hot dinners.'

'Aye, well, he clearly pushed his luck.' Wilfred stepped over the sprawled shape and took her arm, manhandling her back into the kitchen and pushing her down on a chair.

She was crying but he made no effort to comfort her; the smell emanating from her was turning his stomach.

'You did it,' she said again. 'You found him going through your things.'

'What makes you think he was doing that, Mam?' He stared down at her, his eyes cold. 'No parents would steal from their own, would they? No, I came upstairs and he must have been in your room because the next thing I heard was him scream as he fell.'

'No—'

'Yes, I'm telling you that's what happened, all right, and you wouldn't want to call me a liar, not with me being the breadwinner and standing between you and the workhouse. Course, they don't call them places where they stick old folk like you with nowt to their name workhouses any more, but that's what they are sure enough. He was an old soak. Everyone knows it and no one would be surprised he came a cropper. It's more surprising it hasn't happened before now.'

She had stopped crying and now she was staring up at him as though he was the devil himself. Wiping her snotty nose on the back of her hand, she mumbled, 'I need a drink.'

Knowing she didn't mean a cup of tea, he said softly, 'All in good time. I need to get the story straight before I go and fetch the doctor 'cause this'll involve the law an' all. To keep it nice and simple, we were both sitting here having a cuppa when we heard him fall down the stairs, right? It was an accident, pure and simple. That way you get to stay here. Lucky, really, the accident happened when your son had come home in time to look after you.

But a few things'll change here, Mam. First, between us we're going to clean this muckhole from top to bottom and once it's done you'll keep it that way. You'll cook and clean like any other housewife and no one'll step through the door except on my say-so. None of your and Da's cronies, not at any time of the day or night and especially not while I'm at work. Once I'm home of an evening and had me dinner you can get as drunk as a lord, but until then you'll keep sober.'

His mother was gaping at him, her mouth half-open.

'You'll want for nowt but you'll do as you're told and I won't be messed with. Do you understand?'

His words had made her face contract, her eyes narrow, screwed up as though she couldn't believe what she was hearing. 'You – you're not the same lad who went away—'

'No, I'm not,' he interrupted grimly. 'And I tell you now, Mam, you play ball with me and I'll be fair with you, but you start carrying on and playing silly beggars and you'll live to regret it. That's a promise. So . . .' He stared at her, his eyes unblinking. 'What happened here this morning?'

'Your – your da fell down the stairs.'

'And where were you when this accident happened?'

'In here, with – with you.'

'Good.' He nodded. 'We found him like he is now and I told you to sit and have a cup of tea while I fetch the doctor.' He waited a moment. 'So get the tea,' he said sharply, and as she immediately lumbered to her feet, he said again, 'Good, good,' in the manner in which someone would speak to the mentally impaired.

Before leaving the house Wilfred went again into the hall, standing and staring down at the grotesque contorted shape that had been his father. He felt the same sense of deep satisfaction that he had experienced when he had gazed at Farmer Burns after killing him.

He smiled a smile that wasn't a smile at all as he said softly, 'So, I win, Da. I bet that's sticking in your craw right now, isn't it. I wish your passing could have lasted longer and been more painful but beggars can't be choosers and I had to take the opportunity when it arose. I'm sure you appreciate that.' He straightened, throwing back his shoulders. Now that he had time to collect his thoughts he was realizing this couldn't have worked out better if he had planned it. He could remain close to Cora and keep an eye on her, and being next door he'd make sure he got back on the old footing with her mam and da and the rest of them. Her da was disabled now, he wouldn't be able to do what he'd used to, and what was more natural than the next-door neighbour stepping in and helping out? Especially when it was Cora's best friend.

Once he got this stinking hole cleaned and fumigated to the last nook and cranny, he'd paint and wallpaper every room. You wouldn't recognize the place by the time he was finished. New curtains and rugs and bedding, new furniture where needed as well. He'd got enough put by to do all that with plenty left over for a deposit on a house. And if he couldn't buy this place, if the landlord wouldn't sell, then he could take all the stuff with him when he got somewhere else and took a mortgage because he wasn't going to rent for ever and a day. That was a mug's game, besides which, when he asked Cora to marry him he wanted her to know she would have her own place in time, bought and paid for. It would be nice if it could be here, next to her mam an' da, because he knew she'd like that, but they'd have to see.

He had the sudden urge to laugh, to raise his hands in the air and clap for sheer pleasure, but with his mother in the kitchen he didn't. The thought of her brought him frowning to himself. His da had got one thing right when he'd said they weren't good enough for him, and certainly his mam wasn't good enough to associate with Cora. He didn't want Cora to have to be polite, not with a filthy, debauched old scrubber like his dear mam, but for the present it would be canny to bide his time. In a few months, perhaps even a few weeks, a pillow over her face once she was in a drunken stupor should do it, and then it would be plain sailing. With the size of his mam and the way she had drunk herself insensible for years, no one would question that her heart had finally given up. He'd be careful to make sure there wasn't a mark on her. Aye, his mam would be no trouble.

He smiled again. He could hear the neighbours. '*What a shame about Mrs Hutton, her going so quick after him, but that's often the way when a couple's been married that long. The one that's left sort of gives up, strange that. But it's the lad I feel sorry for. Back from the country and losing them both in such a short time. I mean, I know the Huttons weren't the best mam an' da to them boys, but blood's thicker than water . . .'*

Oh, aye, he could hear them all, he thought with a grimace of contempt. Everyone knew what his mam an' da were and how he and his brothers had been kicked and beaten by their da and starved by their mam, but in death they'd acquire sainthood in some quarters. And he could play the grieving son if it suited his purposes.

His smile widened. It was good, this feeling of being in control of his own destiny. He wouldn't let anything or anyone stand in the way of that. You had to be strong to survive in this world, take life by the horns and subdue it and always look out for number one. He took a deep intake of breath and nodded twice. But for now he had to start the ball rolling and fetch the doctor.

Chapter Twenty-Two

'We can never thank you enough, you know that, Etta. Are you going to be all right here by yourself?'

It had been a beautiful warm day, the sky a bright blue with fluffy white clouds. Now it was evening but still warm. The calendar in Etta's kitchen said it was the middle of June, but that was the only way they had of knowing the date. For the last little while they'd lived in total isolation, cut off from the outside world.

It had been true what Etta had told them that first day, Jed thought, as he hugged the little woman goodbye. No one ventured this way and Etta rarely went further than her garden and the copse at the end of it where she collected wood for the range in the kitchen. As she told them, apart from a visit to the nearest town a couple of times a year to buy a supply of flour and sugar and tea which then lasted her for months, she had no need to leave her home. She grew her own vegetables; collected eggs from her hens, milk from Oriel and honey from her bees; and caught the occasional wild rabbit or pheasant for meat. She was self-sufficient and proud of it.

Now she said, a chuckle in her voice, 'Will I be all right by myself? How do you think I managed before you came?' But she touched Jed's cheek in a swift caress to soften the words. While they had waited for Jock's foot to heal sufficiently for them to be on their way, Jed and Neville had busied themselves doing numerous little jobs about the house – mending a kitchen cupboard, sweeping the chimney in Etta's small sitting room, replacing a couple of rotten floorboards, whitewashing the cellar and so on. They had also repaired a gaping hole in Oriel's little barn at the end of Etta's garden, and made the hen coop more secure for the night-time. It had been the least they could do for the diminutive old lady who had not only taken the three men in at great risk to herself, but also looked after them exceedingly well, pressing second helpings on them at every meal and checking Jock's foot umpteen times a day to make sure all was as it should be.

Each of the men had a lump in his throat as they walked down Etta's garden path and out into the lane beyond the front garden. This little house had been an oasis in a sea of violence and madness, rest for their minds as well as their bodies, and she would never know just how much she had done for them, Jed thought as they turned and waved for the last time. If he had told Etta that meeting her had given him hope for the world in the future she would probably have thought he was mad, but it was the truth. They had witnessed such horrific things, unimaginable cruelty and suffering and hatred, but Etta was the other side of the coin.

Jock summed up what they were all thinking as he said, 'If things had been different, if we didn't have to try for home, I could have stayed there for ever. She was a grand little body.'

'Aye.' Jed smiled at his two friends and they smiled back. 'She was that.'

As well as packing them up a large rucksack full of food Etta had provided them with a map which was even more precious than her bread and hard-boiled eggs and cheese. They were heading in a south-westerly direction and were going to walk at night and lie low during the day. They had no idea how the war was progressing as Etta had no wireless, a conscious decision on her part. She and her husband had been perfectly happy without the intrusion of the outside world in any shape or form, and she saw no need to change that, she had told them. Jed didn't blame her. After what he had been through it sounded ideal.

They walked steadily across wild, open country that first night, crossing the border into Germany as the sun rose and spending the day sleeping in a forest area that had plenty of cover. It set the pattern for the following days. They were careful to avoid settlements of any kind and keep off main roads, supplementing what was in the rucksack with anything from the fields and hedgerows that could be eaten. The three of them were in far better shape than on the march, thanks to Etta, but even so they found it hard going at times. They were underweight and still well below par from their time as POWs, and Jed and Neville were more than happy to adjust their pace to accommodate Jock's foot which still had a little healing to do.

Days and nights merged together as they walked deeper into Germany, and now they were relying on what they could steal to eat. Eggs from hen coops, vegetables from gardens and fields, and anything they could lay their hands on when they found a door unsecured in the occasional remote dwelling off the beaten track, places like Etta's little house. They had felt awkward, almost like criminals, the first couple of times they had stolen from someone's home, but they'd told themselves these folk were the enemy and this was wartime. Etta was one in a million, besides which they were in Germany now. In the very lair of the wolf.

They often heard the drone of planes overhead but no sound of bombs falling, but as they were concentrating on avoiding built-up areas that perhaps wasn't surprising. They hoped they were getting closer to the Allied lines all the time and they had seen no German troop movements, but again, the fact that they were skirting any towns or cities meant it was unlikely they would run into any German soldiers.

They had lost track of how many days and nights it had been since they had left Etta's, when one day they were awoken by what were clearly American voices. They had spent the day resting in a copse of trees on the outskirts of a town. From Etta's map, Jed thought the town might be

Neustadt but it could just as easily be Rothenburg or Uffenheim. Etta had advised them to avoid Nuremberg – the city was a hub of Nazi activity – but looking at a map and working out a route in Etta's kitchen was very different from working their way through an alien land in darkness whilst attempting to give a wide berth to its inhabitants.

Jed lay for a moment on the dense bracken and moss he'd slept on, unable to believe that what he was hearing wasn't a dream. But no, they were Americans. He could even hear one of them singing 'My Heart and I'. Badly.

He shook Jock and Neville awake and the three of them wriggled on their stomachs and peered out from their cover to the road some fifty or sixty yards away. A convoy of American soldiers, complete with jeeps and tanks, were rolling along, and from the noise they were making they weren't too bothered about German snipers.

As Neville tried to scramble to his feet, Jed and Jock pulled him down none too gently. The last thing they needed was to be mistaken for part of a German ambush. Trigger fingers could be a mite too quick in wartime and a bullet was a bullet whether fired by friend or foe. Instead, and still under cover of the trees, Jed shouted, 'We're British POW. Don't shoot 'cause we're coming out, all right?'

He repeated it twice and heard someone, a commanding officer presumably, give the order for the unit to halt. Then someone shouted for them to come out with their hands in the air.

As they stumbled from the copse Jed was aware of

several soldiers coming towards them, including an officer who was asking their names and ranks; of the convoy beyond, and – which added to the unrealness of the sudden turnaround in their fortunes – of the sudden flight of a large bird, a pheasant perhaps, in the field on the other side of the road. It rose straight up into the vast expanse of the dusky evening sky, soaring away until it was just a speck in the distance, unconfined and at liberty to go wherever it pleased. He watched it fly into the setting sun and as he blinked he knew that if he lived to be a hundred, the moment and the intensity of what he was feeling right now would be just as vivid. *He was free.*

Compared to how the Americans were clothed and how they looked, the three of them were poor specimens, Jed reflected wryly, as two soldiers presented them to the officer. The American grinned at them before asking how they came to be sleeping rough. As Jed explained their story he saw a look of gradual amazement dawn, and the officer interrupted to say, 'You don't know then?'

'Know?'

'The war's over, guys. It's been over since May seventh, a few weeks. Signed and sealed. Their precious Führer took the easy way out and killed himself, Mussolini was shot by partisans and strung up, and we're in the process of rounding up hundreds of the German generals and hierarchy. It's just the Japs left to be brought to heel now.'

'It's over?' Jed gazed into the young, clean-shaven face. 'Thank God.' He turned to Jock and Neville who were looking equally stunned. Then the three of them were laughing and hugging, oblivious to the Americans who stood there grinning at the three British soldiers who had survived not only Auschwitz but also weeks on the run from the Nazis.

After the three of them had climbed into the back of a truck they were given food and bottles of water and the convoy was on the move once more. Jed had no idea where they were going and he didn't care. The war was over, the Allies had won, Hitler was dead and the Nazis were beaten. What else was there to know?

It was dark when the American tank unit trundled into their camp which had a small airstrip attached to it. It had clearly been used by the Germans until fairly recently when it looked as though it had received a direct hit by the Allies. The airstrip was undamaged but a number of buildings to the north of the camp were blackened shells. However, there were more on the south and west side that were intact, and Jed and the others were taken to one of these on the margin of the site and told it would be their home for a couple of days or so until they were flown out with some other former POWs. The barracks were constructed of wood and would no doubt be freezing cold in the winter, but on a summer's evening like this one they were pleasantly warm and the bunk beds were comfortable. Furthermore, they were in American hands which meant there would be good food and plenty of it, and this was confirmed a little while later when a soldier arrived to escort them to the mess tent where they enjoyed a substantial meal of beef stew followed by rice pudding. It might have come out of tins but it was hot and tasted wonderful.

It was three days before the planes – there were four of them – arrived, and Jed didn't think he'd seen a more beautiful sight than the RAF Dakotas bumping down on the airfield. He and Jock and Neville had got to know the forty or so other POWs who were waiting to go home, and a couple of them they recognized from Auschwitz. These men told Jed they had escaped from the Germans shortly after he and Jock and Neville had, and had made it as far as Nuremberg before the Americans had picked them up. Of the POWs who had continued on the march there was no news. Strangely, the five of them didn't talk about Auschwitz. There was no room for reminiscing about something so ugly, so unbelievably horrific. Even the American commanding officer, when they had been asked where they had been prisoners, had simply put his hand on each of their shoulders in turn and asked no questions when they had said the name of the concentration camp.

Instead, each of them had talked about home, loved ones, even their pets, along with their gardens and allotments and in Neville's case, his prize racing pigeons. Jed had described the farm at this time of the year and how, as a warm summer sun sinks and shadows lengthen, the dark forms of bats appear, fluttering in the half-light and twisting and turning as the edge of night approaches.

He'd talked about the ears of barley and corn appearing, the hill-scarp to the north of the farm at dusk marked by the sunny crowns of trees and long, deeply fret shadows, of meadows ripe with buttercups and daisies and cow parsley, but he didn't mention the one thing that dominated every thought of home. Cora. Or what he was going to do the minute he got back.

As he walked towards the planes, sandwiched between Jock and Neville, he was conscious of other POWs whooping and cheering as they ran past them, eager to get on board. Some of them were carrying their belongings in bags or parcels but apart from Etta's rucksack, which Jock had, the three of them had nothing. Nothing except their lives – which was everything.

The other three planes had already taken off when they climbed into the last Dakota, sitting down on the narrow seats along the side of the ribbed metal interior. This was it, they were going home. Jed looked round. Everyone was smiling but no one was saying much. Perhaps, like him, they still could hardly believe it was happening.

The roar of the engines reverberated through him as the plane began to taxi down the airstrip. He leaned back and shut his eyes, not because he was worried about take-off or flying but because he didn't want anyone to see the tears in his eyes.

Chapter Twenty-Three

'What a shock for poor Wilfred, his mam going so soon after his da, and just when they'd got the house nice and things were settling. He was beside himself when he popped in to tell us earlier, Cora. You'll have to go round and see him later.'

Nancy, Gregory and Cora were sitting at the kitchen table. It was a bitterly cold Thursday afternoon in the first week of November, and Cora's half-day from the shop in Crowtree Road where she now worked; Thursday being the least busy day of the week according to Mrs Gray, the owner of the premises. Despite knowing she was paid well for what she did and that there were plenty of worse jobs, Cora hated every minute.

The sign on the shop door said 'Mrs Gray, Millinery, Mantles & Costumes, Exclusive Fashions'. Mrs Gray and her assistant, Miss Williamson, a tiny, shrivelled-up, bird-like woman whose whole life revolved around her job, were excellent dressmakers and hat-makers. They largely worked in the back of the premises while Cora dealt with clients – 'We don't have customers, Miss Stubbs, only clients' – who came in the front door of the shop. Mr Gray had been dead for a long time. Cora wouldn't have been surprised if he'd died of boredom and was mummified somewhere in the flat upstairs.

Mrs Gray's 'clients' were from the top echelons of Sunderland society, most of them wealthy matrons who had patronized her for donkey's years. They were, without exception, outstandingly aware of their own importance and extraordinarily dull. If nothing else, the last weeks had made Cora even more determined to look into a nursing career, but for the moment the household was in desperate need of her weekly wage and that was that. Her reward for slowly suffocating day by day was on a Saturday evening when she came home and gave her mother her wage packet unopened. Her mam's face would light up with relief, and although her mam had a way of making a penny turn into two, by the next Friday Cora knew she'd be dipping into the little pot on the mantelpiece that held the rent money; it would be replaced as soon as Cora handed over her next wage packet. Her father had been out looking for work but with just one functioning arm it had been hopeless, and his war pension didn't amount to much.

Cora took a bite of her mother's stottie cake. The bread was fresh from the oven and still warm, just the way she liked it. 'And the doctor reckons that Wilfred's mam just went upstairs to sleep and didn't wake up?' she asked Nancy.

'That's what Wilfred said. Poor lass. Mind, as I said to your da, there's worse ways to go, and –' here Nancy lowered her voice as though there were umpteen other people present – 'you can't drink like she did and it not do something to your insides, can you?'

'No, I suppose not.'

'But it's Wilfred I feel sorry for. Poor lad.'

Cora looked at her mother. 'Mam, he's never got on with his mam an' da, you know how they were.'

'Oh, I know, I know. Course I know. Didn't we bring poor Wilfred up most of the time, bless him? He practically lived here, didn't he? But still, it *was* his mam. And like I said, he was cut up about it when he came round after they'd taken her away. He'd put so much work into that house to make it nice for her, and I think with his da gone the two of them were getting along fine.'

'It might have been a shock but I don't think he'll be too upset in a day or two.'

Nancy's reply to this was to look at her daughter and say for the umpteenth time since Cora had walked into the house, 'Poor Wilfred.'

Cora glanced at her father and Gregory winked at her. Wilfred had always been 'poor Wilfred' as far as Nancy was concerned and would for ever remain so.

'Pop round and have a word with him when he gets back from the docks,' he said gently. 'It'll keep your mam happy though personally I agree with you, lass. I can't see Wilfred's mam's passing as anything but a relief to the lad.'

'Gregory!' Nancy looked askance at her husband. 'That's an awful thing to say.'

Obviously Wilfred had still gone in to work then, Cora thought, as she smiled at her father. He'd got a job at the docks through his brothers who both worked there, and had started about the same time she had begun at Mrs Gray's. Both his brothers were married with bairns and he had asked her a couple of times to go round to their respective houses with him and meet everyone, but she had made some excuse or other thus far. She had been trying to distance herself a little from Wilfred but it wasn't easy, especially with him living next door. She had been hoping that once Maria left school next year and got a job, her younger sister could take her place as the main breadwinner and she could go away somewhere to do her nurse's training, a hospital where she could live in. It would be a natural break from Wilfred without her having to say anything to upset him. She had discussed this with Maria who was doubtful.

'I can see him following you wherever you go,' her sister had said flatly. 'Look how he was when you wouldn't commit to seeing him every Sunday afternoon once we were home, and he always manages to pop up anyway.'

Cora sighed. It would be worse now with his mam having passed away and her own mam feeling even sorrier for him. As a sudden thought struck her, she said, 'Mam, don't invite Wilfred round to eat with us every night or anything, will you? I mean, sometimes, of course, but not as a regular thing . . .'

Her voice trailed away at the expression on her mother's face, and when Nancy said, 'All right, lass. What's going on?' she stared at her parents. She had confided in her mother about Jed, everything, right down to him leaving to fight because of what he had done to Farmer Burns to protect her, but she hadn't said a word about Wilfred asking her to be his lass. She had told herself that was because it didn't seem fair to Wilfred and it was a private matter, but now she had to admit the real reason was that she thought her mam, liking Wilfred as she did, would be all for the match and try to push her into his arms. Whether that was right or wrong, she realized now she had to make her position clear.

Taking a deep breath, she said, 'It's like this . . .'

It took a while to tell the full story because she found herself going right back to when they had first been evacuated and Jed had come onto her horizon and how Wilfred had been strange for a time, through to the events of VE Day. When she finished there was silence in the kitchen for a moment or two. She was all prepared for what she thought her mother's reaction would be, so when Nancy said, 'But of course you couldn't think of poor Wilfred in that way, lass. He's not the one for you. Anyone who knows you would see that,' it completely took the wind out of Cora's sails.

'I thought you'd want me to be his lass,' she said lamely.

'Wilfred?' Nancy shook her head. 'No, no. He's a nice enough lad and he's got a heart of gold – look how he was with his mam in the last weeks despite how she's always been with her boys – but you and him. Oh, no, lass.'

Cora glanced at her father and he nodded in agreement with his wife.

Cora relaxed back in her seat, feeling as though a weight had been lifted. With her parents being on her side in this and her mother seeing the situation so clearly, it portended good for the future. Once Wilfred's mam's funeral was over she'd give it a few weeks and then have a word with him and make it absolutely plain where he stood, no matter what he said. It would upset him and she felt awful about that, really awful, because Wilfred was the last person in the world she wanted to hurt, but it was better to be cruel now so as to be kind in the long run. For a start, while he was thinking there was a chance with her, he wouldn't be looking at other lassies.

It was exactly a week later and winter had certainly arrived. The sky looked full of snow and there was a bite to the wind that penetrated any amount of clothing. Now, as Cora walked home treading carefully on the icy pavements, she was almost tasting the beef broth they were having for lunch. No one could make beef broth like her mam. Like her da always said, it warmed the cockles of your heart, and if ever she needed something warm inside her it was today. The small electric fire that she normally had in the front of the shop had broken the day before and it had been as cold inside as it had been outside. In spite of this Mrs Gray wouldn't countenance her keeping her coat on and she had practically frozen, her teeth chattering so much she'd hardly been able to talk. Any customers – sorry, *clients*, she corrected herself bitterly – had been ushered through to the back of the premises to the workshop and dressing room where Mrs Gray and Miss Williamson were as snug as a bug in a rug, thanks to a substantial coal fire in the black-leaded fireplace. She had been counting the minutes to lunchtime, it being her half-day.

Cora sniffed, admitting that she felt more than a little sorry for herself. She knew Mrs Gray and Miss Williamson had numerous cups of tea throughout the working day as a rule but she was lucky if they offered her even one. Normally this didn't bother her unduly although she thought it was a bit mean, but considering she had been in an icebox today she would have thought they might have been a little more considerate. But no.

A few flakes of snow began to blow in the wind as she walked on, wishing with all her heart that it was six months or so in the future and Maria was about to leave school and she, herself, could start her life again. Because this wasn't living, this treading time.

Oh, stop your whining. The self-admonishment was fierce. Fifty-five million dead in the war, countless more like her da maimed and injured, and barely a family in the country that hadn't been ripped apart by tragedy and loss, and here was she griping about her job. But it wasn't just her job.

She stopped, turning her face up to the sky and the snowflakes that were falling more thickly minute by minute.

She had heard it said more than once that time was a great healer, but if that was true she'd experienced nothing of it thus far. She could say that for a large part of the day at Mrs Gray's, and certainly for most of the night hours when she lay awake or dreamed nightmarish scenarios of loss and aching grief, she was thinking of Jed and what might have been.

She began walking again, quicker now, impatient with her maudlin thoughts and life in general. It was Wilfred's mother's funeral tomorrow and Mrs Gray had given her the afternoon off whilst making it clear her wage packet would be docked accordingly. Much as she didn't want to lose an afternoon's pay, she knew she had to go to the funeral for Wilfred's sake. When she had popped round to see him the evening after his mother had passed away he had asked her if she would partner him at the funeral; his brothers had their wives and families, he had said, but he was on his own and was going to find the day difficult. She had agreed – what else could she have done? she thought now – but it had made her all the more determined that once things had settled down she needed to make it clear how she felt.

All the neighbours had contributed to the wake being held after the funeral at Wilfred's house, dipping into their rations to provide food for 'the poor lad' as she'd heard him referred to more than once, and not just by her own mam either. But somehow, and she felt horribly guilty about this, she admitted to herself, she had a niggling doubt that Wilfred's grief over his mother's demise was real. She, more than anyone, had been privy to how much he had hated his mam and da from a little bairn. Could you change so radically in just a few weeks? But it wasn't her concern. She nodded to herself. She would support Wilfred tomorrow and get through the day as best she could, she owed Wilfred that. He *was* her friend when all was said and done.

When she walked into the back yard there was a faint aroma of beef floating on the air and she lifted up her face and sniffed. Unlike in the summer there was no discernible odour from the neighbours' privies, something Cora appreciated more than most, having a keen sense of smell. Her mother had slow-cooked a piece of brisket the day before which they'd had for dinner, and it was with the remains of this that she'd made their lunch. Beef broth and her mam's home-made bread, Cora thought, as she opened the back door, feeling like a bairn again. It had been a regular meal in the past, being cheap and tasty. So much had happened since those far-off days of childhood, but by some miracle her mam and da were back together and even expecting another bairn, and the family were united once more. For the present at least. She had to count her blessings. Her da was a great one for saying that but he was right.

The kitchen was wonderfully warm after the bitterly cold morning she had endured in the shop, and her mother had a cup of tea waiting for her. As she sat down at the table with her da, Nancy passed her an envelope. 'Came in the post,' she said quietly. 'Looks like Rachel's writing.'

Cora took it with a word of thanks but didn't open it straight away. She and her mam had had to agree to disagree about Rachel Burns after she'd told her about Farmer Burns and Enid and the rest of it. Her mother maintained that by looking the other way about her husband's behaviour, Rachel had been complicit in what had happened to Enid and had also put Cora and the other girls at risk. Cora couldn't argue with that – if you looked at it in the cold light of day it was the truth – but she had tried to explain to her mother that nothing was black and white. Rachel wasn't a bad person, she had argued, she had just been under Farmer Burns's thumb and frightened of him like everyone else, but her mother refused to see it that way. It had been her da taking her aside one day and whispering in her ear that he thought Nancy was jealous of the regard she had for Rachel that had persuaded Cora to drop the matter. But she did like Rachel, loved her even, and in spite of leaving Stone Farm had no wish to lose contact with the woman with whom she'd become fast friends any more than she did with Maud, with whom she corresponded regularly.

It was after lunch and before she started on a pile of ironing that she opened Rachel's letter. They had written to each other a couple of times but Cora knew that Rachel, busy as she was from morning to night working and running the farm, barely had a moment to herself let alone time to put pen to paper. Rachel's other two letters, the last one being in August, had been short, just saying how much she missed Cora and the others and how the farm was doing. She now employed three farmhands and a woman who helped in the house and dairy, but said woman, according to Rachel, wasn't a patch on Cora for hard work.

Cora saw straight away that this letter was longer, and she curled up in one of the armchairs in front of the range to read it while her mother busied herself at the kitchen table making a humpty-backed rabbit pie for dinner, and her da sat in the other armchair smoking his pipe and immersed in his paper. The snow was falling more thickly now and although it was barely two in the afternoon the light was muted, the glow from the coal in the open fireplace of the range a deeper red in the semi-twilight. It was cosy, quiet and peaceful, but within moments Cora had sat up straighter, her heart pounding fit to burst.

Nancy had noticed the movement and now she said, 'What's the matter?' but Cora couldn't reply, not even when her father lowered his paper and said, 'Cora, lass? You all right?'

It took her a minute or two to read the letter in full, and when she had finished she still didn't speak but handed it to her mother who was now standing by her father's armchair. Nancy took it and then gasped after reading the first couple of lines, causing Gregory to say irritably, 'Read it out loud, woman, for goodness' sake.'

Nancy glanced at her daughter, whispering, 'Oh, lass,' before raising her voice and beginning to read:

Dear Cora,

I need to tell you right away that what I'm going to say is going to come as a shock and for that reason I'm not going to beat about the bush. Jed is alive. Not only that, he's back home. I've been worrying about whether to write and tell you for weeks, since just after my last letter in fact which is when he came home, but Jack says it's the right thing to do and so here's the full story. Apparently he was taken as a POW after he was injured and transported to one of those terrible concentration camps. The Nazis wouldn't allow any letters in or out and so he had no way of letting anyone know he was alive. Those places were hell on earth as we all know now so what he went through is anyone's guess. His mam says he won't talk about it, not even to his da.

Nancy raised her head for a moment and glanced at Cora who was sitting perfectly still and looking like a ghost, her face drained of colour. Again she said, 'Oh, lass,' before beginning to read once more.

Near the end of the war when the Allies were closing in, the Germans abandoned the camp and took the

> POWs on a march. It was in the dead of winter apparently so how many survived is questionable, poor things. You can't believe what the Nazis have done, can you, but I digress. Anyway, Jed and two of his pals managed to escape after weeks of walking umpteen miles every day and sleeping out in the open in the snow and what have you. They were in Czechoslovakia but on the border into Germany and a Swiss woman who'd been married to a German doctor took them in. One of Jed's pals was injured and this woman helped him recover. When they left her after a number of weeks they travelled across Germany and only found out the war was over when they ran into some Yanks. They were flown back to England eventually but Jed was poorly for a while, after-effects of what he'd been through, but then he came home. You can imagine how his mam and da felt to get him back.

Oh, yes, Cora thought. Yes, she could imagine that, and she was so glad for his mother especially.

> Now I come to the most difficult part of what I have to tell you, lass.

Nancy paused, looking first at Cora who remained sitting with her head bowed, and then at Gregory who was staring up at her. He knew Cora had been in love with a farmer's son who had gone off to war and got himself killed, but that was all. Clearing her throat, Nancy went on:

> When Jed was home I went across to see him and his mam and da and wish them well, to be neighbourly, you know? I thought he might ask after you but he didn't, but his mam mentioned that Wilfred had written to her once or twice. I don't know if you were aware of that? Anyway, there was something I couldn't put my finger on and I came away feeling all unsettled, I can't explain it. I whittled about it for weeks and in the end Jack took me across to see Mrs Croft in the day when the men would be out working so I could have a woman-to-woman chat in private. Well, lass, what she told me was news to me and I reckon it might be to you too. According to Jed's mam, Wilfred had told her that you and him were courting before he left their farm and not only that but you were going to get wed in the future. Then in these letters, he led her to believe you were betrothed and he was getting his house ready for when you married. He said how pleased you were to be able to live next door to your mam and da and because of that he had given up all hope of returning to work at the farm in the near future, but that it was still a dream for him, perhaps in the years to come. He had a way of making his dreams come true, he'd said. Well, I was amazed, so amazed she went and got the letters to show me and there it was in black and white. And there's something else, lass, something important.

Nancy took a deep breath as Gregory muttered, 'He lives in cloud cuckoo land, that lad. I've never heard such tripe. And to write and tell this woman all that. He's barmy.'

No, not barmy, Nancy thought as a little chill shivered down her spine. Clever, very clever. There was more here than wishful thinking. Motioning with her hand for Gregory to be quiet, she began reading again:

> Jed's mam told me that when he got back the first thing he did was to ask about you. Course she felt duty bound to tell him what Wilfred had said before you'd all gone home and then about the letters, and she said the look on his face broke her heart. She's regretted saying anything ever since because she reckons, and he didn't say this, mind, but she's reading between the lines, but she thinks he was going to come and find you and see if you wanted to give him and you a second chance. But once she showed him the letters he shut up like a clam. The only thing he said was that he could understand you wanting to be near your family because they were everything to you. So that's it, lass, and I hope I haven't put my foot in it by writing or offended you if you and Wilfred are thinking along those lines. I wouldn't want us to fall out, not for anything.
>
> Oh, and my other bit of news is that Jack and I are going to get married next year, in the spring we thought. He said we're both too long in the tooth to

waste time and I agree with him. He's going to sell his cottage and smallholding and come and live here and we'll manage the farm together. Him and his wife had no bairns before she died and so there's no one to consider but ourselves. No doubt there'll be a bit of talk in some quarters but Jack says while they're gossiping about us they'll be leaving some other poor beggar in peace. The thing is, I love him, Cora, and that's all that matters, isn't it. And he loves me. If you'll come to the wedding it would make the day for me, lass. I'll let you know the date when we decide, probably May time. So you take care and write and tell me when you can that I haven't upset you, all right? I only want the best for you, I hope you know that.

With love from your friend, Rachel.

There was a moment of deep silence in the kitchen when Nancy finished speaking, and Cora looked up to see both her parents staring at her. It was Gregory who said, 'This lad, this Jed. You still care about him, hinny?'

Cora swallowed. There were no words to describe how she was feeling and so she simply whispered, 'Yes.'

'And I know the answer but I need to ask the question just the same – all this that Wilfred's said, it's just in his head? There's been no arrangement between you, no promises given?'

'None.'

Gregory nodded and Nancy came to sit on the arm of

Cora's chair, putting her arms round her daughter as she said, 'How soon do you want to leave?'

It was one of those moments when she and her mother were perfectly in tune. Gratefully, Cora whispered, 'Tomorrow.' She couldn't wait a moment more than was absolutely necessary. He was alive. She had her miracle. If God never answered another prayer for the rest of her life then that was all right. 'Do you think I'm being awful if I miss the funeral?'

Nancy was amazed Cora could even ask that after all Wilfred had said and done. She would never have expected such cold manipulation from the lad, not from Wilfred who thought the world of her daughter. But then that was the trouble . . .

'No,' she said firmly. 'You must go, lass. It's the right thing to do. However it turns out, it's the right thing. Only don't expect too much, hinny, just in case.'

Cora knew what her mother meant. The reason that Jed had left was still there. He had killed a man because of her. And it was only supposition on his mother's part that he had been going to find her and ask that they begin again. But however this panned out she had to see him. Even if it was only to look into his face one more time before she knew she had to face life without him. But he was alive, warm and breathing, able to feel the sun on his face, to laugh, to eat and drink and live in the countryside he adored. If this didn't work out, that's what she had to remember. She hadn't been the means of him dying. He had come home. *He had come home.* She buried her head in her mother's arms and let the tears come.

Wilfred was humming to himself when the knock came at the back door. When it opened he had composed his face into a suitable mask of grief and his voice was equally subdued when he said, 'Cora, I didn't expect to see you tonight. I thought you said—'

'This isn't about your mam or the funeral.' She stared at him, at this dear friend who had become a stranger. 'I had a letter from Mrs Burns today.'

'Oh, aye?' He didn't like the farmer's wife and he sensed she didn't like him. 'Getting on all right, is she?'

'She's going to be married but that isn't the only reason she wrote.' Cora came fully into the kitchen but when he waved to a chair indicating for her to sit down she continued to stand and face him. 'She had some news she thought I ought to know.'

Wilfred's eyes narrowed. 'Which is?'

'Jed's alive. He was a POW but he's home now, back at the farm with his parents. That's wonderful, isn't it?'

Wilfred's face stiffened. With some difficulty he made himself say, 'Of course.'

'Rachel said when he got back to the farm he asked after me and his mam got the impression he was going to come and see me. That's when she told him about what you had said.'

'What I'd said? I don't follow.'

'About you and me, Wilfred. That we were going out together and going to get married.'

He looked her straight in the eyes. 'She's mad, barmy. I never said that. I might have said I liked you but that was all.'

'And she showed Rachel some letters you had written to her, Jed's mam, that is. About us being engaged and planning to live here, next to my mam and da. Did she write those herself too? How could you lie like that?'

'They weren't lies. I was only saying what was going to happen. You love me, you know you do. And I love you as you deserve to be loved, don't you see? No one could love you like I do.'

'Wilfred, I'm going to see Jed and I shall tell him you and I were never engaged and we're not getting married. I owe him that.'

'You *owe* him?' It was verging on a shriek and Wilfred must have realized this because when he next spoke his voice was calmer. 'You owe him nothing, Cora.' The thought of her going to Jed Croft was sending white-hot knives into his brain. 'He's a nowt, all wind and water. He might look the part but he's got no gumption, no fire in his belly. If he had really loved you he'd have made sure Farmer Burns couldn't touch you again, not gone on about reporting him to the police. The police!' He gave a bark of a laugh. 'Everyone knew they were in Burns's pocket. They'd have done nothing, like they did over that other girl, Enid.'

Cora felt sick. She put a hand on the kitchen table to

steady herself. 'What do you mean?' He couldn't know about Farmer Burns attacking her that day; she must have misunderstood him.

'I killed him, Cora. Farmer Burns, I killed him for you. To stop him hurting you. I did it to protect you because I love you, do you understand now? Burns had to be stopped and so I stopped him. That's what you do if you love someone, really love them. You don't leave them at the mercy of filth like Burns.'

Cora's face was bloodless and she felt dizzy. 'You – you couldn't have. Jed—'

'Jed knocked him about a bit but he didn't have the guts to finish it,' Wilfred said feverishly. 'I was at the farm. I heard you scream but Jed got there first so I listened. I heard it all. And when you and him had gone I went into the barn. Burns was blind drunk and bleeding but he wasn't dead. The things he said about you –' his lips came back from his teeth in a snarl – 'he was scum. And I knew he wouldn't stop till he'd seen you six foot under.'

Cora shook her head dazedly. 'No, Jed—'

'Jed!' Wilfred spat the name out. 'The spineless nowt. He'd have let you carry on living there even knowing what Burns was. And when he thought he'd killed Burns, when I said I knew and that unless he cleared off I'd go to the police and tell them everything, off he went as meek as you like.'

'You *blackmailed* him?' Cora couldn't believe what she was hearing. 'That's why he left?

'He left because he's gutless.'

For a moment Cora couldn't speak. The shock of what he had said was wearing off and a hate such as she'd never experienced before had her wanting to throw herself at Wilfred and claw his face to shreds. He had forced Jed to leave and he had let her torture herself that she had sent the man she loved to his death. And Jed might have been killed. Wilfred had probably been hoping for that. She fought to gain control, her voice brittle when she said, 'You wanted Jed dead. Admit it. Did you tell him he had to join up?'

'Haven't you been listening to a word I've said? He isn't worthy of you, that's what I'm saying. Look, lass, I've been to see the landlord and he's agreed for me to buy this place off him. All the work I've done here, it's for you. I'll make it a little palace, I promise, and right next to your mam an' da. You'll never want for a thing, I promise you, and I'll make you happy. Anything you want, you'll have.'

Cora stared at him. Was he mad? He had to be, he had to be deranged. He had just told her that he had killed Farmer Burns and then made Jed believe he had done it and blackmailed him to leave her into the bargain. Jed had gone to war and been incarcerated in one of those terrible camps, probably suffering the torments of the damned if half the stories in the papers about the concentration camps were true, and then Wilfred calmly talks about them setting up home together?

She had never really known Wilfred. Right from a

bairn when they'd played together and he had practically lived at their house, she had imagined she knew him inside out but she hadn't. There was a whole different side to him, a dark side. It had showed in his face when he had talked about Farmer Burns and Jed. Was it because of what his mam and da had done to him and his brothers?

She felt a spasm of pity for him and it enabled her to speak softly when she said, 'I'm going to see Jed tomorrow, Wilfred, and I shall tell him I still love him, that I'll always love him. He might feel differently about me now – after what he's gone through he'll be a changed man, I know that, but regardless of him and me I will never marry you. I never would have, even before I knew Jed was still alive. I am truly sorry but I just don't feel the way you do.'

'No, no.'

He was glaring at her now and for the first time in her life Cora felt afraid of him. Something had changed in his face; it was as if there was another person looking out from behind his eyes, and she wished she had let her mother come with her as Nancy had tried to persuade her to do. But she had thought that with what she had to tell Wilfred, that would have been cruel. He would feel bad enough without another person present.

'It's because of him you're saying that. You would have married me. It's always been you and me and I know you love me. Other people might try and take you away from me but we're meant to be together. You know that deep down, you *know* it. I won't let you go to him,

Cora. Everything I've done I've done for you, don't you see? I can't live without you.'

'Wilfred, I care about you, I always will, but what you did to Jed was terribly wrong, you must understand that?' Part of her couldn't condemn him for killing Farmer Burns – the man had been the personification of evil – but it terrified her that Wilfred had done it in cold blood.

'If you go to him I'll tell the police he killed Burns and that's why he ran off to join up. I'll see him go down the line for it, Cora. I swear it.'

The fear of him drained away and with it the anger as her pity increased. He was so damaged, she thought, more damaged than she could ever have imagined, like a hurt bairn desperate for love. 'You must do as you feel fit,' she said softly, 'but I am going to him, Wilfred, and I will tell the police everything you've told me if you accuse Jed.'

'You can't leave me. Please, Cora.' Her name was wrenched up from the depths of him and he began to cry, great racking sobs that shook his body as his hands covered his face.

She wanted to go to him, she wanted to put her arms round him and comfort him as she had done so many times when he was a bairn and had come to her black and blue from one of his father's savage beatings. But he was a child no longer. He was a grown man and their ways had to part, for his sake as well as hers. The time for gathering him in to her, like a mother with a bairn, was past. She closed her eyes tight for a moment, hating what she had to do and say, but this had to end now.

'I'm sorry, Wilfred, I really am,' she whispered, and then she turned and walked out of the back door into the yard. She stood for a moment in the snow, wondering if he would come after her and not wanting a scene that the other neighbours might hear, but apart from the sound of his sobs inside the house all was quiet.

Slowly, her head bowed, and feeling torn apart inside, she made her way home to where Nancy and Gregory were anxiously waiting for her. And as she was enfolded into her mother's arms, the tears now streaming down her face and words impossible, her heart broke for the little boy who had never been cuddled like this, never known what a home was, never had a moment of unconditional love in his life from the two people who had brought him into the world.

Chapter Twenty-Four

Cora and Nancy didn't go to bed that night. They sat in the kitchen once the rest of the household was asleep, talking, drinking tea and discussing the ifs and maybes of the future. Nancy was huge now – the baby was due at the end of November – and Cora was anxious that nothing should happen while she was gone, but as Nancy said, there was a houseful of other folk around if she did start early. 'Lass, this is my sixth bairn, I'm an old hand at it so don't you go worrying about me. I have them as easy as shelling peas. I barely had time to pull me knickers down before our Susan popped out.'

Cora smiled as Nancy had meant her to, but in truth she didn't feel like smiling. She was beside herself about meeting Jed. When she saw his face she would know if he still loved her. And how would he react when she told him Wilfred was responsible for Farmer Burns's death, and all that that meant? Wilfred had told Mrs Croft such lies and compounded them in his letters to Jed's mother. Would Jed believe there was nothing of that nature between Wilfred and herself and that she had remained true to him? And the baby could come any time. She shouldn't be gallivanting off to Northumberland. She knew her da and Maria would look after her mam but she wanted to be here for her too. And then there was Wilfred. She couldn't get his anguished face out of her mind. She was angry with him and part of her hated him for what he had done, but the other part still couldn't help caring about him. Loved him even.

A white winter dawn was breaking when Cora brought up the subject of Wilfred again. She had told her parents everything he had said and Gregory had been for going round and giving Wilfred a piece of his mind but she and her mam wouldn't let him. Now, as Cora made some toast for her mother and herself and brewed the umpteenth pot of tea of the night, she said, 'I think I'll go and see how Wilfred is before I leave to catch the train. He was in such a state, Mam.'

'No, don't do that, lass.' Nancy reached out a hand and patted her daughter's arm. If she had spoken the truth she would have said that she wanted Cora as far away from Wilfred as she could get for the moment. It was clear the lad was unbalanced where she was concerned and who knew what he might do? You read of such things in the paper occasionally, crimes of passion they liked to call them. She had already agreed with Gregory that he would see Cora onto the train and stay with her every minute until it left.

Now she said, 'It's his mam's funeral this afternoon and likely he's getting himself composed for that. It might upset him if he saw you again. I'll go round this morning and make sure he's all right, I promise, once you an' your da have left for the station. I'll take him something to eat and see about setting out things for the wake. After the do you had last night a bit of time for him to accept what's what won't come amiss.'

'So you don't think I ought to go to the funeral?'

They had discussed this several times and Nancy's answer was the same. 'No, hinny, I don't. I've told you that me an' Maria will look after him and I won't let your da say anything. He won't be by himself and I think he'll cope better without you there, to be honest. Look, lass –' Nancy lifted her daughter's chin and looked into the deep brown eyes – 'even leaving the matter of the farmer aside, Wilfred's done some terrible things. He could have got Jed killed and ruined both your lives. He's not a little lad any more, he's a man and –' Nancy hesitated for a moment before saying – 'a dangerous one. You have to face that. Now go and get your things together once you've finished your toast and stop worrying. You're doing the right thing in going today and what will be will be.'

Cora flung her arms round her mother. 'I love you, Mam.'

'An' I love you, hinny.' As she said it Nancy gave thanks, as she so often did, that the Almighty had seen fit to restore Cora to her.

At half-past eight that morning Nancy stood looking out of the window before she kept her promise to Cora and went to see Wilfred. It had stopped snowing but the low heavy sky threatened plenty more. Some sparrows were arguing about the scraps that she'd put on the bird table that Gregory had made for her, a sleek blackbird eyeing them from his perch on top of the wall. He looked remarkably like a disapproving headmaster surveying a crowd of unruly students and she had to smile. She loved the birds and she was always attributing human characteristics to them. Gregory laughed at her but she had heard him talking to the regular visitors to the garden when he thought she couldn't hear, so she wasn't the only daft one.

Aware that she was prevaricating because she didn't want to go next door, Nancy made herself put on her coat and boots. Cora and Gregory had left for the station a few minutes ago and the other children were on their way to school. Maria had promised she'd call in at the shop on her way and tell Mrs Gray that Cora was indisposed but hoped to be back at work Monday morning.

Gathering herself together for what might lie ahead, Nancy left the house, treading carefully in the deep snow. Horace had been supposed to sweep the yard that morning before school but had left it too late. That lad! Nancy shook her head. She knew Horace was just counting the days until he left school and could disappear off to Northumberland and begin working on the Crofts' farm or a similar one. There wasn't a day went by that he didn't remind them that he had come home under duress. He could be a pain in the backside, could Horace.

When she reached Wilfred's back door she knocked once and then again. After standing for some thirty seconds or so she tried the handle of the door. It wasn't locked. Entering the house, she called, 'Wilfred? It's Mrs Stubbs. Are you there, lad?'

The kitchen was quiet and the fire in the range was all but out. There had been no preparation for the wake thus far from what she could see. The new table that Wilfred had bought some weeks ago was bare, the six chairs neatly fitted beneath it. Nancy glanced about her. There was still the faint odour of fresh paint hanging on the air and everything was spick and span. She had only been in the Huttons' kitchen a few times when Wilfred's parents were alive and she had felt like getting into a bath of disinfectant afterwards. Now the place was transformed, beautiful you might say.

Nancy called again, venturing into the hall which like the kitchen was sparkling clean with freshly painted cream walls and brand new carpet on the floor. Wilfred had certainly done his mother proud, Nancy thought as she stood wondering what to do. Pity Mrs Hutton hadn't lived to enjoy what a lovely place the lad had made for her. Wilfred might be obsessed with Cora but he wasn't all bad, not if he could let bygones be bygones with his mam and go the extra mile like this.

Thinking Wilfred must have popped out somewhere, Nancy couldn't resist the temptation to see what he had done to the front room. If it was anything like the kitchen and hall it would be grand, she thought, as she guiltily opened the door, aware she was being the thing she hated most, a nosy neighbour. As she poked her head round the door she got a shock to see Wilfred sitting in one of the armchairs of the brand new suite, and she began to say, 'Oh, I'm sorry, lad, I did call but . . .' before her voice dwindled away and her hand went to her mouth to smother the scream she was about to make. He was sitting facing her, his eyes open and his face a grey-white colour and Nancy knew he wasn't breathing, even before she made herself walk across and bend down to touch him.

Whimpering to herself, she stepped back a pace. He was dead, *dead*. She glanced at the coffee table in front of the armchair. Like everything else she had seen thus far it was pristine and modern, and in the middle of the long rectangle of smooth light wood there stood a small squat glass alongside an empty whisky bottle, and a little bottle that had clearly held pills was lying on its side. Nancy picked the bottle up and saw that it had held sleeping tablets, prescribed for Wilfred's mother.

'Oh, Wilfred, Wilfred, Wilfred.' She stood staring at him, her mind racing. He had killed himself. Killed himself because he couldn't have Cora. He was just a young lad and he'd thrown his life away. And then in the next instant she considered how this was going to affect her lass. Cora would be devastated – this could blight her life.

It was a moment or two before she saw the envelope on the mantelpiece with Cora's name on it. After picking it up, she looked at it for more than a minute, wondering what to do. By rights she should give it to Cora unopened but she wasn't going to. Drawing in a shaky breath she left the front room with its staring occupant and walked into the kitchen, pulling out a chair and sitting at the table as her heart thudded fit to burst. Putting one hand to her chest she sat staring at the envelope, aware that she was holding Wilfred's last words to her daughter in her hand. If this letter was full of recriminations it would destroy her lass, she knew it would. Cora was going to feel bad enough as it was.

Decision made, she slit the envelope open and pulled out the single sheet of paper it contained. Closing her eyes tight for a moment she took another shaky breath and then opened them and began to read:

Cora,

How could you leave me for him? After all I've done for you, how could you walk away like that? I love you, I'll always love you and I'll always be with you. Nothing can separate us, not even death. I'll always be there, watching you, you know that, don't you? You'll only have to shut your eyes and you'll feel me there, loving you, wanting you. Godfrey Taylor thought he could move me aside and have you but I fixed him and I tried to fix Jed too, for your sake. Only for your sake. He's not good enough for you and he'll let you down. You'll see. And when he does, remember my words. I had everything sorted for us, Cora. I dealt with my da and my mam so we could be together and I would have given you the sun, stars and moon. All I've done I've done because of you and a love like mine will reach beyond the grave. Giving up my life for you is the final sacrifice and I believe I shall become closer to you than your own skin. Every moment, wherever you are, whatever you're doing, I'll be with you. Closer than he could ever be. At night I shall come to you in your dreams and in the day the wind in your hair and caressing your skin will be my touch, my breath. I'll look at you out of your babies' eyes and see into your soul. You are mine. You will always be mine and I'll be waiting for you, Cora.

Wilfred

Nancy dropped the sheet of paper with a little cry. *This was a curse.* As she watched it flutter to the floor she felt a wave of nausea rise up and staggered over to the deep white sink just in time.

After the sickness was over, she sank down on the chair again, her hand on her belly, and forced herself to bend over and pick up the letter. She read it through twice and with each word the conviction that this sheet of paper carried more than mere words grew. This letter held the power to infect her lass's mind. It was a disease, a canker, and as she swayed back and forth on the chair any remaining sympathy for the boy she had always called 'poor Wilfred' evaporated. This was sick, evil, and if Cora read this it would seed itself like a growth inside her and send out tentacles that would choke everything that was good and clean and wholesome in the future, everything that she and her Jed might share. That bit about looking out of her babies' eyes, that wasn't normal. None of it was normal. In death, even more than in life, Wilfred was seeking to control and manipulate every facet of Cora's life, and to say he would be waiting for her . . .

Nancy shivered, drawing her coat more closely round her, but the chill was from within. After some minutes she stood up. Some of the other neighbours would be calling round soon with their offerings for the funeral; she didn't have long for what she knew she had to do but she was feeling bad. The pains in her stomach that had begun when she had first seen the white figure in the armchair were gathering pace and she knew what they meant. The baby was coming.

She walked back into the front room after putting the letter and the envelope into her coat pocket, and picked up the empty pill bottle from the coffee table, slipping that into her pocket too. It took all her willpower to touch the body, but when she lifted Wilfred's arm rigor mortis had not yet set in. She knew from laying out her own mother that this normally occurred some four to six hours after death, so he must have died after five o'clock, perhaps as dawn broke? No doubt he had waited for some time after Cora had left him the night before, hoping she would return, before then making his plans. She imagined him sitting quietly drinking the hours away before he finished it by swallowing the pills. She shivered again. This was worse, much worse than some spontaneous thing. But the fact that he'd left it so late suited what she had in mind.

Knowing she had to be stronger in mind and body than she had ever been before, Nancy steeled herself and bent to put her arms round Wilfred's waist. As she did so, for a split second she thought she saw a flicker in the wide staring eyes, something dark and malevolent, and so real was it that she stumbled backwards, nearly falling. She straightened, her heart pounding, and when she looked again there was nothing. She had imagined it, she told herself faintly, and was it any wonder after reading that letter?

Again she bent, lifting the body and ignoring the pain ripping through her belly as she sent Wilfred thudding against the coffee table to lie in a crumpled heap at the side of it. His head had made hard contact with the wood but she didn't pause to inspect any damage. Once more forcing herself, she picked up the glass and wrapped one of his hands round it, turning the whisky bottle on its side so that the last drops dribbled out on the wood. Standing back, she surveyed her handiwork.

She saw a young lad who, on the night before his mam's funeral and having only lost his da some weeks before, had drunk himself silly and on trying to get up, no doubt to go to bed, had fallen and cracked his head on the coffee table. An accident. Tragic, terrible, but an accident.

Nancy was breathing hard, the pains in her belly fierce.

That's what she saw, she told herself as she stumbled

out of the room and into the kitchen, but would it be what others, the doctor for one, saw? But she couldn't worry about that now. She had done all she could.

Somehow she made it back to her own kitchen and took off her coat and boots. It had begun snowing again, big fat flakes tumbling out of a laden sky, and she sighed in relief. The snow would fast cover her footsteps just in case anyone noticed them in Wilfred's back yard. Within a short while you wouldn't know anyone had called there this morning.

Reaching in her coat pocket she took out Wilfred's letter and without hesitating threw it into the fire. It flared briefly and then was gone. Next she prised off the label on the pill bottle and disposed of that in the same way before opening the medical box she kept in the kitchen cupboard which held bandages and bits and pieces. She stuffed the bottle at the bottom of it. An empty bottle, innocent and innocuous.

The pains were coming thick and fast now but she pulled on her slippers and put the kettle on the hob before going into the yard and shouting over the garden wall to her neighbour on the other side from the Huttons. She and Flora went back a long way and Flora had had ten bairns; she'd know what to do now because as sure as eggs were eggs this baby was coming within the next hour or so.

Flora poked her head out of the window and when Nancy explained what was happening and that she was alone in the house, gasping between pains, she heard

Flora shouting instructions for her Tom to fetch the midwife before she tore out of her house and into Nancy's back yard, just as Nancy's waters broke in a biblical flood.

With Flora's help she got back into the kitchen but both women knew she would never make it upstairs. This baby was going to be born on the clippy mat in front of the range and unless the midwife had wings on her heels, Flora was going to be the one to deliver it.

The pain she remembered from old had her in its grip and it had taken control like an express train, but as the urge to push became unstoppable Nancy was conscious of a feeling of deep peace over and above the agony. Cora would never read that letter that had carried within it seeds of something terrible. Whether she herself lived or died now, what she had done this morning was between her and her Maker. No one else, not even Greg, would know about it. She had made some unforgivable mistakes in her life but this was not one of them and God knew that. And then she gave herself over fully to the process of bringing new life into the world.

Chapter Twenty-Five

It was getting dark when Cora trudged up the lane that led to Stone Farm later that afternoon. There had been a number of delays on the journey due to the adverse weather conditions, and a couple of times she had doubted the last train would get through when eight-foot drifts of snow either side of the track proved a problem, but eventually she climbed down from the train at the small station in the little market town she had first arrived at years before with her siblings in tow.

Only one other person left the train with her, a tall, rather distinguished gentleman with snow-white hair and an expensive-looking leather overnight bag, and Cora stood on the platform looking about her for the station-master on disembarking. It had stopped snowing just after midday, but the snow was deep and she doubted any taxis would be out on such a night. Quite how she was going to get to Rachel's she didn't know. If the worst came to the worst she supposed she would have to walk but it was miles, and the half-an-hour or so journey by horse and cart through little hamlets and farming country would take much longer by Shanks's pony. Still, if she had to so be it and she had dressed with the weather in mind that morning in her stout if somewhat ugly boots and with several layers beneath her winter coat.

She saw the stationmaster come out of his cottage and exchange a few words with the white-haired gentleman, and as soon as they'd finished she hurried over. He stared at her in surprise. 'I didn't know there was anyone else on the train besides Major Maitcham,' he said before she could speak. 'Where are you bound for, miss, on a night like this?'

She had made up her mind she was going to see Rachel before she went to see Jed, and now she said, 'Stone Farm. Do you know it?'

The stationmaster prided himself on knowing every hamlet and farm within a fifty-mile radius of his station, and now he nodded. 'The Burns place, aye, but even if I call you a taxi there'll not be one willing to take off on them country roads in this snow. Treacherous it is in places. Here, come with me, miss, I've an idea,' and before she could object he had taken her arm and was hurrying her out of the station premises and into the lane beyond. There, just beginning to trundle off in the winter twilight, was a cart pulled by two big powerful horses, with a driver and the white-haired gentleman sitting side by side, deep in conversation.

'Major Maitcham?' As the stationmaster called out the cart stopped and when Cora and her good Samaritan came alongside, the stationmaster said, 'Major, this young lady needs a knight in shining armour and I thought you might fit the bill. She wants to get to Stone Farm which I believe is on the way to the estate, sir? I wondered if you'd be so kind as to drop her off as you pass?'

'Delighted, delighted.' With an agility that belied his years, the major jumped down from the cart and assisted Cora up onto the long plank seat, introducing the other man as his estate manager. Tucking a thick rug round her legs, he said cheerfully, 'Filthy night, isn't it, m'dear, but you can trust old Ned and Zak to get us home safely, isn't that right, McHaffie?'

'None better, sir. None better.'

'That's right, that's right.' The major beamed at Cora and nodded to the stationmaster. 'We'll be on our way then before the next lot comes down. Pity about the snow, m'dear. You'd be riding in more comfort if McHaffie had met me with the car but with the roads as they are it wouldn't cut the mustard. Four wheels are very nice and quite addictive, I might add, but in weather like this nothing beats the horses. Get you from one end of the country to the other, Ned and Zak, and no need to worry about petrol rationing either, what!'

Cora smiled as she thanked the major. She had heard of him from her time in Northumberland and knew he owned a large estate to the west of Stone Farm. She had always imagined the gentry to be somewhat standoffish but the major was lovely. Relaxing a little now she knew she was in safe hands, she waved goodbye to the station-master as McHaffie clicked his tongue at the horses and they began to plod off.

It was a pleasant enough journey. The major was clearly delighted to have a captive audience and he regaled her with story after story of his time in the army. All Cora had to do was to ooh and aah a little at the appropriate pauses which was just as well, because in truth her mind was on Jed and their forthcoming meeting. She had planned to refresh herself at Rachel's and have something to eat before going along to see Jed. It would be more sensible to wait until the following day but she didn't want to be sensible. If she had to battle her way through a bit of snow so what? she told herself stoutly, as her heart continued to race and jump like a mad thing the way it had done ever since she had read Rachel's letter and found out he was alive.

It was dark when they reached the two big wooden gates that were always open and which led to the farm along a winding track. She insisted to the major that she could walk perfectly well from this point, thanked him once more for his kindness and jumped down from the cart without waiting for him to assist her. She stood and watched until the cart disappeared from view and then picked up her bag and walked through the gates. It felt like coming home.

Due to the blanket of snow coating the countryside and a full moon sailing in the sky she could see her way as clearly as if it was daytime. The fields either side of the track were devoid of cattle; all the cows would be housed inside the barns now, and the smooth expanse of unbroken snow glittered in the deep frost that was falling. It was bitterly cold but Cora didn't feel it, not even when the snow came over her boots in parts of the track and began to melt and squelch as she walked.

By the time she reached the farmyard and entered its courtyard she was breathing hard, but she sped across this and through the archway leading to the path to the farmhouse. There she stopped for a moment, a huge lump in her throat. She was so glad to be back, even if it was only for a day or two.

Pulling herself together, she walked up to the front door. It was the first time she had used the big brass knocker; when she had been living at the farm they had all used the kitchen entrance without exception, but somehow that seemed as though she would be taking liberties, having been away so long. There was a light shining behind the closed curtains of the parlour window so she hoped Rachel would hear her. After Farmer Burns had died and she and the others had moved into the bedrooms of the main house, they had often transferred to the parlour once they'd finished their evening meal to read or play games or just sit and talk in front of the roaring fire.

She knocked twice, and when the door opened and she saw Rachel standing there she tried to speak but the lump in her throat choked her.

Rachel's eyes opened wide and then her face split into a Cheshire cat grin as she said, 'Cora, lass, I can't believe it. Come in, come in. You're a sight for sore eyes. Is this about Jed and the letter I sent? I thought you might write but I never expected this. I was so worried I might have put my foot in it about Wilfred.'

Cora was in the hall now with Rachel hugging her, and the older woman still continued to speak as she led Cora into the parlour where the heat from the blazing fire in the grate enveloped her frozen limbs. It was only as Cora shivered convulsively that Rachel stopped her gabbling, pushing Cora down into an armchair as she said, 'You're freezing and no wonder. Here, take them boots off.' She knelt down in front of Cora, removing first one sodden boot and then the other, whereupon she began chaffing her feet still in her wet stockings. 'You take them off while I go and get you a bite to eat, and then we'll talk proper.' Rachel stood up, but again she hugged Cora, saying, 'Oh, it's so good to see you, lass. I can't tell you how often I think of you in a day. Now get warm, get warm,' and so saying she darted out of the room.

Cora sat staring after her friend and she had to smile. She hadn't been able to get a word in edgeways. Rachel was so different now from the dour, waspish creature of yesteryear. She even looked different today. Cora was sure Rachel had put on some weight and it suited her, as did her new hairdo. Gone was the severe bun and instead soft curls framed her thin face, giving it the appearance of being plumper.

By the time Rachel had returned carrying a tray with a big bowl of steaming vegetable soup and several slices of crusty home-made bread on it, Cora had divested herself of her stockings and coat and was toasting her feet on the fender. Rachel beamed at her. 'Get this down you, lass. It'll warm you up from the inside. And while you do I'll fill you in on all the news hereabouts although I daresay there's only one thing you're interested in, eh, lass?'

'Two things.' Cora smiled. 'Your wedding is one of them. I'm so pleased for you both and I wouldn't miss it for the world. Jack's a very lucky man and you can tell him that from me.'

'I'm the lucky one, Cora.' Rachel was suddenly sober-faced. 'He knows all about Bernard and what he was, and about poor Enid too. I told him that poor lass would be alive now if I'd done something, and I should have. I should have. Enid'll haunt me to my dying day, I know that. But he doesn't condemn me like so many would. He said I'm a victim too, that anyone who came into contact with Bernard was intimidated by him. Apparently there was talk about him for years in the village, about what he got up to when he went further afield. I never knew that, but people aren't daft, are they, lass?'

Cora wasn't sure about that. Looking back, she could see she'd been daft, or perhaps too trusting would describe it better, where Wilfred was concerned. Now she said, 'There's something I need to tell you. It all came to light when you wrote me that letter . . .'

Rachel listened without interrupting and when Cora finished speaking they remained quiet for some moments. Then Rachel nodded. 'I had guessed that Jed killed

Bernard, of course, at least we thought it was Jed, didn't we, but anyway, I knew he'd got his just desserts at long last. I can't blame Wilfred for doing him in, in fact I think he deserves a medal for that particular act, Cora, but what followed . . .' Rachel shook her head. 'I always knew that what Wilfred felt for you wasn't normal. It's one thing to care about someone, and from what you told me about his mam and da I'm not saying he didn't have it hard as a bairn, but then so do thousands of others and they don't obsess about a lass to the point of madness. If you had agreed to stay in these parts he'd have stepped into Jed's shoes at the Crofts' farm without a second thought.'

'I know that.'

They stared at each other for a moment more and then Rachel said softly, 'Eat your soup, lass. Now I presume, you being you, you're not about to wait until tomorrow before you go and see Jed?'

Cora grinned her answer.

'I thought as much. Well, I'll sort you out a pair of dry boots. I've still got the ones you wore when you were here and your overalls and socks. I'll bring them through to you in a minute, and when you get back I'll have aired your bed and lit a fire in your room. Once you're ready I'll walk part of the way with you – now don't shake your head like that, I'm going to – and no doubt Jed'll see you back here safe and sound. The drifts are deep in places but as long as you keep to the lane you'll be all right and the farm tracks are mostly clear. I shan't turn in till you get back, just so I know you're all right.'

Cora looked at the woman who had become a dear friend and again it struck her how different Rachel was from the person who had driven them to this farm over five years ago. Softly, she said, 'Thank you, for writing I mean. What shall I do if he doesn't want me, Rachel?'

Rachel looked into the beautiful face and her voice was just as soft as she murmured, 'He'll want you, lass, never you fear. And I think Wilfred only told you half the story. I don't know what he said to Jed to make him leave without saying goodbye, but I would stake my life on the fact that Jed went for your sake and not to save his own skin. That's not the Jed I know. But there, no doubt you'll get to the bottom of everything when you talk to him.'

Talk to him. She was going to talk to Jed; he wasn't dead after all. Suddenly the wonder of it swept over Cora anew and she found she couldn't wait another minute to go and see him. 'Rachel, I'm sorry but I don't think I can eat anything right now.'

'You most certainly can and you will.' It was said as firmly as her mother would have spoken. 'You've had a long journey and it's freezing out there. There is no way I am letting you leave here without something warm inside you. Now you finish that soup up to the last drop while I fetch your things. No argument.'

By the time Rachel returned with her arms full, Cora had drunk the soup and eaten one slice of bread. She had to admit she felt better for it. She changed into the thick warm clothes that had been so welcome on icy-cold winter mornings at the farm when she'd had to struggle out of her nice cosy bed.

Once she was ready, she and Rachel left the house together. Outside, the air was so cold it took her breath away for a moment, but the sparkling cleanness was wonderful, Cora thought, drawing in a satisfying lungful. Even on the coldest day at home the air was tainted from the industry lining the docks, along with the smoke and soot from thousands upon thousands of chimneys in the grids of streets in the town. She had never noticed the quality of the air before she had come to the country, but as soon as she had returned to Sunderland it had been one of the things that grated on her.

The pair of them talked as they walked, but of inconsequential matters for which Cora was grateful. All she could think of was whether Jed would believe her when she said she'd never been Wilfred's lass. Jed's parents were fond of Wilfred, she knew that, and they wouldn't have doubted that what he'd said was true, which unwittingly would have confirmed the lies to Jed. It was all such a tangle, such a mess.

She left Rachel at the boundary of the two farms and walked on in the hushed silence. She could see the silhouettes of the farmhouse and the barns and buildings surrounding it in the distance now, and she actually put her gloved hand over her heart which was thumping so violently she felt it was going to burst out of her chest. How was she going to live the rest of her life if he didn't love her any more, if all that he had been through had changed him and even made him resent that she was the cause of it? Because she was, even if it was indirectly. If Wilfred hadn't loved her he wouldn't have killed Farmer Burns and then convinced Jed he was responsible and forced him to go to war. She shook her head in momentary despair before continuing along the track.

Jed straightened to ease his aching back for a few moments. He had been up at first light and he had worked solidly since then, only stopping briefly to eat the meals his mother had prepared. His face, which had long since lost the boyishness of youth and taken on the grimness of a man three times his age, softened for a moment at the thought of his mam. He knew she was worried about him and although he assured her constantly that he was all right, she was always on at him to rest more. But he couldn't rest. He didn't think he'd ever be able to enjoy a good night's sleep again. No matter how exhausted he was when he fell into bed – and he made sure he was so tired he could barely stand let alone walk – he would toss and turn half the night and the other half plunge into nightmares the like of which he wouldn't wish on his worst enemy.

In spite of the bitter night he was sweating, and now he put down the axe with which he'd been chopping wood for the past hour and flexed his shoulders and neck. One legacy from his POW days was that he was constantly in pain somewhere in his body. The army doctor had warned him of this and said that it was a result of the years of starvation and exhaustion, coupled with the injuries he had sustained. It would get better in time, the doctor had said. How much better he couldn't say but in the meantime plenty of rest, good food and regular painkillers would assist his recovery.

Jed allowed himself a wry smile. Rest was out of the question, he'd go stark staring mad, and he wasn't about to put his faith in the pills the doctor had given him either. They had been quietly disposed of the first day he was back home. Still, he was certainly getting the good food so one out of three would have to do.

After all the snow of the last days it was a beautifully clear night, he thought, lifting his face to the black sky that was alive with hundreds of twinkling stars gathered around the huge white moon. He remembered another night like this when he and Cora had stood in the beech wood under a frosty moon. He had comforted her about her mam leaving her da then and told her that whatever happened to them in the future he would never leave her. And what had he done? He had left her. She must hate him now or at the very least despise him for breaking the promises he had made that night. In spite of everything – her mam, her worry about her da, the uncertainty of the war and their suspicions about Farmer Burns – they had been happy then. Life had been sweet for both of them because they had each other. Hell, he'd been such a fool.

He groaned in the quiet of the night, shutting his eyes and clenching his teeth against the image of her in Wilfred's arms, an image that was with him day and night. He knew his mam and da thought the sun shone out of Wilfred's backside and he hadn't disillusioned them about the lad they'd taken into their home and their hearts – what was the point? If there had been a chance of getting Cora back he would have told them the truth in an instant, even though he knew his mam would be as devastated at him killing Farmer Burns as Wilfred blackmailing him to join up. But it was clear Cora was happy with Wilfred and being able to live next door to her parents and family. She had lost faith in him and with it the love she'd felt. The only thing he could do for her now, the last thing, was to leave her in peace and let her be content and settled in the bosom of those she loved. But it was killing him. Slowly and surely it was accomplishing what even Auschwitz with all its horror had failed to do, and that was to crush the will to live. He couldn't see the beauty in the world around him any more and that frightened him when he thought about it. From a little lad he had revelled in the countryside and the moods of nature, his spirit lifting and soaring like a bird on the wing at the sight of a field of waving corn, a pink-tinged dawn, the autumn mist rolling across newly ploughed earth, or a pale winter sun illuminating frosted spider webs.

He shook his head as he opened his eyes and he was in the act of bending to pick up the axe once more when he looked beyond the woodpile with its covered tin roof and down the track leading away from the farm. He could swear he'd seen a figure in the distance but it must be a trick of the shadows against the white snow. He moved out of the shelter of the woodpile and scrutinized the track through narrowed lids. No one in their right mind would be out on a night like this, he told himself with a little 'huh' at his stupidity. He was imagining things now, on top of everything else.

And then, as the track curved away from the hedgerow and trees bordering a field, he saw the figure again, slightly closer now. There *was* someone. It must be one of the old tramps who passed this way now and again, probably hoping for a hot meal and a night spent in the hay barn. His da always allowed them to spend a night or two in the warm in winter and these fellows had a way of tipping off others of their kind as to where they could get fed and watered. In the past, with the arrogance of youth, he had thought his father was barmy to permit it, but he didn't think like that any more. Kindness didn't cost much but it could be life or death to these poor blighters in such weather.

He had only taken a few steps towards the figure when he became absolutely still. They were probably unable to see him against the shadows of the barn on one side of him and the woodpile on the other, but now the figure was quite distinct against the white snow and there was something about the way it was walking . . .

He rubbed his hand across his eyes, afraid of what he thought he was seeing or rather of the hope that had surged up because of it and how he was going to feel when he was proved wrong, because it was impossible, *impossible* that it was her.

He took a slow step forward, then another, then another, like a blind man. As he emerged from the darkness into clear view, he saw the figure stop for a moment, just a moment, before beginning to try and run, stumbling and almost sprawling on the icy, snow-covered track. He must have called her name because it reverberated in the frosty air, shattering the stillness, and then he was running too.

They met in a wonder-filled embrace as he lifted her off her feet into his arms, crushing her in to him as he said her name over and over between smothering her face in kisses. Her arms were round his neck and she was kissing him back, half-laughing and half-crying but wholly his. How long they stood wrapped up in each other they didn't know, but when, still swaying together but her feet now on the ground, their lips parted, it was as though all the explanations had already been said.

'Cora, Cora.' He stared at her and her face shone like one of the stars above them. 'Oh, my love, my love.'

'I thought you had been killed.' She reached out and touched his face, her hand trembling. 'I didn't know – that you were home, I mean. I came as soon as I heard . . .'

Her words were lost as he took her mouth again with such passion that they were blind and deaf to the world around them, and it was only when they became aware of Jed's father's two sheepdogs barking and jumping up at them that they drew apart once more. Jed gave a word of command to the dogs who immediately quietened, slinking round their legs, and as they looked to the farmhouse they saw his parents standing in the lighted doorway.

'They – they're calling you,' Cora said weakly, barely able to form her words.

Jed raised his hand to his parents but then turned back to her. 'Before we go up to the house I have to tell you,' he whispered. 'I love you, Cora. I always have and I've never stopped loving you, not for a second.'

'And I love you. Everything Wilfred said to your mam and the letters he wrote, it's all lies, Jed. He was always just a friend, nothing more. And Farmer Burns, you weren't responsible for his death. It was Wilfred, Jed. All the time it was Wilfred.' She gulped as she added, 'I'm sorry, I'm so sorry.'

'No, don't ever say that to me. You've nothing to be sorry about. Come on, we'll go and talk inside, but Cora?' He stopped again and looked deep into her eyes. 'Are you sure, about Farmer Burns?'

She nodded.

He swore softly as he put his arm round her. 'I'd like five minutes alone with Wilfred Hutton,' he said grimly. 'I always knew there was something wrong about that day. I hit Burns to be sure, but not hard enough to kill him. I thought it must have been one of those freak accidents in the end, but it makes sense now.' And then he pulled her hard in to him for another fierce kiss. 'But what am I saying?' he murmured against her lips. 'Nothing matters now. We're together at last and I won't let you go again.'

Entwined, they walked up the track towards the two figures standing in the doorway, the dogs bounding ahead of them and into the house. It was Jed's mother who called to them, saying, 'Cora, lass, what a surprise. The dogs heard something and we let them out but we never expected this. Come in out of the cold, the pair of you and have a hot drink. We'll go in the sitting room, there's a nice fire in there.'

Jed winked at Cora as they followed his parents through the hall and into the sitting room. 'She's bursting to know what's happened,' he whispered, 'but I bet Da's told her not to rush in where angels fear to tread.'

Cora smiled but in truth she felt more than a little intimidated by Jed's parents. Wilfred had told them a pack of lies but would they believe that? She couldn't blame them if they had reservations about her now. She hoped they would accept that Wilfred had only ever been a friend, the boy next door who she had grown up with and loved as a brother, but it was a tall ask. And now they were going to hear about Farmer Burns and Jed thinking he'd killed the farmer, along with the blackmail that had caused Jed to go to war with everything that had ensued thereafter. If she was his mother she wouldn't feel too kindly to the girl who was the catalyst for it all.

In the event she needn't have worried. Over hot milky cocoa and Jed's mother's teacakes, the four of them talked for over an hour. There was shock and fury from Jed's parents but this was directed at Wilfred, the lad they had treated as one of their own; for Cora they had nothing but sympathy and compassion. Their son was a different matter. Jed got a lecture from his father on the folly of not coming to him on the day of the farmer's death, and Mrs Croft said nothing which was perhaps even more damning than her husband's anger.

Jed sat with his head bowed. He knew exactly how his parents were feeling, but the lowered head was not because of remorse because he had disappointed and upset them by not confiding in them, but because he needed to hide the light in his eyes that would have told them he didn't care about anything but that Cora had come to him.

It was just after nine o'clock when the older couple left them to go upstairs. Jed's father smiled at Cora and told her he was expecting to see a lot more of her in the future now everything was sorted, but Deborah Croft put her arms around the lass who held her son's happiness in her hands and whispered, 'He needs you more than you will ever know, dear. He was dying inside before you came.'

'Me too, Mrs Croft,' Cora whispered back.

They looked at each other for an infinitesimal moment and then Jed's mother gave the slightest of nods as she touched Cora's cheek in a swift caress before turning and leaving with her husband.

'What was that about?' Jed had been standing across the other side of the room in front of the fire and now he came over to her, taking her into his arms. 'What did she say?'

'Nothing really. She just loves you, that's all.'

'And I love you.' His arms, telling of his hunger, crushed her in to him and for long moments they were lost in each other, both of them barely able to believe they had weathered the storm and come into safe harbour.

'Jed?' After a while she drew back in his arms, lifting her hands and cradling his face. 'Was it bad, your time as a POW? I want to know it all, to understand.'

'Perhaps one day.' Now was not the time. This was too perfect, too precious. 'But for now I need to get you back to Mrs Burns so you can get some sleep. We've got tomorrow to talk – we've got endless tomorrows.'

'You won't shut me out? I know that's what some POWs do, to get through, but I want to share it with you in some small way.'

'I won't shut you out.' And when she continued to stare at him without speaking, he said again, 'I won't shut you out, I promise. How could I? You're part of me, part of the fabric of my being, my soul. How could I shut you out?'

Now she flung her arms round his neck, reaching up on tiptoe and covering his mouth with hers with such passion that her emotion shook both their bodies.

It was a long time later, after they had loved and talked and loved and talked again when he said once more, 'I need to get you back to Mrs Burns. It's late and you must be tired. She'll have my guts for garters, you know that, don't you?'

Cora giggled. 'She's waiting up for me,' she admitted.

'Now she tells me.'

Once in the hall Cora pulled on her coat and wrapped her muffler round her neck, her hat low over her ears, but the bitter cold of the frosty night still made her gasp as she stepped outside. They walked hand in hand along the track where just hours before she had trod with such apprehension, and Stone Farm was within sight when Jed stopped, pulling her in to him as he murmured, 'Do you remember that other night? It was just like this. Cold and frosty and beautiful. I told you I loved you beyond words and that what we had happens once in a lifetime. Do you remember?'

She nodded. She remembered.

'I promised you I would never leave you and I broke that promise. Can you forgive me?'

'There's nothing to forgive.'

'Will you marry me, my love, and soon? Next summer? As soon as Maria gets a job and can take your place at home?'

She smiled at him in the light of the moon, the glinting sparkle of the frost like diamond dust and their icy breath mingling as she said, 'Yes, yes, yes,' with such fervour that a roosting bird in the hedgerow rustled its protest at being disturbed. Jed was her life and she wanted nothing more than to be his wife. It would be hard work, being a farmer's wife, but she felt she had been born for it. The towns and cities held nothing for her now; here she could breathe and grow into the person she was meant to be. She was home.

Chapter Twenty-Six

It was the middle of August and post-war Britain was seeing dire warnings about the shortage of coal for the forthcoming winter; rationing increased with grim messages of greater austerity by the government and there were strikes here and there all over the country. Councils were seeking aid to rebuild towns and cities; police and Ministry of Food enforcement officers were cracking down on black marketeers; and fifty thousand servicemen were queueing up for a divorce as the epidemic of unfaithfulness during the war years came to light.

The country was in a mess, Gregory remarked grimly to Nancy as he sat reading his newspaper in Rachel's parlour on the morning of Cora's wedding. He emerged briefly from the article on the fortune being earned in the sale of nylons, chocolates, perfume and other scarce goods by unscrupulous ne'er-do-wells to shake his head at his wife and sigh despondently, before saying again, 'Aye, a real mess,' and returning to the paper.

And she supposed he was right, Nancy thought from

her place on the sofa opposite Gregory's armchair, but somehow, with everything so right for her immediate family, she couldn't summon up the concern she perhaps ought to feel. She glanced at the downy head of the baby at her breast as contentment flooded through her like a warm toddy. Douglas was a supremely happy baby and rarely cried unless he was hungry.

There was Cora, she mused, as the baby's mouth pulled strongly at her breast, about to wed the man she loved and take up her new life as a farmer's wife, and Jed's mam and da seemed to think the world of her already. Their Horace, to his great delight – and if she admitted it, Nancy confessed, great relief on her part – was to finish his last year's schooling in Northumberland while he lived with Cora and the Crofts at Appletree Farm, ready to take up the job Mr Croft had lined up for him this time next year. Horace had been a different boy since Cora had told him what she had arranged. She hadn't even had to nag at him to do his chores over the last months. Having left school, Maria was starting work as a receptionist at a dental practice in Holmeside the following week, and Mr Turner, the dentist, had promised he would train her as a dental nurse in due course which Maria was thrilled about.

Nancy gave a little shudder. She'd hate that herself, messing about in people's mouths, but Maria was drawn to all things medical and seemed over the moon about the opportunity. But the icing on the cake, and something none of them could have foreseen, was that Gregory had been approached in the spring by an old army colleague whose family owned a hotel in Roker. Gregory had served under the captain in Tobruk and on one occasion had been instrumental in saving his life, something which Gregory had forgotten but which Captain Fletcher had not. On leaving the army after the war the captain had taken over the family business and had, in his own words, decided to search out a fellow native. The fact that the Fletchers owned a string of first-class hotels all over the north-east and Gregory was as poor as a church mouse was neither here or there. The captain had offered Gregory the job as lift attendant at the hotel, and the monthly salary to go with it had made Gregory's eyes pop out of his head. Nancy had never had the opportunity to tell the captain what the job had meant to her husband's self-esteem but she suspected he knew anyway. He was a nice man, Captain Fletcher, she thought to herself. A very nice man.

Douglas had filled himself to bursting and had fallen asleep at her breast. She settled the baby in her arms and was just rearranging her clothing when Rachel came into the room. They had met for the first time the afternoon before when she and Gregory and the rest of the family had made the journey from Sunderland for Cora's wedding. She hadn't expected to like the woman Cora regarded as almost a second mother, and she didn't, but she was honest enough to admit that it was her problem and not Rachel's.

Now, as Rachel said, 'Cora wondered if you could help her get ready,' Nancy forced a smile, before passing

Gregory his son and walking into the hall. There Rachel caught up with her, taking her arm as she murmured, 'Could I talk to you for a minute before you go up?' Whereupon she led the way to the kitchen.

As Nancy entered, Rachel waved her to a chair but Nancy remained where she was, just inside the door. 'What is it you wish to say?' she said politely, trying to keep the antagonism which she knew was completely unwarranted from sounding in her voice. She knew she had been cool with Rachel but she just couldn't help it and she fully expected that the other woman was going to take her to task. So when Rachel said softly, 'It's about Wilfred,' Nancy's eyes widened.

'Wilfred?' Her voice was high with surprise and realizing this she turned and shut the door before moving fully into the room. 'What about him?'

'I received a letter from him, after – after he'd died. He must have posted it that evening, knowing what he was going to do.'

Nancy stiffened. Wilfred's death was officially an accident.

'It was unpleasant.' Rachel shook her head. 'No, more than unpleasant. I had never liked Wilfred and he didn't like me, but that aside, it – well, it was unhinged.'

Nancy sat down in the chair Rachel had gestured to when they had come into the kitchen. Her legs suddenly felt weak. 'What did it say?'

'Among other things, that I would be damned for all eternity for my part in breaking him and Cora up and that he would haunt me until the day I died. Unexplained things would happen, he said, and I would know it was him, watching me and waiting. Unhinged, like I said, but there was no doubt that he absolutely believed what he had written. He expected to be able to reach beyond the grave. Nancy –' Rachel paused. She was fully aware of how Cora's mother felt about her. 'Wilfred's passing? It wasn't an accident, was it?'

Nancy shook her head.

'Wilfred said he'd left a letter for Cora.'

'He did. I destroyed it and she doesn't know it existed.'

'Was it bad?'

'It was a curse, evil. If she'd read it she would never have been able to get it out of her mind.'

Rachel nodded. 'How did you find it before anyone else?'

Nancy breathed out slowly. 'Cora must never know.'

'Of course she must never know. That's why I've never mentioned his letter to me.'

'You destroyed it?'

'Immediately.'

'Well,' said Nancy quietly. 'It was like this . . .'

The telling didn't take long. Outside the open kitchen window the birds were singing and the sky was blue, and in the fields surrounding the farm the scent of trees and wild flowers was sweet and warm winds rustled the ripening ears of corn. It was a beautiful day, and to the two women in the kitchen the darkness they were discussing was all at odds with the summer morning.

There was silence for a few moments after Nancy finished speaking, and then Rachel whispered, 'Thank you for telling me. Do you think Cora suspects he killed himself?'

'Why? Has she said anything to you?'

'No, no.' Rachel shook her head. 'She told me it was an accident, that he got drunk and fell and hit his head. She said she felt awful because she thought he got drunk on account of her telling him she was coming to see Jed, but I said it was far more likely because he had lost his da and then his mam in such a short time.' Rachel looked at Nancy. 'And to think he did them in – it doesn't bear thinking about. And that poor lad who liked her, losing his legs an' all, and then blackmailing Jed to join up.'

Neither of them mentioned Farmer Burns.

Nancy stood up. 'I'd better go up, no doubt she's all a dither, and . . . thank you for saying nothing about Wilfred's letter to you.'

'I care about Cora. Very much.'

'Aye, I know you do.' It cost Nancy something to add, 'And she cares about you too,' but it was in that moment that they became friends.

Cora was an exquisite bride. She was wearing her mother's wedding dress, and so alike were they that Nancy had barely had to alter a stitch of the lace and satin gown. When the music began and she walked down the aisle on her father's arm Jed turned from his place at the front of the church next to Jock who was his best man, and such was the look on his face that everyone reached for their handkerchiefs. Indeed the only one who wasn't in tears was Cora; her face was radiant and her eyes starry, and Jed didn't think he had seen anything so beautiful in his life.

After the service in the little parish church all the guests followed the bridal horse and trap that was decked out with white ribbons and wild posies to Appletree Farm. Jed had his arm round her as they drew near to the farmhouse, and as Cora gazed at the lovely old building, its walls almost hidden by vines and climbing roses, she remembered the first time she had seen it. It had been a warm summer's day then too, and she had been captivated by the beauty of the house that had spoken of peace and joy and comfort to the unhappy bewildered girl she'd been then. And now it was her home and Jed was her husband.

She turned to him, her face alight with happiness. 'I love you so much,' she whispered, 'so very much.'

He tightened his arm around her, his other hand holding the reins, bending his head and kissing her as he murmured, 'It would be impossible to express how much I love you, my darling.' And as she smiled and lay her head on his shoulder, he knew a moment of deep thankfulness that nothing had marred this day for her.

Only his father knew about the letter he had received after Wilfred had died; its contents had been too vile to show to his mother. They had burned it and it hadn't been mentioned between them from that day to this, but in a way the letter had achieved the very opposite of what its writer would have wanted in that it had brought him and his father closer. It had shown his father what he had been up against with Wilfred Hutton as nothing else could have done, destroying any last remnants of doubt that Wilfred hadn't actually meant to send him to his death.

As he brought the horse and trap to a halt, he jumped down and then lifted Cora into his arms, twirling her round before setting her on her feet. 'Welcome home, Mrs Croft,' he said softly as the rest of the procession began to arrive. 'Prepare to be carried over the threshold shortly.'

Jed's father was having a little cottage built in the grounds of the farm for himself and Jed's mother which would be ready for them in the autumn when they'd move out of the farmhouse. They had insisted they wanted the young couple to take the main house and make it their own for themselves and any future children they might have. Cora had won her mother-in-law's heart for ever when she'd said she wouldn't want to alter a single thing in the farmhouse, but Jed had several things in mind. An indoor privy both upstairs and downstairs, he'd told Cora one evening when she'd travelled up for the weekend, along with converting one of the bedrooms into a big bathroom with running water on tap. 'And later an extension at the back of the house overlooking the garden,' he'd enthused. 'The ground floor being a sunroom with big doors we can throw open in the summer, and the first floor consisting of our bedroom suite with our own bathroom and private sitting room.' She had smiled and hugged him and told him his plans were wonderful, but all she really wanted was to be his wife and live and work with him on the farm. A partnership in every way as modelled by Jed's parents. And bairns, she had added firmly. She wanted lots of bairns. At least three little boys and three little girls. Jed had laughed and said he'd do his best but perhaps they ought to get the wedding day over first?

Cora thought of this now as she stood arm in arm with her new husband and watched her family and friends coming towards them. Even Etta had made the journey from Czechoslovakia to be with them, and Maud had arrived the day before and was staying with Rachel and Jack at the farm for a few days. It was the perfect day, and she suddenly felt a sharp sense of regret and loss that Wilfred wasn't among the throng. But the old Wilfred, her best friend and childhood companion. Not the Wilfred who had emerged when she had met Jed and fallen in love with him, the Wilfred who had professed such great love for her while attempting to ruin her life by forcing the man she adored to leave her for the horrors of war. That individual would always have constituted a very real threat to her Jed. She had never seen it so clearly before. And so it was time to say goodbye to both the Wilfreds she had known. The hurt little boy and the dangerous man. And somehow, she hadn't been able to let go of the first until this very moment, because at the bottom of her she had been rent with pity and sorrow, and guilt too, because she hadn't been able to make things right for him. But that was a betrayal of Jed.

She glanced at her husband. His features showed the ravages of what he had been through and he looked ten, twenty years older than he was. Still handsome, still her Jed, but damaged. If she lived a hundred lifetimes she would never be able to make it up to him – what loving her had cost him.

Softly, so softly that the words were merely a silent breath, she whispered, 'You have no hold on me any more, Wilfred, and I won't think of you again. I'm going into the future and nothing of you can come with me.'

A sudden breeze came from nowhere, caressing her face and lifting her veil, but she smoothed it into place, suddenly impatient for the rest of the day to begin, and the breeze disappeared. And as her mother and father and Maria and Rachel reached her, hugging her and laughing and surrounding her and Jed with their love, she felt free for the first time in her mind and spirit since the day, many years before, when as a small bairn she had taken a crying little boy into her arms and comforted him with childish hugs and kisses.